On a Wicked Dawn

Stephanie Laurens

piatkus

st romance stories **Stephanie Laurens** read were set
the backdrop of Regency England, and these continue
t a special attraction for her. As an escape from the
rld of professional science, Stephanie started writing
cy romances, and she is now a *New York Times*, *USA*
and *Publishers Weekly* bestselling author.

nie lives in a leafy suburb of Melbourne, Australia, with
her husband and two daughters, along with two cats,
speare and Marlowe.

more about Stephanie's books from her website at
www.stephanielaurens.com

On A Wicked Dawn

The Bar Cynster Family Tree

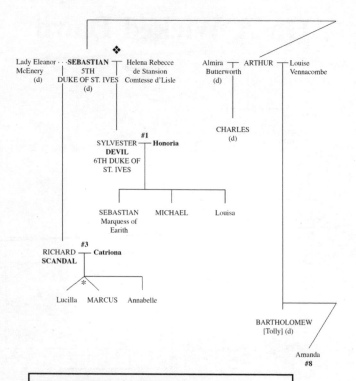

Lady Eleanor··**SEBASTIAN**┬ Helena Rebecce
McEnery | 5TH de Stansion
(d) DUKE OF ST. IVES Comtesse d'Lisle
(d)

Almira ┬ ARTHUR ┬ Louise
Butterworth Vennacombe
(d)

#1
SYLVESTER ┬ **Honoria**
DEVIL
6TH DUKE OF
ST. IVES

CHARLES
(d)

SEBASTIAN   MICHAEL   Louisa
Marquess of
Earith

#3
RICHARD ── **Catriona**
SCANDAL

✳

Lucilla   MARCUS   Annabelle

BARTHOLOMEW
[Tolly] (d)

Amanda
#8

THE CYNSTER NOVELS

#1 *Devil's Bride*   #6 *All About Love*
#2 *A Rake's Vow*   #7 *All About Passion*
#3 *Scandal's Bride*   #8 *This Volume*
#4 *A Rogue's Proposal*   #9 *On a Wicked Dawn*
#5 *A Secret Love*
❖ *Special—The Promise in a Kiss*

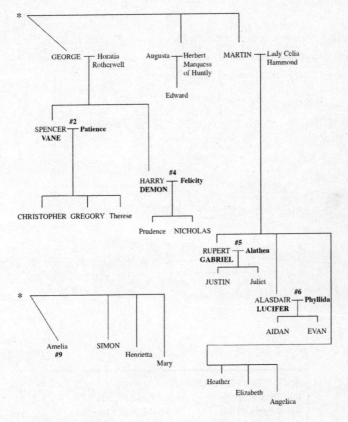

MALE CYNSTERS in capitals   * denotes twins

Chapter One

Mount Street, London
3 a.m., May 25, 1825
He was drunk. *Gloriously* drunk. More drunk –
drunker – than he'd ever been. Not that he made a
habit of inebriation, but last night, or more specifically
and especially this morning, was a once-
in-a-lifetime occasion. After eight long years, he was
free.

Lucien Michael Ashford, sixth Viscount Calverton,
sauntered along Mount Street, nonchalantly twirling
his ebony cane, a smile of unfettered joy curving his
lips.

He was twenty-nine, yet today qualified as the first
of his adult life, the first day he could call said life
his own. Even better, as of yesterday, he was rich.
Fabulously, fantastically – legally – wealthy. There
was not a great deal more he could think of to wish
for. If he hadn't been afraid of falling on his face, he
would have danced down the deserted street.

The moon was out, lighting the pavements, casting
deep shadows. About him, London lay sleeping, but
the capital, even at this hour, was never truly silent;

1

from a distance, distorted by the stone facades all around, came the jingle of harness, the hollow clop of hooves, a disembodied call. Although even here, in the most fashionable quarter, danger sometimes lurked in the shadows, he felt no threat. His senses were still operational, and despite his state he'd taken care to walk evenly; any watching him with felonious intent would see a tall, sufficiently well built, gracefully athletic gentleman swinging a cane that might, and indeed did, conceal a swordstick, and move on to more likely prey.

He'd left his club in St. James and the company of a group of friends half an hour ago, electing to walk home the better to clear his head of the effects elicited by a quantity of the very best French brandy. His celebrations had been restrained owing to the simple fact that none of said friends – indeed no one other than his mother and his wily old banker, Robert Child – knew anything of his previous state, the dire straits to which he and his family had been brought by his sire prior to his death eight years before, the perilous situation from which he'd spent the last eight years clawing his way back, and from which yesterday he'd finally won free.

The fact they'd had no idea what he was celebrating had not prevented his friends from joining him. A long night filled with wine, song, and the simple pleasures of male companionship had ensued.

A pity his oldest friend, his cousin Martin Fulbridge, now Dexter, earl of, wasn't presently in London. Then again, Martin was doubtless enjoying himself at his home in the north, wallowing in the benefits accruing to a recently married man; he had married Amanda Cynster a week ago.

2

Grinning to himself, Luc mentally – superiorly – shook his head over his cousin's weakness, his surrender to love. Reaching his house, he turned to the shallow steps leading to the front door – his head spun for an instant, then righted. Carefully, he walked up the steps, halted before the door, then hunted in his pocket for his keys.

They slipped through his fingers twice before he grasped them and hauled them forth. The ring in his palm, he shuffled the keys, frowning as he tried to identify the one for the front door. Then he found it. Grasping it, he squinted, guiding it to keyhole ... after the third try, it slid home; he turned and heard the tumblers fall.

Returning the keys to his pocket, he grasped the knob and sent the door swinging wide. He stepped over the threshold—

A dervish erupted from the black hole of the area steps – he caught only a fleeting glimpse, had only an instant's warning before the figure barreled past him, one elbow knocking him off-balance. He staggered and fetched up against the hall wall.

That brief human contact, deadened by layers of fabric though it was, sent sensation rushing through him, and told him unequivocally who the dervish was. Amelia Cynster. Twin to his cousin's new wife, longtime friend of his family's whom he'd known since she was in nappies. An as-yet-unmarried female with a backbone of steel. Cloaked and hooded, she plunged into the dim hall, came to an abrupt halt, then whirled and faced him.

The wall behind his shoulders was the only thing keeping him upright. He stared, astounded, utterly bemused ... waited for the effect of her touch to subside ...

3

She made an angry, frustrated sound, dashed back to the door, grabbed it, and propelled it shut. The loss of the moonlight left him blinking, eyes adjusting to the dark. The door closed, she swung around; her back to the panel, she glared – he felt it.

'What the devil's the matter with you?' she hissed.

'*Me?*' Easing his shoulders from the wall, he managed to find his balance. 'What the damn hell are *you* doing here?'

He couldn't even begin to imagine. Moonlight streamed in through the fanlight, passing over their heads to strike the pale tiles of the hall. In the diffused light, he could just make out her features, fine and delicate in an oval face, framed by golden curls tumbling under her hood.

She straightened; chin rising, she set the hood back. 'I wanted to speak with you privately.'

'It's three o'clock in the morning.'

'I know! I've been waiting since one. But I wanted to speak with you without anyone else knowing – I can hardly come here during the day and demand to speak privately with you, can I?'

'No – for a very good reason.' She was unmarried, and so was he. If she wasn't standing before the door he'd be tempted to open it and ... he frowned. 'You didn't come alone?'

'Of course not. I've a footman outside.'

He put a hand to his brow. 'Oh. Good.' This was getting complicated.

'For goodness sake! Just *listen*. I know all about your family's financial state.'

That captured his immediate and complete attention. Noting it, she nodded. 'Exactly. But you needn't worry I'll tell anyone – indeed, quite the opposite.

4

That's why I needed to speak with you alone. I've a proposition to put to you.'

His wits were reeling – he couldn't think what to say. Couldn't imagine what she was going to say.

She didn't wait, but drew breath and launched in. 'It must be plain, even to you, that I've been looking about for a husband, yet the truth is there's not a single eligible gentleman I feel the least bit inclined to marry. But now Amanda's gone, I find it boring in the extreme continuing as an unmarried young lady.' She paused, then went on, 'That's point one.

'Point two is that you and your family are in strait-ened circumstances.' She held up a staying hand. 'You needn't try to tell me otherwise – over the past weeks I've spent a lot of time here, and generally about with your sisters. Emily and Anne don't know, do they? You needn't fear I've told them – I haven't. But when one is that close, little things do show. I realized a few weeks ago and much I've noticed since has confirmed my deduction. You're in dun territory – *no!* Don't say a word. Just hear me out.'

He blinked – he was barely keeping up with the flow of her revelations; he didn't at present have any brain left over to cope with formulating speech.

She eyed him with typical acerbity, apparently reas-sured when he remained mute. 'I know *you* are not to blame – it was your father who ran through the blunt, wasn't it? I've heard the grandes dames say often enough that it was a good thing he died before he crippled the estate, but the truth is he did bring your family to *point non plus* before he broke his neck, and you and your mother have been carefully preserving appearances ever since.'

Her voice softened. 'It must have been a Herculean

task, but you've done brilliantly – I'm sure no one else has guessed. And, of course, I can see why you did it – with not just Emily and Anne, but Portia and Penelope, to establish, being known as paupers would be disastrous.'

She frowned as if checking a mental list. 'So that's point two – that it's imperative you and your family remain among the *haut ton* but you don't have the wherewithal to support such a lifestyle. You've been hanging on by your fingernails for years. Which brings me to point three. You.'

She fixed her gaze on his face. 'You don't appear to have considered marrying as a way to repair your finances. I imagine you didn't want to burden yourself with a wife who might have expensive expectations, quite aside from not wanting to burden yourself with a wife and any associated demands at all. That's point three and the reason I needed to speak with you privately.'

Gathering herself, she tipped her chin higher. 'I believe that we – you and I – could reach a mutually beneficial agreement. My dowry's considerable – more than sufficient to resuscitate the Ashford family fortunes, at least by enough to get by. And you and I have known each other forever – it's not as if we couldn't rub along well enough, and I know your family well, and they know me, and—'

'*Are you suggesting we marry?*'

His thunderstruck tones had her glaring.

'Yes! And before you start on about how nonsensical a notion it is, just consider. It's not as if I expect—'

He missed whatever she wasn't expecting. He stared at her through the dimness. Her lips continued to move; presumably she was talking. He tried to listen, but his mind refused to cooperate. It had frozen – seized – on the one vital, crucial, unbelievable fact.

She was offering to be his wife.

If the sky had fallen he couldn't have been more shocked. Not by her suggestion – by his reaction.

He wanted to marry her – wanted her as his wife.

A minute ago, he hadn't had a clue. Ten minutes ago, he would have laughed the idea to scorn. Now ... he simply *knew*, with an absolute, unwavering, frighteningly powerful certainty. A feeling that rose through him, stirring impulses he always took care to keep hidden behind his elegant facade.

He refocused on her, truly let himself look at her, something he now realized he'd not previously done. Previously, she'd been an irksome distraction – a female to whom he was physically attracted but could not, given his then lack of fortune, ever conceivably approach. He'd consciously set her aside, to one side, one woman he knew he could never touch. Forbidden, and even more so because of their families' close ties.

'—and there's no need to imagine—'

Golden ringlets, rosebud lips, and the lithe, sensual figure of a Greek goddess. Cornflower blue eyes, brown brows and lashes, skin like the richest cream; he couldn't see in the dimness but his memory supplied the image. And reminded him that behind the feminine delicacy lay a quick mind and a heart he'd never known to be at fault. And a spine of pure steel.

For the first time, he let himself see her as a woman he could take. Have. Possess. To whatever degree he wished.

His reaction to the mental image was ruthlessly decisive.

She was right about one thing – he'd never wanted

7

a wife, never wanted the emotional ties, the closeness. He did, however, want her – of that he entertained not the slightest doubt.

'—any reason to know. It'll work perfectly well – all we need do—'

She was right there, too – the way she'd framed her proposition, it could indeed work. Because she was offering, and all he had to do was ...

'*Well?*'

Her tone jerked his mind from the primitive plane on which it had been wandering. She'd folded her arms. She was frowning. He couldn't see, but he wouldn't have been surprised if she was tapping her toe.

He was suddenly very aware that she stood within arm's reach.

Her eyes narrowed, glittering in the weak light. 'So what's your considered opinion – do you think our marrying is a good idea?'

He met her gaze, then raised one hand, lightly traced her jaw, tipped up her face. Openly, unhurriedly, studied her features, wondered what she would do if he simply ... he fixed his gaze on her eyes. 'Yes. Let's get married.'

Wariness stole into her eyes. He wondered what she'd seen in his face; he reassembled his social mask. Smiled. 'Marrying you' —his smile deepened— 'will be entirely my pleasure.'

Releasing her, he swept her a magnificient bow—

A mistake. One he had only the most fleeting inkling of before his vision went black.

He collapsed on the floor at her feet.

Amelia stared at his crumpled form. For one moment, she was completely at a loss – half expected him to rise and make some joke. Laugh ...

He didn't move.

'Luc?'

No answer. Wary, she edged around until she could see his face. His long lashes were black crescents smudged over his pale cheeks. His brows, the planes of his face, looked oddly relaxed; his lips, long, thin, so often set in a severe line, were gently curved ...

She let out her breath in an exasperated hiss. Drunk! *Damn* him! When she'd wound up her courage, come out so late at night, stood in the cold dark for hours, then managed to get through her rehearsed proposition without a single fluster – and he was *drunk*?

In the instant before her temper took flight, she remembered he'd agreed. Perfectly lucidly. He might have been giddy, but he hadn't been incapable – indeed, until he'd fallen, she'd had no idea, hadn't been able to tell from his manner or his speech. Drunks slurred their words, didn't they? But she knew his voice, his diction – he hadn't sounded the least bit odd.

Well, the fact he'd kept quiet and let her talk without interruption had been odd, but it had worked to her advantage. If he'd made his usual barbed comments, picked at her arguments, she'd never have got them all out.

And he'd agreed. She'd heard him, and, more importantly, she was sure he'd heard himself. He might be all but unconscious now, but when he awoke, he'd remember. And that was all that mattered.

Euphoria – a sense of victory – seized her. She'd done it! Staring down at him, she could hardly believe

9

it – but she was here, and so was he; she wasn't dreaming.

She'd come to his house and made her proposition, and he'd accepted.

Her relief was so great it left her giddy. A chair stood nearby, against the wall; she sank onto it, relaxed back, and studied his recumbent form.

He looked so peaceful, slumped on the tiles. She decided it was a good thing he'd been drunk – an unexpected bonus; she was perfectly certain he didn't normally imbibe to excess. The concept was so un-Luc-like; he was always so rigidly in control. It must have been some special occasion – some friend's great good fortune or some such – to have resulted in his present state.

His long limbs were tangled; his face might look peaceful, but his body ... she sat up. If she was going to marry him, then presumably she should ensure he didn't wake with a cricked neck or a twisted spine. She considered him; shifting, even dragging him, wasn't an option. He was over six feet tall and broad-shouldered and while he was rangy and lean, his bones were typical of men of his background – heavy. The remembered thud as they'd hit the floor assured her she'd never manage to meaningfully move him.

With a sigh, she stood, gathered her cloak, and walked into the drawing room. The bellpull was by the mantelpiece; she tugged it, then returned to the door. Almost closing it, she stood in the dark drawing room and watched.

Minutes ticked by. She was about to go back and tug the bellpull again when she heard a door squeak. A glimmer of light appeared down the corridor

10

leading to the kitchens; it steadily grew brighter. Then its bearer halted, gasped, then with a muttered exclamation hurried forward.

Amelia watched as Cottsloe, Luc's butler, bent over his master, checking the pulse at his throat. Relieved, Cottsloe straightened and stared; she hoped he imagined Luc had been in the drawing room, rung for assistance, then staggered into the hall and collapsed. She waited for Cottsloe to summon a footman. Instead, the old man shook his head, picked up Luc's cane, and set it on the hall table along with his candle.

Then Cottsloe bent and tried to heft Luc to his feet.

Amelia suddenly realized there might be reasons Cottsloe, kind old Cottsloe, who doted on Luc and the whole family, might not want to summon help, might not want it known that Luc was drunk. But it was ludicrous – Cottsloe was in his fifties, shortish and tending toward rotund. He managed to get Luc half-upright, but there was no way he could support such a heavy and unwieldy body far, especially not up the stairs.

Not alone.

With an inward sigh, Amelia opened the door. 'Cottsloe?'

With a hiss, he turned, wide-eyed. Slipping through the door, she waved him to silence. 'We had a private meeting – we were talking, and he collapsed.'

Even in the dimness, she saw the old man's blush.

'I'm afraid he's a touch under the weather, miss.'

'Indeed, he's quite drunk. If I help, do you think we can get him upstairs? His room's on the first floor, isn't it?'

Cottsloe was nonplussed, uncertain of the propri-

11

eties, but he did need help. And Luc had first call on his loyalty. He nodded. 'Just along from the top of the stairs. If we can get him that far . . .'

Amelia ducked under Luc's dangling arm and hauled it across her shoulders. She and Cottsloe staggered until they'd hefted Luc upright; supporting him like a sack of meal between them, they turned toward the stairs. Luckily, Luc regained some degree of consciousness; when they reached the first stair, he got his feet under him and started, with their assistance, to climb, albeit in a sagging, lurching way. Amelia tried not to think of what might happen if he fell backward. Pressing against him, steadying him, brought home just how solid and muscled he was underneath his elegant clothes.

Guessing which way his stagger would send him next, and countering his tipping weight, became a game that left both her and Cottsloe puffing by the time they gained the top of the stairs. Their charge remained oblivious, his lips gleefully curved, his brow unfurrowed under his midnight black hair. His eyes hadn't opened. Amelia was sure that if she and Cottsloe both let go, Luc would crumple in a heap once more.

Between them, they steered him down the corridor, then Cottsloe reached ahead and flung open a door. Her hands sunk in Luc's coat, Amelia pulled, then shoved, and sent him reeling into the room; she hurriedly followed, hauling to keep him from sprawling facedown on the floor.

'This way.' Cottsloe tugged Luc toward the huge four-poster bed. Amelia pushed. They got him to the bed, then had to shuffle him about. Finally, he stood with his back to the bed.

They both let go; he stood there, swaying. Amelia

placed her palm against his chest and pushed. Like a felled tree he toppled, landing flat on his back on the silk counterpane. The counterpane was quite old, but looked comfortable; as if to illustrate, Luc sighed and turned, snuggling his cheek into the midnight blue softness.

On another sigh, every last remnant of tension left his body. He lay relaxed, lips curved as if hugging some pleasant memory close.

Despite all, Amelia felt her lips lift. He was so atrociously handsome, the silky locks of his jet-black hair feathering his pale cheeks, his long-fingered hands relaxed by his face, his long body lying bone-less in oddly innocent slumber.

'I can manage now, miss.'

She glanced at Cottsloe, nodded. 'Indeed.' She turned to the door. 'I'll let myself out. Don't forget to bolt the front door on your way down.'

'Of course, miss.' Cottsloe followed her to the door; with a bow, he saw her out.

As she descended the stairs, Amelia wondered what poor old Cottsloe thought. Regardless, he wasn't the sort to spread rumors, and he'd learn the truth soon enough.

When she and Luc announced their betrothal.

That thought was stunning – even though it had been her goal, she still hadn't assimilated the fact she'd attained it, and so easily. Collecting the footman she'd left waiting by the area steps, she headed home through the quiet streets.

Dawn was not far off when she slipped into her parents' house in Upper Brook Street. The footman was an old friend who, having a lady friend himself, quite understood – or at least thought he did; he wouldn't give her away. By the time she reached her room she was so buoyed by her success she could have danced.

Undressing quickly, she slid between her sheets, lay back – and grinned widely. She could barely believe it, yet she knew it was true. Luc and she would marry, and soon.

To be his wife, to have him as her husband – even though she'd only faced the fact recently, that had been her unacknowledged dream for years. At the beginning of this Season, she and her twin, Amanda, despairing of fate ever handing them the right mates, had decided to take matters into their own hands. They'd each formed a plan. Amanda's had been straightforward and direct; she'd followed her path to Dexter; last week she'd married him.

She, Amelia, had had her own plan. Luc had been in her mind from the outset, a nebulous yet recognizable shadow, but she'd known the difficulties she would face with him. Having known him all her life, she was well aware that he had no thoughts of marriage – no positive ones, anyway. And he was smart, clever – far too quick, too mentally resistant, to be easily manipulated. Indeed, he was unquestionably the last gentleman any sane lady would set her heart upon.

That being so, she'd determinedly divided her plan into stages. The first had been to establish beyond all doubt who was the right gentleman for her – which of all the eligibles within the *ton*, regardless of whether they were thinking of marriage or not, was the one she wanted above all others.

Her search had brought her back to Luc, left her with him and only him in her sights. The second stage of her plan involved getting what she wanted from him.

That was not going to be easy. She knew what she wanted – a marriage based on love, on sharing, a partnership that extended further and reached deeper than the superficialities of married life. Ultimately, a family – not just the amalgam of his and hers, but theirs, a new entity.

All that she wanted, with a desire that was absolute. How to persuade Luc to fall in with her plans, how to bring him to share her aspirations ...

A novel strategy – one he wouldn't immediately see through and counter – had clearly been necessary. She'd realized that getting him to marry her first and fall in love with her subsequently was the only way forward, yet how to accomplish the former without the latter had initially stumped her. Then she'd noticed the oddity of Emily's and Anne's gowns. After that, alerted, she'd noticed any number of minor details, until she was sure beyond all doubt that the Ashfords needed money.

Money she had in abundance; her considerable dowry would pass to her husband on her marriage.

She'd spent hours rehearsing her arguments, laying out the salient facts, reassuring him that theirs would be a marriage of convenience, that she wouldn't make unwanted emotional demands, that she was prepared to let him go his own way as long as she could similarly go hers. All lies, of course, but she had to be hardheaded; this was Luc she was dealing with – without those lies, she could see no chance of getting his ring on her finger, and that had to be her first goal.

A goal she'd almost realized. Outside her window,

the world was stirring. Her heart light, buoyed by a feeling of rightness, of satisfaction and triumph, she closed her eyes. And tried to rein in her joy. Gaining Luc's agreement to their wedding was not an end, but a beginning, the first active step in her long-range plan. Her plan to translate her most precious dream into reality.

She was one step – one big step – closer to her ultimate goal.

Five hours later, Luc opened his eyes, and remembered with startling clarity all that had happened in his front hall. Up to the point of that unwise bow; after that, he recalled very little. He frowned, struggling to pierce the fog shrouding those latter moments – out of the mists, he retained a definite impression of Amelia, warm, soft, and undeniably female, tucked against his side. He could remember the pressure of her hands on his chest . . .

He realized he was naked under his sheets.

His imagination reared, poised to run riot – a quiet tap distracted him. The door eased open. Cottsloe peeked in.

Luc beckoned, waited only until Cottsloe closed the door to tersely inquire, 'Who put me to bed?'

'I did, my lord.' Cottsloe clasped his hands; his eyes were wary. 'If you remember . . .'

'I remember Amelia Cynster was here.'

'Indeed, my lord.' Cottsloe looked relieved. 'Miss Amelia helped get you upstairs, then she left. Do you wish for anything at this time?'

His relief was greater than Cottsloe's. 'Just my washing water. I'll be down to breakfast shortly. What time is it?'

'Ten o'clock, my lord.' Crossing to the window, Cottsloe drew back the curtains. 'Miss Ffolliot has arrived and is breakfasting with Miss Emily and Miss Anne. Her ladyship has yet to come down.'

'Very good.' Luc relaxed, smiled. 'I've some good news, Cottsloe, which, needless to say, must go no further than you and Mrs. Higgs, if you would be so good as to pass the word to her.'

Cottsloe's face, until then set in typical butler imperturbabilty, eased. 'Her ladyship did whisper that there'd been some encouraging developments.'

'Encouraging indeed – the family's afloat again. We're no longer run aground, and even more than that – financially, we're once again precisely where we should be, where we've pretended to be all these years.' Luc met Cottsloe's steady brown eyes. 'We're no longer living a lie.'

Cottsloe beamed. 'Well done, my lord! I take it one of your investment ventures was successful?'

'*Extravagantly* successful. Even old Child was bowled over by *how* successful. That was the note I got yesterday evening. I couldn't speak to you then, but I wanted to tell both you and Mrs. Higgs that I'll make out drafts to you both for all your back wages this morning. Without your unfailing support, we'd never have weathered the last eight years.'

Cottsloe blushed and looked conscious. 'My lord, neither Mrs. Higgs nor I is in any hurry over the money—'

'No – you've been more than patient.' Luc smiled disarmingly. 'It'll give me great pleasure, Cottsloe, to at last be able to pay both of you as you deserve.'

Phrased in that way, Cottsloe could do nothing but blush again and acquiesce to his wishes.

17

'If you would both come to the study at twelve, I'll have the drafts waiting.'

Cottsloe bowed. 'Very good, my lord. I'll inform Mrs. Higgs.'

Luc nodded and watched as Cottsloe retreated, silently closing the door. Sinking into his pillows, he spent a moment thinking grateful and fond thoughts of his butler and his housekeeper, who had stood unwaveringly behind the family throughout their time of need.

From there, his thoughts wandered to his change of circumstances, his new life ... to the events of the past night.

Mentally checking his faculties and his physical state, he confirmed everything was in working order. Bar a faint headache, he felt no aftereffects from the previous night's excesses. His hard head was the only physical characteristic he'd inherited from his wastrel sire; at least it was a useful one. Unlike all the rest of his father's legacy.

The fifth Viscount Calverton had been a dashing, debonair ne'er-do-well whose only contribution to the family had been to marry well and sire six children. At forty-eight, he'd broken his neck on the hunting field, leaving Luc, then twenty-one, to take over the estate, only to discover it mortgaged to the hilt. Neither he nor his mother had had any idea the family coffers had been ransacked; they'd woken one morning to find themselves, not just paupers, but paupers heavily in debt.

The family properties were all prosperous and productive, but the income was eaten by the debts. There had been literally nothing left on which the family themselves might survive.

Bankruptcy and a sojourn in Newgate threatened.

18

Out of his depth, he'd put aside his pride and appealed to the only person who might have the talent to save them. Robert Child, banker to the ton, then aging, semiretired but still shrewd – no one knew the ins and outs of finance better than he.

Child had heard him out, considered for a day, then agreed to help – to, as he put it, serve as Luc's financial mentor. He'd been relieved yet surprised, but Child had made it clear he was only agreeing because he viewed the prospect of saving the family as a challenge, something to enliven his declining years.

He hadn't cared how Child wanted to see things, he was simply grateful. Thus had commenced what he now considered his apprenticeship in the world of finance. Child had been a strict yet immensely knowledgeable mentor; he'd applied himself and gradually, steadily, succeeded in eroding the huge debt hanging over his and his family's future.

Throughout, he, his mother and Child had had a firm understanding that no circumstance, no detail, could ever be allowed even to hint publicly at the family's state. While he and his mother had agreed readily on the grounds of the social consequences, Child had been even more adamant – one whiff of poverty, and they would be dunned, their secret would out, and the flimsy house of cards that he and Child had painstakingly erected to keep the family ahead of their creditors would come crashing down.

By unstintingly applying themselves to keeping up their facade, with the costs initially underwritten by Child himself, they'd succeeded in maintaining their status. Year by year, their financial position had improved.

Eventually, as the burden of debt had shrunk, under Child's guidance, he'd moved into more speculative investments. He'd proved adept at sizing up risky opportunities and making large profits. It was a dangerous game, but one in which he excelled; his latest venture had proved more rewarding than his wildest dreams. His ship had very definitely come in.

His lips twisted wryly as his mind scanned the years – all the hours he'd spent poring over account books and investment reports in his study while the *ton* imagined he was indulging with opera dancers and Cyprians in company with his peers. He'd come to enjoy the simple act of creating wealth, of understanding money and how it grew. Of creating stability in his family's life. The undertaking had been its own reward.

In many ways, yesterday had been the end of an era, the last day of one chapter in his life. But he'd never forget all he'd learned at Child's feet; he wasn't about to eschew the rules that had governed his behavior for the past eight years, nor was he likely to desert an arena in which he'd discovered not only an unexpected expertise, but his own salvation.

That conclusion left him facing forward, looking into the future. Considering what he wanted from the next stage of his life – considering what Amelia had offered.

He had, through all the years, set his face firmly against marriage as a way to refill the family coffers. With his mother's support and Child's acquiesence, he'd reserved that option as a last resort, one he was deeply relieved he'd never had to pursue. Not, as Amelia had supposed, because of the potential expectations of a wealthy wife, but for a far more entrenched, deeply personal reason.

Put simply, he just couldn't do it. Couldn't even

20

imagine it, marrying a lady for such a cold-blooded reason. The very idea left him chilled; an instinctive, deeply compelling aversion rose at the mere thought. Such a marriage was not one he could live with.

Given that, given his code that had precluded any thoughts of marriage while he was incapable of adequately supporting a wife, he'd spared no real thought for the institution.

A small voice whispered that he had thought of Amelia – not as a wife, but as a woman he'd expected to have to stand by and see married to some other gentleman. As always, the thought left him uncomfortable. Arms over his head, he stretched full length, deliberately shifted his mind, and felt the constriction about his chest dissolve.

Thanks to some peculiar quirk of fate, she wasn't going to marry another – she was going to marry him.

That prospect was very much to his liking. He hadn't considered the fact that yesterday's victory left him free to pursue marriage if and when he wished, until she'd suggested it. But now she had ... now she'd *offered* ...

He wanted to marry her. The impulse that had risen last night at her words – the instinct to seize and claim her – had diminished not one whit in the intervening hours. If anything, it had grown more definite, an amorphous urge solidifying into conviction and rock-like resolution. Now he was debt-free, now he was rich, marrying her was, at least as far as his instincts were concerned, not just permissible but highly desirable. He felt no aversion, but rather an unexpected degree of impatience.

Mind racing, he mentally constructed the future as he would have it, Amelia centrally featured as his

21

wife, then turned his mind to achieving that goal. The hows, whys, wherefores ...

Accustomed as he was to checking every action for potential ramifications, the problem was immediately apparent. If he told her he no longer needed her dowry, what reason could he give for wanting to marry her?

His mind simply stopped, remained stubbornly blank, refused to countenance the reason by even thinking it. He grimaced, changed tack, tried to see his way forward ...

Correcting her mistake, thus freeing her from their verbal contract, and then attempting to win her back was a fool's agenda. He knew how she'd react; she'd be mortified, and would very likely avoid him for the next several years, something she was perfectly capable of doing. Yet at some primal level, he already thought of her as his, already seized if not yet claimed; the concept of releasing her, lifting his paw and letting her go ...

No. He couldn't – wouldn't – do it.

He knew where they stood at the moment – he needed to find a way forward from there, toward their wedding, and had no intention of taking a single step back. When it came to her, his instincts were unequivocal in their refusal to be lenient; she'd offered, he'd accepted, *ergo* she was his.

Could he tell her the truth but decline to release her? Confess he no longer needed her dowry but insist they marry anyway?

She wouldn't accept that. No matter how insistent he was, how hard he argued – no matter what he said – she'd feel he was only being kind, sparing her the pain of rejection ...

He grimaced again, folded his arms behind his head. There was enough truth to that to make it impossible to argue – not with her; she knew him too well. He would indeed do much – given his heretofore lack of interest in marriage, possibly even that – to avoid hurting her. Females such as she, females he cared about, needed to be protected – that was one of his most fundamental beliefs. The fact they might argue, rail, and disagree was beside the point; such resistance held no power to sway him.

The only way he might convince her he wasn't being kind was to admit and explain his desire to have her as his wife.

Once again, his mind seized. He couldn't even explain that desire to himself, did not understand whence its power sprang; the idea of admitting to the type of desire that of itself impelled a man to marriage, in words, to her – the object of said desire – evoked a resistance every bit as rock-solid as his intention to wed her.

He knew her, and the females in her family, very well; such an admission would be tantamount to handing over the reins to her, not something he would willingly do this side of hell. He wanted and would have her to wife, but he was implacably opposed to giving her any unnecessary hold over him.

The fact that others of his kind had ultimately succumbed and done so, most recently Martin, floated through his mind; he ignored it. He had never been inclined to let emotions or desires rule him; if anything, the last eight years had forced him to master them even more rigidly. No woman was capable of overriding his will; no woman would ever control him.

Which left him staring up at the canopy, toying

with his remaining option. He considered, analyzed, extrapolated, predicted. Formulated a plan. Searched for and found the flaws, the hurdles; evaluated them, devised the means to counter them.

It was not an easy or straightforward path, yet it was one that led to his desired destination. And the price was one he was prepared to pay.

He hesitated only long enough to run one last mental assessment; he saw nothing to deter him. Knowing Amelia, he had no time to lose. If he wanted to retain control of their interaction, he needed to act immediately.

Throwing back the covers, he rose. Dragging a sheet off the bed, he wound it around his hips as he crossed to the desk before the window. Sitting, he drew a sheet of fine paper from one pigeonhole and picked up his pen.

He was sanding the note when a footman entered with his washing water. Luc glanced up, then turned back to the note. 'Wait a minute.'

He folded the note's corners, then dipped the pen in the inkstand and wrote her name. Waving the note to dry the ink, he turned to the footman. 'Deliver this immediately to 12 Upper Brook Street.'

Chapter Two

'Why the museum?' Amelia asked as she approached him.

Reaching out, Luc closed his fingers about her elbow and turned her around. 'So we can converse in reasonable privacy, in public, and anyone seeing us will imagine we've simply and innocently come upon each other. No one ever imagines assignations occur in the museum. I'm here, clearly under duress, escorting my sisters and Miss Ffolliot – *no*! Don't wave. They're going to wander and meet me later.'

Amelia glanced at the three girls at the other end of the room, staring wide-eyed at a display. 'Does it matter if they see us?'

'No. But having seen you, they'll expect to join us, and that would be counterproductive.' He urged her through an archway into a room devoted to Egyptian artifacts.

Transferring her gaze to his face, she noted his expression was, as usual, uninformative. His dark hair, black as pitch, was perfectly groomed; not a trace of dissipation marred the beauty of his classical features. Impossible to guess that ten hours before

25

he'd been drop-at-her-feet drunk.

How to frame her question? Why are we assignating?

Looking ahead, she mentally girded her loins. 'What did you want to talk about?'

The glance he threw her was sharp and dark. He drew her to a halt by the side of the room, in front of a case filled with pottery. 'I would have thought, after our meeting last night, that the subject would be obvious.'

He'd changed his mind – woken up, realized what he'd said, and was going to take it back. Hands clasped, fingers gripping tightly, she raised her chin, fixed her eyes on his. 'There's no point telling me that you were so drunk you didn't know what you were saying. I heard you, and you heard yourself. You agreed – and I intend holding you to it.'

He blinked, frowned – then his frown grew blacker. 'I've no intention of claiming diminished responsibility. I wasn't so drunk I didn't know what I was doing.'

'Oh.' His acid tones left little doubt he was in earnest.

'That's not what we need to talk about.' His frown still lingered.

Hugely relieved, she fought to hide the fact, schooling her features to simple interest. 'What, then?'

He glanced about, then took her arm and urged her on, strolling slowly. Because of his height, he had to look down to speak to her, rendering their conversation private regardless of the public setting. 'We've agreed to marry, now we need to take the next steps. Decide on how and when.'

26

She brightened; he wasn't going to renege on their agreement. Quite the opposite. The sensation of her heart soaring was distracting. 'I'd thought in a few days. You can get a special license, can't you?'

His frown returned. 'What about a wedding dress? What about your family? A few days – doesn't that seem a mite precipitate?'

She halted, met his gaze, set her chin. 'I don't care about a dress, and I can talk my parents around. I've always wanted to be a June bride, and that means getting married within the next four weeks.'

His eyes narrowed; she knew – could see in his dark blue eyes – that he was debating some point, but, as usual, she couldn't tell what.

'Four weeks will work – four days won't. Just consider – what will people think when they suddenly learn, out of the blue, that we're marrying in such unseemly haste? Such behavior will raise the question of why, and there are only two possible answers, neither of which will endear the match to your family or, indeed, to me.'

She considered ... reluctantly conceded. 'People would suspect money was at the heart of it, and after all your hard work hiding your family's state, that's the very last thing you'd want.' She sighed, looked up. 'You're right. Very well – within four weeks then.' It would still be June.

Luc gritted his teeth, gripped her arm, and led her on. 'I wouldn't want them to think the other, either.'

Her brows rose. 'That you and I ...' She blushed lightly.

'Aside from anything else, no one would believe it.' He kept her moving when she tried to stop and face him. 'Pretend we're looking at the exhibits.'

27

She turned her gaze to the glass cases lining the walls. 'But we've known each other for years.' Her voice sounded tight.

'And have shown not the smallest sign of having any interest in developing a relationship closer than that of family acquaintance – precisely. We need to lay some groundwork, and if you've set your heart on four weeks, then we'll do it in four weeks.' She glanced up; he hurried on before she could argue. 'Here's my plan.'

He'd expected to have two months or more to accomplish it, but four weeks ... he could seduce any woman in four weeks.

'We need society simply to accept our marriage – there's no reason it won't. As far as anyone knows, we suit to a tee. All we need do is lead them to the realization gradually, before we make any announcement.'

She nodded. 'Don't startle the horses.'

'Exactly. As I see it, the easiest, most believable path for us to follow is for me to start looking around – I won't need to look far for my eye to fall on you. You were bridesmaid to my groomsman at Martin and Amanda's wedding. You're in Emily and Anne's company much of the time. Given we've known each other for so long, there's no reason I can't fix my interest on you more or less at first glance.'

Her expression told him she was following his reasoning, seeing the picture he was painting. 'Then,' he stated, 'we go through the customary stages of courtship, although as you insist on a June wedding, it'll have to be a whirlwind one.'

A slight frown marred her brow. 'You mean we should pretend that we're ... attracted in the usual way?'

There wouldn't be any pretense involved, not if he

had any say in the matter; he fully intended their courtship – her seduction – to be real. 'We do the usual things – meet at balls and parties, go on outings, and so on. With the Season slowing down and Emily and Anne to be entertained, we won't have any difficulty inventing occasions.'

'Hmm ... that's all very well, but do we really need four weeks?' They'd reached the corner of the room; she halted and faced him. 'Everyone already knows *I've* been looking around.'

'Indeed – that will fit, too.' He looped his arm in hers and drew her on, still progressing slowly as if scanning the cases. 'We can mutually notice each other, and go on from there. You've had plenty of experience flirting over the last years – just play it by ear and follow my lead.'

She narrowed her eyes at him; her chin set. 'I still don't see why we need take *four weeks*. I can pretend to fall in love in one.'

He bit his tongue on an unwise rejoinder and narrowed his eyes back. 'Four weeks. You offered, I accepted, but I call the play from now on.'

She halted. 'Why?'

He met her belligerent gaze, held it. When she simply glared back, unwavering, he quietly stated, 'Because that's the way it's going to be.'

He was adamant about that, and not at all averse to having the point broached thus early in their relationship. With any other woman, it wouldn't need to be stated, but Amelia was a Cynster – wise to have the lines drawn, the chain of command established. And this was undoubtedly the moment; she couldn't argue, not without risking what she'd already gained – his agreement to their wedding.

Abruptly, nose elevating, she looked away. 'Very well. Have it your way. Four weeks.' She stepped out, not waiting for him to take her arm. 'But not a day more.'

The stipulation reached him as she walked on; he didn't immediately follow, instead grasped the moment to tamp down the impulse she had, all but deliberately, evoked. He couldn't press her yet – not for a week or so. But once he had her tied up tight . . .

She paused, ostensibly to study a case of knives; he watched her, noting the way the light glinted on her curls.

Deception was not the best foundation on which to base a marriage, but he'd told no lies, and wouldn't; he'd merely omitted mentioning a pertinent fact. Once she was his and he was sure of her, then he could tell her the truth – once her feminine heart was committed, she wouldn't care *why* they were marrying, only that they were.

None of that, of course, required a public courtship. Whether he seduced her now or after they wed made no difference to his plan. However, while he felt no qualms over her imagining that he was marrying her for her money – given it was her idea in the first place – he had an absolute aversion to society imagining any such thing. That, in his lexicon, would be unacceptable conduct, conduct unbefitting a gentleman. Not only would the image be a lie, letting society think he was marrying her purely for monetary reasons, without any real affection, wouldn't reflect well on her. Especially coming hard on the heels of Martin and Amanda's love-inspired union.

In his view, she deserved better.

With a haughty toss of her curls, she moved on. He stepped out, prowling in her wake, his longer strides eating the distance between them despite his languorous pace.

She deserved to be wooed, resistant and suspicious though she was, impatient and dismissive. And it would give him the opportunity he needed to tie her to him with something other than prosaic pragmatism. With something that would render his reason for wedding her inconsequential.

By declining to examine what that reason was, he hoped it would remain in its nascent state, ephemeral – less demanding. Why such a compulsion had surfaced now, why it was so focused on her, the sudden realization that she was the only wife he wanted all contributed to his underlying unease; despite the craving she and that reason evoked in him, she'd shown no sign of any reciprocal emotion.

Yet.

Reaching her side, he took her hand. Met her gaze as she faced him. 'I'll need to meet with Emily and Anne soon – it'll be better if they don't see us together.'

She arched a brow. 'Plotting?'

'Indeed.' He held her gaze, then bowed. 'I'll see you at the Mountfords' tonight.'

She hesitated, then nodded. 'Until tonight.'

He pressed her fingers, then released them. She turned and looked at the glass case.

Two heartbeats later, he left her.

There was one person who had to know the truth. On returning home, Luc glanced at the clock, then repaired to his study and busied himself with various financial matters awaiting his attention. When the clocks chimed four, he set aside his papers and climbed the stairs to his mother's sitting room.

She would have been resting, but she always rose at four o'clock. Reaching the upstairs gallery, he glimpsed Mrs. Higgs in the front hall below, heading for the stairs, a well-stocked tray in her hands. At his mother's sitting room door, he tapped; hearing her voice bid him enter, he opened the door.

She'd been reclining on the chaise, but was now sitting up, rearranging cushions at her back.

A still beautiful woman, although her dramatic coloring – black hair, fair complexion, dark blue eyes the same as his – had faded, there remained some indefinable quality in her smile, in her fine eyes, that reached out to men and made them eager to serve her. A quality of which she was not oblivious but had not, as far as he knew, employed since his father's death. He'd never understood his parents' union, for his mother was intelligent and astute, yet she'd been unswervingly faithful to a shiftless wastrel, not just during his life, but to his memory, too.

She saw him and raised both brows. He smiled, entered, then held the door for Mrs. Higgs, who inclined her head and swept past to set her tray on the low table before the chaise.

'I've brought two cups, as it happens, and there's plenty of cakes – will you be wanting anything more, m'lord?'

Luc surveyed the small feast Higgs was busily laying out. 'Thank you, Higgs, no. This will be sufficient.'

His mother added her smiling thanks. 'Indeed,

32

thank you, Higgs. And is everything in train for dinner as we discussed?'

'Aye, ma'am.' Higgs straightened and bestowed a beaming smile on them both. 'All's well on the way, and everything's right with the world.'

On that triumphant note, she bobbed and whisked herself out of the room, closing the door behind her.

His mother's smile deepened; she held out her hand and he gripped it, felt her fingers curl tight. 'She's been bouncing about all day as if she was eighteen again.' Lifting her gaze to his face, she continued, 'You brought us around, my son – did I tell you how proud I am of you?'

Looking down into her lovely eyes, glowing and suspiciously bright, Luc quelled a schoolboy urge to shuffle his feet and duck his head. He smiled easily, squeezed her hand, then released it and waved dismissively. 'No one is more relieved than I.'

He sat in the armchair facing the chaise.

Minerva's shrewd gaze traveled his face, then she reached for the teapot. 'I've invited Robert to dine tonight – that was an excellent idea. We'll be serving at six – early for us, but you know how he is.'

Luc took the cup she held out to him. 'Emily and Anne?'

'I've told them they've been gadding rather too much. As we've no formal dinner to attend tonight, I suggested they nap until seven, then have dinner in their rooms before they get ready for the Mountfords' ball.'

Luc's lips twitched. His mother was as ruthless a manipulator as he.

'Now.' Minerva sat back with her cup, sipped, then fixed her gaze on his face. 'What's troubling you?'

He smiled easily. 'I doubt you would call it "trouble" – I've decided to marry.'

She blinked, stilled, then widened her eyes. 'Correct me if I'm wrong, but isn't that decision somewhat sudden?'

'Yes, and no.' He set down his cup, wondering how little he could get away with revealing. His mother was remarkably acute, especially when it came to her offspring. The only one she'd been unable to read well was his brother Edward, recently banished for crimes they all still found hard to comprehend.

Shifting his thoughts from Edward, he glanced at his mother. 'The decision's recent in that prior to yesterday, as you know, I was in no position to think of marriage. The notion's not recent in that I've had my eye on the lady in question for some time.'

Minerva's gaze remained steady. 'Amelia Cynster.'

It was an effort to mask his shock. Had he been *that* unknowingly transparent? He pushed the thought aside. Inclined his head. 'As you say. We've decided—'

'Wait.' Minerva's eyes grew round. 'She's already agreed?'

He backtracked. 'I came up with her briefly last night.' He avoided mentioning where; Minerva would imagine he'd looked in at some ball. 'We met again this afternoon and took our discussions further. It's tentative, of course, but . . .' No matter which way his mind darted, he could see no way to avoid making a reasonably clean breast of the whole. He sighed. 'The truth is, she suggested it.'

'Great heavens!' Brows flying, Minerva looked her question.

'She'd seen through our facade. From a lot of little

34

things, she realized we were hard-pressed. She wishes to marry, reasonably and well – I think Amanda's marriage has left her lonely in a way she's never been before – but she feels no compelling wish to marry any of the eligibles lining up to pay court to her.'

'So she thought of you?'

He shrugged. 'We have known each other for a very long time. Realizing our family's financial straits, she suggested a marriage between us would serve all our ends. She would become my viscountess, and gain the status of married lady, and the family finances would be repaired.'

'And what of you?'

Luc met his mother's dark eyes. After a moment, he said, 'I'm agreeable.'

She didn't press for more; she studied his expression, then nodded, and sipped. After a long moment, she met his eyes again. 'Am I right in assuming you haven't told her you're now fabulously wealthy?'

He shook his head. 'It would create a not-inconsiderable degree of awkwardness – you know how she'd feel. As it is ...' He stopped himself from shrugging again, picked up his cup, and sipped instead. Prayed his mother would not further pursue his motives.

She didn't, not with words, but she let the silence stretch; her gaze, dark, shrewd, and understanding, remained on him – he felt it like a weight. He had to fight not to shift in the chair.

Eventually, Minerva set her cup on her saucer. 'Let's see if I have this straight. While some men pretend to love or at least to a pretty passion to conceal the fact they're marrying for money, *you* propose to pretend you're marrying for money to conceal—'

'That's merely temporary.' He met her eyes, and felt his jaw firm. 'I will tell her, but I prefer to choose my own time. Naturally, her confusion will remain entirely between us – as far as society and all others are concerned, we're marrying for the customary reasons.'

Minerva held his gaze; a minute passed, then she inclined her head. 'Very well.' Her voice held a note of compassion. She set aside her cup, her expression gentle. 'If that is what you wish, I will engage to say nothing that will preempt your revelation.'

That was the undertaking he'd come there to get; they both understood that.

He nodded, finished his tea. Minerva leaned back and chatted on inconsequential matters. Eventually, he rose and took his leave of her.

'Don't forget.'

He heard the murmur as he reached the door; hand on the knob, he looked back.

She hesitated; although he couldn't see it, he sensed the frown in her eyes. Then she smiled. 'Dinner at six.'

He nodded; when she said nothing more, he inclined his head and left.

Later that evening, they walked into the Mountfords' ballroom and joined the queue waiting to greet their host and hostess. Beside Minerva, Luc glanced around. The ballroom was fashionably full, but he couldn't see any head of bouncing golden ringlets.

Behind him, Emily and Anne were sharing breathless confidences with Anne's best friend, Fiona

Ffolliot. Fiona was a neighbor's daughter from Rutlandshire; her father's property adjoined Luc's principal estate. Fiona had come to London for part of the Season with her widowed father; they were staying with General Ffolliot's sister in Chelsea. Although well-to-do, the family was not well connected; Minerva had offered to take Fiona about with Emily and Anne, so she could see more, and be seen by more.

Luc had approved. Having Fiona artlessly breezy beside her gave Anne, always timorous and shy, more confidence and in some measure released Emily, older by a year, from Anne's side. It seemed likely that Emily would receive an offer from Lord Kirkpatrick at the end of the Season. They were both young, but the match would be a good one, and was looked upon with favor by both families.

The line of guests shuffled forward. His mother leaned nearer, lowering her voice so that no one else could hear. 'I think our dinner was an unqualified success. A nice way to set the seal on our past affairs.'

Luc arched a brow. 'Prior to burying them?'

Minerva smiled and looked away. 'Precisely.'

After an instant's pause, he continued, 'I'll still be seeing Robert – I don't intend giving up my interest in such endeavors.'

His mother opened her eyes at him, then smiled and patted his arm. 'Darling, if your interests truly lie in that direction – rather than the other – then I'm certainly not going to complain.'

The laughter in her voice, the light that now glowed undimmed in her eyes – the way her spirits in the space of a day had lifted – made all his hard work worthwhile. As he led her on to greet the Mountfords, and heard Emily and Anne's gowns shushing as they followed, Luc mentally acknowledged that, despite the trials of the years – despite his father's efforts and those more recently of Edward – he was yet a lucky man.

And about to get luckier. The thought echoed in his mind when, having settled his mother on a chaise beside Lady Horatia Cynster, Amelia's aunt, he finally caught sight of his bride-to-be. She was whirling down a country dance, oblivious as yet of his presence. Curls jouncing, she was laughing up at Geoffrey Melrose, her partner; Luc wasn't enamored of the sight.

His sisters' and Fiona's hands had also been claimed; they, too, were on the floor. Luc fixed his gaze on Amelia, waited . . .

She glanced around, saw him – and missed her next step. She quickly looked away, readjusted to the dance; she didn't glance his way again. However, at the end of the measure, she glided over to join his sisters. As throughout this Season both she and Amanda had been assiduous in easing Emily's and Anne's way – a selfless act for which he was more grateful than he had any intention of ever telling either twin – no one saw anything unusual in her making one of their circle.

Not one gossipmonger so much as raised a brow when he strolled across the ballroom to join the group.

They were a colorful and handsome company; the three younger girls, all brown-haired, all somewhat shorter than Amelia, wore gowns of pastel blue and pink, petals surrounded by the gentlemen's darker coats. At the center, Amelia glowed in a silk gown of muted gold. The shade emphasized the ivory perfection of her skin, turned her hair a more definite gold, made her eyes a more intense, more startling blue.

Emily's, Anne's, and Fiona's partners had lingered to chat; three other young gentlemen had come up, hoping to secure the girls' hands for the next dance. To Luc's irritation, Melrose had followed Amelia, and Hardcastle had ambled up, casting covetous eyes over her slender form. Hiding his instinctive snarl behind an easy smile, he bowed to Amelia, nodded to both gentlemen, adroitly maneuvering so he ended by Amelia's side.

She noticed, but other than one glance, gave no sign. After casting a comprehensive glance over his sisters, Fiona and their beaux, he left them, for once, to fend for themselves and turned his attention to Amelia.

To eliminating a potential problem.

'I heard,' he murmured into the first lull in the conversation, 'that Toby Mick was likely to meet The Gnasher at Derby.'

Amelia stared at him; Melrose looked slightly shocked. It was an unwritten rule that gentlemen did not discuss such bloodthirsty subjects as the exploits of the Fancy in the presence of ladies.

Hardcastle, however, positively vibrated with pent-up enthusiasm. He bent a pleading look on Amelia. 'You don't mind, do you, my dear?' Without waiting for any reply, he pounced. 'It's quite true – I had it from Gilroy himself. They say it'll be all over in three rounds, but—'

Melrose was torn. Luc merely waited, feigning mild interest, pretending not to notice Amelia's sharp glance.

39

'And there's talk that now they've doubled the purse, Cartwright is considering throwing his hat into the ring.'

The mention of the latest contender was too much for Melrose.

'I say! But is there really any likelihood of that? I mean, it's not as if Cartwright needs the outing – he was in action only two weeks ago on the Downs. Why risk—'

'No, no! You see, it's the challenge.'

'Yes, but—'

Luc turned to Amelia. Smiled. 'Would you care to stroll?'

'Indeed.' She gave him her hand.

He tucked it possessively in his arm. The other two barely broke off their argument to acknowledge their farewells.

'You're wicked,' she said the instant they were out of earshot. 'One of the matrons will overhear, and then they'll be in trouble.'

He raised his brows high. 'Did I force them to it?'

'Humph!' Amelia looked ahead, and tried to quell the fluttery sensation that had developed in her stomach. It couldn't be nervousness; she was at a loss as to its cause.

Then Luc leaned nearer, guiding her around a trio of gentlemen. The sudden *frisson* that flashed down her side – the side he'd brushed – opened her eyes.

Of course! She'd never been this physically close to him, except when he'd been *non compos mentis*. He was now wide-awake, and closer than the merely polite; she could sense him, hard, strong, and very male, a potent living force beside her.

A distracted moment later, she realized the emotion

40

evoked by his nearness wasn't panic, or fear, but something far more giddy. Decidedly more pleasurable.

She glanced at his face. He felt her gaze and looked
down. Then his gaze grew intent; his eyes searched
hers.

Her lungs seized.

The introduction for the first waltz cut through the
conversations. Luc glanced up; she dragged in a huge
breath.

Held it again as he looked back at her. His fingers
closed about her hand; he lifted it from his sleeve,
then elegantly bowed, his eyes never leaving hers.
'My dance, I believe?'

At that precise instant, she would have felt far safer
dancing with a wolf, but she smiled, inclined her
head, and let him draw her to the floor. What had
Amanda called him? A leopard?

And lethal to boot.

She had to agree with her twin's estimation as he
gathered her close and steered her into the swirling
throng.

Her chest felt tight; her skin came alive. Her wits
were giddy, her senses taut. With anticipation, expectation. Of what, she wasn't sure, but that only
increased the excitement.

It was ridiculous – they'd waltzed before, on
numerous occasions, yet it had never been like this.
Never before had his eyes, his attention, been
focused, fixed on her. He didn't even seem to hear the
music, or rather, the music became part of some
sensory whole that included the way their bodies
revolved, swayed, touched, brushed as he effortlessly
guided them down the long room.

Never before had she been so aware; never had she

waltzed like this, with him or anyone else. Drawn into the music, into the moment, into ...

Something had changed. Something fundamental – he wasn't the same man she'd danced with before. Even the planes of his face seemed harder, more chiseled, more austere. His body seemed more powerful, the fashionable screen more transparent. And there was something in his eyes as they rested on hers – something ... she couldn't place it, but her instincts recognized enough to make her shiver.

He felt it; his lids lowered, long lashes screening his dark eyes. His lips twisted wrily; his hand shifted on her back, reassuring, soothing.

She stiffened. 'What are you about?'

The words tumbled out before she'd thought, their tone as suspicious as her glance.

Luc opened his eyes wide, resisted the urge to laugh – to ask what the hell she *thought* he was about. Then the implication struck, and all thought of laughing fled – but he still had to fight to hide his possessive gloat, to keep a smug smile from lifting his lips. Despite his efforts, it must have showed; he quickly moved to dampen the temper building in her eyes. 'Don't worry – I know what I'm doing. I told you this afternoon, just follow my lead.'

He shifted his hand on her back again, drawing her closer as they went through the turns. 'I won't bite, but you can't expect me to change my spots overnight.'

Or, indeed, at all, but he left that unsaid. After a moment, the grim look in her eyes eased; he felt her relax once more into his arms – indeed, relax more than before.

'Oh – I see.'

He sincerely doubted it. He didn't either; it took him a few moments to follow her train of thought, then he realized – she thought the effect he knew he was having on her was simply part of his ... mystique. The natural outcome of the application of his popularly acclaimed talents.

In part, she was right, but that didn't fully explain her reaction, or his. Or his to hers, for that matter.

Experience, and his was extensive, told him she was remarkably sensitive, stunningly responsive. The fact that had startled her strongly suggested such responses had been limited, at least thus far in her life, to him.

Hence his surge of appreciation. She was a sensual prize, untouched, unawakened, and she was his, all his. Small wonder he felt like gloating.

He knew, had known for years, that the response she evoked in him was stronger, different, more powerful than with any other woman he'd met. In all those years, concentrating on subduing his own reactions, he'd never thought to look for hers. Why so? He'd never thought of pursuing her.

Before.

It took effort to resist the impulse to draw her closer still and push ahead with his plan to tie her to him sensually, yet the wisdom of the years warned that going too fast would risk her guessing his plan – and resisting. She'd become even more suspicious than she had been a moment ago.

However, if he took things gradually, seduced her step by deliberate step, then she, now thinking her responses merely the norm, the usual, nothing out of the ordinary ... by the time she realized the strength of her own desire, she'd be too addicted to break free,

43

too enthralled to quibble over why they were marrying, even when he confessed he didn't need her dowry.

The music wound down and they slowed. His senses, every last ounce of his awareness focused on her. On the physical her, on the promise inherent in her slender form, on her skin, her eyes, her lips – the cadence of her breathing.

His, all his.

He had to force his arms to release her, had to screen his intent behind the black veil of his lashes. Had to smile easily, tuck her hand in his arm, and turn back to the other guests. 'We'd better stroll.'

She looked slightly put out. 'There's no one I really want to meet.'

'Nevertheless.' When she glanced at him, he murmured, 'We can't instantly, after one perfectly ordinary waltz, cleave to each other's company.'

She grimaced, then waved ahead. 'Very well – lead on.'

He did, much against his wishes, especially knowing it was against hers, too. But a plan was a plan, and his was sound. He found a knot of mutual friends; they stood and conversed with their customary facility. They were both at home in this sphere; neither needed the other's support.

It came as a surprise when he realized he'd retreated from the conversation, content to listen to Amelia's chatter, to her laughter and quick-witted sallies. She had a tongue almost as keen as his, and a mind equally agile; he was taken aback at how often she voiced his silent thoughts.

He caught a glance or two directed their way, and inwardly smiled. His relaxed but watchful presence by her side was not going unremarked. By dint of strolling on at just the right moment, he kept her to himself for the next dance; watching the other dancers twirl through a reel, they strolled about the floor.

Unfortunately, he couldn't, yet, keep her to himself entirely. Lord Endicott appeared and, with an irritatingly pompous air, claimed the second waltz.

He had to endure the sight of her smiling and laughing up at Endicott for the entire measure. Then, at the end of the dance, the witless woman didn't return to him; he had to stalk after her.

When Reggie Carmarthen appeared through the crowd, he very nearly fell on his neck. Reggie was not at all surprised to find him pushing Amelia into his arms for the next dance; they all knew each other well.

Consequently, when he reappeared at the end of the dance to reclaim Amelia's hand, Reggie looked stunned.

Amelia grinned and patted Reggie's arm. 'Don't worry.'

Reggie stared at her, then at him. Eventually, Reggie mumbled, 'Whatever you say.'

Impatient though he was, he bided his time. He didn't chase off Reggie, a safe companion, even though Reggie kept slanting glances at him, expecting him to bare his teeth. Together with some others, they went into supper, filling one of the larger tables, exchanging easy, good-natured banter. He sat beside Amelia, but other than that, was careful to make no overly possessive gestures.

They returned to the ballroom just as the orchestra struck up for the next waltz. He smiled, with easy charm solicited Amelia's hand.

Amelia returned his smile and bestowed her hand – just as Lord Endicott, who'd been barreling toward them, reached them.

'I'm so sorry.' She smiled at his lordship. 'Lord Calverton was before you.'

Lord Endicott bore the loss gracefully; he bowed. 'Perhaps the next dance, then?'

She let her smile deepen. 'Perhaps.'

Luc pinched her fingers. She turned from his lordship. Her eyes met Luc's – she glimpsed a hardness, a something that made her breath catch – then he lifted his gaze and nodded to Endicott. Then he led her to the floor.

She didn't get another chance to look into his face until they were whirling down the room. His eyes – a true midnight blue – were always difficult to read; when half-screened by his distractingly long, thick lashes, guessing their expression became impossible. But the planes of his face were hard, uncompromising, not aloof as they usually were ...

'What *is* the matter? And don't say nothing. I know you better than that.'

Hearing her words, she realized they were even truer than before; she now knew the tension investing his lean frame was not usual.

'It would help our cause considerably if you could refrain from encouraging other gentlemen.'

She blinked. 'Endicott? I wasn't—'

'Not smiling at them would be a good start.'

She stared at his face, at his hard expression and even harder eyes – he was serious. His acerbic tone told her he was in one of his tempers. She had to struggle not to grin. 'Luc, do listen to yourself.'

46

His eyes met hers briefly; he frowned. 'I'd rather not.'

He drew her closer – a fraction too close for propriety – as they revolved through the turns. And didn't ease his hold as they swept back up the room.

Being held so firmly, whirled through the dance so effortlessly, was distractingly pleasant, yet ... she sighed. 'All right – how do you want me to behave? I thought I wasn't supposed to pretend to fall in love with you all in one week. Are we rescripting our performance?'

It was a moment before he answered, through his teeth, 'No. Just ... don't be so animated. Smile vaguely, as if you're not really focusing on them.'

When she could keep her lips straight, she looked at him, nodded. 'Very well. I'll try. I take it,' she murmured as the music slowed, 'that I'm supposed to focus on you?'

She caught his eye, thought the blue darkened, saw his jaw set. He gave her no answer. Instead, one hand locking about hers, he towed her from the floor.

Eyes widening, she saw the terrace doors approaching. They were open. The flagged terrace beyond was bathed in moonlight. 'Where are we going?'

'To advance our script.'

Chapter Three

He led her onto the terrace, where numerous couples were strolling, taking advantage of the mild night. The moon, a silver half disc, rode high, bathing the scene in shimmering light.

Luc glanced around, then wound her arm in his and turned along the terrace. 'It's customary,' he said, as if in answer to the question in her mind, 'for courting couples to spend time together in conducive surrounds.'

Conducive to what? She glanced at him, but he said no more. She looked ahead. 'Do you think anyone's noticed yet?'

'They have, but it'll take a few nights to convince them there's more to our interaction than mere socializing.'

'So how do you propose advancing our script?'

She felt his glance. 'All we need do is follow the age-old plot. The gossips will wake up soon enough.'

Age-old plot. She was perfectly certain his version would differ significantly from hers. Not that she intended arguing with what she hoped his plan would be – not when it bade fair to fall in so well with hers.

They continued along the increasingly sparsely populated terrace; most couples remained within the area illuminated by the ballroom's light. At the terrace's end, Luc cast a swift glance about, then closed his hand hard over hers; three long strides, drawing her with him, and they were around the side of the mansion. Shallow steps led down, then the terrace continued beneath a loggia supporting a rioting white rose.

Once beneath it, they were screened from above, and from anyone on the terrace. The garden beyond the loggia was deserted, the room that gave onto it dark, not in use.

They were alone. Private.

Luc halted, drew her to face him. She looked up, caught only the briefest glimpse of his face as he bent his head and, one hand cradling her jaw, set his lips to hers.

Gently.

The fact penetrated her whirling mind; she'd braced for an assault. She'd been kissed before; in her experience all men were greedy.

Not Luc.

Not that she doubted, not for one instant, that he would want, and would take, more, but he didn't grab, seize, demand. He lured.

Touch by touch, caress by caress. It was she who moved into him, into the kiss. His hand shifted from her jaw to her nape, long fingers hard against her sensitive skin. His other hand still grasped hers, fingers twining, locking.

His lips moved on hers, subtly shifting, encouraging . . . unthinking, she parted her own; he surged in. Not aggressively, yet powerfully. His habit of slow grace seemed even more pronounced in this arena. Every movement was unhurried, languid, yet laced with absolute mastery.

She shivered, realized how completely he'd captured her – her wits, her senses. She couldn't see, couldn't hear – was distant from the world and had no wish to go back, no wish to be distracted from the sheer wonder of the kiss. As if he understood, he angled his head and pressed deeper, drew her with him.

Excitement shimmered through her. The intimacy touched her; she found herself eagerly, wantonly, surrendering her mouth – pleasure coursed through her when he took. Claimed.

That was what he'd wanted, intended to achieve with his advancing of their 'script.' He'd moved to set his mark on her, a first declaration, a preliminary statement of absolute intent.

She was in absolute agreement. He'd set the scene, pledged his troth – now it was her turn. If she would.

She wasn't sure how to do it. Tentatively, she stepped nearer; her bodice brushed his coat. The steely tension holding him increased; the fingers at her nape tightened ... with an inward shrug, she boldly kissed him back.

And he froze.

Emboldened, she sent her free hand sliding up to his shoulder, then higher still to trace his lean cheek. She pressed another long, tempting kiss on him, then flicked her fingers free of his slackened grip. Lifting that arm, she draped it on his shoulder, slid her fingers into his silky hair – and stepped closer yet, kissed him more determinedly—

His arms closed around her. He didn't crush her,

yet there was no disguising the possessiveness behind the act. She twined her arms about his neck, but she didn't need to hold him to her; she offered her mouth again and he took control, wrested it from her.

His next kiss curled her toes.

Heat flooded her. Not in a searing rush but in a steady relentless tide. It poured down her veins, filled her up, took her over ... she clung, and drank, felt her senses slide beneath the heating waves. Let herself sink against him, hard as steel beneath his elegant clothes, felt the vise of his arms close in.

His languidness – always a veneer – had flown. Every kiss seemed deeper, stronger, like a current steadily eroding her ability to resist. Not that she was resisting, a fact he knew. He didn't demand – he asked for no permission at all – but simply took, claimed, opened her eyes, ripped aside the veils, and showed her how far a simple kiss could go.

She was with him every inch of the way.

It was the tensing of her fingers at his nape, the arching of her spine – the sudden, blinding need to take the kiss much further – that jerked Luc back to reality. To sanity.

What the hell were they doing?

Abruptly, he drew back, broke the kiss. Struggled to draw breath, to steady his whirling head.

Couldn't do it with her in his arms, with her slender, pliant, oh-so-feminine body pressed so invitingly to his. His heart thundered. He forced his arms to unlock, forced his hands to grip her waist and set her back from him.

She swayed; he steadied her as she blinked at him in surprise.

He dragged in a huge breath. 'We—' The word

51

came out as a strangled rumble. He cleared his throat
– clogged with desire – managed to growl, 'It's time
we returned to the ballroom.'

'Time?' She stared at him, then glanced about.
'How do you know? There's no clock.'

'Clock?' For one instant, he couldn't imagine ...
then he shook his head. 'Never mind. Come on.'

Grabbing her hand, he towed her along, then up the
steps to the terrace. Hauling in another breath, he
paused, feeling his wits slowly falling back into place.

Into working order, where they hadn't been for the
past God-knew-how-many minutes.

There were still couples wandering. Setting
Amelia's hand on his sleeve, he steered her toward
the ballroom. She was breathing more rapidly than
usual, but when they reached the area where light
spilled out and he ran a critical eye over her, she
seemed remarkably composed. Her cheeks were rosy,
her eyes huge and bright, and her lips, if one looked
closely, were swollen, yet the image she projected –
of a young lady mildly starry-eyed – would serve
their purpose well.

They reached the ballroom doors; he stood back to
let her precede him. She stepped past, then paused,
looked back. Her eyes met his, briefly searched, then
steadied.

He felt sure she was about to speak, but instead,
she smiled. Not just with her lips, but with her eyes.

Then she turned and walked into the ballroom.

He stared, then silently swore and followed her.
She'd smiled at him like that once before; as before,
the hair at his nape had lifted.

He'd intended it to be a simple kiss. What it had

turned into ... memories of that had kept him awake half the night.

The clocks chimed twelve noon as Luc crossed his front hall. There were documents and reports awaiting him in his study; he'd make a start on them before lunch and get his mind off its obsession.

He was reaching for the study doorknob when he heard her laugh. He knew the notes well, could at any time make them ring in his mind. For one instant, he thought that was what he'd heard – his imagination teasing him. Then he heard the voice that went with the laugh, not precise words, but the tone, the cadence.

Glancing along the hall, he listened. Amelia, his mother, and his sisters. Fiona, too. He strained his ears but heard no one else. Not an at-home, then, but an informal morning visit by a friend of the family.

The documents on his desk called to him. Some orders he needed to deal with by that evening; others were urgent bills he could at last pay. Responsibility urged him to the study; a deeper, more primitive instinct pointed in a different direction.

Last night she'd gone along with his edict, acquiesced readily and let him steer their path – up until that kiss. Their supposedly simple first kiss. *Then* she'd overset his plans. It hadn't been he who'd turned the exchange into a flagrantly sensual prelude – and if it hadn't been he, it had to have been she.

That fact disturbed him not a little. If she could challenge his rule in that sphere, what else might she attempt?

Which led to the exceedingly pertinent question of what she was doing in his drawing room that morning.

*

Amelia glanced up as the drawing room door opened. She smiled delightedly, made no attempt to hide her approbation as Luc entered, saw them, then shut the door and strolled up the long room to where they sat before the windows.

Her companions looked and smiled, too, his mother on the chaise beside her, Emily, Anne, and Fiona on two chairs and an ottoman ranged before them. Her intended presented the sort of picture any lady would smile at. His blue coat of Bath superfine fitted him superbly, displaying his shoulders to advantage, drawing attention to his narrow hips. His long, muscled thighs were encased in buckskin breeches which disappeared into Hessians shined to a mirror gloss. The contrast between his pale skin and the absolute blackness of his hair and brows was dramatic even in daylight.

He nodded to the three girls; skirting them, reaching her side, he inclined his head to his mother as he held out one long-fingered hand.

Her heart thumped as she laid her fingers across his, felt his close strongly.

He bowed. 'Amelia.'

Within their homes, they could use their given names; while his tone would not have alerted the others, not even his mother, she caught the warning note – saw it echoed in his eyes as he straightened and released her.

She let her smile brighten. 'Good morning. Have you been riding?'

He hesitated, then nodded, stepping back to lean against the nearby mantelpiece.

'Would you like some tea?' his mother asked.

Luc glanced at the tray on the table. 'No, thank you – nothing.'

54

Minerva gracefully relaxed against the chaise. 'We've just been discussing the latest invitations. Despite the Season winding down, there seem quite a few interesting events planned for the last weeks.'

Luc raised a disinterested brow. 'Indeed?'

Amelia looked up at him. 'Even though there are only three or so weeks to go, I doubt we'll be short of diversions.'

He looked down at her, into unbelievably innocent blue eyes.

'It's all so exciting!' Fiona, bright as a button, bobbed in her chair, distracting him. Her brown curls were caught up in the same style Anne favored – she looked more than just familiar ... then he realized she'd borrowed one of Anne's spencers.

'At least the balls aren't quite so crowded anymore,' Anne put in.

Fiona swung to face her. '*Not* as crowded?'

'Definitely not,' Emily confirmed. 'They were much worse – truly crushes in every sense – at the height of the Season.'

'So was your come-out a crush?' Fiona asked.

Minerva smiled. 'Indeed – it was a very well attended affair.'

She glanced up at him; Luc met her gaze and shared her proud smile. He still inwardly shuddered at the disruption and effort his sisters' come-out had entailed, but at least he could now pay for it.

'It was such a pity you missed it.' Anne caught Fiona's hand. 'So odious of your aunt to insist you go to visit your cousins instead.'

'Now, now, girls,' Minerva intervened. 'Fiona is staying with her aunt, and Mrs. Worley has been very kind in sparing her to us so often.'

55

Anne and Fiona accepted the rebuke meekly, but it was clear their poor opinion of Fiona's aunt choosing to take her to visit relatives in Somerset during the critical week had not altered.

'I heard there's to be a balloon ascension in the park the day after tomorrow.'

Emily's information distracted the girls; Minerva sat back, watching with fond affection as they discussed the event.

Luc paid their ramblings little heed; his gaze on Amelia's golden head, he wondered ... she was watching the younger girls, smiling at their excitement. 'Would you like to view the spectacle?'

She looked up, met his eyes – read them, and colored delicately. She glanced at the girls. 'Perhaps we could make a party?'

Luc inwardly grimaced, but gracefully nodded when his sisters looked eagerly his way. 'Why not?' It would serve as a reasonable first outing to which he could publicly squire Amelia.

Fiona whooped; Anne smiled. Emily laughed. They fell to discussing the details.

Under cover of their excited chatter, Amelia glanced up and met his gaze, a certain consciousness in her eyes ...

'Actually, we've just been discussing ...' His mother captured his attention before he could fathom the reason behind *that* particular look. Minerva smiled and held his gaze. 'As Amanda has gone north and won't return this Season, and as I've got to escort these giddy girls about, then it makes eminent sense for Amelia to join us, especially when Louise has clashing engagements.'

He managed to keep his expression impassive, then he looked again at Amelia. She met his gaze over the rim of her cup, then lowered it and smiled brightly. 'It seemed the most obvious idea.'

'Indeed. So Amelia will be joining us here tonight, then we'll all go on to Lady Carstairs's rout.' His mother raised a brow at him. 'You hadn't forgotten, had you?'

He straightened. 'No.'

'I'll order the carriage for eight, then – we should all be able to fit.'

Amelia set down her cup and spoke to Minerva. 'Thank you. I'll be here before eight.' She smiled, then extended the gesture to the girls. 'But now I really must go.'

Luc waited, suppressing his impatience while she farewelled his mother and sisters. When she turned to him, he waved to the door. 'I'll see you out.'

With brief nods to his mother and the girls, he stalked after her to the door, reached around her and opened it, then followed her into the hall. A quick glance showed no footmen about; shutting the door, he caught her gaze. 'You agreed to follow my lead.'

She opened her eyes wide. 'Weren't you intending for me to join your mother and sisters at some point?' Turning toward the front door, she started pulling on her gloves. 'It seemed an opportunity waiting to be grasped.'

'Quite.' He prowled by her side as she headed for the door. 'But *at some point*.'

She halted, looked at him. 'Which point?'

He frowned. 'Possibly after the balloon ascension.'

She raised her brows, then shrugged. 'Tonight was sooner. Anyway' —glancing down, she struggled with one of the tiny buttons closing her gloves— 'it's done now.'

Impossible to argue that. Luc told himself it didn't really matter. They reached the front door; he opened it. She was still struggling with her glove.

'Here – let me.' He grasped her wrist, sensed more than heard the quick intake of her breath. Felt the *frisson* that sheered through her as his sliding fingertips found the gap in the cuff of her recalcitrant glove, found her bare skin.

He met her gaze, then, gripping, slowly raised her hand and looked at the difficult button.

She remained absolutely immobile – he didn't think she even breathed – while he dealt with the tiny closure. The button slipped into place. He looked up, caught her gaze – deliberately rubbed the fine leather, smoothing the button into place, his thumb riding slowly back and forth over the sensitive inner face of her wrist.

Her eyes sparked; she twisted her wrist – he released her. She looked down, gathering her skirts.

Thrusting his hands in his pockets, he lounged against the doorframe. 'I'll see you tonight then. Before eight.'

'Indeed.' She inclined her head, but didn't meet his gaze. 'Until then.'

Head rising, she stepped out and descended the steps. Reaching the pavement, she turned for her home and waved one hand; her footman came quickly up the area steps, nodded to Luc, then fell in behind her.

Luc dispelled the frown that had been about to form; straightening, he shut the front door – only then did he let his lips quirk. She might have taken it upon herself to initiate the next step, but he still held the whip.

Satisfied, he headed for his study. Passing the side table at the back of the hall, he paused, contemplated the polished surface. Where was his grandfather's inkstand? It had stood there as long as he could recall ... perhaps Higgs in her annual spring cleaning frenzy had taken it for polishing and put it somewhere else. Making a mental note to ask her sometime, he strode on – to the business still waiting behind his study door.

'Are you sure Minerva has room for you in her carriage?'

Amelia glanced across her bedroom and smiled at her mother. 'She said she'd use her traveling carriage. There'll be just the six of us.'

Louise considered, then nodded. 'None of you is stout, after all. I have to say it'll be a relief to have a quiet night at home. I still haven't recovered from the rush of Amanda's wedding.' After a moment, she murmured, 'I suppose I can trust Luc to keep an eye on you.'

'Indeed. You know what he's like.'

Louise's lips quirked. Then she straightened. 'No, no!' Amelia had grabbed up her reticule and shawl and was hurrying toward her – she waved her back. 'Stop and let me see.'

Amelia grinned and halted. She slid the cords of her reticule over one wrist, draped her shimmering shawl about her shoulders, then she stood straight, head high, and pirouetted. Then she glanced at Louise.

Louise nodded approvingly. 'I was wondering when you were going to wear that. That shade becomes you.'

59

Amelia broke from her pose and hurried to the door. 'I know.' She kissed her mother's cheek. 'Thank you for buying it for me.' Stepping on down the hall, she smiled over her shoulder. 'I have to rush – I don't want to be late. Good night!'

Louise watched her go, a smile on her lips, a softness in her eyes. When Amelia had disappeared down the stairs, she sighed. 'You don't want to miss the chance of setting him back on his heels – I know. Good night, my dear, and good luck. With that one, you'll need it.'

Decked out in black coat and black trousers, ivory cravat and silk waistcoat, Luc was standing in the front hall looking up the stairs at the head of which his mother and sisters, and Fiona, all dressed for the evening, were finally congregating, when he heard Cottsloe open the front door. Assuming Cottsloe was checking to see if the carriage had arrived, he didn't glance around.

Then he heard Cottsloe murmur, 'Good evening, miss,' heard Amelia's light reply.

He swung around, mentally thanking the gods she'd arrived—

His mind stopped, literally seized, in the instant his gaze touched, locked on her.

She was a vision to confound not just his senses but his wits. His mind's slate remained blank, as blank as his expression, as his eyes devoured. As every instinct he possessed hungered.

Wanted . . .

She turned from greeting Cottsloe and glided toward him, head rising, golden ringlets tumbling down her back, brushing her shoulders. His fingers

60

curled. She lifted her gaze to his, smiled with easy familiarity – as if she always appeared in his front hall in the guise of a sea goddess, some acolyte of Venus Aphrodite given flesh, blood, and cornflower blue eyes.

Ringlets, eyes, and face he knew, but as for the rest ... had he ever truly seen her before? He'd certainly never seen her dressed as she now was.

Her gown was fashioned from shimmery silk gauze so light it shifted with every breath, so sensuous it draped every curve lovingly, outlining the lushness of breast and hip, of sleek thigh and curvaceous derriere. The color was a pale, silvery blue-green. A ruffle of the same material formed the bodice; another ruffle rippled around the hem. Expertly cut, the gown emphasized the indent of her waist, pouring over her like water, clinging, coruscating ...

For one fanciful moment, she appeared to be clothed in nothing more substantial than sea foam, as if, at any moment, the waves would retreat, the breeze sigh, the foam melt ...

An illusion, but such a good one he found he was holding his breath.

He couldn't see any sleeves or straps, then realized they were there but transparent; her bare shoulders and the delectable upper swells of her breasts seemed to rise out of the froth of the bodice, for all the world as if it would be a simple matter to peel the gown down ...

She reached him, stopped before him, screened from the others; from behind came exclamations from his sisters and the clattering of their now-eager descent.

He dragged his gaze up to Amelia's eyes.

She met it, a teasing smile on her lips. Raised one delicate brow. 'Are you ready?'

Her voice was low, sirenlike ...

Ready?

He stared – into eyes that were nowhere near as angelic as he'd expected. Before he could narrow his, her smile deepened, and she stepped past him to greet his mother and sisters.

Leaving him to grapple – to wrestle back under control – a veritable horde of instincts he'd been only dimly aware he possessed. He swung around, hands rising to his hips as he considered her. His mother and sisters would read his stance as impatience; they were already late. Amelia would know better, but ...

He didn't, in that instant, care what she knew or guessed. If he'd had any chance of being obeyed, he'd have ordered her home to change. No matter how late it made them. But the enthusiastic approbation that ... *gown* for want of a better word was receiving from his assembled female relatives made it clear they didn't view the ensemble as he did.

It was scintillating, but in his opinion better suited to a boudoir than a damned rout. And he was supposed to squire her around for the rest of the evening? And keep his hands to himself?

Keep every other man's hands off her?

Him and half the Guards.

He scowled, and was about to ask pointedly where her shawl was, in a growl to go with the scowl, when he realized it was draped over her elbows. A shimmering, glimmering fantasy that, as she flipped it up over her shoulders and turned with his mother, ready to depart, only added to the allure of that gleaming gown.

Ruthlessly shackling his temper, and more, he waved them all to the front door. 'We'd better get going.'

His sisters and Fiona grinned forbearingly at him as they trooped past, imagining his black mood to be occasioned by their tardiness. His mother swept after them, an amused look in her eyes, taking care not to meet his.

Amelia glided in Minerva's wake; drawing level with him, she smiled, and continued on.

He stood for a moment, watching her hips sway under the shimmering gauze, then inwardly groaned and followed.

If he'd been thinking – thinking at all – he'd have got down the steps faster; when he stepped onto the pavement, the three girls had already piled into the carriage and taken their seats. He handed his mother up, then gave Amelia his hand, supporting her as she stepped up to the carriage, by long habit looking down at the right moment to glimpse the flash of bared ankle before she let her skirts fall.

He was more than 'ready' when he climbed into the carriage; he was uncomfortably hard. A situation that grew considerably worse when he realized that the space they'd left for him was next to Amelia, between her and the carriage's side. There was only just enough space sitting three to each seat; the girls, crowded on the forward seat, already had their heads together, chattering animatedly. Impossible to make them change places – what excuse could he give? Instead, gritting his teeth, he sat – and endured the sensation of Amelia's hip riding against his, of her

63

slender, distinctly feminine thigh pressing against his, that godforsaken gown shifting, discreetly tantalizing, between them.

All the way to the Carstairs house down by the river at Chelsea.

The Carstairses owned a large house in Mayfair, but had elected to use their smaller property with its long gardens reaching down to the river for this summer night's entertaining.

They greeted their hostess in the hall, then joined the other guests in a long reception room running the length of the house. The room's rear wall was comprised of windows and a set of doors presently open to the gardens. Said gardens had been transformed into a magical fairyland with hundreds of small lanterns hung in the trees and strung between long poles. A light breeze off the river set the lanterns bobbing, sent the shadows they cast swaying.

Many guests had already yielded to the invitation of the softly lit night; turning from surveying the company, Luc looked at Amelia – and immediately determined to do the same. She'd appeared stunning enough in the even light of his front hall. Under the glare of the chandeliers she looked like ... the most delectable delight any hungry wolf could dream of.

And there were plenty of hungry wolves about.

Inwardly swearing, he gripped her elbow, cast a cursory glance at his sisters. Ever since their come-out, successful as it had been, he'd become, if not less protective, then at least less overtly so. Emily had found her feet; Anne, naturally quiet, remained so. He felt comfortable leaving them to their own devices, and Fiona would be safe in their company.

He'd check on them later.

'Let's go into the garden.' He didn't look at Amelia, but sensed her glance, sensed her underlying amusement.

'If you wish.'

He did glance at her then, sideways, briefly; the smile in her voice was manifest on her lips, lightly curved. The temptation to react – to kiss that teasing smile from those luscious lips – was frighteningly strong. He quelled it. With a curt nod for his mother, already settled with her bosom-bows, he grimly steered Amelia down the room.

To reach the doors giving onto the gardens they had, perforce, to travel the length of the room. It took them half an hour to manage it; they were constantly stopped by ladies and gentlemen, the ladies to comment on her gown, some genuinely complimenting, others ingenuously exclaiming over her daring in wearing it, the gentlemen to flatter and compliment, albeit largely in nonverbal vein.

When they finally won free and gained the terrace doors, Luc's jaw was set, his expression unrelentingly grim – at least to Amelia's eyes. She could sense the breadth and depth of his temper, could sense his increasingly strained control.

Considered ways to further exacerbate it.

'How pretty!' She stepped onto the terrace flags.

Luc's fingers slid from her elbow – where they'd been locked ever since they'd arrived – to her wrist, then he grasped her hand and came up alongside, placing her hand on his sleeve – trapping it there. 'I hadn't realized their gardens were so extensive.' He scanned the shadowy walks leading down and away. 'You can barely hear the river from here.'

'Just a faint lapping and the occasional splash of

oars.' She was looking around herself. 'It appears they're having the dancing out here.' She nodded to a group of musicians, resting with their instruments at one end of the wide terrace.

'Let's stroll.'

If they didn't, others would soon join them; she had no interest in conversing with anyone but Luc. Even with him, she'd prefer to exchange something other than words, and the garden promised to be the best venue for that. She went down the terrace steps at his side.

The gravel walks spread in numerous directions; they took the least frequented, leading away under the leafy branches of a grove. They walked through successive bands of moonlight and shadow; she held her tongue, aware of Luc's gaze, aware that it returned as if against his will to her bare shoulders, to the bared upper curves of her breasts.

She wasn't surprised when he eventually growled, 'Where the devil did you find that gown?'

'Celestine had it brought in from Paris.' She glanced down, fluffed up the ruffle that formed the bodice, supremely conscious that his gaze followed her every move. 'Different, but hardly outrageous. I like it, don't you?'

She glanced up; even in the dim light she saw his lips thin.

'You know damned well what I – and every other male present this side of senility – think of that gown. Think of you in that gown.' Luc bit his tongue, stifling the words: *Think of you out of that gown.* Narrow-eyed, he glared at her. 'As I recall, we'd agreed that *you* would follow *my* lead.'

She opened her eyes wide. 'Isn't this' —slipping

her hand from beneath his, she spread her shimmering skirts— 'along the path we're supposed to walk – that society expects us to tread?' Halting, she faced him. They were far enough from the terrace, and there were no other guests in the vicinity; they could speak without restraint. 'Isn't it expected that I'd wish to dazzle you?'

His eyes couldn't get any narrower; he gritted his teeth, spoke through them. 'You're dazzling enough without the gown.' What was he saying? 'I mean an ordinary, *usual* gown would have sufficed. That' — with one finger, he indicated the scintillating garment — 'is going too far. It's too dramatic. It doesn't suit you.'

He meant that things dramatic didn't suit her; Amanda was dramatic, Amelia was ... whatever she was, it was something else.

Courtesy of the overhead branches, her face was in shadow, even when she lifted her chin. 'Oh?'

There was nothing in the syllable to suggest she'd taken offense; indeed, her tone seemed light. It was the set of her chin that sent a warning snaking down his spine, sent him rushing into speech, disguising his disquiet behind an exasperated grimace. 'I didn't mean—'

'No, no.' She smiled. 'I quite understand.'

That smile didn't reach her eyes. 'Amelia—'

He reached for her hand, but with a silken swish, she turned back along the path.

'I really think, if that's the tack you believe we should take, that we ought to get back to the terrace.' She continued in that direction. 'We wouldn't want any of the gossipmongers to overinterpret our state.'

He caught up with her in two strides. 'Amelia—'

'Perhaps you're right and we should take this more slowly.' A note had crept into her voice, one that gave him pause. 'That being so . . .'

They'd reached the terrace; she stopped before the steps in a patch of light cast by the lanterns. He halted beside her, saw her scan the platoon of guests waiting on the flags for the orchestra to start up. Then she smiled – not at him. 'Indeed.' Glancing his way, she inclined her head in dismissal. 'Thank you for the walk.' Turning, she started up the steps. 'Now I'm going to dance with someone who does appreciate my gown.'

Chapter Four

The words reached Luc a second too late for him to grab Amelia back. Gaining the terrace, she plunged into the crowd; although he followed in a flash, by the time he located her she was part of a group, chatting animatedly with Lord Oxley, one hand on his lordship's arm.

The musicians chose that moment to strike up; the introduction to a cotillion had the guests quickly forming into sets. Jaw clenched, Luc retreated to where shadows draped the house wall; folding his arms, he leaned his shoulders against the wall, and watched Amelia – his bride-to-be – dip and sway through the figures.

That wretched gown floated about her, a fantasy of shimmering light. He saw at least two accidents caused by gentlemen getting distracted. The emotions that scored him were not familiar, the tension gripping him only partially so. Desire he was accustomed to, could deal with without effort, but this other ...

His temper felt raked, rawly sensitive. Overreactive, yet he was rarely that. How had she so easily provoked him to this state?

At least the damned dance wasn't a waltz.

That thought had him cursing. The next dance almost certainly would be – and he didn't trust himself to take her in his arms, not in public, not in that excuse for a gown. Yet he knew perfectly well what would happen if he tried to endure watching her waltz – in that gown – with some other man.

Comprehensively cursing all women – Cynster females especially – he watched and waited. And planned.

Amelia knew he was watching her; she only smiled more brightly, laughed and charmed Lord Oxley, but only so far. She had no intention of exchanging his lordship for one difficult viscount. Luckily, Luc couldn't be totally, incontrovertibly, sure of that.

At the end of the dance, she studiously avoided looking Luc's way, instead encouraged other gentlemen to gather around. She was watching Mr. Morley bow over her hand when Luc strolled up.

The instant Morley released her fingers, Luc appropriated them, directed a negligent, possibly bored nod her way, then wound her arm with his and set her hand on his sleeve – leaving his hard palm heavily over it.

She opened her eyes wide. 'I wondered where you were.'

His dark eyes met hers. 'Wonder no more.'

The four gentlemen who'd surrounded her looked from him to her, confusion in their faces. They would know she'd entered the house on Luc's arm, but would have assumed their association was as before – a convenient family connection, nothing more.

Nothing deeper.

The currents now surging between them, around them, spoke otherwise.

Wishing his eyes were easier to read, she smiled at Luc – then directed her delight at her cavaliers. 'Have you heard about the balloon ascension?'

'Indeed, yes!' Lord Carmichael replied. 'It's to be held in the park.'

'Day after tomorrow,' Mr. Morley supplied.

'Perhaps, my dear, I could offer my new phaeton as a conveyance.' Lord Oxley puffed out his chest. 'Quite seven feet off the ground, y'know – you'll have an excellent view.'

'Indeed?' Amelia smiled at his lordship. 'I—'

'Miss Cynster has already agreed to attend the spectacle in company with my sisters.'

She glanced at Luc, brows rising, faintly haughty.

He met her gaze, added, 'And me.'

She held his dark gaze for an instant longer, then let her lips curve and inclined her head. Turning back to Lord Oxley, she gestured helplessly, easing her rejection with a smile. 'As I was about to say, I'm afraid I've already accepted an invitation to attend with the Ashfords.'

'Ah, well – yes.' Lord Oxley shot a puzzled glance at Luc. 'I see.' His tone suggested he hadn't the foggiest clue.

A screech from a violin alerted the crowd to the upcoming waltz.

'My dear, if I might beg your indulgence—'

'If I might be so bold, Miss Cynster—'

'Dear lady, if you would do me the honor—'

Mr. Morley, Lord Carmichael, and Sir Basil Swathe all broke off, glanced at each other, then looked at Amelia.

She hesitated, waited – then lifted her chin. 'I—'

Luc pinched her fingers trapped under his hand.

71

'My dear, I came to fetch you – Mama desires you to meet an old friend.'

She looked at him. 'But the waltz ...?'

'I fear this old friend is quite elderly and must leave soon. He's rarely in London.' He glanced at her four cavaliers. 'If you'll excuse us.'

No question, of course; he barely waited for her to murmur her good-byes before drawing her away. Not onto the dance floor, where she'd wanted to go – with him – but doggedly back into the house.

Inside the doors of the long reception room, she halted, refusing to be dragged farther. 'Who is this old friend your mother wants me to meet?'

Luc glanced at her. 'A figment of my imagination.'

Before she could respond, he changed direction, urging her to a door. 'This way.'

She was intrigued enough, hopeful enough, to let him steer her through, into a short passage that eventually joined a corridor running parallel to the reception room on the other side of the house. Rooms opened off it to both sides.

Her hand locked in his, Luc made for a door halfway along the corridor, on the side farthest from the reception room. Opening the door, he looked in, then stepped back and swept her before him – she had no real option but to enter the room. He followed on her heels.

She looked around. The room was a parlor boasting comfortable sofas, chairs, and low tables. Long curtains framed the windows, undrawn, allowing pale moonlight, faint but pervasive, to illuminate the scene.

One in which no other soul breathed, bar them.

She heard a muted click. She swung around in time

72

to see Luc slide something into his waistcoat pocket. A glance at the door confirmed the lock was the sort that would normally have a key in it. It no longer did.

A most peculiar sensation flickered over her skin, slithered down her spine. She lifted her gaze to Luc's face as he closed the distance between them.

She was not going to let him fluster her, make her act like some mindless ninny he could manage with disgustingly arrogant ease. Folding her arms beneath her breasts, uncaring of the fact that pulled the ruffle forming her bodice tight, she lifted her chin. 'What's this all about?'

He blinked, halted, apparently uncertain. Then she realized he wasn't looking at her face. A fact he quickly rectified, lifting his eyes to meet hers.

'This,' he stated, through clenched teeth, 'is about *that*.'

She frowned. '*That*?'

His features grew grimmer; his eyes, so dark, burned. 'We need to discuss our tactics. The steps we're going to take to manipulate the *ton* into believing our marriage is anything but arranged. We need to discuss the order in which we're going to take those steps. *And* we need – definitely need – to discuss the small matter of timing.'

'Timing?' She widened her eyes. 'Surely it's simply a matter of taking our agreed steps in their appropriate order, and if the opportunity presents to move faster—'

'No! *That* is where we disagree.'

He was still speaking through his teeth. She frowned – pointedly – searching his face. 'Whatever is the matter with you?'

Luc looked long and hard into her wide blue eyes,

and couldn't tell if she was teasing. 'Nothing,' he ground out. 'Nothing that any normal – no, never mind!' He raked back his hair, then realized what he was doing and let his hand fall. 'The important thing we're going to discuss and agree on is the pace of our little charade.'

'Pace? What—'

'It can't go too fast.'

'Why not?'

Because that risked revealing far too much. He locked his gaze on her stubborn face. 'Because going too fast will raise questions – questions we'd rather weren't asked. Like is there any reason for my sudden pursuit of you – I've only known you for how long? Twenty something years? Too fast, and people will wonder what's behind it. And my possible motives are the least of it. I told you from the start, this needs to be convincing, and that means slow. Four weeks. No shortcuts.'

'I thought you meant we could take *up to* four weeks, not that it *had* to take four weeks.'

'People need to see a steady progression from mild interest, to awareness, to decision, to confirmation. If they don't see any motive – if we don't give them a good show – they won't accept it.'

All nonsense, of course. If she had any more gowns in her armoire like the one she was wearing, no one would wonder at his sudden decision.

On the thought, his gaze lowered; he frowned at the offending article. 'Have you any more gowns like that?'

She glared, then looked down at her gown, spread the skirts. 'What is it about this gown that so irks you?'

He had wisdom enough to know to keep his lips shut; instead, he heard himself growl, 'It's too damned inviting.'

She seemed taken aback. 'Is it?'

'Yes!' He'd thought the effect bad enough in his hall, and even worse under the chandeliers. Yet the worst, most dizzying effect was now, in half-light. He'd noticed it under the trees; it had been partly to blame for his unwise words. In poor light, the gown made her skin shimmer, too, as if her bare shoulders and breasts were part of a pearl, rising from the froth of the sea. Offered, waiting for the right hand to recognize and seize, take, reveal the rest that the gown concealed ...

Small wonder he could barely think.

'It's ...' He gestured, struggling to find the right words to talk his way out of this morass.

She was looking down, considering. 'Inviting ... but isn't that how I should look?'

It was the way she lifted her head and met his gaze – head-on, direct – that shook his laggard wits into place. His eyes slowly narrowed as he considered – her words, and her. 'You know.' He took a menacing step toward her. She dropped her skirts and straightened, but didn't step back. He halted and glared down into her eyes. 'You know damned well how you – in that damned gown – affect men.'

Her eyes widened. 'Well of course.' She tilted her head, as if wondering at his thought processes. 'Whyever did you imagine I'd worn it?'

He made a strangled sound – the remnants of the roar he refused to let her hear. He never lost his temper – except, these days, with her! He pointed a finger at the tip of her nose. 'If you wish me to marry

75

you, you will not again wear this gown, or any like it, unless I give you leave.'

She held his gaze, then drew herself up, folded her arms—

'For God's sake, don't do that!' He shut his eyes against the sight of her breasts rising even higher above the rippling edge of her bodice.

'I'm perfectly decent.'

Her tone was clipped, distinctly acid.

He risked lifting his lids the veriest fraction; his gaze, predictably, locked on the ivory mounds flauntingly displayed by the distracting gown. Her nipples had to be just—

'Anyone would think you've never seen a lady's breasts before – you can't expect me to believe that.' Amelia kept her delight at his susceptibility firmly in check. Not hard; she didn't like the direction this discussion was taking.

His gaze was unabashedly locked on her breasts; beneath the thick fringe of his sooty lashes, his dark eyes glittered.

'At this point, I don't much care what you believe.' There was a quality in his voice, in the slowly and precisely enunciated words, that made her still, that alerted every instinct she possessed.

His gaze slowly rose, and fixed on her eyes.

'I repeat: if you want me to marry you, you will not again wear this gown, or any like it.'

She lifted her chin. 'I'll need to some time – toward the end—'

'No. You won't. Need to. Or do so.'

She felt her jaw lock, could almost feel her will and his collide, but while hers was like a wall, his was like a tide – it flowed all around, surged, tugged, weakened her foundations. She knew him too well, knew she couldn't push him and didn't dare defy him at this point.

It didn't happen easily, but she forced herself to nod. 'Very well.' She drew in a breath. 'But on one condition.'

He'd blinked, his gaze lowering; he jerked it back up to her face. 'What condition?'

'I want you to kiss me again.'

He stared at her. A moment passed. 'Now?'

She spread her hands, widened her eyes. 'We're here – completely private. You locked the door.' She gestured to her gown. 'I'm wearing this. Surely our charade suggests a certain script?'

Luc looked into her eyes – he was perfectly sure he'd never felt so torn in his life. Every instinct, every urge, every demon he possessed wanted nothing more than to seize the slender body so provocatively displayed and feast. Every instinct bar one. Self-preservation was the only naysayer, but it was screaming.

Increasingly hoarsely.

There was no way he could argue his way out of her suggestion. Aside from anything else, his mind baldly refused to be a party to that much deceit.

He lifted his shoulders, making it look like a shrug, in reality trying to ease the tension that had already locked every muscle. 'Very well.' His voice was even, his tone commendably nonchalant. 'One kiss.'

One rigidly controlled, absolutely finite kiss.

He reached for her; she stepped toward him. Before he could catch her and hold her back, she was in his arms, her distracting gown shushing against his coat, her supple figure stretching against him as she reached up and twined her arms about his neck.

Bending his head, he found her lips, covered them – all without the slightest thought. His hands gripped her waist, but his arms were powerless to ease her away from him. Their lips melded and the compulsion to instead draw her closer grew.

She parted her lips under his, and he did.

Let his hands slide over the sumptuous silk, over the curves it concealed, then he deliberately drew her against him, molding her softness to his much harder frame. Drew her breath from her, then gave it back, took her mouth slowly, thoroughly.

He sensed not the slightest hesitation through their increasingly explicit exchange; her tongue boldly met his with a ladylike eagerness that was unfeigned and oddly tempting. Enticing. As if she and she alone could offer him something his experienced senses had never encountered before.

As if she was confident of that, knew it with a sureness that left no room for doubt.

Her body remained pliant yet vibrant in his arms; not passive, yet limited in her ability to script their interaction purely by lack of experience. He could sense through her lips, through her responses, an unfettered commitment to the pleasures inherent in the kiss. To inciting, as she had before, subsequent delights.

That he'd expected; that was where he drew his line. This time, he was prepared for her pushy nature – for her attempts to lure him into rushing headlong into a situation his finely honed instincts were strongly warning would not be one he was accustomed to. This woman was to be his wife; nothing –

no temptation – would ever be sufficient to make him forget that, and all its connotations.

For all his experience, his instincts urged caution. In this arena, he was no more experienced than she – and he had more to lose.

As she returned his kisses avidly, Amelia had no thought of winning or losing; she'd demanded the kiss purely to enjoy it, and to learn more. More of the dizzying delight he so effortlessly conjured, that seemed to warm her from her bones to her skin.

Their second kiss was indeed living up to her expectations. He seemed to have accepted holding her close; her senses purred at the pleasure inherent in having all that hard muscle and heavy bone surrounding her, pressed to her breasts and the swells of her thighs, his arms banding her shoulders and back. She was tempted to wriggle closer still.

He hadn't even tried to turn the kiss into a single peck, as she'd suspected he might. She had absolutely no doubt he was, instead, enjoying the exchange – the succession of caresses, him to her, her to him – every bit as much as she.

So what came next? The thought floated through her mind; she followed it. Mentally caught her breath, then kissed him back even more flagrantly – distracted him long enough to press closer still, to sink against him, her breasts flush against his chest.

The pressure eased the ill-defined ache that seemed to be burgeoning in her breasts; she shifted slightly, seeking further relief. His arms had instinctively tightened, supporting her. As the tide of the kiss shifted, he kissed her back – with greater fire, with the promise of flames. She inwardly gasped, felt his arms ease, his hands slide ... suddenly knew what

79

next she wanted, what next she needed from him.

His hands rose, palms tracing upward from her hips to her waist, then higher, sliding to her sides . . .

Where they stopped.

And reversed direction.

Before she could think, he ravaged her mouth, briefly, thoroughly, then he eased back from the kiss and lifted his head. Set her back from him, his hands at her waist, steadying her.

He met her wide, blinking stare, searched her eyes, then raised one brow, as ever faintly arrogant. 'Enough?'

She could barely breathe; her head was whirling, her pulse thudding. But she understood what she saw in his face; his implacability was no news to her. Letting her lips curve, she boldly drew one finger down his cheek, then stepped back. 'For now.'

With that, she turned toward the door. 'We'd better get back, don't you think?'

Luc did, but it took a moment to get his body to obey. He felt buoyed, reassured; he'd set himself to walk an extraordinarily fine line, one she was clearly intent on dragging him over, yet he'd triumphed – a not inconsiderable feat, considering the provocation. Joining her, he hunted out the key, opened the door, and held it wide.

Head high, a satisfied smile on her lips, his temptress swept past him; he let his gaze assessingly travel her slender length, then followed, closing the door, making a mental note to send around to Celestine regarding any similar gown she might produce. Marriage, after all, lasted a long time – only sensible to ensure he enjoyed it.

*

Deep in the gardens close by the river, a young lady slipped through the trees. Reaching the river wall, high and built of stone, she followed it to the corner of the property.

There, beneath a large tree, a gentleman waited, a denser shadow in the gloom. He turned as the young lady came up.

'Well? Do you have them?'

'Yes.' The young lady sounded breathless; she raised her reticule, a larger than usual affair, and opened it. 'I managed to get both pieces.'

The items she drew forth glinted as she handed them to the gentleman. 'You will send all you can get for them to Edward, won't you?'

The gentleman didn't answer, but turned the objects in his hands, holding up first one, an ornate gold inkstand, then the other, a gold-and-crystal perfume flask, to the fitful light filtering through the leaves.

'They'll fetch a few guineas, but he'll need more than that.'

'More?' Lowering her reticule, the young lady stared. 'But ... those were the only pieces Edward mentioned ...'

'I daresay. But poor Edward ...' The gentleman slid the two objects into the capacious pockets of his driving coat and sighed. 'I fear he's trying to be brave, but you can imagine, I'm sure, what it's like for him. Banished by his family, cast into a foreign gutter and left to starve, forgotten, with not a friend in the world—'

'Oh, no! Surely not. I can't imagine ... I'm sure ...' The young lady broke off. She stared through the dimness at the gentleman.

Who shrugged. 'I'm doing all I can, but I don't

81

move in these circles.' He looked through the dark garden to where the fairy lights began, and farther, to where the elegant throng was dancing and laughing on the terrace.

The young lady drew herself up. 'If I could help more ... but I've already given all the money I have. And there aren't that many precious little objects lying about Ashford House, not ones that rightly might be Edward's.'

The gentleman was silent for sometime, his gaze on the dancers, then he turned to the young lady. 'If you really want to help – and I'm sure Edward would be eternally grateful – then there's plenty more items like these two that could help him, and that they' —with his head, he indicated the faraway crowd— 'would like as not never miss.'

'Oh, but I *couldn't* ...' The young lady stared at him.

The gentleman shrugged. 'If that's the way it is, then I'll tell Edward he'll have to manage on his own, that no matter what rat-infested, flea-ridden hovel he's now forced to live in, despite all the blunt his family and their friends have, there's no help for him here. He can give up all hope—'

'No! Wait.' After a moment, the young lady sighed, a whispering surrender. 'I'll try. If I see any little things that might suit—'

'Just pick them up and bring them to me.' The gentleman glanced at the house. 'I'll be in touch about where we can next meet.'

He turned to leave – the lady put out a hand and caught his sleeve. 'You will send the money to Edward straightaway – and tell him that I at least care?'

The gentleman studied her earnest expression, then nodded. 'It will mean a lot to him, I'm sure.'

With a bow, he turned and walked away through the trees. The young lady sighed, looked up at the distant terrace, then lifted her skirts and headed back to the house.

'Your pardon, ma'am, but Lord Calverton, the Misses Ashford, and Miss Ffolliot have called.'

Louise looked up. Amelia blinked. They were sitting at their ease in the morning room at the back of the house, Louise reading a book, Amelia on the chaise perusing the latest issue of *La Belle Assemblée*.

From the comfort of her armchair, Louise shrugged. 'Show them in here, Colthorpe.' As the butler bowed and retreated, Louise smiled at Amelia. 'Given it's the Ashfords, we may as well relax.'

Amelia nodded absentmindedly, her gaze on the door. Luc had said nothing about calling this morning. After they'd returned to Lady Carstairs's reception room, he'd remained by her side, subtly but definitely *there*, until the end of the night. The Ashfords had dropped her at her parents' door; Luc had escorted her up the steps, bowed with his usual bored languor – and said not a word about any future engagement.

The door opened; Emily, Anne, and Fiona gaily bustled in. Amelia shut the periodical and laid it aside. Luc strolled in, impeccably turned out in a dark blue coat, breeches, and Hessians, as always darkly, dangerously handsome. The girls very correctly greeted her mother; Amelia tried to catch Luc's eye, but beyond a swift glance as he'd entered, he didn't look her way.

Then he was bowing over Louise's hand, greeting her mother with his usual polished grace. Alert, Louise waved him to the chaise; instead, he misinterpreted the gesture – purposely, Amelia was sure – and bowed. 'Amelia.'

She returned his nod, then watched in bemusement as he chose the armchair alongside her mother's and sat. The three girls fluttered over to perch around her. Luc turned to Louise; the girls turned to her.

'It's a lovely day outside.'

'So very pleasant. Just a light breeze.'

'We'd thought to take the air in the park, but Luc suggested—'

What Amelia wanted to know was what Luc was suggesting to her mother.

Smiling at the tableau of her daughter surrounded by the younger girls, all chattering, Louise looked at Luc and raised her brows. 'I take it you don't find keeping an eye on Amelia as well as your sisters and Miss Ffolliot in the evenings too much of a trial?'

Luc met her gaze, succinctly replied, 'No.' Amelia was a trial, but he would manage. 'Your daughter does, however, have a stubborn streak, and a tendency to go her own road, as you're doubtless aware.'

'Naturally.' Louise looked intrigued.

He directed his gaze across the room, to where Amelia was listening to his sisters' and Fiona's entreaties. 'She gets on well with my sisters, and my mother, too, of course, which makes things easier.'

'Indeed?' The faint amusement in Louise's voice assured him she'd followed his change of tack; she knew quite well what 'things' he was referring to.

'I had hoped,' he returned his gaze to Louise, 'that

you would approve.' He paused, then smoothly continued, 'I thought a jaunt to Richmond, given the weather is so clement, would be a welcome diversion. We're taking the open carriage, of course.'

He awaited Louise's verdict. She regarded him for a disconcertingly long time, but eventually smiled and inclined her head. 'Richmond, then, if you think it will serve.'

That last comment had him inwardly frowning, but he got no chance to probe for an explanation – he wasn't even sure he wanted one; Louise turned and spoke to the girls, who'd already outlined their plans to Amelia.

Louise indicated her approval. Amelia stood, shooting a sharp glance his way. 'I'll have to change.'

He rose. 'We'll wait.'

Crossing the room, he opened the door and held it for her. Pausing in the doorway, she looked up at him, suspicion in her eyes. He smiled. Screened from the others, he flicked her cheek. 'Hurry up.' After a fractional pause, he added, 'I guarantee you'll enjoy it.'

Her eyes searched his, then she elevated her nose and left.

Ten minutes later, she returned, in a gown of sprigged muslin, cherry red against white. Three flounces adorned its hem; the bodice fitted snugly, and the sleeves were tiny puffs. A bright red ribbon was threaded through her curls, a wider ribbon of the same shade was wound about the handle of the parasol tucked under her arm. Luc gave silent thanks that she didn't favor bonnets; he'd make sure that when they walked, she kept the parasol shut.

She was pulling on red kid gloves; half boots of the

same shade were on her feet. She looked delectable – good enough to eat.

He rose. The two younger girls were by the window, examining the small ornaments laid out on the wide sill; he collected them with a glance and turned to where Emily was chatting with Louise. 'We'd better make a start.'

They made their farewells, then he waved his charges on, closing the door as he followed them into the hall. The girls bustled on, beaming at Colthorpe as he opened the front door for them. Reaching out, Luc captured Amelia's hand, twined her arm with his. Glanced down as she looked up at him. 'You'll enjoy the drive.'

She raised a skeptical brow. 'And the hours at Richmond spent following those three?'

He smiled and looked ahead. 'Those you'll enjoy even more.'

This time, he dictated where they would all sit. The three girls dutifully took the seat behind the coach-man, facing Luc and Amelia. As the coach rolled off, Amelia cast him a suspicious glance, then opened her parasol, deploying it to shade her face.

The girls chatted and looked about, exclaiming at the sights as the carriage turned south, crossed the river at Chelsea, then rumbled west past villages and hamlets. Although the girls were only a foot away, seated as she was with Luc, Amelia felt no compelling need to listen to their conversation.

Luc said nothing, looking about idly, elegantly at ease beside her. He had to keep his distance to avoid her parasol; compensating, he'd spread his arms, one along the carriage's side, the other along the back of the seat.

She wondered what he was up to, but as the miles

rumbled uneventfully by, she relaxed. Only then did she realize how tense she'd become – how intense she'd been for the past several months, doggedly pursuing her plan. Her plan, which had landed her here, where she wished to be.

With the right gentleman beside her.

She'd just come to that realization and let a small smile curve her lips, when Luc's fingertips brushed the soft tendrils exposed at her nape. She froze, couldn't quite hide her reactive shiver. As usual, she'd worn her hair pulled into a topknot, but it was naturally curly, so tiny locks sprang loose, feather-light, sensitive to the touch.

Turning her head, she intended to frown, but the look in Luc's eyes distracted her. Intent, he watched her; his fingertips shifted, stroked again.

'What are you smiling at?'

The light in those dark eyes wasn't teasing; he wanted to know. She looked forward, would have shrugged but ... she didn't want him to take his hand away. 'I was just thinking ...' She gestured to the bucolic scenery through which they were rolling. 'I haven't been out to Richmond for years. I'd forgotten how restful the drive can be.'

She glanced back at him, again found herself trapped in his eyes.

'You gad about too much.' His eyes remained on hers, his fingers firmed. 'From now on, you won't have to.'

She had to smile; trust a man to imagine that the only reason ladies 'gadded about' was in pursuit of them. 'There'll still be the Season, and making appearances. More or less obligatory, after all.'

The girls were engrossed with their own topics; he and she could converse freely.

'Only up to a point.' He paused, then coolly stated, 'In the coming months I think you'll discover there's other activities more to your taste than whirling around ballrooms.'

She had absolutely no doubt to what activities he was alluding; his gaze was anything but cool. Meeting it, she arched one brow. 'Such as?'

The look in his eyes stated very clearly: that's for me to know and you to learn.

'Oh, look! Is that Richmond village?'

They both turned to see Fiona pointing; Amelia inwardly cursed. She glanced at Luc, but he retrieved his arm and turned away. The moment was gone.

Or so he led her to believe. Only when they were strolling in the girls' wake under the spreading oaks and beeches did she realize he had another agenda beyond entertaining his sisters – one that involved only them.

They were under a large oak that hid them from view, the girls ahead, already clear of the shadows, when Luc tugged her to a halt, spun her to him, and kissed her, swift, hard and all too sure.

Then he released her, resettled her hand on his arm, and strolled on.

She stared at him. 'What was that for?'

He looked at her, eyes glinting from beneath his lashes as they passed into the sunshine. 'I didn't think I needed a reason.'

She blinked, faced forward. He didn't, of course. Not to kiss her, or ... anything else.

He had a fertile imagination – the rest of the day passed in giddy absorption in what became a light-hearted game. At first, when his long fingers found the gap in her glove cuffs, and stroked, toyed, with caresses that were so innocent it was hard to comprehend why they felt so illicit, she couldn't see any reason to discourage him; she was more concerned with trying to predict just what he would be at next – what sensitive spot he would choose to tease – with a breath, with a touch, with a kiss.

Later, after they'd lunched at the Star and Garter, then, as the afternoon waxed glorious, started down the hill, she concluded that, for propriety's sake, she had to at least protest. The sliding, glancing passage of his hand over her hip, over the curve of her bottom, covered only by a thin layer of muslin and a silk chemise, was explicit enough to make her blush. She knew perfectly well no one else could see, however . . .

Yet when she grasped the moment as they passed under another useful tree and turned to him, lips opening on a rebuke – she found herself in his arms being thoroughly kissed. Kissed witless; when he released her, she'd forgotten what she'd wanted to say.

Lips curving wickedly, he tweaked a curl, and, one hand on her bottom, turned her toward the carriage.

She kept her parasol up all the way home to hide her blush from his sisters. The man was a rake! His fingers now rested not at her nape but even more possessively, heavy at the curve where her shoulder met her neck.

The most amazing discovery was that she liked his fingers there – liked feeling his touch, the weight of his hand. The sensation of skin to skin.

The realization kept her silent – occupied – all the way home.

Chapter Five

The surest way to manage Amelia was, not just to keep the reins in his hands, but to use them. To drive her, distract her, so she didn't have time to filch said reins from his grasp.

That established, Luc escorted her, together with his sisters and Fiona, to the balloon ascension, and through judicious dalliance kept her on tenterhooks the entire time – kept her attention riveted on him. She didn't even notice the other gentlemen who unsuccessfully vied for her smiles.

The following day, confident he now had her measure, confident he could keep her distracted sufficiently to draw out their unexpected courtship until the ton yawned, nodded, and thought no more of it, he agreed to escort his mother and sisters, Fiona, Amelia, and her mother, to the Hartingtons' *al fresco* luncheon in the grounds of Hartington House.

After counting heads, he sent a note to Reggie, inviting him, too, to make one of their party. Reggie arrived in Mount Street just as the ladies, young and old, chattering like starlings, descended the front steps of Ashford House. By the curb, the Cynster landau stood waiting, along with Luc's curricle.

Following his female responsibilities down the steps, he smiled at Reggie. Who could count as well as he.

Reggie met his gaze as he strolled up. 'You owe me for this.' Reggie had already bowed to Minerva and Louise, both friends of his mother's. He nodded, a touch resignedly, at the younger girls. The footman handed them up. Reggie turned to Amelia as she halted beside him.

She'd only just realized Luc's strategy.

Reggie caught her eye. 'Have fun. But think twice before agreeing to anything he says.'

She grinned and pressed Reggie's hand, then watched as he climbed into the landau, taking the last seat beside Louise. Luc gave the coachman directions, then returned to her side as the landau rumbled off.

It was replaced at the curb by Luc's curricle. He handed her up. She shuffled along, then he joined her. Taking the reins, he nodded to his groom. The pair of matched greys were released; they tossed their heads – Luc calmed them, then, with a flick of his wrist, set them trotting in the wake of the landau.

She had to smile. 'Poor Reggie.'

'He'll enjoy himself hugely being the undisputed center of attention while he regales them with the latest gossip.'

'True.' She glanced at Luc's chiseled features. 'But if you find escorting us such a trial, why did you suggest it?'

He turned his head; his eyes met hers. His message was quite clear: don't be daft. The glint in the midnight blue depths clearly stated that he had plans for Lady Hartington's *al fresco* luncheon, plans that

91

had nothing to do with food.

When he looked back at his horses, her heart was beating faster, her mind awash with fanciful imaginings, her nerves tensing with a blend of excitement and anticipation she'd never felt with anyone but him. The effect left her pleasantly expectant, sunnily confident, as they rolled through the streets.

Indeed, as she cast a surreptitious glance over her companion, negligently handsome in a drab, many-caped driving coat thrown over a dark blue morning coat, his long legs encased in tight-fitting buckskin breeches and glossy Hessians, long fingers firm on the reins as he expertly guided the frisky greys through the crowded thoroughfares, she couldn't think of anything she needed to make her day more complete. She had the right man and, if she'd read that glance correctly, his promise of pleasure to come.

Smiling, she sat back and watched the houses go by.

Hartington House lay to the west amid gently rolling fields. The house stood in an extensive park with large trees, a lake, and many pleasing vistas. Lady Hartington was delighted to welcome them; Luc assumed his customary bored expression, projecting the image that, in view of the number of females attending from his family, he'd felt obliged to lend them his escort.

They joined the other guests on the wide terrace overlooking the lawns, passing through the crowd, nodding, and exchanging greetings. Although Luc remained by her side, his expression, and that air of a man condemned to an afternoon of polite boredom, remained, too.

Amelia glanced at him as they emerged at one side of the crush, in relative if temporary privacy. 'I hesitate to mention it, but if you want the *ton* to believe you've fixed your eye on me, shouldn't you be looking rather more *interested* in spending time by my side?'

She pretended to admire the distant lake; from the corner of her eye, she saw his lips twitch, felt the weight of his gaze as it rested on her face.

'Actually, no – that might, I feel, be stretching the bounds of the believable. *Not*,' he smoothly continued as she swung to him, eyes flashing, lips parting on an incensed retort, 'because my wishing to spend time in your company is not believable' —he captured her gaze— 'but because the idea I would allow it to show, like some smitten puppy lolling at your dainty feet, is just a touch incredible.' He raised one black brow. 'Don't you think?'

A callow youth, an eager puppy – she couldn't remember him ever being like that. Throughout his career, he'd always been as he was now – arrogantly distant, aloof – cool. As if there was steel beneath his elegant clothes, concealing and distancing the flesh-and-blood man.

She had to agree; she didn't have to like it. Haughtily inclining her head, she looked away.

Luc fought not to grin knowingly. Sliding his fingers around her wrist, he stroked, then set her hand on his sleeve. 'Come – we should circulate.'

While they talked to first this group, then that, he cataloged the company. There were few of his ilk present. One or two older men, like Colonel Withersay, intent on bending a pretty widow's ear, and many youthful pups attending in their mothers'

93

trains, still rosy-cheeked, stammeringly eager to hold a girl's reticule while she adjusted her shawl. No husbands – none would have been expected. Given that the Season was drawing to a close, the wolves' attention was also elsewhere; Luc doubted many of his peers were yet awake. Certainly not out of bed, whoever's beds they were gracing.

When Lady Hartington rang a bell, summoning them down to the lawns, where an array of culinary delights was set forth on trestle tables, he led Amelia down and, with his habitual distant grace, assisted her in assembling a plate of select morsels, simultaneously piling his own plate high. Preserving his attitude of resigned boredom – gaining a narrow-eyed, remarkably suspicious look from Reggie – he remained beside Amelia, exchanging mild comments with those who joined them.

Giving all the matrons who, driven by instinct, invariably watched such as he no inkling that he harbored any intention of working his wiles on any of the sweet innocents present – certainly not on the fair beauty by his side.

The sun rose higher; the day grew warmer. Her ladyship's culinary offerings were consumed with relish, as was her wine cup.

As he'd expected, once their visceral hunger was satisfied, all the young things developed a longing to explore the famous grotto by the lake. Their mothers wanted nothing more than to stay seated in the shade and exchange desultory conversation. It consequently fell to Reggie and a host of bright-eyed youths to escort the bevy of giggling girls across the lawns, through the trees, and around the lake to the grotto.

He didn't have to say a word; all he had to do was

wait for the moment his mother and Louise looked across to where he and Amelia remained seated at a table to one side of the lawn. The giggling girls had gathered into a brightly hued pack and were bustling across the lawns, parasols bobbing, a few dark coats amid the crush.

His mother caught his eye, raised her brows. Louise merely looked amused.

As if responding to a maternal hint, he assumed his most weary expression and glanced at Amelia. 'Come – we should follow.'

She was the only one close enough to read his eyes, to gain any sense that acting as overseeing gooseberry was not his goal. Her gaze fixed on his face, she gave him her hand. 'Indeed – I'm sure the grotto will be fascinating.'

Luc didn't reply, but rose and drew her to her feet. The sun was beaming down; he had to let her put up her parasol, then, side by side, some distance in the rear, they set off to follow the chattering horde.

He wondered whether anyone bar Louise had correctly interpreted his mother's questioning look. Minerva wasn't the least worried about her daughters; her question had more to do with what *he* was about. She couldn't fathom his tack, and was wondering ...

He had every intention of leaving her guessing. There were some things mothers didn't need to know.

The lawns ended in a belt of parkland; beyond, the lake lay flat and reflective under a cerulean sky. Once in the trees' shade, he slid his hands into his pockets and slowed his pace, his gaze on the group ahead.

Amelia glanced at him and slowed, too. 'I've never been to the grotto. Is it worthwhile?'

'It won't be today.' Luc nodded at the gaggle ahead. 'They'll be there.'

The distance between them and the group was steadily increasing.

'However, if you've a mind to be adventurous ...' He slanted her a glance. 'There's somewhere else we might go.'

She met his gaze calmly. 'Where?'

He took her hand and drew her away, through the trees, through a stand of shrubs onto a narrow path that twisted and turned, eventually climbing the man-made hill into the base of which the grotto had been carved. The hilltop formed part of the created land-scape; a stone seat with a thyme cushion was placed to give a superb view over the fields to the west. Laurels had been groomed to shade the bench; with an appreciative sigh, Amelia sat and furled her parasol.

From far below came a distant giggle, carried on the updraft from the lake. After surveying the land-scape, Luc turned; his dark eyes briefly surveyed her, then he sat beside her, leaning back, at ease, one arm along the back of the seat.

Amelia waited, then turned her head and studied him, relaxed, outrageously handsome with the breeze feathering his dark hair, a potent and dangerous attraction in the long lines of his sprawled limbs. After a moment of considering the view, he looked at her. Met her gaze, searched her eyes.

She was about to say something – very likely some-thing caustic – when he lifted his free hand. He reached for her face, but didn't touch. Instead, his fingers twined with a ringlet bobbing by her ear. He wound the lock taut, then, very gently, tugged.

Captured her gaze as he drew her closer, and closer, until those long fingers slid about her nape, urging her nearer, until she drew so close her lids lowered, her lips parted, her gaze fell to his lips. Until at the last his thumb slid beneath her jaw and tipped her face up, and those long, lean lips met hers.

He hadn't moved but had encouraged her to come to him; it was the same with the kiss. His lips moved on hers, hard, assured; he lured her with promises, with teasing glimpses of all she could have, all the pleasures he could give her, and would. If she wished it.

If she made the decision and came into his arms, parted her lips, and offered him her mouth. Gave herself to him ...

She shifted nearer, her parasol sliding from her lap as she raised her hands to his chest, leaned nearer yet, and let the kiss deepen, encouraged him further. A thought flitted through her brain – this was why he was so successful with the *ton's* ladies, why they flocked to him, vying for his attention.

He knew he didn't need to press, that all he had to do was invite, raise the possibility, and any lady who had ever got close enough to sense the sheer virility of his body, to feel his fingers stroke her wrist, to experience the sensation of his lips on hers, would accept.

Unlike other ladies, she knew him well, knew the image of lazy, undriven sensuality was a facade. Even as he drew her deeper into the giddy pleasures of their kiss, his fingers sliding free of her curl, his hands stroking down to her waist, gripping and lifting her more definitely to him so she was all but lying atop him as he eased back against the seat, she was well aware that that facade was wafer-thin, that he was perfectly capable of pressing, of demanding, commanding a surrender, of ultimately taking all he wished.

The power was there, the power to compel any woman to be his – to want to be his. She could feel it in the shifting muscles of his chest as his arms closed around her, locking her lightly to him, could feel it in the lips that continued to hold hers – effortlessly. An inherently male power, primitive, a touch frightening – scarifying, given that that very power was one she would have to contend with, deal with, treat with, every day for the rest of her life.

She shivered at the thought. He sensed it. A fractional hiatus was all the warning she got, then his hands firmed on her back, his lips and tongue hardened, and he ravished her mouth, ripped her senses from her – and she could think no more.

Could only follow mindlessly where he led, into a whirlpool of sensation, of steadily increasing desire. She gasped, tried to pull back and find her mental feet; his hand left her back to slide once more along her throat, cupping her nape, tangling in her curls as he ruthlessly drew her back into their kiss, into the rising flames.

Their heat was insidious, beckoning, tempting ... she sank into them. Relaxed, let go ...

Sighing softly into his mouth, she gave up any thought of managing the moment, settled, instead, simply to let herself feel. Experience the too-knowing caress of his fingertips down her throat, down over the exposed skin above her neckline, down over the curve of one breast. Those wandering fingers traced, teased, then returned to flirt with the tiny ruffle

98

edging her bodice. A longing was growing inside her, unfulfilled; she shifted, murmured, the sound trapped between their lips.

He understood. His fingers returned to the swell of her breast, and traced again, more slowly. Again, then again; each time his touch grew heavier with intent while her flesh firmed and her skin heated. Then his fingers curved, and he cupped her softness.

Sensation flashed through her, immediately melting into a warm tide that spread like warmed honey through her. His wicked fingers tensed, flexed – he closed his hand, then kneaded; nerves she didn't know she possessed came alive. Pure pleasure washed through her when his other hand left her back to minister to her other breast. Eyes closed, her mouth all his, still captured in the drugging sensuality of a slow, deep kiss, she gave herself up to the sensation of his hands on her breasts, to the heat and the fire slowly building, to the tightness, the ache he both evoked and appeased.

It was a revelation that anything could feel quite so good, quite so satisfying, yet there was more, she knew, more she yet wanted, more her awakening body yearned for. Within minutes, she was very certain – more she had to have.

Luc broke their kiss, but only to skate his lips along her jaw to find the delicate hollow beneath her ear. He didn't need to think to know what she wanted – to know that he could take as he wished. Beyond a distant watching brief to ensure their privacy, which, given the composition of Lady Hartington's company, he was certain would remain undisturbed, his senses were focused on the woman in his arms, on the tantalizing promise of the svelte body beneath his hands.

He'd had women aplenty, yet this one ... he put the difference he was too experienced not to notice in the strength of his own desire down to the fact she had for so long been a forbidden delight. A forbidden delight he could now sample, and subsequently savor whenever he wished. However he wished. That thought, barely conscious, fueled his need, but he shackled it, played to hers instead, confident in the knowledge that ultimately he would have all he wanted, all he wished – every wicked dream completely and thoroughly satisfied.

Her shallow breaths stirred the hair at his temple, caressed his skin with tendrils of temptation, evocative as sin. He sent his lips lower, cruising the length of her throat, along skin like ivory silk, delicate and fine. Pressing his lips to the base of her throat, he found her pulse beating under that fine skin, a speeding tattoo that urged him on, as did the small fingers that clenched on his chest, creasing his shirt, the rake of her nails just enough to awake a need of his own, to have her hands on his bare skin.

The thought of naked skin sent his attention to the mounds that filled his hands. Full and firm, heated, swollen. The buttons of her bodice were straining, easy to slip free; the ribbon straps of her chemise were fastened with tiny bows that unraveled at a tug.

A quick shuffle of fingers and hands, and her naked breasts were in his palms. She gasped; her lashes fluttered, but she didn't open her eyes. Didn't look down.

Lips curving, he raised his head, found her lips again, unsurprised when she kissed him ravenously. Riding the tide, he waited, then slid deep and took command, once again sent her senses whirling while his hands played, and learned her. Found the peaks of her breasts, ruched tight, tweaked gently, then slowly squeezed ... until she gasped again, until she broke the kiss and lifted her head, struggling for breath.

He ducked his head, let his lips trail down her throat, over the fine skin covering her collarbone, then lower still to the soft upper curve of her breast. The heat of his lips touched her and she stilled, quivering ... he didn't pause but licked, then laved, then opened his mouth and took the peak in, curled his tongue about the tip, and gently rasped.

The sound she made was neither gasp nor sob but pure shocked surprise. Pleased surprise. He continued to feast, holding her steady over him, watching her face from beneath his lashes as he pleasured her – and himself. His first taste of her flesh would remain blazoned in his mind – the piquancy of knowing no other had ever tasted her, touched her, like this.

He'd gradually urged her upward; her hip now rode against his stomach, one slender, decidedly feminine thigh caressing his rampant erection. She could not be unaware of his state, yet he sensed no retreat, no sudden maidenly reserve – no panic.

A fact that only sharpened his desire, a desire that flared when he caught a glimpse of bright sapphire beneath her lids, and realized she was watching. Watching him pay homage to her breasts, watching him feast on her bounty.

He caught her gaze, held it.

Deliberately curled his tongue about one tight bud, deliberately, and slowly, rasped – just hard enough to shatter her composure – then he suckled, and she caught her breath on a gasp. Closed her eyes. Slid one hand from his chest to his nape; head bowing, she held him to her, a surrender as explicit as the quiver that raced through her when he drew her flesh deeper still.

His hand left her breast, sliding down, over her hip, pausing to caress her derriere before sliding around, along her thigh, reaching for her skirt—

She sank against him, soft, pliant, urgent – a flagrant invitation.

Between them, he splayed his hand over her upper thigh, tensed to slide his fingers inward, searching—

He stopped. Remembered.

Where they were – what they were supposed to be doing.

Taking things one step further.

Not ten.

He lifted his head, found her lips, and kissed her – took a dark pleasure in ravaging her mouth, taking from her in that way what he would not yet take from her more explicitly.

Yet.

He stiffled his groan, his body's protest, with that promise. This was only a temporary state – a tactic in his greater campaign. A campaign he was determined to win without granting her any concessions.

Forcing his hands from their absorption, he gripped her hips and held her to him, stealing a moment to glory in her suppleness, in the evidence of how well she would, when the time came, suit him, taking in the womanly warmth that ultimately, when the time came, would ease his pain.

Sensing him drawing away through their kiss, she broke it herself, lifting her head to look down at him.

She frowned. 'What's the matter? Why have you stopped?'

He debated the wisdom of suggesting that, all things considered, she should be thanking him he had. Lying beneath her, he studied her face, taking in the fact that fate was having a hearty laugh at his expense. She didn't want him to stop – she'd be quite happy if he drew her back down, kissed her swollen cherry red lips, and—

It took serious willpower to drag in a breath. 'Timing.'

The flash in her eyes jerked his wits into action. 'As in' —he lowered his gaze to the tempting white mounds inches from his face— 'we wouldn't want to rush things to such an extent that you were overwhelmed.'

Settling one arm across her hips, anchoring her to him, he sent the fingers of his right hand dancing across the edge of her gown, teasing, tantalizing, flirting anew.

She shivered, watching through downcast eyes. 'Overwhelmed?'

The frown in her eyes was fading, but hadn't yet disappeared.

Surreptitiously watching her face, he chose his words carefully. 'There's so much to experience, so much I could show you, and after the first time, it's never quite the same. Never so . . . excruciating in its novelty.'

The frown remained.

Hooking a finger into her loosened bodice, he drew the fabric down, reexposing one pert nipple. With the pad of his thumb, he circled the aureole, applying just the right degree of pressure.

Her lids fell; she caught a shaky breath. 'Oh. I see.'

'Hmm. Given our situation, I thought you might prefer to take the long road, see all the sights, visit all the temples along the way' —he caught her gaze— 'so to speak.'

Huge, ever-so-slightly dazed cornflower blue eyes blinked at him. 'Are there a lot of ... temples?'

His lips curved spontaneously. 'Several. Many are missed because people rush.' He shifted his hand to her other breast and repeated the subtle torture, holding her gaze all the while, intensely aware of the ripples of sensual tension he was sending spiraling through her. 'We have three weeks yet ... it seems only sensible to see all we can. Visit as many temples as we can. As many places of worship.'

Her eyes held his. He was aware to his bones of every breath she took, of the rise and fall of the soft flesh beneath his fingers, of the throb of her heartbeat against his chest, and that deeper throb between her thighs, in the heated spot above his abdomen.

Her lashes fluttered down and she sighed. On the exhalation she went all but boneless, sinking against him, all resistance flown. Her hips shifted, the inner faces of her thighs quite deliberately caressing him.

He managed not to react, but one part of his anatomy was beyond his control. She peeked at his face, ran the tip of her tongue over her lower lip. 'I would have thought you'd be more urgent.'

He managed not to grit his teeth. 'It's a matter of control.'

'Well, you're the expert, I suppose ...'

He couldn't manage any reply. She glanced down, and he realized his thumb had seized – he set it sliding again, around and around.

'Is there really that much more to savor?'

'Yes.' Not a lie. His gaze had fixed once more on one tightly ruched nipple; it was an effort to draw enough breath to sigh. 'But we've run out of time today.'

He tweaked her chemise back up. With a resigned sigh of her own, she helped him set her gown to rights. But when he reached for her waist and gripped, intending to lift her from him, she stayed him, sliding one hand past his jaw, curling her fingers into his hair.

She looked down into his eyes, studied them, her gaze direct, then she smiled. 'Very well – we'll do it your way.'

Leaning down, she kissed him – long, lingering, and sweet. As she lifted her head, she whispered against his lips, 'Until next time ... and the next temple on our way.'

He was a man it was impossible to manipulate or drive; she'd known that for years. The only way to deal with him was to take whatever he offered, and work it to her own ends.

Thus Amelia concluded. Consequently, she reassessed Luc's insistence on a courtship of four weeks, focusing, this time, on the opportunities such an undertaking might afford her. Opportunities she hadn't, prior to Lady Hartington's *al fresco* luncheon, realized existed.

Those opportunities were not inconsequential.

What price a gentleman – one as experienced as Luc Ashford – promising to open a lady's eyes – slowly? Step by step. In a nonoverwhelming way.

Her attitude to his stipulation of four weeks underwent a dramatic change.

He'd agreed to marry her, to make a June bride of her; she knew he would. With her primary goal secured, there was no reason she couldn't participate in extracurricular developments – and the prospect he'd laid before her was beyond her wildest dreams.

She spent the next day in a pleasant daze – reliving, planning, wondering ... by the time she curstied to Lady Orcott that evening, then, on Luc's arm, followed his mother into her ladyship's crowded ballroom, she was biting her tongue against the urge baldly to ask which particular temple lay on their immediate horizon.

'There's Cranwell and Darcy.' Luc steered her toward the group containing those two gentlemen, cronies of sorts.

Amelia acknowledged the introductions. Miss Parkinson, a serious but wealthy bluestocking, was also present; she nodded, her gaze lingering disapprovingly on Amelia's gown of apricot silk.

The same gown incited Cranwell's and Darcy's immediate if unspoken approbation, possibly accounting for Miss Parkinson's disaffection.

'Daresay,' Cranwell drawled, dragging his gaze from the gown's low neckline and the expanse of her upper breasts it revealed, 'that like us, you're finding the tail end of the Season fatiguing?'

She smiled sunnily. 'Not at all. Why, just yesterday I spent a delightful afternoon discovering new landscapes at Hartington House.'

Cranwell blinked. 'Ah.' He would know to a rock what amenities Hartington House afforded. 'The grotto?'

'Oh, no.' Laying her hand fleetingly on his arm, she assured him, 'These were much more interesting, much more novel and enticing vistas.'

'Indeed?' Darcy shifted nearer, clearly intrigued. 'Tell me – were these vistas to your liking?'

'Very much so.' Her eyes full of laughter, she let her gaze slide to Luc. He was wearing his bored social mask, but his eyes . . . she let the curve of her lips deepen, then looked back at Darcy. If Luc insisted on dawdling through the evening chatting with friends before consenting to show her the next temple along their way, he would have to bear the consequences. 'Indeed, I fear I'm addicted – I'm eager to experience my next revelation.'

Noting shrewdly speculative glints in both Cranwell's and Darcy's eyes, she smiled at Miss Parkinson. 'New landscapes are so fascinating when one has the time to examine them, don't you think?'

Without a blush, Miss Parkinson replied, 'Indeed. Especially when in the right company.'

Amelia brightened. 'Quite. That goes without saying, I believe.'

Miss Parkinson nodded, her lips perfectly straight. 'Only last week, I was at Kincaid Hall – have you visited the folly there?'

'Not recently, and definitely not in the right company.'

'Ah, well – you should be sure to take advantage should the opportunity arise.' Miss Parkinson rearranged her shawl. 'Like you, my dear Miss Cynster, I'm quite looking forward to the upcoming house parties – so many opportunities to further one's appreciation of nature.'

'Oh, unquestionably.' Delighted to have found such a ready wit with whom to spar, Amelia was happy to further their game, one that was making all three gentlemen decidedly uncomfortable. 'It's a pleasure to be able to further develop one's understanding of natural phenomena. All ladies should be encouraged to do so.'

'Assuredly. While it used to be thought that only gentlemen had the required understanding to appreciate such matters, we are lucky to live in enlightened times.'

Amelia nodded. 'These days, there's no impediment to any lady's broadening her horizons.'

How long they might have continued in such vein, discomfiting their male listeners, none of whom dared interject, they were destined never to learn; the orchestra chose that moment to start the introduction to a cotillion. All three men were eager to end the conversation; intrigued by the possibilities suggested, Lord Cranwell solicited Miss Parkinson's hand.

Lord Darcy bowed to Amelia. 'If you would do me the honor, Miss Cynster?'

She smiled and gave him her hand, at the last throwing an innocent smile at Luc. He wasn't enamored of cotillions, and as they could still only dance twice with each other in one night, he'd wait for the waltzes.

His eyes, very dark, met hers briefly; he nodded a crisp acknowledgment as Darcy led her to join one of the rapidly forming sets.

While she danced, twirled, smiled, and chatted, Amelia considered that nod – or rather, its underlying quality. A certain tension now lay between them, a nuance of emotion not previously present. By the end of the cotillion, she'd decided she approved.

Darcy was perfectly ready to monopolize her, but Luc reappeared and, with smooth arrogance and not a single word, reclaimed her hand, setting it on his sleeve. Darcy's brows rose fleetingly, but he was too wise to press; Luc's actions spoke of an as-yet-unannounced understanding.

She smiled and chatted, but after a few minutes, Luc excused them and drew her away. They ambled through the crowd; glancing at his profile, she hid a smug smile and patiently waited.

Through innumerable encounters with friends, through the first waltz, and supper. By the time Luc drew her into his arms for their second, and last, waltz of the night, she'd lost all touch with patience.

'I thought,' she said, as they whirled down the floor, 'that we agreed to start exploring new vistas.'

He raised a brow – as usual, wearily. 'This venue is somewhat restricting.'

She wasn't that innocent. 'I would have thought an expert in the field, such as you are so widely purported to be, would be up to the challenge.'

The subtly emphasized words rang warning bells. Luc met her eyes, something until then he'd avoided; he had no need to see the irritation sparking in the blue. There was no evidence of stubbornness in her face – no set jaw, no tight lips – no change at all in the expectant tension that from the moment he'd met her in his hall earlier that evening had invested the supple body now supported in his arms; nevertheless, he could sense that steely strength of purpose he knew she possessed burgeoning by the instant.

Lifting his head, he scanned the room. 'The opportunities are limited.' Orcott House was not large; the ballroom was of simple design.

'Be that as it may ...'

He looked at her, again met her eyes. Confirmed

that the threat he'd thought he'd heard beneath her words was intentional. Instinctively replied, 'Don't be foolish.'

If he could have called back the words, he would have – instantly. But she'd surprised him – left him inwardly blinking at the preposterous notion that she might cross swords with him – *him* of all men – her goal being to force him to indulge her in some shameless dalliance ...

The idea was crazy – upside down and inside out. Totally contrary to how the world operated – his world, at least.

The sudden flash of blue fire that lit her eyes suggested he prepare himself for upside down. Inside out. And worse.

Amelia smiled sweetly as the waltz ended. 'Foolish? Oh, no.' She stepped out of his arms as they halted, registering the fact that his fingers started to flex, wanting to seize her, that he had to force himself to let her go. Her eyes on his, she let her smile linger as his hands fell from her; she turned away, holding his gaze to the last. 'I've something more potent in mind.'

Outrageous provocation was what she intended, what she served up in lavish degree. She was twenty-three, and in this arena thoroughly experienced – there was little she dared not do. Especially with Luc on her heels.

She flirted and teased to the top of her bent – and watched his temper rise. It was never easy to provoke it, or him – he was far too controlled, even to his emotions. But he didn't like seeing her smiling and laughing, inviting the attention of other men. He definitely didn't approve of her leaning close, letting

110

her natural charms invite inspection – an invitation other gentlemen saw no reason to refuse.

After six years in the ballrooms, she knew exactly which men to choose, which she could incite and tease with abandon and a clear conscience. The same males were the best for her purpose in another sense – they were the most likely to step in and pick up the gauntlet she made no bones about throwing down.

She was courting no risk – that she knew. There was not a chance Luc would allow any other man to seize that which he considered his.

The only question that remained was how long it would be before he capitulated.

And seized her himself.

Twenty minutes was the answer. Deserting one group of stunned rakes with an openly seductive laugh, she stepped back, ignored Luc at her shoulder, and set off through the crowd. An instant later, she heard a muttered curse – not a polite one – as Luc, on her heels, saw the group she now had in her sights. The gathering included Cranwell, Darcy, and Fitcombe, another of his peers.

He said not a word, just seized her hand, hauled her to the nearest wall, flung open a door she hadn't even noticed – one used by the servants – and stalked through, towing her behind him. Two shocked footmen carrying trays dodged about them, then Luc threw open another door, one leading into a normal corridor, dark and unlighted. He stepped through, pulled her after him, then slammed the door shut, spun her about, and backed her against it.

She blinked into his face, now devoid of any polite mask – or indeed, any politeness at all. His eyes were narrow, dark shards boring into hers; his lips were set

111

in a thin line. Stripped of all softness, the chiseled planes were forbidding, shadowed, harsh in the gloom.

'What do you think you're doing?'

The words were hard, incisive, his voice deep and menacing.

She held his gaze, calmly replied, 'Getting us here.'

With one forearm braced on the door, his other hand at her waist, holding her immobile, he leaned closer, his face intimidatingly inches from hers, a bare inch between their bodies.

Intimidated was not what she felt, a fact she allowed him to see.

His expression grew grimmer. 'What the hell do you imagine you'll experience in a dim corridor?'

She held his gaze, slid her hands up, curled her fingers into his lapels, then raised her brows, and evenly stated, 'Something I haven't experienced before.'

A blatant challenge, one he answered so swiftly her head spun.

His lips claimed hers, hard, forceful. She expected to be crushed against the door, but although his hand remained, pinning her against the panel, keeping her precisely where he wished, he didn't close the distance between them, didn't use his hard body to trap hers.

He didn't have to, didn't need to – just the kiss, blatantly sexual, unforgivingly explicit, was enough to rip her wits away, to shred any thought of escape. Likewise any thought of further provoking him.

Appeasing him – she hadn't intended to, yet quickly found herself doing precisely that, driven to it

112

by the unrelenting demand of his lips, his tongue, of his unquestioned expertise. He knew precisely what he was doing – even more, he knew what he was doing to her. He gave no quarter but quickly, efficiently, ruthlessly drove her to the point where surrender was her only option.

She tried to slide her arms up and wind them about his neck, but his hand at her waist, braced to preserve the small distance between them, prevented that. Instead, she spread her fingers and slid them into his thick hair, marveling at the feel of the heavy silky locks tumbling through her digits. Drew him deeper into their kiss – gave him all he wished. Invited him to take more.

She didn't even feel his fingers on her laces, only registered the fact he'd been busy when he shifted and the hand that had risen to cradle her face drifted down, hard fingertips trailing down her throat, down to the low neckline of the gown – only then did she realize her bodice was gaping. His knowing fingers didn't hesitate, but slid beneath the silk, seeking and finding, then he eased one breast free, his fingers already tight about the pebbled tip.

His touch was possessive and sure. He tweaked, rolled, kneaded, until she was inwardly gasping, reeling, the sensations aroused by his hand at her breast clashing with those evoked by his ceaseless, devastatingly persistent possession of her mouth. Of her lips. Of her breath.

She was close to fainting when he lifted his head, only to duck lower and take the sensitive bud he'd tortured into the hot wetness of his mouth. To lick, lave, suckle – until, head back against the door, she could no longer mute her cries.

He stirred then; the hand cradling her breast slid away. Then he rested it, palm flat, fingers splayed, on her stomach. Kneaded in a way she hadn't expected – hadn't expected to make her knees weak.

Eyes closed, her fingers clenched in his hair, she gasped as his lips tugged at her nipple. Then his fingers slid lower; her legs quaked.

Suddenly, it was only the iron grip of his hand at her waist that was keeping her upright, pinned against the door.

Through two layers of silk, his questing fingers found her curls. Stroked, teased, in some odd way taunted. Parted them. Heat pooled within her, deep between her thighs. His fingers didn't pause but continued their gentle probing, touching soft flesh that no other had ever touched, albeit through the screen of silk.

He didn't part her thighs, didn't press his hand between. His mouth was still hot, greedy on her breast, distracting her. Then, with one fingertip, he touched her – touched some spot she hadn't known she possessed – gently, knowingly. Persistently.

The sharp sensation of his mouth at her breast, the novel, wholly unexpected, shockingly intimate caress of that marauding fingertip all but brought her to her knees.

Her skin felt afire, her lungs had long seized. Then his finger slowed, and he pressed – breathless, she gasped his name.

To her surprise, he lifted his head – not to look at her, but to stare down the corridor.

Then he cursed softly, straightened, drew his hands from her. She started to slide down the door.

He cursed again and grabbed her. 'There's someone coming.'

The words were a low hiss; he was almost as quick setting her bodice to rights as he had been disarranging it. That done, he spun her around, held her to him, hauled open the door, and bundled her through before him. He shut the door carefully, silently ...

They stood in the now dark and deserted servants' corridor, his arm around her waist, holding her against him. She clung to his arm even though she no longer needed the support.

From beyond the door came voices, footsteps – a group of people passed by in the corridor where less than a minute ago they had been.

The footsteps faded; Luc heaved a relieved sigh. Close – too close. He glanced at Amelia, silent and alert; without a word, he urged her on toward the door into the ballroom.

'Wait.' He stopped her just before the door. They could hear the sounds of the ball still in full swing. It seemed like eons since they'd left.

She'd halted before him. Even in the darkness, he had no trouble redoing her laces, neatly tying them off.

When he lowered his hands, she glanced at him, then turned and stepped nearer. One hand touching his cheek, she stretched up and kissed him lightly. 'No more?' she murmured as their lips parted.

He didn't attempt to mute his growl. 'That was more than enough for one night.'

Chapter Six

More than enough torture. He doubted she realized the effect she had on him, especially when he had her under his hands, his to do with as he pleased. He had absolutely no intention of telling her, or of letting her guess.

He wasn't that foolish.

Inwardly wincing at the memory of what had transpired the last time he'd uttered that word, he watched his torment trip down Lady Hammond's dance floor in a country dance. Her partner was Cranwell; ever since Lady Orcott's ball five nights ago, Cranwell and the others with whom she'd flirted had grown overtly attentive. They were watching to see if he'd lose interest and walk away, then they'd pounce.

Stifling a dismissive humph, he focused on Amelia. She was enjoying herself as she always did these days – bright-eyed and expectant, anticipating the moment when he'd whisk her off somewhere private, and they would grab as many minutes of illicit indulgence as they could.

Compounding frustration wasn't his idea of fun, yet he wasn't about to invite another display of her talents like the one she'd staged at the Orcotts'. He'd capitulated as soon as he'd realized she'd found a real chink in his armor and taken the necessary steps to deal with her, albeit under duress.

Subsequently, he'd accepted that he had, at least in part, to dance to her tune. By letting her believe he was, he remained in control of their interludes, specifically how far those interludes went.

Which, thus far, was no further than at Lady Orcott's.

Self-preservation was a wise and sensible goal.

Feminine fingers touched his sleeve; knowing who it was, he turned, drawing his mother's hand into the crook of his arm.

She smiled. 'Come, my son – let's stroll a little way.'

He raised his brows faintly but complied; simultaneously, he scanned the room, checking on Emily, Anne, and Fiona. Amelia might claim the best part of his attention, but he hadn't forgotten his responsibilites.

'No, no – they're well. Indeed, very creditably engaged. It's you – and the lady you've been watching – I wanted to speak with you about.'

'Oh? Why?'

'I've been approached by no less than three of the senior hostesses, as well as any number of the lesser gossips. Speculation is rising that the relationship that in the past existed between you and Amelia has undergone a fundamental transformation.'

His lips twitched; that was an accurate way of describing it. 'On what evidence do the good ladies base such speculation?'

'It's been noted that you're both spending an

117

unusual amount of time together, that you, especially, have gone out of your way to facilitate that, and, of course, it's been noted that you both have a tendency to disappear from the central venue, to return within a reasonable time, admittedly, yet that frequent fact is viewed with suspicion.'

'That sounds as it should at this point.' Luc glanced at Minerva. 'What have you said?'

She opened her eyes wide. 'Why, that you've known each other for years and have always been close.'

He nodded. 'It's possible you might actually start wondering yourself . . .'

Minerva raised her brows. 'Just what date are you aiming for?'

There was a note in her voice that had him temporizing, 'Well, not just me—'

'Luc.' Minerva fixed him with a straight look. 'When?'

He knew when to capitulate; he'd had recent practice. 'About the end of the month.'

'And the ceremony?'

He set his jaw. '*By* the end of the month.'

Her eyes opened wide, then a thoughtful expression swept her face. 'Ah. I see. That does explain a few things.' She refocused on his face, then patted his arm. 'Very well. At least I now know what to expect – and how to manage the gossips. You may leave them to me.'

'Thank you.'

She caught his eye, then smiled and shook her head. 'You'll go your own road, I know, but beware, my son. Marriage for you will not be as easy as you think.'

Still smiling, she left him. Luc watched her go, a frown in his eyes, one question in his mind. Why?

Women. A necessary evil, or so he'd come to accept. He could define precisely what the necessary parts were. As for the rest, one simply had to learn to deal with them – it was that or be driven insane.

To enliven the next day, they'd organized a picnic at Merton. A picnic – he knew what that meant. Bucolic delights – like rocky or marshy ground, or trees with unhelpfully rough bark, or inquisitive ducks – all obstacles he'd met with in his callow youth.

He was long past those days – long past picnics.

'I'll take a decent chaise in a conservatory any day.'

'What was that?'

He glanced at Amelia, beside him on the curricle's seat. 'Nothing. Just muttering.'

Amelia grinned and looked ahead. 'I haven't been to Cousin Georgina's in years.'

She was looking forward to it, to the chance of spending more than a few rushed minutes with Luc. She wanted – very definitely – to take their interaction further, to learn more of the magic he conjured, to wallow in the sensations he knew so well how to invoke. Ultimately, to travel further down their road and visit the next temple.

Since Lady Orcott's dim corridor, progress had been minimal, primarily due to lack of time. At least, that's how it seemed, although in truth, she never had the slightest idea of time passing once Luc's lips were on hers.

Let alone his hands on her body, clothed or otherwise.

Nevertheless, she'd learned one or two things. Such as, despite the fact he physically desired her, that iron will of his stubbornly intervened and left him firmly in control, not just of her but of himself, too. Even when he'd reduced her to a gasping, witless, boneless heap, he could still hear and function as if he were merely out riding. Indeed, that was a very apt analogy – he loved riding, but never lost control.

Undermining that control, seeing him in the throes of a passion as hot and mindless as what he induced in her, was a very tempting proposition.

She glanced at him, studied the strong line of his jaw, then smiled and looked ahead.

The drive leading to Georgina's villa lay around the next bend. Luc turned the curricle in between the gateposts; the drive led to a circular court before the villa's front door.

Georgina was waiting to greet them. 'My dears.' She enveloped Amelia in a scented embrace and kissed her cheek. Then she smiled, and gave Luc her hand. 'The last time you were here, you fell out of the plum tree. Luckily, you didn't break any bones.'

Luc straightened from his bow. 'Did I break any branches?'

'No, but you did eat a great many of the plums.'

Amelia slipped her arm in Georgina's. 'The others are following in the carriages. Can we help with anything?'

The answer was no, so they sat outside on the terrace and sipped cool drinks until the others arrived. As well as Luc's sisters and Fiona, and Minerva and Louise to keep Georgina company, young Lord Kirkpatrick and two of his friends had been invited, along with Reggie, and Amelia's brother Simon. And three of their cousins, Heather, Eliza, and Angelica, together with a few of their friends.

The carriages rolled up, the occupants joined them on the shady terrace, and the picnic party swelled to a sizable group, full of laughing, chattering good cheer.

Luc viewed the gathering with mixed feelings. He was thankful his two youngest sisters, Portia and Penelope, had remained at home in Rutlandshire. They hadn't come to London with the family primarily because of the cost; after his recent windfall, he'd toyed with the idea of sending for them, but at fourteen and thirteen, they were supposed to be attending their lessons. Penelope would be, her nose buried in some tome, but on a day like this, Portia would be out with his prize pack of hounds. If they'd been here, at this party, he'd have been forced to keep a strict eye on them both – and endure their incessant and often pointed teasing. Just as well those two sharp-eyed nuisances were safely far away.

'Luc?'

Amelia's voice drew him back to Merton; he blinked, and saw her silhouetted against the glare of the sunlight washing over the lawns. She was wearing a thin muslin gown, perfect for the warm day; the bright light behind her turned the fabric translucent, revealing the shapely curve of one breast, the indentation of her waist made all the more definite by the delectable swell of her hips, followed by the long, slender lines of her legs.

He had to draw breath before he succeeded in dragging his gaze back up to her face. She tilted her head, studying him, a light smile on her lips. She gestured with a plate. 'Come and eat.'

With a nod, he got to his feet – slowly – using the instant to shackle his hunger, sudden, rampant, unexpectedly vital. He hadn't realized it had grown to this extent, to the point where its spurs had real bite, driving him to seize.

He joined her; to her right lay the open doors to a dining parlor where a feast was spread. Many of the company were filling their plates, chattering incessantly; others, plates in their hands, were heading out to the chairs and tables assembled on the lawn.

Relieving Amelia of the plate, he met her gaze, blue eyes wondering. With his other hand, he caught her fingers, raised them and pressed his lips to the tips. Let her, but only her, see the real nature of his hunger in his eyes.

Hers widened. Before she could say anything, he lowered her hand, and turned her to the table. 'So what's the most delectable delight?'

Her lips twitched, but she calmly informed him the stuffed vine leaves were particularly good.

They filled their plates, then joined the others on the lawns. The next hour sped by in easy converse. Good company, excellent food, fine wine, and a bright summer day; there were no jealousies or tensions in the group – they all relaxed and enjoyed the occasion.

Eventually, their appetite for food sated, the younger crew – all bar the older ladies, Luc, Amelia, and Reggie – decided on an expedition to the nearby river. A walk through the gardens joined a country path to the riverbank; Simon, Heather, Eliza, and Angelica all knew the way. The party rose in a flurry of pastel muslin flounces and frilled parasols, the young gentlemen eagerly assisting.

'No need to rush,' Louise advised them. 'We've hours before we need to leave.'

Smiling, Minerva nodded her own permission.

Most set off in close file through the gardens; Heather and Eliza descended on Reggie.

'*Do* come along – we want to hear all about Lady Moffat's wig.'

'Did it really fly off at Ascot?'

Always ready to gossip, Reggie allowed himself to be led away.

Luc raised a brow at Amelia. 'Shall we?'

She raised a brow back, a speculative gleam in her eye. 'I suspect we should, don't you?'

He rose and drew out her chair. Neither of them had any intention of walking as far as the river, yet with every evidence of reluctantly doing their duty and watching over their juniors – who in this company needed no watching – they ambled, side by side, in the group's wake.

They left the lawns behind; when the gardens hid the house from view, Luc paused on a crest in the walk. Ahead, the others straggled in groups of three and four, stretching away toward the golden fields and the distant green ribbon of the river.

Simon's voice reached them; he and Angelica were debating the likelihood of again meeting a family of fierce ducks encountered on their last visit.

Luc glanced at Amelia, waiting beside him. 'Do you want to see the river, complete with ducks?'

Her lips curved. 'I've seen it all before.'

'In that case, which way is the orchard? Maybe we can identify the tree I fell out of on my last visit?'

She waved to another path, leading to the left a little way along. 'At the very least, the plums will be ripe.'

123

He stepped off the main walk in her wake. 'It isn't plums I'm thinking of tasting.'

She threw him a haughty, challenging glance, and forged on.

He smiled, and followed.

The orchard was a seducer's delight – large old trees heavily in leaf surrounded by a high stone wall, it was far enough from the house to ensure privacy, uphill and far enough from the path to the river to make it highly unlikely any of the others would come that way.

Once beneath the trees, they were all but invisible to anyone outside the orchard. Amelia had been right; the plums were ripe. Reaching up, Luc plucked a plump one. He saw Amelia glance his way; he handed it to her, then searched and found another for himself.

'Hmm – delicious.'

He looked at Amelia as he bit in; she was right again – the sun-warmed fruit was heavenly. Eyes closed in appreciation, she swallowed; red plum juice stained her lips.

Opening her eyes, she took another bite. The juice overran her lip, one drop trickling down from the corner.

He reached out and caught the drop on his fingertip. She blinked, focused – then leaned forward and took the tip of his finger between her lips, and sucked lightly.

His lungs – all of him – seized; for one instant, he was blind. Then he blinked, hauled in a breath, managed to lower his hand – and saw, beyond her, the orchard's crowning glory, at least for their purpose.

A small summerhouse, it had clearly been placed in

the center of the orchard to capitalize on the privacy.
The orchard was on a slope, so the summerhouse had
views over the distant fields and river, but the trees
all around ensured no one could see in.

Many of Merton's villas had been built by gentlemen for their mistresses; Luc was only too ready to
exploit someone else's good planning, especially as he
doubted he could keep his hands off his fair companion for much longer, and although the grass beneath
the trees grew lush and thick, and little fruit had thus
far fallen, grass stains on a lady's gown was a telltale
sign.

He gestured to the summerhouse. He didn't have to
say anything – she was as eager as he. Turning, she
led the way. Lifting her skirts, she climbed the three
shallow steps, then smiled and went forward, swinging around to sit on the heavily padded sofa placed to
enjoy the view.

She looked up at him, a gentle curve to her lips, a
questioning, challenging lift to her brows. He paused
in the archway for only a second, then strolled
forward and joined her.

Not as she'd been expecting. He didn't sit beside
her, but placed one knee on the cushions, leaned over
her and, one hand framing her face, tipping it up, set
his lips to hers.

He was in no mood for polite playing, for pretending to a distance that no longer existed between them.
One thing their shared kisses over the past five days
had wrought was the dropping of certain barriers; her
lips, and she, were his whenever he wished. He knew
it; so did she.

She responded ardently, as she always did. Her
lips parted beneath his, inviting him in, welcoming

and warm. She tasted of plum, rich and sweet; he plundered and drank, easing down to the cushions, his hip beside hers.

Her arms twining about his neck, she leaned back against the cushioned arm, back against the arm he slid around her. They were both hungry, frustratingly starved; there was no reason they couldn't now feast.

For long moments they did simply that, appeasing the appetites evoked but left unfulfilled through the preceding days. But that wasn't enough to slake his hunger. Or hers.

He was so caught in the kiss, in the honeyed splendor of her mouth, he didn't realize she'd – once again – taken the lead. Taken it upon herself to open his shirt and lay his chest bare. A fleeting moment of coolness was the only warning he had before her palms made contact – and shook him to his soul.

He drew back from the kiss, struggling to breathe, distracted, his senses caught by the sensate thrill of her bold and brazen exploration.

Her touch was not shy but avid – greedy as she spread her fingers wide and flexed them, pressing into the wide muscle banding his chest, then sliding up, then across, possessively tracing as if he were a slave she now owned.

For one instant, held in thrall, he wondered if that were true.

Then he caught his breath, and took advantage of her distraction to reassert control, to drag his mind free from the drugging delight of her touch. Slipping free the buttons of her straining bodice, he laid bare the firm mounds he'd grown quite familiar with, but only in dim light. He paused, took a moment to savor their perfection, the translucent skin, the blue veins beneath, the pale rose of her lightly puckered nipples. He blew on one, and watched it tighten, then bent his head and feasted some more.

Her breath catching on a gasp as he rasped one sensitive bud, Amelia let her head fall back, one hand still splayed on his chest, the fingers of the other sunk in his black hair. Eyes closed, lips parted as she struggled to breathe, she gloried in the no-longer-novel sensations, delighted in the simple intimacy, now a familiar delight, and waited, expectant, excited – fascinated – for more.

His hot mouth moved over her breasts, aching and swollen, nipples excruciatingly tight. Heat welled within her, grew and swelled until it demanded release.

She shifted restlessly beneath him, waiting, wanting . . .

When she could wait no more, she drew her hand from his chest, searched and caught his wrist, tugged his hand from her breast, insistently drew it down to her stomach. She didn't need to give him further directions; his fingers tensed, kneaded lightly, then slid farther down to touch her as he had before, teasing the fine curls beneath her gown.

Combined with the play of his lips, mouth, and tongue on her breasts, the tantalizing caress of his fingertips was . . . more than pleasant. But there was still more – more that she'd yet to experience; she knew it, and wanted it – now.

Especially as her nerves were growing tighter, tenser, coiling in some indefinable way . . . until she ached. Yearned.

She lifted her hips, deliberately forcing his fingers deeper between her thighs.

He glanced up from ministering to her breasts; his eyes glinted darkly.

She caught his gaze. 'More.' When he didn't immediately comply, she insisted, 'I know there's more. Show me. Now.'

There was something going on behind those dark devil's eyes; despite the light, they seemed almost black. Quite impenetrable.

Then he raised one brow; he shifted, deserting her breasts to lean over her once more.

'If you insist.'

The growl feathered her lips in the instant before he took her mouth again. She hadn't been expecting it, didn't have a chance to brace herself against the sudden onslaught. Not physical but sensual, a powerful tide that whirled her wits away, that left her incapable of doing anything beyond feeling and reacting.

Beyond sensing the altered tenor of the kiss, the shift that had left him blatantly dominant, seizing and claiming as he wished. Each deep slow thrust had her shuddering, yet in a different way; the shift of his coat and shirt against her bare breasts was a new sensation. Then he angled his chest, pressing close for an instant, and the intervening fabric was gone, pushed aside. The heat of his chest, the crinkly, raspy black curls met her swollen breasts.

Sensation speared through her; he shifted again and the peaks of her breasts turned fiery with delight, one step away from pain as he deliberately abraded them.

It was then she felt his hand on her thigh, and realized he'd flipped up her skirts. Cool air touched her calves but she cared not at all, her every sense intent on the gentle caress of his fingertips upward along her inner thigh.

He touched her curls and she shivered; he ran one fingertip down through them, and her nerves leapt. Then his

lips firmed, and he drew her back into the kiss; she tried to resist, to let her mind follow his fingertips instead, but he ruthlessly captured every last shred of her awareness and anchored them, her, in the passionate engagement of their lips and tongues, the increasingly intimate merging of their mouths.

When he finally allowed her to resurface, not completely but just enough to sense again, her thighs were parted, his hand was between, his fingertips sliding over heated flesh that was swollen and quite wet.

It was a shocking discovery, one of dizzying delight. He didn't release her lips, but kept her with him in the kiss while his fingers played. But it wasn't just play; beneath the drugging sensuality, the consistent delight, lay a possessiveness, a primitive drive that she sensed despite his efforts to disguise it. To keep it veiled, concealed – hidden.

It was there in the tension that held him, that locked his muscles and left him rigid. There in the heavy weight of his erection against her thigh, in the steely power in his hand as he parted her folds and caressed her. She sensed it in the building heat he held back from her, kept screened from her, as if to protect her from the flames. Flames he was accustomed to dealing with, but which she had yet to experience.

If the choice had been hers, she would have asked for the flames – they beckoned with an addictive glory. But she could do no more than accept what he gave her, take what he offered – what he allowed.

She was too desperate to argue, too caught in the

129

sensual web he'd woven. She needed more. Now. He seemed to understand. He parted her slick folds and opened her, gently probed the entrance to her body until she thought she'd scream, then slowly, boldly, slid one long finger into her.

In some dim part of her brain, she'd expected the penetration to ease her need, and for some few minutes it did. But then the subtle friction of that probing finger, sliding languidly back and forth, ignited another want, another need – one even more desperate than the last.

He purposely built it, stoked it, until she was clinging, her nails sinking into his arms, her body arching under his. A captive, certainly, one ready to yield, to surrender.

And she did.

The implosion of sensation, the sudden release, the tide of sensual heat that engulfed her, took her unawareness, caught her up, whirled her high, into some sensual heaven.

The ease, the physical peace that suffused her, was unfamiliar, yet she embraced it eagerly and relaxed in his arms, only dimly aware when he withdrew his hand and flipped her skirts down.

His lips remained on hers, hard, too knowing, yet the heat was dying; she could sense him bringing the barriers down, shutting her off completely from the furnace and the flames.

When he finally lifted his head, she was waiting. Raising one hand, she speared her fingers through his hair, and held him near. Forced her weighted lids to rise, studied his eyes.

Even from this close, she couldn't read them.

'Why did you stop?' His gaze dropped to her lips;

she tightened her hold on his hair. 'And if you mention time or timing, I'll scream.'

His lips curved, then he met her eyes. 'Not time. Temples.' He put out his tongue and ran the tip along her lower lip. 'We haven't reached that temple yet.'

She didn't take his explanation well, but grudingly forebore to argue; she seemed to have accepted that at least in this arena, she couldn't dictate to him.

The afternoon was mild; they had plenty of time. He slumped back and rearranged her so she lay atop him, her back to his chest, cradled in his arms as her skin cooled and her wits lazily drifted. A moment of blessed peace he seized for himself. Placed as she was, she couldn't see his face – couldn't see the glances he slanted at hers.

He was trying to regain his bearings, and didn't want her to know he'd lost them. Didn't want her to guess, as she might if she saw him looking uncertain, that he was ever so slightly at sea.

Even on this sea, one he'd successfully navigated more times than he could count.

Women, the having of them, had never truly mattered – not in any specific way – in the past. He'd assumed having Amelia would be, if not precisely the same, then not seriously different.

Yet the blind need that had gripped him only moments past was new. Blind lust, blind desire – those he was familiar with – but blind need? That was something else. Something that had never before afflicted him. He couldn't logically explain why the need to possess her and only her had suddenly become so acute. So absolutely necessary.

He didn't know how deep this unfamiliar emotion

ran. He didn't know if he could control it – or if, ultimately, it would control him.

That thought left him wary, even more wary than before, yet as the minutes ticked past and the afternoon waned, the soft warm body, so elementally feminine, in his arms, in spite of all, soothed him.

She'd lost all physical distance; she was utterly content in his arms, even though her bodice was still open, her breasts delightfully exposed. He felt his lips curve; he definitely approved of her this way. The temptation to raise a hand to the soft mounds and play was real, yet ... the end of the day was not that far away.

Eventually, they stirred and after righting their clothes, headed back to the villa. She led the way, as she so often did. Just before they reached the main walk, he stopped her; close behind her, he bent his head and pressed his lips briefly to the curve of her throat.

She said nothing, but looked around, her eyes meeting his as he straightened. Then she smiled – that odd, glorious, womanly smile that always left him suspicious – and blithely turned and headed on.

They reached the lawns a few minutes before the others straggled back, tired and weary but smiling. They all piled back into the carriages. Although the girls' chatter had died, Reggie begged for relief so Luc took him up behind them in his curricle. The faster equipage soon left the carriages far behind.

They were trotting into London when Reggie yawned and stirred. Luc grinned. 'Did you hear anything worth learning?'

Reggie humphed. 'Only some tale about a snuffbox gone missing at Lady Hammond's and some precious

132

bud vase that Lady Orcott's misplaced. You know what it is, though – it's the end of the Season and things have got moved and people have forgotten where they put them.'

Luc thought of his grandfather's inkstand. Reggie was undoubtedly right.

Chapter Seven

The evening of the next day loomed as a disaster; if Luc could have avoided the Countess of Cork's masquerade, he would have, but the old harridan was a longtime friend of the family – attendance for him was compulsory. That being so, there was no argument powerful enough to prevent Amelia attending, too; she was – and had made it perfectly clear she was – flown with high hopes for the evening.

Ascending the steps of the Cork mansion with Amelia, cloaked and masked, on his arm, he was uncomfortably aware of the irony; he'd never felt so torn in his life. At least his mother, and hers, and their cronies, would not be attending. Tonight was largely for those of his and Amelia's ilk, and those more youthful who aspired to similar status.

Handing their invitations to the butler, he ushered Amelia into the crowd thronging her ladyship's front hall. Those new to such entertainments had paused there; masked and unidentifiable in dominos, they were looking around, trying to recognize others. A hand at her back, he urged Amelia on.

'The ballroom,' he said when she hesitated and

glanced back at him. 'It'll be less packed in there.'

At one point, he had to take the lead and shoulder a way through, but his prophecy proved correct; in the ballroom, they could at least breathe.

'I'd no idea it would be such a crush. Not so late in the Season.' Up on her toes, Amelia was craning her neck, trying to get her bearings.

'If masquerades aren't crowded, they tend to miss the mark.'

She looked at him. 'Because it's too easy to guess who everyone is?'

He nodded brusquely and took her arm. Not that anyone would have trouble identifying her regardless of the crowds; those cornflower blue eyes, wide behind her mask, were distinctive, especially when combined with the flash of golden curls beneath her domino's hood.

'Here.' Halting, he tugged her hood forward, further shielding her face and hair.

She looked up at him. 'It doesn't really matter if people guess who I am. I've already found my partner for the night.'

True, but ... 'Given your hopes for the evening, it would be wiser to avoid drawing unnecessary attention our way.'

She was wearing a half mask; he watched her face clear, saw a seductive smile curve her lips as she inclined her head. 'On that I must bow to your greater experience.'

Sliding her hand onto his arm, she came alongside – into the position where he now expected her to be; he felt most comfortable when she was there, beside him, her hand on his sleeve. Stifling a sigh, he consented to stroll down the ballroom.

135

In more normal circumstances, he would be assessing the room and the house for places to which he might later whisk the lady he had on his arm so they could indulge in private pleasures. Tonight, with the lady who currently commanded most of his waking thoughts, he was more concerned with, if at all possible, avoiding precisely those same pleasures.

'Amelia.' Nothing for it but to take up the slack in her reins. And try to turn her. 'Despite what you're thinking, we're still rolling too fast down our chosen road.'

It was a moment before she looked up at him, and by then her chin had set. 'You aren't, by any chance, going to suggest we backtrack?'

'No.' He knew she'd never accept that. 'But ...' How to explain that despite what he'd led her to believe, there were only so many temples prior to intercourse at which it was possible to worship? At least while retaining his sanity. 'Take it from me, we can't go much further than we've already gone. Yet.'

To his surprise, she didn't stiffen, fix him with a glare, and argue. Instead, she halted, faced him; her eyes searched his, then she smiled – one of those smiles that every instinct he possessed distrusted – and stepped closer so they could converse without being overheard.

'Are you saying you won't seduce me yet?'

He felt his face harden; his eyes locked on hers, he thought carefully before confirming, 'Yet.'

Her smile deepened; she stepped closer still. Raised a hand and laid her fingers along his cheek. 'Stop being so noble.' She kept her voice low, a sirenlike murmur. 'I'm perfectly ready to be seduced. By you.'

136

She studied his eyes, then tilted her head. 'Is it because you've known me for so long?'

It was so tempting to say yes – to claim that as his excuse and trade on her empathy.

'It's got nothing to do with how long I've known you.' He bit the words out, but she didn't take umbrage, instead simply waited, her eyes steady on his, her brows faintly rising in question.

Her hand had fallen to his chest; she was so close, she was almost in his arms. A quick glance around confirmed that, despite his distraction, his rake's instincts had been functioning normally; they were at the end of the ballroom in a shadowy alcove where a corridor joined the main room. In the circumstances, it seemed natural to slide his arms around her and keep her where she was.

While his mind raced, trying to formulate a reason she'd accept for delaying her seduction until he'd come to grips with what said seduction now meant – would mean – to him. 'I've only been openly wooing you for ten days. Full-scale seduction at this point would be distinctly precipitate.'

She laughed and settled against his chest, her face tilted up to his. 'Why? How long do you usually take to inveigle a lady into bed?'

'*That* is not the point.'

'True.' Her smiling eyes remained on his. 'But if we did indulge, who would know? I'm not going to come out in spots, or convert into a simpering ninny, or do anything else to alert anyone to the fact.'

He wasn't worried about her changing – he was worried about him. About his lack of understanding, potential lack of control, of the primitive need she evoked in him. That need was even now driving him

137

to fall in, immediately if not sooner, with her plans. That need wanted her beneath him, wanted her surrender – wanted her.

But it was a need unlike any he'd ever known – infinitely more powerful, more compelling. It was a need that drove him as no desire ever had.

He looked into her eyes. 'Believe me, we need to put off your seduction, for at least another ten days.'

Amelia listened to the words, even more listened to his tone. Hard, ruthless – decided. Yet he'd said the words, discussed the point – he hadn't just tried dictatorially to force her to fall in with his plans. That, she was well aware, was his more customary mode of dealing with females. Explaining himself, even as poorly as he had – hardly surprising given he got so little practice – had never been his style. Yet he'd tried. Tried to gain her cooperation rather than insisting on her obedience.

So she continued to smile at him. 'Another week and more?' She couldn't imagine it, didn't believe it would happen. After their recent interactions, especially in Georgina's orchard, especially that last, unexpectedly revealing kiss on the path back to the villa, she was confident matters between them were progressing precisely as she'd hoped. As she'd dreamed. He certainly viewed her as a woman – a woman he desired – but there was more to their interaction than that.

As a loving future husband, he was coming along perfectly – far more so than she'd expected at this relatively early stage. Which suggested she should treat his current vacillation with some degree of magnanimity.

Letting her lips curve more definitely, she reached

up and wound her arms about his neck. 'Very well. If you wish.'

The suspicion that flashed into his dark eyes made her smile even more; she drew his head down, drew his lips to hers. 'For the present, let's leave things to develop as they will.'

Their lips met, sealing the agreement; Luc could barely believe his luck. Indeed, as their lips clung, then parted, only to come together again, driven by mutual need, one part of his mind was viewing his relief with cynical skepticism.

Which continued when they lifted their heads and, by unvoiced agreement, joined the couples on the dance floor for the first waltz. As he whirled her down the room, aware to his bones that she was simply enjoying the moment, enjoying the sensation of being in his arms, swept away by the music, he couldn't but suspect her acquiescence.

The last time he'd tried to deny her, to slow their slide into intimacy, she'd stuck her nose in the air and swanned off to flirt with other men. Luckily, at a masquerade, while the possibilities to do the same were theoretically unlimited, in practice, she was already in his arms – and at a masquerade, there was nothing to stop him from keeping her there.

He was an accomplished rake; holding a lady's attention, fixing it, not on him but on the illicit ruffling of her senses that a masquerade so lent itself to, was all but second nature. Sliding into the habit – touching her, caressing her beneath her voluminous domino, stealing kisses in the shadows – required no thought. And when they both grew too hungry to be satisfied with what could be accomplished in the ball-room, he saw no danger in finding a quiet nook in which to further indulge their senses.

He didn't see the danger at all.

Habit had him leading her to a small study – a room so small no one else would consider it. Even better, a room with a lock, one he turned. A desk sat to one side of the narrow room; in the room's center stood a large admiral's chair with a black leopardskin spread before it.

With a laugh of pure expectation, Amelia put back her hood and flipped the sides of her domino back over her shoulders. Stepping past her, he dropped into the admiral's chair. Tugging his mask free, he tossed it aside and reached for her.

She came onto his lap, into his arms in a froth of slippery silks, eagerly reaching for his face to bring it to hers. His lips on hers, he found the ties of her domino and quickly undid them; the heavy cloak slid down and away to pool on the floor at his feet. She dispensed with her half mask, flinging it blindly away, then she wriggled closer yet, sank against him, her hands on his chest, her lips teasing and taunting – flagrantly tempting.

He answered her challenge avidly, ready enough to take what ease they could. They'd attended tonight intending to spend the time in each other's company; there was nothing else they needed to do.

His hands roved her sleek body, roved her curves, possessing as he would. She kissed him with unfeigned delight, openly encouraging.

All too soon they were giddy, both of them, but not from Lady Cork's champagne. Their kisses grew headier, more evocative; she grew softer, he commensurately harder. He'd made a logical rational decision that indulging her with kisses and caresses was only fair; no sense in forgoing such simple pleasures. At no point had he entertained the notion that she could, no matter how hard she tried, overcome his determination not to seduce her.

And she didn't – he wasn't sure she even tried.

It wasn't she who tumbled them from the chair onto the leopardskin rug. It wasn't she who trapped herself beneath him. However, that done, breathless, dizzy, and expectant, she willingly obliged him by dealing with the fiendishly tiny closures of her bodice, revealing her breasts, encouraging him to admire, caress, and taste, once he'd indicated that was his aim.

He'd touched her breasts before, viewed them, feasted on the soft flesh, but before she hadn't given herself to him – he'd simply taken, and she'd acquiesced.

Perhaps it was that, that sublime gesture of acceptance, that caused the change, the irresistible, irreversible alteration in the tenor of their exchange.

The switch caught him unawares, caught him with his defenses, if not down, then in temporary abeyance. Before he understood, before he saw the danger, his lips were on hers, hard and demanding, his hand on her breast, equally insistent, his body heated and hard holding her down, his intention brutally clear.

Before he could think, they both went up in flames.

He'd been there before, in desire's furnace; even though she hadn't, she showed no fear. He kissed her more ravenously, more explicitly than he ever had before; she met him and urged him on.

Her hands were frantic, clenched in his hair, then his shirt was undone and her palms spread across his chest, fingers flexing, sinking in as he rolled, then squeezed one

141

pebbled nipple tight, tighter ... until she broke the kiss with a gasp, her body arching under his.

A flagrant invitation – the need it evoked, primitive and unrestrained, slammed into him, rolled over and through him, and shook his laggard wits into place.

One instant of blind clarity was all he gained, but it was enough to realize their present situation was not her fault, but his. In his mind, he knew she was his – his to take whenever he wished, here, now, if that was what he wanted.

He wanted – with a need so acute it was a physical hurt. He hadn't expected his own instincts to betray him, delivering up to him that which was, here and now, his deepest desire.

He could have her now, here; even as his lips returned to hers, even as his body moved over hers, one thought flashed through his mind: and what then? He wasn't ready to face it – this need she drew forth, and all that might flow from it. He didn't know enough yet to feel secure. Indulging it just once might condemn him to ... what? He didn't know.

And while he didn't know ...

He'd been a captive of the flames often enough to know how to manage them. Now he'd realized the danger, his will was still strong enough to escape the web his own talents had spun.

There was, of course, a price – one he set about paying unstintingly.

Amelia knew this had to be very close to the very last temple on their road. Beneath the staggering heat, an urgency had gripped them – both of them; it drove them on. Her senses could barely cope, yet seemed to have expanded, heightened; her skin was oversensitized, yet greedy for every touch.

142

She was acutely conscious of her tortured breathing, and his; it was as if their kisses were all that anchored them in the world – they clung to the exchanges as if their lives depended on it. As for their bodies, hers had melted, all resistance gone; his in contrast had only grown harder, as if the steely strength normally infusing his muscles had coalesced into rock-hard rigidity.

Hot, rock-hard rigidity. From the lips ravaging hers, to the hand kneading her naked breast, to the hard columns of his legs tangled with hers. His erection, as hard and hot as the rest of him and even more rigid, was a potent promise of all she hoped would come.

When his hand left her breast, slid over her hip and started to gather and lift her skirt, she stopped breathing entirely – caught in a vise of anticipation, excitement, and sheer overwhelming desire.

A new feeling, that last – never before had she wanted this, not with any other man. With Luc, it was meant to be – she didn't question that; she knew it in her bones.

She felt the touch of cool air; shifting over her, he pushed her skirts and chemise to her waist, leaving them bunched there, his hand sliding immediately to her curls, then farther. His tongue thrust deep into her mouth as he cupped her; the bold rhythm he set up distracted her for an instant – the instant in which he opened her body and slid one finger into her softness.

Her body, no longer hers, reacted, her hips lifting against him. But he didn't let her senses free, holding them to the steady thrusting rhythm of his tongue, echoed by that bold finger.

The heat within her built, and built, until she

simply had to break free and breathe. He lifted his head, let her lie back, gasping, panting – she would have writhed but his weight held her down.

She felt him come up on his elbow and shift back. Cracking open her lids, she looked – and saw him looking down to where his hand rhythmically flexed between her naked thighs. His knee held them spread; as she watched, his gaze roamed over her hips, over her bare stomach, up over her midriff, over her rucked skirts to her breasts, still exposed, the peaks tight, pointed, their fine skin flushed.

His expression was hard, etched, driven, yet something in his gaze, in the line of his lips, suggested a softness, an intangible emotion she hadn't before seen in him. Then his gaze rose and touched her face, locked on her eyes.

Between her thighs, his hand shifted; slowly, deliberately, he probed deeper. Then his thumb caressed, circling that spot he'd so often teased.

She caught her breath, closed her eyes, tensed. Then forced her eyes open, forced her limp arms to obey as she reached for him. 'Come to me – now.'

She caught his shoulders and tugged but he didn't shift. His lips twisted in a half smile. 'Not yet.' He glanced down again to where his hand played between her thighs, then he slid from her grasp and shifted farther back. 'There's one more altar at which I've yet to worship.'

What he meant she couldn't imagine, but as he immediately bent his head and set his lips to her navel, she didn't have breath, wits, or inclination to ask. He planted kisses over her stomach, then wended his way lower, rendering the already hot skin more fevered.

The unanticipated caresses, unquestionably illicit,

drugged her mind, tantalized her senses. But when he withdrew his hand from between her thighs and set his lips to her curls, she jerked, suddenly unsure. 'Luc?'

He didn't answer.

The next touch of his lips made her shriek.

'*Luc*!'

He paid not the slightest heed – within seconds, she'd lost all hope of stopping him, lost all wish to do so – lost her mind, lost her wits into a maelstrom of physical sensation.

She'd never dreamed that such a thing could be, that a man would touch her like this, there, let alone that he would. She'd wanted him to make her his, and in all ways bar one, he did – in the end, she surrendered, let him take her as he wished, gave herself up to his expertise and floated on the tide of erotic delight he conjured.

Boneless, all resistance stripped away, she let him feast. As ever, his liking for the slow and deliberate, the deliberately thorough, held sway – he took all and more, wound her so tight she thought she would expire, then, at the last, when she could feel the bright glory she'd once before experienced bearing down, about to sweep her away, he entered her with his tongue, too slow, too knowing, and flung her into ecstasy.

Later, he simply held her, and when she tried to protest, kissed her deeply, letting her taste her essence on his lips and tongue.

'Not yet' was all he said.

Later still, they returned to the ballroom where he insisted they waltz and wait for the unmasking so all would know that yes, they were there, in the ballroom where they were supposed to be, then, very correctly, he escorted her home.

Luc called in Upper Brook Street the next morning, only to learn that Amelia had gone walking in the park with Reggie. He debated for all of two seconds, then headed for the park. He had to talk with her. Privately, but preferably in a safe, public setting.

He saw her before she saw him. She was standing on the lawn with a group of ladies and gentlemen. Pausing under a tree, partially screened by its leafy branches, he considered – her, him, what he was doing there.

Trying to buy time. Time to learn, to understand. To find answers to questions like: when had having a woman become synonymous with commitment? And now it so very strangely was, what did that mean?

He knew very well that the equation would not add up that way with any other woman, yet with Amelia ... that's the way it was. No matter what he tried to pretend, no matter what he wished. He'd spent half the night forcing himself to face that truth. And trying to see beyond it.

The first thing he'd seen was the Hightham Hall house party he, Amelia and their mothers and his sisters were committed to attend – three days of unfettered summer entertainments starting tomorrow. At this stage, such a house party was the last thing he needed.

Time was what he needed – time to come to grips with his need for her, to understand it well enough to manage it, to control it. Instincts warred whenever he was close to her – he wanted her, now, yet on another plane knew that was dangerous. It wasn't she who

146

was dangerous, but what she made him feel, and what that feeling might do to him. Being controlled by his emotions was not something that had ever threatened before – and he was adamant he wouldn't allow even this to develop to that extent.

So he was here to sue for mercy. Temporarily.

He sauntered out of concealment just as the group broke up. Lady Collins and Mrs. Wilkinson were late for a luncheon; he greeted them only to bid them farewell, using the distraction of their leaving to greet Amelia and appropriate her hand.

Reggie, on Amelia's other side, noticed, but pretended not to; as the two ladies departed, he tugged down his waistcoat. 'Don't know about you, but I wouldn't mind stretching my legs. How about a stroll to the Serpentine?'

The others – Mrs. Wallace, Lady Kilmartin, Lord Humphries and Mr. Johns – greeted the suggestion favorably; as a group, they turned down the graveled path leading to the water.

It wasn't difficult to drop back, to slow their steps until there was sufficient distance between them and the others to talk freely.

Amelia cocked her head, lifted a questioning brow. 'I presume there's something on your mind.'

The smile that flirted about her lips, the glint in her blue eyes, suggested she knew very well what thought had leapt into his brain the instant he had her to himself again, a soft, female body by his side. Ruthlessly, he squelched it, but didn't take his eyes from hers. 'Indeed.'

His tone made her blink. Before she could start speculating, he continued, 'The Hightham Hall house party. Tomorrow.'

The light that leapt into her eyes had him hurrying on, 'We need to be careful. I know what you're thinking, but while the venue might appear at first glance to be greatly amenable, in reality, such a crowded and cramped house poses dangers all its own.'

Head tilted, she'd listened, her gaze steady on his face. Now she looked ahead. 'I had thought that the house party was all but fated in terms of our direction.' She glanced at him. 'Are you telling me that view is incorrect?'

He nodded. Somehow, he had to convince her not to take advantage of the amenities afforded by a major house party to tempt him further – he felt certain she would try. His aim was to prevent that, in case she succeeded. 'The prospect seems ready-made, I grant you, but—'

The others strolled ahead; luckily the Serpentine Walk was quite long. Amelia held her tongue and listened – to what anyone knowing Luc would instantly recognize as a plethora of nervous excuses. From him, given the subject of their conversation, the fact was astonishing.

'I can assure you the outcome risks being far less satisfactory than you might hope.' He glanced at her, saw her rising brows, mentally replayed his words, hurriedly amended, '*Not* in terms of immediate enjoyment, but—'

That he didn't want to take advantage of the house party to further their interaction, to take what surely *had* to be the ultimate step, was crystal clear. Why was less so.

She let him talk without interruption, hoping to learn more. The situation, his reaction, was so unlike what she'd been expecting – what, knowing him, she

148

had every reason to expect – she was more puzzled than dismayed. This was the man she wanted to marry; he was proving to have more layers than she'd imagined – it behooved her to pay attention.

'Ultimately, we have to consider the fact that any action likely to result in rumors besmirching your name must be avoided at all costs.'

He sounded so pompous, she had to fight to keep her lips straight. They reached the end of the Serpentine's banks; the others had turned back toward the lawns. Luc halted, and drew her to face him. His eyes searched hers. 'You do see, don't you?'

She studied his dark eyes, confirmed he was indeed worried, but about what she couldn't be sure. Nevertheless, she knew how to respond. She smiled reassuringly. 'You know perfectly well I would never do anything to besmirch my name.'

He wasn't so sure of her that he jumped to conclusions; his eyes searched hers for confirmation that she meant what he hoped she did. She let her smile deepen and patted his arm, then glanced up the Walk. 'Now you'd better take me back before Reggie starts wondering if he did the right thing in allowing us to be alone.'

Their mothers had decreed their party would set out for Hightham Hall at nine o'clock the next morning. Reggie's mother was feeling unwell, so he, too, was joining them. To Luc's mind, that still left him in charge of too many females with insufficient male support – every one of those females could twist Reggie around her little finger.

Together with Reggie, he stood on the pavement and resignedly watched the two traveling carriages

149

sink on their axles as box after box was added to their loads.

'Dashed if they'll wear the half of it.' Reggie glanced at the four horses harnessed to the Cynster carriage, which had arrived fifteen minutes earlier already burdened with Amelia's and Louise's trunks and boxes. 'Just hope the cattle're up to it.'

Luc humphed. 'No danger there.' Both his and the Cynster stables contained only the best. 'But it's going to add at least an hour to the journey.' Hightham Hall was in Surrey, on the banks of the Wey.

Reggie watched a footman hand another bandbox up to the Ashford coachman. 'Assuming we make it at all.'

A flurry of activity drew their eyes to the front door; excitedly chattering, Luc's sisters and Fiona, as usual one of the party, eagerly descended the steps. Luc looked beyond them, caught Cottsloe's eye. The butler stepped back into the house to speed the summons for Luc's curricle.

Reggie was counting bodies; Luc broke the news that he and Amelia would travel separately. Reggie looked surprised. 'Wouldn't have thought you'd bother – there'll be plenty of room.'

Luc met his eyes. 'You've forgotten to count the maids.'

Reggie blinked, then groaned.

As she followed her mother and Luc's onto his front steps, Amelia saw Reggie's pained expression, so typical of fashionable males embarking on a trip with female relatives that she had no difficulty guessing his thoughts. Luc's expression was equally typical, but of himself – hard, impassive, impossible to read.

But then he glanced up and saw her, and hesitated, as if suddenly uncertain. She brightened; smiling, calm, and assured, she continued down the steps to his side.

The next moments were filled with orders and organization, with the questions of who would go where debated and decided, then all the others were handed up to the coaches; Luc shut the last door and stepped back.

'We'll be ahead of you before the river,' he told Reggie, who nodded and saluted.

Luc signaled to his coachman; the man swung his whip, the horses leaned into the traces, and the heavy coach ponderously rolled forward. The Cynster carriage followed just as Luc's groom appeared, driving his curricle. The curricle drew up alongside them. Luc watched the coaches until they'd turned the corner, then glanced at her.

She was waiting to catch his eye, to raise her brows, faintly challenging. Stepping close, she murmured, 'Stop worrying – everything will be perfectly all right.'

He was a full head taller; his shoulders were so broad, standing this close, he shielded her completely. This close, she could feel the sheer male strength of him all but vibrating around her, like a humming in the air she could feel. This close, and the potent sexuality that lurked beneath his elegant facade was rawly apparent, just short of a physical threat.

And despite all of that, there she was, reassuring him over their intimate relationship. Over the pace of said intimate relationship.

Did irony get any more delicious?

Her smiling assurance had the opposite of its

intended effect; his dark eyes – still difficult to decipher, but she was getting much better at it – grew even more wary. His brows lowered in more obvious suspicion.

Valiantly resisting an urge to laugh, she smiled into those watchful eyes and patted his arm. 'Do stop scowling – you'll scare your horses.'

That got her a grim look, but he did stop frowning and handed her up to the curricle. She settled her skirts, decided the sun was not yet high enough to warrant opening her parasol. After exchanging last-minute words with Cottsloe, Luc joined her; in short order, they were away.

He was an excellent whip, an instinctive driver, but she knew better than to chatter and distract him while he tacked through the morning traffic. As he'd predicted, they passed the two coaches just past Kensington; so much heavier and less maneuverable, the latter had to stop frequently and wait for their way to clear.

Thankful she was in the curricle, in the open air, she let her gaze drink in the myriad sights; although she'd seen them many times, now, with Luc beside her, poised on the threshold of her dearest dream, every view, every detail her eyes beheld seemed more alive, brighter, more heavily imbued with meaning.

They reached Chiswick and turned south, crossing the river to Kew, then journeyed on, heading south and west, into the countryside. As the houses fell behind, the brightness of the summer morning enveloped them, and there still seemed no need for talk – for idle chatter to fill the moments.

That was one thing that had changed. She'd counted the days – fourteen had elapsed since the dawn on which she'd taken her courage in her hands and bearded him in his front hall. Before then, she'd have felt compelled to converse, to keep some measure of social contact between them.

Much had changed in the past days; they no longer needed conversation as a bridge between them.

She glanced at him, swiftly took in his expression before looking away; he was absorbed in his driving – she didn't want to draw his attention. She didn't want him thinking about her, brooding about their relationship and how that should or should not progress. How and when the next step should occur. They would both do much better if he left that to her.

Their peculiar discussion in the park the previous day had given her a great deal to think about. The amazing fact that he wished to delay their intimacy in the teeth of his desire – and hers – had been initially so incomprehensible that she'd had to think long and hard before she'd felt confident she'd correctly identified all the reasons behind it.

Once she had ... once she'd realized there could only be two reasons, and that neither was, in her opinion, sufficient to justify another week of dallying, far from feeling downhearted, she'd felt buoyed – with expectation, with a determination to bring their no-longer-necessary wooing to an end.

He'd denied being influenced by having known her for so long, and to some extent she accepted that as true. However, he'd always viewed her as he did his sisters and other gently reared females; they were to be protected from all danger. The wolves of the *ton* always featured as a prominent danger; given Luc now expected her to become his wife – and had had fourteen days to accustom himself to the notion – then

153

it was hardly surprising if his definition of danger now extended to himself, and his wolflike, in other circumstances reprehensible, desires.

Poor dear, he was simply confused – caught in the proverbial cleft stick by his inherent, intrinsic warrior-male instincts. She understood; she could recall some of her cousins being similarly torn. Hoist with their own petard, indeed.

It wouldn't do to laugh – they all took such matters so seriously. And besides, if she was to succeed in getting him to put aside his chivalrous scruples, provoking his temper was the last thing she should do.

His second reason was one she understood even better – a simple case of stubborn male will. He'd decreed from the first that for social acceptance they would need four weeks of public courtship; the fact they'd patently succeeded in two weeks – as evidenced by the encouraging reactions of all the senior matrons over the past week – was not going to change his mind.

She wasn't, in fact, intending to argue that point; as long as they married in June, she would gain what she wished from their wedding.

Their wedding, however, was not in her mind equated with their intimacy. The latter could precede the former, as in truth it so often did. They had made their decision, and society approved; as long as they did not flaunt the fact, neither society nor their families would bat an eyelid.

That, she had no doubt, Luc knew – or would if he allowed himself to consider the matter impartially. But with both his instincts and his will driving him, impartiality was clearly beyond him.

It therefore fell to her to take matters in hand. To

bring their stalled wooing to a satisfactory end, to advance his script through the last scene – the one he'd unexpectedly balked at. If she hadn't been so sure he desired her – wanted her as she wanted him – she would not have been able to face the task with the calm certainty presently infusing her.

'There it is.'

Luc's words jerked her from her thoughts; looking ahead, she saw the twin towers of Hightham Hall rising above the trees. A stone fence bordered the lane; a little way along, they came to a pair of open gates. Luc turned his horses in, then they were bowling along the graveled drive, watching the large sprawling house draw near.

The butler, grooms, and footmen were waiting; a coach had just disgorged its occupants – as they drew up, it rumbled away. A groom ran to the greys' heads; Luc threw the reins to another, then stepped down.

He turned and lifted her from the carriage. For one moment, while Lady Hightham's minions scurried about them, unstrapping the bags from the curricle's boot and carting them indoors, Luc held her fast between his hands, a fraction closer than propriety allowed – close enough for her to sense the very physical response that flared between them. To which he was paying not the slightest attention; his features a touch grim, he searched her face.

'You do agree, don't you?' His eyes held hers. 'No further advances for at least the next week.'

She smiled gloriously up at him; if they'd been alone she'd have pressed herself to him and kissed his worries away – perhaps it was as well they were surrounded. Raising a hand, she caressed his cheek.

'I told you – stop worrying.' Turning toward the house, she held his gaze. 'You have absolutely nothing to fear.'

Stepping out of his hold, she headed for the house. He watched her for a long moment, then she heard the scrunch of his boots as he followed her, felt his gaze on her back. The curve of her lips deepened; he didn't – wouldn't – believe her; unfortunately, he knew her too well.

Lifting her head, she went up the front steps, wrestling with the one burning question that yet remained: How was she to seduce a man who, given his legendary career, must have seen it all?

Chapter Eight

She'd come prepared. Even so, she would need to take him by surprise.

They'd arrived in good time – it was barely noon when, with Luc at her heels, she entered the drawing room where their hostess was entertaining those already present.

'Mama and Lady Calverton are yet on the road,' Amelia replied to Lady Hightham's inquiry. 'Luc drove me down in his curricle,'

Her ladyship beamed, and patted the chaise beside her. 'Do sit down, dear – you must tell me all your news!'

Amelia sat, hiding a grin as Luc coolly ignored her ladyship's archly teasing gaze; after bowing over her hand, he strolled off to join a group of similiar gentlemen who'd taken refuge by the windows. Amelia let him go. She'd been to house parties aplenty; she knew the timetable as well as he.

The ladies chatted avidly while more guests arrived; the Calverton and Cynster coaches rolled up just in time for the customary late luncheon.

Following that came the period when the gentlemen

sloped off to some masculine den to lie low while the ladies got themselves settled. This first afternoon was a time for feminine organizing – learning which room they'd been assigned, ensuring their gowns were properly shaken and their maids had found them and laid out their brushes. Also for learning who was quartered around them, and where chaperons and dangerous gossips were stationed.

Later that evening, those ladies intent on pursuing an illicit liaison would find some opportunity to divulge their whereabouts to their partners in desire. Whatever might transpire did so over the ensuing days; it was, therefore, the structured, accepted, and expected norm that nothing remotely scandalous ever occurred on the first afternoon of a house party.

Reaching the room assigned to her – a delightful bedchamber at the end of one wing, helpfully close by a secondary stair – Amelia found that her maid, Dillys, had obeyed her instructions to the letter. Her gowns were already hanging, her brushes neatly laid upon the dressing table. The garment she'd asked to be left out was draped upon the bed. In return for working like a Trojan ever since she'd set foot in the house, Dillys was to get the afternoon off – so she could cast her bright eyes over the footmen, stealing a march over the other maids.

Hands clasped, Dillys stood waiting at the end of the bed, eager for her thoroughness to be approved of so she could be off.

Closing the door, Amelia noted the other little touches she'd requested all in place. 'Very good. Now – one last thing.'

From her reticule, she drew out the note she'd scribbled in the parlor downstairs. 'When the clocks strike three, give this to the butler. The direction's on the note – simply say I asked that it be delivered immediately.'

'At three o'clock.' Dillys took the note.

Amelia glanced at the clock on the mantelpiece; the hands stood at two-forty. 'Whatever you do, *don't* forget. I'll ring when next I need you.'

Grinning, Dillys bobbed and departed, closing the door behind her. Amelia turned to the bed, and the garment laid out upon it.

The three heavy bongs emanating from the longcase clock in the corner of the library drew Luc from his absorption. He glanced at the other gentlemen slumped about the large room; except for two idly discussing some curricle race, the rest had their eyes closed. Some were even snoring.

Half their luck; he couldn't relax enough to nod off. Holding a news sheet before his face, he'd pretended to be catching up on events; in reality, his mind was engrossed with its now-habitual obsession.

Her image blossomed in his mind – that gentle smile that in recent days had flirted across her lips whenever he attempted to reinforce the line he'd drawn *vis à vis* herself and him. Every time that smile bloomed, he had to shackle an urge to kiss it from her lips. And then ...

Inwardly cursing, he jerked his mind off the very track he'd insisted they would not follow. Yet. Sometime, definitely – just not yet. Unfortunately, ingrained habit was hard to break; simply being here, at a house party, a venue all but expressly designed to further the end he was so determined to delay only added to the already considerable strain of desisting. Resisting.

159

He shouldn't have come. Having done so amounted to self-flagellation with a very prickly scourge. Just how prickly he'd only realized when he'd held her between his hands in the forecourt – knowing they were here, in a venue he could so easily exploit to gain the ease his body longed for, in a house that was not his, not hers, and where she wasn't, courtesy of her mother's presence, specifically under his protection.

Just how strong his desire to have her had grown, he'd only then fully comprehended.

Only to have her tease him.

Eyes narrowing, he replayed yet again all she'd said, heard again the tenor of her assurance.

He trusted her not one jot. He'd be watching her closely; from this evening on, he'd keep his guard high . . .

A moment later, he grimaced and surreptitiously shifted. His body was trapped in the most peculiar vise. On the one hand, he was champing at the bit to have her, on the other, he was desperately reining back, fighting to postpone the very moment he so desired. If anyone had suggested he was capable of contorting himself to this extent, he'd have laughed in their faces.

The door opened. The supercilious butler looked in, saw him, entered, and shut the door. Crossing the floor, the man offered his salver. 'For you, my lord. I was told it was urgent.'

Luc nodded his thanks and lifted the folded square. The man had spoken quietly; none of those resting had been disturbed. The two chatting glanced over, then resumed their discussion. The butler bowed and retreated. Luc laid aside the news sheet and opened the note.

*

160

Luc – Please come to my room at once.

                                                          A.

P.S. It's on the first floor at the very end of the west wing at the top of the stairs at the end.

He frowned, read the note again, then refolded it and slipped it into his pocket.

He might not trust her, yet ... she couldn't have even settled in. Maybe the lock on her trunk had jammed – no, it had to be something more serious. Perhaps she'd mislaid her jewelry case. Perhaps ... perhaps she was in some more dire trouble.

Stifling a sigh, he rose. Whatever was behind her summons, she presumably needed him specifically, and the note, hastily scribbled in pencil on a scrap of paper, bore little resemblance to an illicit invitation. With a nod to the two men still awake, he walked from the room.

He found the stairs at the end of the west wing. At this hour, there were few about whose notice he needed to avoid – all the ladies were in their rooms, fussing and unpacking and harrying their maids.

He climbed the stairs and found the right door. Very softly, he tapped.

And heard her call, 'Come in.'

He opened the door. The room was large. Sunlight streamed in through two sets of windows, both with their curtains wide. To the left stood the bed, a largish four-poster with diaphanous white curtains presently roped back. The counterpane was of sprigged ivory satin. A jumble of lace-trimmed pillows was massed welcomingly at the bed's head. A dressing table and stool were set against the wall

161

beyond the bed. In the room's center a round table boasted a vase of white lilies, their scent perfuming the air. The area to his right, containing an armoire and dressing screen, the fireplace and a chair, was in relative dimness, the shadows darker in contrast with the brightness elsewhere.

His quick survey failed to locate Amelia. Hovering on the threshold was too dangerous; frowning, he stepped in and closed the door. He opened his mouth to say her name – a movement in the dimness caught his eye.

Caught his breath – every muscle he possessed froze, rigid with ...

Not exactly shock yet something a long way beyond surprise.

She'd been standing by the edge of the screen, in the deepest shadows. He'd missed seeing her because of the brightness streaming in, the brightness into which, unhurriedly, she moved.

His mouth dried as he realized what she was – and wasn't – wearing. His gaze had locked on her; his wits, driven by instinct, had brutally focused. On the slender ivory goddess, her charms in no way concealed by the translucent silk robe hanging open from her shoulders.

She walked toward him; he couldn't move – couldn't drag his gaze from her. She wore not a stitch beneath the sheer robe, the delights of her body boldly and brazenly displayed.

For him.

The knowledge shook him. He knew he should turn and escape, now, yet he stood rooted to the spot as she neared, incapable of turning away, of refusing what she was so blatantly offering.

She didn't stop until her breasts met his chest, until

her silk-screened thighs brushed his. Reaching up, she looped one all but bare arm about his neck; her other hand splayed on his chest, she met his gaze fearlessly. Expectantly.

His control quaked; he managed to draw enough breath to rasp, 'You *promised* ...'

Her lips curved gently – that sweet, understanding, patronizingly challenging smile. 'I told you there was no reason to worry – and there isn't.'

Without conscious direction, his hands fastened about her waist, his intention to put her from him immediately corrupted by the feel of her – the warmth of her skin reaching through the delicate silk, the suppleness, the reality of her body under his hands, so nearly skin to skin.

Sheer seduction.

He knew it – saw the truth, and her understanding, in her face, in the brightness of her blue eyes, in the inherently feminine set of her lips.

Felt the reality rise through him in response, a desire infinitely stronger than any that had come before, a passion immeasurably more compelling.

He made one last attempt to cling to reason, to whatever the reason was that had made him deny this. He could no longer recall what it was, from where or what it sprang.

Her gaze fell to his lips. He dragged in another breath. Opened his lips—

She stretched up, drew his head down, brought her lips close to his – murmured, 'Stop thinking. Stop resisting. Just—'

He covered her lips with his, stopped her last entreaty; he didn't need to hear it. He kissed her voraciously, deliberately let the reins he'd been gripping so desperately slide – simply let go. Could do nothing else. Hands splaying, sliding over the fine silk, he closed his arms about her, pulling her close, molding her to him.

Let his senses exult – let them free.

She was right – there was no point trying to resist, not this. Any chance he'd had of escaping had died the instant he'd set eyes on her, on all she was so set on offering him. All but naked in his arms, she clung, and returned his kisses greedily, avidly – flagrantly encouraged him to seize, take, and claim.

Her heart soaring, Amelia felt his arms lock tight, felt, in the lips bruising hers, hard and demanding, his decision. His surrender. He straightened, locking her to him; without interrupting the kiss, he lifted her and walked to the side of the bed.

Halting, he let her down, sliding her body down his, his hands cupping her bottom, pressing her to him, molding her softness against his erection while his tongue plundered her mouth, wreaking havoc with her senses. Within her, heat bloomed, burgeoned, grew – but this time she wanted more.

This time, she wanted it all.

She drew back from the kiss, found breath enough to gasp, 'Your clothes.'

Hands on his chest, she pushed his coat wide, trapping his arms. With a curse, he let her go, stepped back, wrenched the coat off and flung it aside.

The violence behind the movement had her blinking. He noticed, and stilled. His eyes, dark, burning, narrowed on hers, then he reached for her; palm curving about her jaw, he tipped up her face, drew her close. He studied her eyes – she didn't try to mask her curiosity. He bent his head, murmured,

'You should beware of what you ask for. You might get it.'

She met his lips brazenly, hoping she would – hoping she would meet the wildness she'd glimpsed so fleetingly a moment before. It was a part of him she'd always known was there, lurking behind his facade, a part he kept most deeply hidden – a vibrant, ruthless vital part she suspected was closest to his real nature.

A nature she'd always found fascinating – something different, illicit, veiled. At base, it was why she found him so attractive, why he and only he would do for her.

That revelation was simply there, its truth resonant and clear. She acted on it, grappled with the buttons of his shirt and yanked the halves apart, splayed her hands and touched, searched, grasped – purred with satisfaction. The skin under her palms was hot, the muscles beneath it rigid and locked. His chest was a wonder of rasping black hair and male hardness; her lips, her mouth, flagrantly welcoming, urgently inciting, she filled her hands and filled her senses.

He stripped off his shirt, but made no move to take charge; taking that as acquiesence, she moved on.

Spreading her hands wide, reaching around to hold him to her as he plundered her mouth, his hands closing about, then provocatively kneading the globes of her bottom. The long muscles framing his back flexed like steel beneath her wandering hands. She ran them down, marveling, then followed the heavy line of his ribs forward to caress the rippling bands across his abdomen. They flickered at her touch; he sucked in a breath as she sent her fingers questing lower. Held that breath as she lightly traced the line of his erection.

His attention shifted – she sensed it. He stilled, but didn't stop her when she reached for the buttons at the waistband of his breeches. The tenor of their kiss changed; he was breathing more shallowly, his senses distracted . . .

Inwardly smiling, she slid one hand inside the opened flap, and found him. Rigid, as she'd expected, yet so hot, and with skin so very fine . . .

They both held to their kiss, yet their attention was not there, but on her questing fingers as she explored, and learned. Solid, as wide as her wrist, he more than filled her hand. Closing her fingers, she circled him, and felt him shudder.

She experimented, taking her time even though instinct warned that commodity would be limited, that the surge of heated passion she could feel rising through him, evoked, provoked by her touch – even though he ruthlessly held it back, soon, the dam would break.

And he'd let the tide loose, let it sweep her up, sweep her away.

He proved strong enough to give her the moment, to take advantage himself, despite her continuing ministrations. She was only dimly aware when he stripped her robe from her, releasing her prize to free her arms from the silk only to take him in hand again. Only to set her mind to provoking him further.

Luc clenched his jaw and endured, while his control grew more brittle by the second. She was still a novice, thank the gods, but even so, her instincts were sound, and her hands pure heaven. Yet her body promised ecstasy, and that was his fell aim. That, and more.

He couldn't fault her arrangements; the light was a

boon, letting him see her, all of her, now, and later, when he finally had her beneath him. When he finally took her.

The thought sent another surge of heat, of pure unadulterated desire rising through him, hardening and lengthening that part of his anatomy that was currently the object of her fascination even more. She noticed, hesitated; he looked down as she sent her thumb stroking over his aching head.

He didn't need to look to know she'd found a latent drop. Before she could think further, let alone act, he caught his breath, nudged her face up and found her lips again, drew her into a drugging kiss, then ruthlessly, deliberately, let the walls fall, seized and devoured, claimed her mouth, her lips, and sent her senses spinning.

Capturing her wrist, he drew her hand from him, then drew her close, then closer, reveling in the sensation of her silken skin caressing his chest, his arms, his erection, while he plundered her mouth, holding her and her senses captive. She couldn't break free, and wouldn't. From here on, their script was his to dictate.

Amelia knew it; she was helpless against not just his strength, but the power he controlled. She didn't fight it – had no intention of doing so, now or ever. This was what she wanted – for him to make her his. Far from resisting, she sank into his arms, gave herself up to the commanding kiss, surrendered and waited, nerves tight with anticipation, for him to claim her.

He seemed to know; he wasted no more time. Breaking the kiss, he lifted her, placing her on her knees on the edge of the bed. Before she could even

167

wonder, he ducked his head and set his lips to her breast. Set his hot mouth to one peak and suckled fiercely.

Her head fell back; her gasp shivered through the room. He feasted like a king, knowing her his slave. His hands, tight about her waist, held her steady, then one hand released and left her; the other slid to her hip and closed, hard, anchoring her, pressing her down so she sat on her ankles.

He laved her breasts, suckled, nipped – tortured the tightly pebbled peaks, his hot mouth pressing heat again and again beneath her skin. Her hands closed on his skull, holding him to her; it was only when he drew back and straightened that she realized he'd pulled off his boots and stripped off his breeches.

As naked as she, he was suddenly there, standing before her. She felt her eyes go round as she took in the sight, drank in the glory. She started to reach for him but he reached for her; gripping her waist, he raised her on her knees, drew her to him and found her lips again. Drew her once more into the heat of his embrace, into the flames and the fire, the heated, dizzying game of conquest and delight.

He conquered while she rode the wave of delight he evoked. She was with him, matching him kiss for kiss, breath for gasping breath as the kiss dissolved into an expression of raging needs, an inferno of unfettered desire. His hands roamed her curves, brutally explicit, no facade, no veneer, to mute his driving need. A need she gloried in, without thought or inhibition wantonly incited.

The feel of his hard body, hot and urgent about her, against her, the evidence of his desire never more real, shredded the last vestiges of modesty, swept away the last primitive restrictions, all remaining reservations.

He urged her back, one knee rising and pushing between hers, parting her thighs. His muscled thigh, raspy with crinkly hair, rode against her curls; her breath caught, tangled in her throat. He deliberately shifted, pressing against that sensitive spot, knowingly winding her tight ...

Until she gasped and let her head fall back, struggling to ride the sensual tide. Her skin was flaming, her body melting, her nerves tightening unforgivingly, her senses in disarray. Something else, something beyond all her experience, was filling her, driving her; a hot fire was consuming her from within. He pressed her back to the bed and she went eagerly, wanting, wanting ... he followed her down, his other knee joining the first in forcing hers apart, spreading her thighs so he could settle between.

The touch of his thighs, crinkly hair abrading the sensitive inner faces of hers, made her force her lids up. He held himself over her, arms braced. He was glancing down to where they would join; the set of his face, angular planes stripped by desire to those of a ruthless conqueror, hard, unrelenting, elementally male, sank into her mind.

He shifted fractionally; between her thighs she felt the touch, the pressure of the broad blunt head she'd earlier admired, felt its inherent strength and heat as it parted her swollen, slippery folds. He glanced at her face, caught her gaze. Turning fully back to her, braced above her, her gaze trapped in his, he flexed his hips and pressed in.

Just a little way. Then he smoothly withdrew – she clutched his sides. He uttered a gravelly laugh. 'This is where, I believe, I'm supposed to tell *you* not to worry.'

He reversed direction on the words, but again halted only a little way in. Just enough to tantalize, to drive her insane. She sucked in a breath, let it out as he again withdrew. 'I'm not worried.'

One black brow arched, then he lowered his head; she lifted her lips to meet his. In the instant before they made contact, he murmured, 'You should be.' Then he covered her lips, took her mouth, but kept the caress light, leaving her senses open and aware, trapped prey for the mesmerizing sensations he pressed on her, flexing his hips, gliding in, then back, just inside the entrance to her body.

Until she writhed and lifted, her body arching, wanting more. Until she couldn't stand any more of his teasing, until she was wet and open and so hungry with desire, so aware of the yawning emptiness inside her that she tried to break from the kiss, sank her nails into his sides when he refused to let her.

Abruptly she found herself kissed so ravenously she lost all touch with the world. His tongue deep in her mouth, he plundered, ruthlessly shackling her. She felt his strength gather, felt his hips shift, settling more heavily between hers. Then he thrust powerfully.

She cried out, the sound smothered in their kiss. He didn't stop but drove on, all the way in, steadily pushing deep, stretching her, impaling her. She couldn't breathe except through him; her mind struggled to take in what seemed impossible, the sensation of him hard and strong, embedded deep within her, filling her fuller than she'd imagined could be.

Before she caught her breath, he drew back, then

170

pressed in again; she tensed, expecting the same sharp pain, but it didn't eventuate. Yet she still found herself struggling – tensing against the welling pressure inside, the inherent force as he filled her again.

He repeated the exercise, then released her lips; his eyes, ebony under his lashes, glinted down at her as, the weight of his lower body holding her immobile, he again withdrew and slowly, even more powerfully, entered her.

She felt every inch, every last fraction as he filled her, felt her body tighten until she arched.

'Relax.' Bending his head, he touched his lips to the corner of hers. 'Lie back and let it happen. Let your body learn.'

Despite the words, it was a growled command, one she had little choice but to obey. He continued to move above her, within her; gradually, her defensive tension unwound.

And the intimacy of the moment caught her. Slid into her mind as he slid more and more easily into her body, as the hair at his groin tangled with her curls. As she felt the first stirrings of submerged passion, a *frisson* of reawakening desire.

She glanced up, caught his eye – it was the wrong moment for awareness to strike, yet it did. Full awareness of her nakedness, her vulnerability, of how essentially helpless she was in the face of his strength, trapped beneath him, her thighs wide.

What he saw in her face, she had no idea, yet although the harsh, set planes of his face never softened, the line of his lips did.

'Stop thinking.' He quoted her words back at her, then withdrew from her completely, only to return in the same heartbeat, more forcefully than before, until

171

he was fully seated, jerking her slightly, sending a streak of sensation through her, giving notice of his intention, and the pleasure to come.

Still holding her gaze, he came down on his elbows, letting his body down atop hers. 'Stop resisting.'

She did; the feel of him, so close, so real, reassured her – the warmth of his body, the contradictory comfort she drew from his muscled strength, washed through her and swept away the last of her maidenly fears. In truth, she was a maiden no longer. She was his.

She would have smiled but her face felt too tight; instead, she sent her hands sliding around to spread on his back. Holding tight, she lifted her face to his, breathed against his lips, 'Show me then. Now.'

His lips quirked in the instant before they met hers. The kiss was long, deep – undisguised. 'Stay with me then,' he murmured, and took her mouth, then took her body again.

And again.

And again. The relentless repetition fed a whirlwind inside them, a hungry, compelling tide of need. It combined with the restless flames of desire, flaring anew, stronger, more powerful, now unrestrained, unrestricted, then the power coalesced.

And erupted.

Into a firestorm.

A raging, uncontrollable conflagration where the physical, sensual, and emotional swirled, where lips melded, tongues tangling, hands gripping, their bodies merged and came together, locked and fused, driven to give, driven to take, driven to be one.

The force was frightening, thrilling, utterly

compelling. She moaned; he gasped. She sank her nails into his back and arched wildly, taking him deeper, wanting him deeper, satisifed only when he thrust harder, faster, ever more powerfully.

He sank one hand into her hair and held her down, ravaged her mouth as he plundered her body. Beneath him, she squirmed, hot, urgent – wild to provoke him further.

It wasn't a game, but a fiery dance of desire, the recognition of a need beyond desperate, a need beyond her knowledge, a need that had to be fulfilled.

A need he seemed to share, equally driven, equally susceptible.

That welling need pulled them down, out, away from the world, onto a plane on which nothing beyond them and that need existed. On which nothing bar the fusion of their bodies was real, their senses held, locked, overwhelmed by the slickness, the heat, the gasping urgency, the spiraling tension. The steadily escalating excitement.

She would have given anything to grasp the bright triumph, the pinnacle of fulfillment that hovered and beckoned, just out of sensual reach. He drove her on, and she sobbed; he thrust deeper yet and her body closed hungrily, holding him, tightening yet more ...

And she suddenly felt it – let go, let herself ride the tide, joyously let it sweep her up, let it claim her soul and take her to the stars. Her body imploded in heat and glory, shards of sensation flashing down every nerve to melt in satiation just under her skin. Golden joy suffused her; the wave crested and she held tight – felt him thrust deep and hold still, holding her there, in glory, then the wave slowly ebbed.

Luc dragged in a breath, eyes closed tight as he felt the last spasms of her completion fade, then his body took charge, no longer his to command, driven by a need he couldn't control, a need he had to slake.

A need to make her his, to bind her to him – to have her and know her to a degree beyond the carnal. To command her surrender. Complete and absolute.

With his.

He couldn't stop himself from reaching for the gilded fruit, even though enough of his mind yet functioned to warn that, once tasted, he'd crave it again and again. Not even the certainty of lifelong addiction could turn him from his goal – bracing his arms, lifting above her, he watched as he loved her, watched her body take him in, cradle him, hold him. Watched her sumptuous, pearlescent curves lift and ease as she rode his thrusts, felt her acceptance as he spread her thighs wider and filled her deeper yet.

Release came on a long wave, a tsunami of feelings that built and rose and finally broke, pouring about him, crashing through him as he shuddered and filled her, spilled his seed deep inside her, then slumped, exhausted, wrung out beside her – more deeply sated, more deeply at peace, than he'd ever been in his life.

They were both exhausted. The sun sank low, slanting through the windows, illuminating their tangled limbs as they lay wrapped together, too drained to stir, and waited for life to reassert itself, waited for the world to start turning.

Slumped on his back, Amelia a warm silken bundle beside him, her head cradled on his chest, Luc idly played with her curls, and tried to think.

Tried to define just what had happened, and what it meant.

The most frightening thing was he couldn't even define what 'it' was – the force that had risen out of nowhere and driven him – he suspected them, but couldn't be sure. She, of course, thought it only normal; he knew better. The point that exercised him most was that it had felt like it belonged, as if such a force was a natural part of him and her – a natural element in their physical interactions. An element that had elevated the latter to heights sufficient to stun even him.

He closed his eyes, tried not to think of the moment he'd first slid into the heat of her, or the moment he'd finally been able to thrust as deep inside her as he'd wished, and feel her close lovingly about him. She'd been so damned tight – easing her into letting him ride her freely had taxed his will, yet the result had been worth every iota of restraint . . .

Swallowing a groan, he opened his eyes and stared at the canopy. He was hard and throbbing, but he couldn't have her again, not with dinner drawing near . . .

The thought focused his mind on where they were, on the hour, the house. The company. All things he could define. Lifting his head, he glanced across the room – at the door he hadn't locked. Now he was listening, he heard the shuffles and scrapes of distant footfalls.

'Mmm . . .' She stirred drowsily. Then her hand drifted from his chest, down over his torso—

He caught her wrist, manacled it. 'We haven't time.' Folding back her arm, he hefted her up, then brushed back her tangled hair. Met her gaze,

175

brilliantly blue, lazily sensual, noted her lips, swollen and red. 'I'll have to leave before the other ladies start emerging. One thing – there's blood on the coverlet.'

She smiled smugly. 'It's all right – it's mine. I brought it. I'll just take it home again.'

Lips compressing, he narrowed his eyes, remembered her transparent wrap – not something her mother had bought her for Christmas. She'd planned, and planned well – witness his current position. 'Very well.' He rolled, taking her, too, pinning her beneath him – not that she struggled. He caught her hands, raised them, pressed them back to the bed on either side of her head, and kissed her – deeply, thoroughly, as he wished.

She undulated beneath him, sinuously sirenlike. Ending the kiss, he lifted his head and used his weight to hold her still. 'Not now.'

'Surely we have time—'

'No.' He hesitated, looking down at her, then bent his head, trailed a kiss to her ear, and whispered, 'Next time I have you, I plan on taking at least an hour, and we'll have to gag you, because I promise you'll scream.'

Drawing away, he studied her face. She simply stared back at him, thoughts whizzing behind her eyes.

He smiled – wolfishly. Then he lifted from her and left the bed.

Amelia couldn't remember a single thing about the first night's dinner.

After Luc left her bedchamber, first checking that no one was about to see him flit down the stairs, she'd bestirred herself. Discovering a number of unexpected aches and twinges in muscles she hadn't known she possessed, she'd decided on a bath – a nice long soak during which she could dwell on what her twin had once confirmed as a magical moment.

Magical indeed – she'd fallen asleep in the tub. Luckily, Dillys had roused her and bundled her into her gown, dressing her hair high before directing her to the drawing room; if left to herself . . .

A curious, delightfully pleasant aura had suffused her, making thought, or indeed any exertion seem unnecessary. She'd had to fight to keep a silly, far too-revealing smile from her face. Up until, joining the assembled guests in the drawing room, she'd set eyes on her soon-to-be betrothed.

Rising from curtsying to their hostess, she'd moved to join Emily, speaking earnestly with Lord Kirkpatrick, and immediately felt Luc's gaze. She'd followed it to its source; he was standing chatting with a lady and three gentlemen on the other side of the room.

He met her gaze; despite the distance, she sensed the frown in his. Knew for a fact that he wasn't attending to the comments bandied before him. Then he seemed to recollect himself, hesitated, then addressed himself to the conversation about him.

That glimpse of uncharacteristic uncertainty left her wondering – raised questions in her mind, very quickly left her uncertain, too.

'We're planning on walking to the edge of the Downs tomorrow morning.' Lord Kirkpatrick looked at her hopefully. 'It's not all that far, and the views are said to be magnificient. Perhaps you'd like to join us?'

177

'Tomorrow?' She glanced at Emily, and saw a similar hope in her eyes. 'I hadn't really thought . . .' Another glance confirmed that his lordship and Emily both wanted her, a supporter of their blossoming romance, to accompany them so they could spend the time together without a bevy of others looking on. 'That is . . . yes, I would like to get out, weather permitting.'

'Of course – weather permitting.'

Both his lordship and Emily beamed with gratitude.

Amelia inwardly sighed, resigning herself to a morning of bucolic pleasures tramping through fields and meadows. There were other pleasures she would have preferred, but . . . she had no idea what Luc was thinking, much less what he was planning for tomorrow.

She felt the touch of his gaze and turned, only once again to sense his brooding frown. Not that such an expression was permitted to mar his Byronic beauty, but she could feel its leaden weight. Again, once their gazes had touched for a moment, he looked away – supposedly distracted by those he was standing with, in reality . . .

What was he thinking? Emily and Lord Kirkpatrick didn't need her assistance, so she could safely stand beside them and try to work it out. Reviewing all that had occurred through the lazy afternoon, and trying to see it through Luc's eyes, she was assailed by a sinking feeling.

Should she have screamed? Or was the boot on the other foot and, on reflection, had he not liked her forwardness? Had she been *too* accommodating? Was that even possible with a man – a rake – like him?

Had she, through sheer inexperience, done something he hadn't appreciated?

178

Was that why he'd left, surely earlier than necessary? He'd been adamant – immovably so – over not indulging with her again, yet he'd been perfectly capable. That wasn't the sort of behavior she'd expected, not from a man of his reputation. She was well aware that since his late teens, he'd had his pick of women, and had never been averse to taking his choice.

Her stomach had tightened, not pleasantly; an even more horrible thought flitted through her mind. Was his dark brooding an indication that he regretted coming to her –

regretted all that had occurred that afternoon?

The thought caught, took root, blossomed, blocking out all else. She tried to catch Luc's eye, but he didn't again glance her way. Indeed, he kept his distance. The gong sounded, and the company transferred to the dining room. As one of the more senior peers present, Luc had to escort one of the grandes dames in; she found herself half a table away from him.

She had to laugh, converse, and put on a gay face – everyone, especially her sharp-eyed mama, expected her to be happy and carefree. She hoped she made a good job of it, but in truth had little idea – all through the meal, her heart was steadily sinking, her mind engrossed with the questions of where they were now, and if he would come to her room that night so she could rid herself of her uncertainties.

Small wonder she remembered not one bite, not one word.

The ladies rose and repaired to the drawing room, leaving the gentlemen – a goodly company – to pass the port. Smiling, she joined the younger girls, Anne, Fiona, and three others, letting their chatter wash over her as she waited for the gentlemen to return, waited for Luc to come to her – to speak, to make arrangements to meet again, privately or otherwise.

The gentlemen returned; Luc did not.

She forced herself to behave normally, to take tea and continue to chat, while inwardly considering and discarding all thoughts of seeking him out. Hightham Hall was huge and rambling; she had no idea where he might be, nor yet where his room was situated. Impossible for her to find him.

He, of course, could find her.

When the youthful crew were encouraged to retire, she stifled a yawn and, citing the drive down as the cause of her tiredness, seized the chance to retreat to her room.

Once there, she changed into a long, lawn nightgown. After shooing Dillys off to her own rest, she blew out her candle and went to the window. Drawing the curtains wide, she waited, watching the wash of moonlight move slowly across the floor.

It finally occurred to her that no matter how early she retired, he wouldn't risk coming to her room until much later – until all the *grandes dames* along the corridor retired, too, and fell asleep. Muttering a curse, she marched to the bed and climbed in. Pulling the covers up over her shoulders, she wriggled and fussed with the pillows, then settled her head on them.

If she fell asleep, Luc would just have to wake her – she was quite sure he would.

Closing her eyes, she sighed, and settled down to wait.

Chapter Nine

The morning sun slanting through the uncurtained windows woke her. She had plenty of time to join Emily and Lord Kirkpatrick on their excursion to the Downs.

They were returning to the house, the sun high in the sky, hot and somewhat exhausted from what had proved an adventurous ramble, when she saw Luc – on the back terrace, hands on his hips, clearly waiting for them.

More precisely, waiting for her; when Emily and his lordship went up the steps, Luc merely nodded distantly. With a wide-eyed glance back at her, now trailing in the rear, the younger couple escaped. Leaving her to cope with a hardened rake who was giving a very good imitation of an aggravated Zeus.

With a jaunty, positively saucy smile, she climbed the steps, swinging her hat by its ribbons. His lips thinned, his expression grew grimmer as he took in her disheveled appearance, the flush in her cheeks, the curls clinging to her brow and throat. She had a fairly good idea of the picture she presented, but was in no mood to pander to his thoughts, whatever they might be.

'Where the devil have you been?'

The inquiry was growled through gritted teeth.

She waved with her hat. 'Up on the Downs. The views are quite breathtaking. You should go and take a look.'

'Thank you, but no – I'll take your word for it. It might have been wise to mention your little expedition – why the hell didn't you tell me you were swanning off?'

She met his gaze. 'Why should I?' The 'you're not my keeper' she left unsaid.

He heard it, however; his jaw clenched. She wasn't close enough to be certain, but she thought his eyes had gone black. They did when he was angry; also when he was ...

'I wanted to speak with you.' The words were even, their tone one of considerable temper severely restrained.

She raised her brows. 'About what?' Nose elevating, she turned along the terrace.

He swung across her path. 'I would have thought—'

The lunch gong clanged. With a not very well suppressed oath, he glared at the house, then at her. 'There are one or two matters I want to get straight with you. After lunch, *don't* disappear.'

She wasn't of a mind to be dictated to, but she kept her eyes innocently wide and carefully stepped around him so he was no longer between her and the house. Then she shrugged. 'As you wish.'

With a swish of her skirts, she turned haughtily away.

His fingers shackled her wrist. He didn't move,

didn't speak, just held her immobile and waited for her to turn back to him.

After a long moment, she did; her own temper had flown – she could feel it – and more – simmering just beneath her skin.

Her eyes flashed, clashed with his; their gazes locked, held.

'Don't.'

It was a primitive, fundamental, all-encompassing warning; he made not the slightest effort to veil its nature.

She felt her breasts swell, felt their wills collide – and knew, had absolutely no doubt, that his was the stronger. She'd never crossed his temper before, but she knew it existed – the other side of that wildness she coveted; she couldn't have one without the other.

But if she had to take him as he was, he would need to reciprocate.

Lifting her chin, she twisted her wrist – he released her, but slowly, enough to underscore that he did so only because he wished it.

'If you'll excuse me, I must change.' With a nod, she turned to the house. 'I'll see you after lunch.'

An hour after the company had quit the luncheon tables, Luc halted at the bottom of the central stairs and silently and comprehensively cursed. Where in all Hades was she? He'd quartered the house, checking every last reception room, inadvertently surprising a number of other couples; he'd then spent a heated half hour combing every likely spot in the gardens. All to no avail.

Dragging in a breath – shackling his temper, suppressing it so he could think – he backtracked.

She'd been at luncheon, arriving late after changing her limp walking dress for a fresh and cool apple green muslin gown. Seeing it, he'd wished he'd gone with her – followed her from the terrace and peeled the walking dress from her damp flesh . . . instead of feasting on cold meats and strawberries, he could have been feasting on fruits more to his taste . . .

Suppressing the resulting mental images, he forced his mind back to the luncheon party under the trees. He'd watched Amelia from afar, not daring in his present mood, and hers, to get within sniping distance – God only knew what she might provoke him to say. Or worse, do. Then, just as the party started to break up, old Lady Mackintosh had collared him. She'd insisted on introducing him to her niece – a flashy, overconfident young lady very aware of her charms. Charms she'd clearly intended to use to capture him.

He'd been tempted to tell her she had no chance; he'd never been attracted by unsubtle women. To his cost.

The thought had made him glance around – only to realize Amelia had gone. He'd forced himself to disengage with an appearance of civility, then had set out to hunt her down.

So here he was, an hour later, and no further forward.

She'd known he wanted to speak with her – she'd promised not to disappear. He considered the possibility that she might have set out to flout him deliberately – and reluctantly dismissed it. She wasn't stupid.

So . . . if she was patiently waiting for him somewhere . . .

He closed his eyes and quietly groaned. Surely not?

It was the last place he'd think of – demonstrably so – yet given the direction in which her mind had so consistently been working ...

Visiting her bedchamber last night had, to his mind, figured as too dangerous. Not only had he been laboring under the weight of unwelcome surprise over how easily she'd seduced him, how easily his need of her had overridden his will, as well as the fact she'd planned and committed the deed without a blink, against his expressly stated wishes, he'd also been grappling with the unexpected and unsettling emotions she'd stirred to life. He'd had no wish to speak with her before he'd had time to think. And only a cad would have gone to her so soon with anything more than conversation on his mind.

The notion of having a cozy chat in her room without laying a hand on her, without her laying a hand on him, had been laughable. Yet a whole night of thinking had got him precisely nowhere.

Five minutes this morning had changed that, crystallized his thoughts wonderfully – the five minutes after breakfast during which he'd realized, then confirmed, that she wasn't in the house.

Not even the discovery, much later, that she'd gone off to play gooseberry for his sister had improved his mood.

A basic, primitive, fundamental mood he had absolutely no wish to discuss. Especially not with her.

God only knew what was going to happen next.

Opening his eyes, he heaved a resigned sigh, and headed straight out of the house.

Descending the front steps, he turned onto the path that led around the west wing. There were too many ladies, young and old, wandering the corridors to attempt an approach from inside. Luck was with him; when he entered through the garden door, there was no one in the small hall at the bottom of the secondary stairs. He took them two at a time. At the top, he paused, and carefully looked around the corner, down the upper corridor. It, too, was temporarily empty. He was at her door, easing it open, in a heartbeat; whisking around it, he had time for only the briefest glance before turning to silently close the door.

She was there, on the bed – the green of her dress, the gold of her curls had confirmed it.

The door safely shut, he turned, grimly holding back his irritation ...

She was asleep.

He realized before he'd taken even one step – one arm lay draped across the counterpane, a different one from yesterday, her fingers, lightly curled, in a patch of sunshine. Hand and arm were totally relaxed, the deep relaxation achieved only in sleep.

His feet took him to the side of the bed, to where, beyond the diaphanous swatches, he could stand and look down on her.

She was lying on her side, her cheek pillowed on one hand. Her curls, pure gold, framed her features, delicate, fine, rendered in alabaster silk. Her long lashes, light brown, lay still in slumber; her cheeks held a faint blush, courtesy of her morning's excursion. Soft and vulnerable, fractionally parted, her lips tempted and tantalized ...

How would she react if he kissed her? Roused her from her nap but didn't let her open her eyes. Pulled her from one dream, to another, and from there into ecstasy.

He shifted his gaze, let it roam. Drew a slow breath. The rise and fall of her breasts, soft mounds revealed above her round neckline, confirmed just how deeply she slept. His gaze traveled on, over the indentation of her waist, over the swell of her hips, down the sleek curve of her thighs.

She'd kicked off her shoes. Her bare toes, bare feet, peeked from under the hem of her gown. He studied them, the graceful arch, the pearly nails – he was reaching to touch when he stopped, and drew back.

If he woke her – here, like this – what then?

They wouldn't talk, even though verbal communication had supposedly been his goal; he knew himself better than that. Yet wouldn't she – she who knew him too well – wonder at his change of tack?

Glancing around, he saw the stool before the dressing table; stepping back, he sat, leaned back, settled his shoulders against the table behind him – and let his gaze rest on her while he considered the questions that had plagued him since he'd last been in this room.

Since he'd had her, and discovered there was more to his need than mere lust. More than desire, more than passion.

Just what the emotion, so elusive yet so powerful, that had threaded through his need and, like a clinging vine, shackled it, and him, was, he didn't know. He suspected his cousin Martin could give it a name; that was more than he could, for he'd never believed that emotion – the one the poets glorified – existed, at least not for him. He'd never felt it before.

Yet it or something like it had hold of him now, a disconcerting, discomfiting experience. If he'd been given a choice, he'd have avoided it – turned down the opportunity to experience it. Why any sane man would willingly accept what he could foresee developing without at least putting up a fight was a continuing mystery.

When she realized ... if she guessed that he hadn't, in fact, been looking for her to speak with her, but had fabricated the excuse to explain his reaction to not knowing where she was, to learning that her attention had not been firmly fixed on him when his was so obsessively fixed on her, what then? Would she see through him?

His gaze shifted to her face, to the delicate features relaxed and at peace. Had she already guessed?

He recalled their words on the terrace. She'd reacted to his anger – illogical unless one invoked that telltale emotion, a fact that did not improve his view of its qualities and only deepened his distrust – yet she'd responded with straightforward anger of her own, irritated by what she'd seen as his domineering stance. If she'd realized the truth of why he'd been so exercised, she'd have been smug.

He stared at her face and the minutes ticked by; gradually, he relaxed, his tension draining away.

An odd contentment stole over him as he watched her sleep. The idea of waking her still teased, but ... it was barely twenty-four hours since he'd been buried deep inside her, and he knew just how deep. On top of that, she'd gone hiking God knew how far all through the morning. Small wonder sleep had claimed her.

He studied her, then smiled. Rising, he stretched, then headed for the door. Let her sleep, let her refresh herself – then he could claim her night hours with an unfettered conscience.

A sudden thought stopped him just before the door – if she woke and thought he hadn't found her, she'd come searching for him, expecting him to be angry. She'd be braced for a clash – not helpful, given his revised plan.

Swinging back into the room, he confirmed there was no escritoire. Digging out his note tablet and a pencil, he scanned the room, then saw what he needed. He considered, then wrote four words: *Tonight at midnight. Here.* Tearing off the sheet, he replaced tablet and pencil in his pocket as he crossed to the center table.

Selecting one of the white lilies whose exotic perfume hung heavy in the room, he broke off most of its stem, curled the note around the stub as he returned to the bed.

Amelia was still deeply asleep. She didn't stir when he gently threaded the lily's stem, carrying his note, into her curls so the flower lay just behind her ear.

He stood looking down at her for some minutes more, then silently left the room.

Midnight was a long time coming.

Amelia waited with feigned patience through afternoon tea, followed by a few hours of charades, then dutifully dressed and allowed herself to be distracted by Mr. Pomfret all through dinner.

When Luc joined her in the drawing room, she suppressed a sigh of relief and waited for him to single her out; instead, he merely stood by her side and conversed easily with Lady Hilborough, Miss Quigley, and her fiancé, Sir Reginald Bone.

She kept waiting, lips curved, teeth mentally gritted. He'd wanted to talk to her; he'd been insistent and irritated, ready to make some point. Now he was behaving as smoothly as usual, as if not an ounce of temper – or wildness – lurked behind his sophisticated mask. She swallowed a humph, then nearly groaned aloud when, clapping her hands, Lady Hightham urged them to gather around for some music.

Music? At this time? Oh, please . . .

But no helpful deity heard her plea; she had to endure a full two hours of harp, pianoforte, and harpsichord – she even had to make a contribution herself, one she kept severely abbreviated. She was no longer a *young* young lady, one needing to impress potential suitors with her talents. On top of that, her husband-to-be was not, she knew, particularly partial to music, and thus unlikely to be swayed by her skill with the keys.

When she returned to her chair in the back row, Luc, at ease in the one beside it, his long legs stretched out, ankles crossed, met her gaze, then raised a cynical brow. 'Supposedly it soothes the savage breast.'

With calm deliberation, she sat, and quietly informed him, 'I would infinitely rather it incited, instead.'

He had to smother his surprised laugh, but the sound made her feel insensibly better.

A few moments later, under cover of a particularly noisy crescendo, he murmured, 'Did you get my note?'

She glanced sideways at him; he was facing forward, his gaze on the pianist. 'Yes.'

'Good. In that case . . .' Uncrossing his legs, he sat up. 'I'm off – I've had enough of this.' His fingers closed about her wrist; his eyes met hers as he raised it and pressed his lips fleetingly to the inner face. 'Until later.'

With that promise – its nature underscored by the expression in his eyes – he released her, rose, and unobtrusively left the room.

She followed him with her eyes, and wished she could follow him in person. Instead, with a resigned sigh, she settled back to listen to the rest of the performances.

It was as well that she did; when the ladies finally decreed they would retire, she noted Lady Hilborough, Lady Mackintosh, and others of their ilk sharply observing that although Luc was absent, she was still among them. A fortunate circumstance; those ladies were most deserving of the tag 'gossipmongers' and would undoubtedly recount any suspicious happenings, heavily embroidered, to the *ton* at large on their return to town.

While everyone knew of, and indeed expected, scandalous doings at house parties, that did not mean that those who indulged could hope to escape social censure were they unwise enough to have their behavior remarked. Thus far, she and Luc had given no one any grounds for comment.

Climbing the stairs beside her mother and his, Amelia realized he would definitely expect to keep it that way. And she agreed. Consequently, when the house grew silent a full hour before midnight, she gathered the last shreds of her patience. And waited.

A rattle at her window woke her. She'd nodded off in the chair before the hearth. She glanced at the clock, squinting in the weak light of the single candle she'd left burning; it was ten minutes past midnight.

The rattle came again; she glanced at the door, but the sound definitely came from her curtained windows.

Rising, reassuring herself that she'd latched the windows earlier, she tiptoed to one side of the pair and peeped out past the heavy curtain.

A familiar dark head greeted her. With a muttered, 'Good heavens!' she rushed to pull the curtains wide and unlatch the tall windows. Luc hauled himself up to sit on the window ledge, then swung his legs into the room. Signaling her to silence – she'd been so surprised she'd simply stared to that point – he rose and crossed silently to the door; she watched, dumb-founded, as he very, very carefully eased the key on her door around. Then he straightened and turned; she presumed he'd locked the door, but she hadn't heard the tumblers fall.

She looked back at the window, went to the ledge and peered out, and down. A thick creeper covered the outside wall; no mystery how he'd reached the window. Why was another matter.

'Latch it again and draw the curtains.'

His voice came to her, soft and dark, from the shadows behind her. Ignoring the shivery thrill that raced down her spine, she hurriedly obeyed. Then she turned – and found herself in his arms. She pushed back to look at his face. 'Why—'

'Sshh.' He bent his head and whispered, 'Lady Mackintosh is haunting the bottom of the stairs.'

She drew back to stare at him. 'She isn't?'

The look he threw her spoke volumes. 'You don't think I risked climbing that damned creeper just to look romantic?'

His disgusted tone made her giggle.

He hauled her close, smothered the sound with a kiss – a kiss that quickly shifted from practical maneuver to seductive exchange, from light caress to long, slow, explicit invasion.

When he finally released her lips, he murmured, 'We'll have to keep quiet.'

'Quiet?' she breathed.

He kissed her briefly, demandingly. 'Totally and absolutely silent,' he confirmed. 'No matter what.'

The tenor of that last phrase, the words a hot whisper feathering her hungry lips, made it clear he hadn't forgotten his declaration that, this time, she'd scream.

The essential contradiction tightened her nerves, made her wish she could question him, but he was kissing her again, drawing her deeper into the exchange, his arms closing around her.

When he finally paused to let her breathe, she did, and quickly said, 'I thought you wanted to talk.'

In answer, he took her mouth, her lips, again. His hands wandered over her back, her hips – he drew her tight against him, molded her to him, making it patently clear rational discussion did not feature on his immediate agenda.

Her head was spinning when he drew back from the kiss – purely to deal with the knotted tie of the robe she'd worn over her nightgown. 'Tomorrow.' He touched the tip of his tongue to the corner of her lips, lightly probing – an erotic little touch that had her breath catching. 'We can talk then.' He briefly transferred his attention to the other corner of her lips, then captured them fully, making them cling to his.

'Tonight' —his voice was so low, so deep, she

wasn't sure she heard so much as felt the words resonating inside her— 'we have more important matters to explore.'

He kissed her again, his hands moving over her shoulders, sliding her robe away. Arms freed, she reached for him – for his coat. She felt the smile on his lips when he finally consented to notice her tugging and release her long enough to shrug the garment free. She let it fall to the floor, aware that his fingers had fastened on the tiny buttons down the front of her nightgown.

Without letting her free of the kiss, he steered her, the long hard columns of his thighs herding her around and back, step by step, until the backs of her thighs hit the bed. He trapped her there, his legs outside hers, his chest a wall before her. Catching her hands, he drew them down, then releasing them, swiftly drew the halves of her nightgown, now gaping to her waist, over her shoulders and partway down her arms, effectively anchoring them to her sides.

She would have pulled away from the kiss and slipped her arms free, but he didn't let her. Didn't let her retreat from the demanding kiss; instead, he captured her awareness completely by closing both hands about her breasts.

He knew precisely what he was doing, knew how to focus and hold her attention, how to blend the now-familiar sensations evoked by his lips and tongue, by his wicked fingers and hands, into a symphony that built at first along well-remembered lines, then swelled into something hotter.

Something different.

Something wicked and just a touch wild.

That promise of wildness held her absolutely, drew

her in, drew her to commit unreservedly to their play. She kissed him back avidly, eagerly, as blatantly voracious as he – his response was instantaneous, a towering tide of heat and urgency that poured through him, and her, and swept them both away.

She could reach as far as his waist; grasping, grabbing, she tugged his shirt from his waistband. He took his hands from her long enough to shrug out of his waistcoat, unbutton the shirt, strip it off, and toss it aside. She didn't wait for him to gather her to him but boldly pressed close, eager to feel his chest against her breasts, all but purring through their kiss as she sinuously rubbed against him, glorying in the raspy friction and the tight tingling that spread beneath her sensitized skin.

His hands closed on her shoulders; the kiss turned incendiary. Her breasts were swollen and hot – as hot as the hard muscles of his chest to which she wantonly pressed them. She sensed a growl in his throat, then his hands dived down her back, his arms pressing her nightgown wide, pushing the garment lower as he ran his hands down her back, blatantly possessive, down over her waist, the small of her back, over the curves of her hips to close, hard and urgent, over the globes of her bottom.

He kneaded provocatively; their lips fused, tongues dueling, not for supremacy but for mutual delight. Then he lifted her; her nightgown slid down her legs as he raised her. He held her tight against him, her naked stomach cushioning his erection; they both clung and gloried in the moment, in the flagrant promise of what was to come, then he tipped her back and they fell on the bed.

Luc kept his lips on hers, trapping her laughing

gasp. He grasped handfuls of her hair and held her down so he could ravage her mouth – and take one long moment to savor the feel of her naked and squirming beneath him. He used his weight to subdue her, kissed her long and hard, then swiftly drew back. 'Wait.'

The hissed whisper echoed through the room. She lay there, wide-eyed, golden curls in bountiful disarray, the soft candlelight playing over the even richer bounty of her body, naked and waiting – all his. She watched as he sat and dispensed with his shoes – carefully setting them aside. No thumps. Then he stood and stripped off his breeches, flinging them to join his coat.

He turned back to the bed, and surprised her delicately licking her lips. Her gaze was fixed a long way south of his face. He would have laughed, but didn't dare; instead, he crawled back on the bed, back to her, running his hands slowly up the sides of her bare legs, his mind quickly scripting all that was to come – he would have to keep his lips on hers the entire time.

She started to reach for him, to pull him down to her; he grasped her waist and lifted her. Startled, she would have gasped, but he sealed her lips with his, drank her surprise, then arranged her as he wished. She acquiesced; through their kiss he could sense her curiosity. Her hands touched his shoulders, drifted down his chest as he set her on her knees before him.

He held her there and shuffled forward to sit on his ankles, his spread thighs on either side of her knees. One hand splayed in the small of her back, he pressed her hips to his stomach so his rigid erection throbbed in the valley between her thighs – safe for the moment from her wandering hands.

She seemed fascinated by his chest – he let her explore while he took his own time exploring the wonders of her mouth, the sleekly feminine planes of her back, the decidedly evocative curves of her bottom. He touched her as he wished, knowing when her breath hitched, when her attention refocused on his hands, and on what he was doing. On the soft dew that dampened her heating skin, on the tightness of the pebbled peaks of her breasts that he knowingly brushed to aching hardness with his chest, on the tautness of her stomach when he pressed a hand between them and evocatively kneaded, on the wetness his questing fingers encountered when he speared through her curls and touched her. Opened her, probed her.

All the while holding her lips with his.

When her hips tilted against his hand, when her nails sank into his shoulders, he drew his fingers from her, slid both hands to the backs of her thighs, gripped, and lifted her to him, laying her spread thighs over his, bringing her hips to his abdomen. Instinctively, she grasped his hips with her knees – slowly, he let her down until her knees rested on the coverlet.

She took control of the kiss, surprising him, pressing a burning caress on him, one nothing short of a flagrant invitation. It sank through him, distracting him; she reached down and closed one small hand around him.

His heart stopped, then she eased her hold and caressed, then closed her hand again. Caught, trapped, he let her play, unable to summon the strength to stop her. There was a sense of dedication, of wonder and joy in her touch that snared his jaded mind, that prevented him from cutting short a moment that, given who she was, what she was, was frankly somewhat shocking. How long she held his senses in thrall he didn't know; only when he was aching, throbbing with the need to sink into the haven of womanly warmth that hovered but a few inches above, did he shift his hands, closing them about her hips, taking control of their kiss again.

Or attempting to – she didn't, this time, willingly yield, as she usually did. Instead, she met him, matched him – rather than draw her hand from him, she braced her other hand on his upper chest, and guided his erection to her entrance.

They both held their breaths, forgot to breathe.

The instant her swollen folds enveloped his head, she let go and he surged in – then stopped, and, chest laboring, let her, as she wished, slide her knees farther past his hips and sink, slowly, inch by inch down, taking him in willingly, eyes closed, lips on his, impaling herself on him.

He let her do it; held back the raging impulse to seize her hips and fill her deeply – instead, muscles flickering with the strain of desisting, he savored the gift of her body as she gave it, as she opened and eased about him, sank lower yet, her breath catching in her throat as she realized how high inside her he was.

When she could go no farther, she shuddered beneath his hands, then wrapped her arms about his neck and kissed him – openly, deeply – in absolute surrender. She was clinging to her wits, to her senses, by a thread.

He let his hands firm on her hips; holding her

immobile, he thrust the last inch to embed himself fully – drawing a shattered gasp from her. He drank it in, aware to his bones of the precious moment, of the emotion that welled through him, through her, in that instant of complete giving, of unconditional acceptance.

It held them, a shimmering net more evident this time than before, stronger, more definite. As he moved within her, as she brazenly adjusted and moved on him, the net tightened and locked about them.

And it was no longer a question of who was driving whom, but what was driving them – and even then, there was no real question. He accepted it; he had no choice. Lungs laboring, heart thundering as their dance escalated, the sheer intensity of sensation all but blinding, he didn't need to think to know that this was what he wanted, what he desired above all else.

She closed hotly about him, pressing low, taking him all; he sank his fingers into her hips, held her down, and thrust deeper still. Their mouths had merged, frantic with the need to smother her moans, his groans, their gasps. He shifted one hand to her breast, closed hard about the firm mound, found her nipple and squeezed – and felt her shudder.

Felt her arch, felt her body tighten, the spiraling tension ratchetting up another notch . . .

Amelia thought she'd go mad, demented, if she couldn't reach the glory beckoning so strongly, if her body didn't achieve the satisfaction she knew existed just out of her reach – soon. Yet Luc held off the moment – how, she didn't know – until she was all but weeping with need. His hand, as hard and demanding on her breast as his lips were on hers, his body slowly, tirelessly plundering hers to the same relentless rhythm with which his tongue plundered her willing mouth, he held her there, on the cusp of completion, while, emperor-like, he savored her.

On a moan, she surrendered, gladly, wantonly. Let her mind slide, let her senses free. Abandoned to the moment, to the clawing, rapacious need, she simply wanted him there, inside her, linked with her, as deeply as he wished. Her thighs spread wide over his, his hand wrapped about her hip, fingers gripping as he held her so he could plunder even more deeply, the fingers of his other hand on her breast, torturing one nipple so lightning speared through her to the same steady rhythm, all underscored her vulnerability.

A vulnerability that touched her, trailed cool fingers over her naked, undulating flesh, and made her shudder, yet beneath it, behind it, through her very surrender to it, came a joy, a wonderment, a triumph more satisfying than anything she'd dreamed.

And it was real. She sensed it through their kiss, through the merging of their mouths, their joint devotion to this moment in all its glory.

The sensation of him filling her, of him being there, strong and alive, buried within her, had become an addiction, a potent, demanding one. The slow slide of his erection, hot, rigid, and powerful, again and again pressing in, filled her mind with desire, filled her body with heat, filled her soul with a nameless craving.

She clung to him and gave herself up to the wonder, to him. Concentrated on using her body intimately to caress him as he was so devotedly, equally intimately, caressing her.

Her body tightened again, one more notch –

suddenly she couldn't breathe, couldn't make her lungs work.

She tried to pull back; Luc caught her, ruthlessly held her to the kiss, releasing her breast, sinking his hand into her hair, holding her tight. He gave her his breath, gripped her hip, pressed her fully down.

And thrust deep.

She screamed.

He drank her keening cry as she came apart in his arms, cresting the wave, riding high. With a calculated rhythm of thrust and grind, he ruthlessly drove her on. And on, until she shattered again, this time completely; linked deep in their kiss, for one fleeting instant, he could have sworn he glimpsed her soul.

And then he was there, too, soaring from the pinnacle, plunging into the whirlpool, the fire, and the glory. The mind-wiping ecstasy of primitive passions slaked, of the deepest sensual sexual gratification.

Never had it felt so profound, so draining, so complete.

Never had he known such deep contentment.

Such abiding joy.

It still held him when he awoke, hours later. It was still dark outside, and inside, too; the candle had long guttered. Instinct warned him dawn was close; he would have to leave her soon.

But not yet.

They lay slumped in her bed, cocooned in the coverlet. She lay curled beside him, her cheek on his chest, one arm reaching across, her hand spread as if to hold him. A warm, feminine weight alongside him, his wife in fact if not yet legally.

He shifted, turned to her. Took great pleasure, a purely male delight, in gently stirring her body to life. She shifted, still asleep, restless but not knowing why; he smiled and moved over her, nudged her thighs apart so he could settle between.

She woke as he entered her; her breath caught, her lashes fluttered, opened wide, then, as he pressed deeper, fell. Her fingers clutched his shoulder; her spine arched. He found her lips and kissed her – and she sighed. Her body relaxed and let him in – let him slowly penetrate her warmth until he was fully sheathed, then she closed lovingly about him.

He held still, savoring again that inexpressible joy that, once again, had infused the moment.

Her hand stole down his back to his hip, then lower. She tilted her hips fractionally; her hand gripped, urging him on.

Stifling a smile, he complied, moving slowly on her and within her; their lips remained fused yet this gentle morning coupling was a time for soft sighs, not screams.

She crested slowly, easily, with a soft female urgency; he followed close, joining her in the warm sea of satiation.

Later, he drew away, soothing her protests with a kiss. He quickly dressed, then leaned over her to whisper, 'There's a bench on the north shore overlooking the lake. Meet me there at eleven.'

Through the gray light of dawn, she blinked at him, then nodded, and drew him down for one last kiss.

It was too early for heroics – he left by the door.

Chapter Ten

'There you are, m'lord – that ought to do it.'

Luc accepted the bouquet of apricot and yellow roses, the stems wrapped and tied with agapanthus leaves, with a grateful nod. He passed a silver coin to the old gardener. 'Worth every penny.'

The old man grinned. 'Aye, well, I knows how it is when a young lady needs to be persuaded-like.'

His lady didn't need persuading, but distracting. Luc inclined his head. 'As you say.' Leaving the gardener, he headed for the lake.

It was nearly eleven o'clock; from the rose garden to the lake was not a short distance. As he rounded the corner of the west wing, he glimpsed a figure in a white muslin gown, curls gilded by the morning sunlight, appear briefly on the path that circled the lake. She passed out of sight, screened by the bushes that bordered the ornamental water; he lengthened his stride.

At least this morning he knew where she was – just where she was supposed to be.

Just where he wanted her.

Last night, more precisely the hours he'd spent

with her, had eradicated all lingering doubts over what now was the best way forward. There was no point carping over the fact she'd seduced him; impossible to pretend he hadn't enjoyed it. The fact he – his will – hadn't been strong enough to resist her temptation spoke for itself; there was no point denying he wanted her in that way – and no sense wasting time before bringing the situation back under his control.

Especially given the confirmation of last night.

She hadn't realized. Hadn't seen, wasn't experienced enough to know that what they shared – the way they shared, that emotion that welled and flared between them when they came together – was not the norm. She'd never been with a man before; she was a sexual innocent – a novice. Why would she guess?

As long as he didn't tell her, didn't reveal how much deeper his involvement with her went, she never would.

Which meant he was safe. He could have her, along with all she brought him, that unnameable well of emotion, could claim her and it and allow it to grow, develop as he wished, all under his control. That he coveted it as well as her was not in question; the entire package called to his conqueror's soul. As matters had fallen out, he could have the whole without making any sacrifice beyond that which he'd already been prepared to make.

All he needed to do was marry her.

Quickly.

And whisk her off to Calverton Chase, where he could learn to handle her and their newfound emotion in safe isolation.

The need for a quick wedding was obvious – if he didn't want her to guess how he felt, he had to avoid situations that would make him react in ways that would, at least to her, educated by her mother, her aunts, and her cousins' wives, scream the truth. He'd been lucky once; he couldn't count on fate smiling twice. Limiting the time they spent in society before their wedding was an essential element of his plan.

Once he'd settled into his role as her husband, once he better understood the practicalities of controlling this emotion that now bound them, then when they returned to London and the *ton* later in the year, he'd know how to manage. Without giving her a weapon with which to manage him.

His best way forward was crystal clear.

The path had been steadily climbing; now it opened into a clearing, high above the lake. Amelia was sitting on the seat facing the distant house, scanning the lawns and the walks – wondering where he was.

So engrossed was she in searching for him, she didn't sense him draw near.

Until he stepped around the seat, swept her an elaborate bow, then offered her the bouquet. 'My dear Amelia, will you do me the inestimable honor of consenting to be my viscountess?'

Reaching for the flowers, she froze, blinked, searched his eyes, then took the bouquet and glanced around.

Lips quirking, he sat beside her. 'No, we don't have an audience, or at least, not an immediate one.' He nodded toward the house. 'No doubt someone will see us and take note, but there's no one else up here.'

Cradling the blooms, Amelia held them to her face and inhaled. Then she looked at him. 'I thought we'd already agreed to marry?'

Still watching the house, he shrugged. 'I thought you deserved a formal offer.'

After an instant's hesitation, she coolly replied, 'You didn't go down on your knees.'

He met her gaze. 'Take what you can get.'

Still puzzled, she searched his eyes.

He faced forward. 'Anyway, I meant immediately.'

If she'd been surprised before, now she was stunned. 'But I thought—'

'I've changed my mind.'

'Why?'

'You mean aside from the little matter of spending last night in your bed? And, of course, that wasn't the first time we'd indulged.'

She narrowed her eyes. 'Indeed – aside from that. *That* doesn't necessitate an immediate trip to the altar, as we both well know.'

'True, but it does raise the question of why not. Why not get married immediately, so we can indulge as we wish, without me having to risk my neck climbing creepers? I'm no lightweight, and besides, what will we do when we get back to London?'

What was going on? 'Stop trying to distract me.' He was still gazing at the house. 'The reason we weren't going to get married for at least the next two weeks was because you didn't believe society would accept our attachment and not look for other reasons.'

'As I said, I've changed my mind.'

At the cool, *arrogant* statement, she raised her brows to the absolute limit.

He was watching from the corner of his eye. His lips thinned, then he inclined his head. 'All right. You were right. The old biddies have accepted us as a couple – indeed, they're expecting an announcement. We don't need to play at wooing any longer.' He looked at her; both his eyes and his expression were uncompromisingly hard. 'Don't argue.'

Their gazes locked, and she bit her tongue. He was right. *Take what you can get.* She would, especially as it was precisely what she'd wanted. She could go on as she'd planned from here.

'Very well.' She looked at the flowers, raised them to her face, and breathed in their perfume. Over them, she met his eyes. 'Thank you, kind sir, for your proposal. I will be honored to be your wife.'

The flowers' perfume was heavenly; she closed her eyes for an instant, savoring it, then looked again at him. 'So – when should we wed?'

He shifted and cast a frowning glance at the house. 'As soon as humanly possible.'

Their decision to marry quickly was going to be interpreted as primarily if not solely due to his impatience.

By the time they quit Hightham Hall late that afternoon, that much was clear; even though they'd said not a word, their intentions had somehow been divined. After being twitted for several hours by every lady, young and old, Luc bundled Amelia into his curricle, left Reggie, greatly entertained, to see to his mother, her mother, his sisters, and Fiona, and escaped.

As he tooled his curricle down the drive, he felt like he was fleeing.

Amelia, beside him, parasol deployed, a smile on her face, wisely held her tongue as he negotiated the narrow lanes; he felt her occasional glance, knew she sensed his underlying irritation.

When they reached the main road to London,

however, she asked, 'How long does it take to get a special license?'

'A few days. Less if one can arrange an audience quickly.' He hesitated, then added, 'I've already got one.'

She glanced at him. 'You have?'

Keeping his gaze on his horses, he shrugged. 'We agreed to wed by the end of June – given we weren't going to announce the fact three or more weeks in advance, we were going to need a special license regardless.'

Amelia nodded, pleased that he'd thought ahead – that no matter how things had seemed, he'd been as committed to their marriage as she.

'More to the point, how long will it take you to make your preparations?' He glanced at her. 'Your gown, the arrangements – the invitations, and so on.'

She opened her lips to airily dismiss such details, then hesitated.

He noted it; his gaze traveled her face, then, lips twitching, he faced forward. 'Indeed. There are the families' expectations – both yours and mine – to satisfy. Let alone society's.'

'No – society's expectations we need not regard. Neither you nor I need do so, not with our age and standing, and at this stage of the year, so late in the Season, the *ton* will accept our wish to marry quietly.'

He inclined his head. 'So what have you been planning?'

Although even, his tone warned her there was no point pretending she didn't have it all worked out. 'I'd thought, if you're agreeable, to be married at Somersham.'

His brows rose. 'In the old church, or the chapel?'

He'd visited often enough to know Devil's principal estate. 'The church – that's where most Cynsters have been married. Old Mr. Merryweather – do you remember him? Devil's chaplin? – he's rather ancient, but I'm sure he'd be delighted to officiate. And, of course, all the staff there are used to managing that sort of gathering – they've had plenty of experience.'

He glanced at her. 'But not, I imagine, at such short notice.'

'Honoria will cope, I'm sure.' She ignored the suggestion, heavy in his manner, that Honoria might be holding herself – and her staff – in readiness. 'So the ceremony, the wedding breakfast, and my gown are easy to arrange.'

He looked back to his horses. 'The invitations?'

'I'm sure your mama will already have given the matter some thought. She's hardly blind.'

'And your mother?'

'Likewise.' She glanced at him, but he didn't meet her eye. 'Four days is the minimum if we send the invitations by messenger.'

'Today's Thursday ...' After a moment, he glanced at her. 'How about next Wednesday?'

She considered, then nodded. 'Yes – that will give us an extra day or two ...' She paused, then looked at him. 'We'll have to make some announcement.' When he merely nodded, his gaze on the road, she inwardly grimaced and broached the one hurdle she could see. 'We'll have to be prepared, when we speak with my father, to explain the matter of your funds.'

The glance he threw her was so swift, she didn't catch it; his leader jibbed, and he had to pay attention to the reins.

She drew breath and forged on, 'If it was just my father, that would be easy enough, but there's also my cousins – Devil and the others. They'll check, I'm sure, and they've all sorts of contacts ... we'll need to be prepared to defend our case, even though I'm quite sure they'll all agree in the end. But if they do become difficult, there's no reason, within the family, that we can't make it plain that we've been intimate. It's hardly likely to shock them after all, but it will force them to see that we're in earnest and quite committed, and ... well, you know what I mean.'

Luc didn't look her way; she could tell nothing from his profile, his expression was as impassive as ever. 'In birth, title, and estate, you're precisely the sort of gentleman they always wanted us – me and Amanda – to marry. The fact that your current funds are low is not significant, given the size of my dowry.'

She'd said all she dared, all she felt she must. Biting her lower lip, she considered his stony profile, then concluded, 'They may grumble at first, but as long as we make it perfectly plain we're determined to wed, they'll agree.'

His chest swelled as he drew in a breath. 'We said Wednesday.' He looked at her, his eyes narrow, his gaze hard. 'I want you to promise by all you hold holy that you will say nothing to anyone about our engagement until I give you leave.'

She stared at him. 'Why? I thought we agreed—'

'We have. That's definite.' He glanced at the road, then back at her. 'I want to put some arrangements of my own in place first.'

She blinked, but could understand ... she nodded. 'Very well – but if we're set on Wednesday, then how long will it be before we're free to speak?'

He flicked the reins; the greys lengthened their stride. He glanced at the sky. 'Impossible to do anything tonight. It'll have to be tomorrow.' He glanced briefly at her. 'I'll do what I need to do, then I'll call on you tomorrow afternoon.'

'What time?'

His lips set. 'I don't know. If you go out, leave a message – I'll find you.'

She hesitated. 'All right.'

A minute passed, then he looked at her, met her gaze. 'Believe me, it's necessary.'

There was something in his eyes, some trace of awkwardness, a tinge of vulnerability, that made her reach out, lay her palm on his cheek, then stretch up and touch her lips to his.

He had to glance at his horses the instant their lips parted, but he caught hold of her hand, then, reassured as to the greys, raised it to his lips and placed a kiss in her palm. He curled her fingers as if to seal the kiss in; his fingers about hers, he held her fist for a moment, then released her.

'Tomorrow afternoon. Wherever you are, I'll find you.'

He should have told her. By all the tenets of acceptable behavior, he should have spoken, and explained he wasn't the pauper she thought him.

The next morning, as he descended the front steps of his house and set out for Upper Brook Street, Luc faced the unpalatable fact that the tenets of acceptable behavior did not extend to Amelia's reaction. Without a cast-iron guarantee that she would still agree to be his bride once she'd learned the truth, he wasn't about to offer it.

211

Indeed, after their sojourn at Hightham Hall, he was even more wary of rocking their rowboat at this point in time, of giving her any excuse to balk or back away from the altar. One afternoon and one night had altered his perspective; where before he'd *thought* her desirable, very likely the right lady for him, after those two interludes, he *knew*.

He was absolutely adamantly set against giving her any chance of escaping him. Of doing anything other than becoming his wife.

On Wednesday next.

After that, he'd have plenty of time in which to find the right moment to tell her the truth.

Assuming she ever truly needed to know.

That last phrase whispered through his brain; he thrust it aside, refused to dwell on it, knowing it for the coward's way out.

He wasn't a coward – he would tell her, one day. Once she loved him, she'd understand and forgive him; that's what love was all about, wasn't it? All he had to do was encourage it in her, and all eventually would be well.

Reaching the front steps of Number 12 Upper Brook Street, he glanced up at the door, then determinedly climbed to the porch and rang the bell.

He'd sent a message earlier; Lord Arthur Cynster, Amelia's father, was expecting him.

'Come in, my boy.' Arthur rose from the chair behind the desk in his library and held out his hand.

Going forward, Luc shook it. 'Thank you for seeing me on such short notice, sir.'

Arthur humphed. 'I'd be given short shrift if I hadn't.' Blue eyes twinkling, he waved Luc to a chair beside the desk. 'Sit down.' Resuming his seat,

Arthur grinned. 'What can I do for you?'

Luc returned his smile easily. 'I've come to ask for Amelia's hand.'

That – getting out the words he'd never thought to say – was the easy part. Arthur beamed, and said the expected things; he'd known Luc from childhood and viewed him from a position similar to that of a distant uncle.

Amelia's wish to marry at Somersham Place the next Wednesday— 'That's her choice, and I'm happy to indulge her' —had Arthur's brows rising, but he accepted his daughter's stubbornness without a blink.

They eventually got to the financial aspects.

Luc drew a folded letter from his pocket. 'I asked Robert Child for a declaration, in case you'd heard any rumors that the current position of the Calvertons had been adversely impacted by my father's activities.'

Arthur blinked, but accepted the document, opened it and read. His brows rose. 'Well, my word. No need to worry on that score.' Refolding the letter, he held it out to Luc. 'Not that I'd expected to.'

Luc reached for the letter; Arthur didn't immediately let go. Luc met his gaze – very blue, very worldly – over the document.

'I didn't imagine you had any financial worries, Luc. Why, then, this letter?'

Arthur released it and sat back, waiting, patient and paternal. It had been sometime since Luc had faced such an interview.

He knew better than to lie – wouldn't have done it anyway. 'I . . .' He blinked, then steeled himself. 'The fact is Amelia imagines I'm very much less wealthy than I am. In short, she thinks her dowry

213

plays a part, indeed, is significant, in cementing our union.'

Arthur's brows had risen high. 'But that's clearly not so.'

There was a smile – a definite smile – flirting at the corner of his future father-in-law's lips; Luc felt the ground firm beneath his feet. 'Indeed. However, I don't, at this juncture, wish to ... rattle her with that revelation.'

Leaning back, he gestured to the paper lying folded on his knee. 'She'll court no danger of penury by marrying me, but you know what she – indeed, ladies generally – are like. We came to our understanding unexpectedly and rapidly – there wasn't a suitable moment, earlier, to correct her misapprehension. Now ... as she wishes to marry so soon, I would prefer not to broach the matter at this time—'

'On the grounds that she's likely to dig in her heels, insist on reexamining every last detail, and generally make your life a misery because she misunderstood, and very likely not agree to marry in June, and subsequently hold the fact against you for the rest of your days?'

He hadn't followed the outcome quite that far; it was no difficulty to look aggrieved. 'In a nutshell, yes. So you see the problem.'

'Oh, indeed.' The twinkle in Arthur's eyes suggested he saw more than Luc would wish, but was prepared to be understanding. 'So how do you see us proceeding?'

'I was hoping you would consent to keep the matter of my wealth in confidence, at least until I've had a chance to break the news to her.'

Arthur pondered, then nodded. 'Given we're

concealing wealth rather than the lack of it, and given it's in her own interests in the sense of the timing, I can see no reason to refuse. The only problem I foresee is the settlements. She'll see the figures when she signs.'

'Indeed, but I would suggest that, with your agreement, there's no reason the figures she sees can't be percentages.'

Arthur considered, then slowly nodded. 'No reason at all we can't do it that way.'

Arthur heard the front door shut behind Luc. Relaxing in his chair, he fixed his gaze on the clock on the mantelpiece. Less than a minute had elapsed when the door to the library opened and Louise entered, bright-eyed and eager.

'Well?' She came around the desk to perch on the edge, facing him. 'What did Luc want?'

Arthur grinned. 'Precisely what you told me he'd want. They've apparently set the date for next Wednesday, if we're willing.'

'Wednesday?' Louise blinked. 'Drat the girl – why didn't she mention that this morning?'

'It's possible Luc might not have wished to have his thunder stolen.'

'Most men prefer to have the way paved.'

'Not all men, and I wouldn't include Luc in that category.'

Louise paused, then nodded. 'Indeed. That's to his credit.' She fixed her gaze on Arthur. 'So everything's settled, all is in order, and you're satisfied he's the right man for Amelia?'

His gaze drifting to the door, Arthur smiled. 'I have absolutely no reservations whatsoever.'

215

Louise studied his smile, then narrowed her eyes. 'What? There's something you're not telling me.'

Arthur's gaze shifted to her face; his grin widened. 'There's nothing you need know.' Reaching out, he caught her by the waist and drew her onto his lap. 'I'm just delighted that there's demonstrably more to what's between them than simple lust – and that's how it should be.'

'More than just lust?' Louise looked into his eyes, her own gently smiling. 'Are you sure?'

Arthur drew her lips to his. 'You taught me well enough to recognize the signs – Luc's chin deep in love, and the intriguing thing is, he knows it.'

On gaining the pavement, Luc checked his watch, then, somewhat grimly, set out for his next appointment. Grosvenor Square lay at the end of Upper Brook Street; he was admitted to the mansion midway along the north side by a majestic figure.

'Good morning, Webster.'

'My lord.' Webster bowed. 'His Grace is expecting you. If you'll come this way.'

Webster led him to Devil's study and opened the door. 'Lord Calverton, Your Grace.'

Luc walked in. Devil rose from a chair by the fireplace. Although they knew each other reasonably well, their acquaintance stemmed from their families' social closeness, from moving in the same circle. Devil, his brother and cousins – the six who'd formed the legendary group known as the Bar Cynster – were all older than Luc by several years.

As Luc joined him, Devil grinned. 'I hope you've no objection to talking before my daughter?'

Shaking Devil's hand, Luc looked down at the

moppet, dark curls jouncing as she bounced on the rug before the hearth, huge pale green eyes shifting from his face to her sire's and back again. Taking the wooden cube she was chewing from her mouth, Lady Louisa Cynster favored him with a huge smile.

Luc laughed. 'No, not at all. I can see that she'll be discreet.'

One of Devil's dark brows quirked; he resumed his seat, waving Luc to the chair opposite. 'Will discretion be required?'

'In part, yes.' Luc met Devil's gaze. 'I've just come from Upper Brook Street. Arthur has consented to a match between myself and Amelia.'

Devil inclined his head. 'Congratulations.'

'Thank you.'

Luc hesitated; Devil prompted, 'I take it that isn't why you're here?'

Luc met his gaze. 'Not precisely. I came to request that neither you nor any other of Amelia's cousins mention to her just how wealthy I am.'

Devil blinked. 'You recently landed a windfall – Gabriel checked. He was jealous. In fact, he proposed that, if the breeze did blow that way and you became one of the family, that he should conscript you, and Dexter, too, into the business.'

Luc knew which business Devil was referring to; the Cynsters ran a combined investment fund rumored to be fabulously successful. He inclined his head. 'I'd be happy to consult, if Gabriel wished it.'

Devil eyed him shrewdly. 'So what's the rub?'

Luc explained, much as he had with Arthur; Devil, however, was less easygoing than his uncle.

'Do you mean she thinks you're marrying her for her dowry?'

217

Luc hesitated. 'I doubt she thinks I'm marrying her only for that.'

Devil's eyes narrowed even more; he sat back in the chair, his gaze unrelenting. Luc met it without flinching.

'When are you going to tell her?'

'After the wedding – when we're at Calverton Chase and things have settled into some semblance of normality.'

Devil thought long and hard. Louisa, as if sensing her father's disaffection, crawled to him, grabbed hold of the tassel trim of one large boot, and hauled herself up, waving and batting her block. Distracted, Devil lifted her onto his lap where she sat propped against his chest, green eyes wide, the block once more in her mouth.

Devil leaned back. 'I'll agree not to say anything, and warn the others not to queer your pitch on one condition. I want your assurance that you will definitely tell her – specifically, in words – before you and she return to town in the autumn.'

Luc raised his brows. 'Specifically, in words ...' He turned the phrases – with the particular emphasis Devil had given them – over in his mind. Realized just what Devil meant. His expression hardened. 'You mean ...' —he spoke softly, distinctly— 'that you expect me to declare myself – to her – before we return to town?'

Devil held his gaze – and nodded.

Luc felt his temper rise – felt trapped, caught, not just by Devil, but by fate.

As if sensing his thoughts, Devil murmured, 'All's fair in love as well as war.'

Luc allowed one brow to rise. 'Indeed? Then

perhaps you can advise me – how did you tell
Honoria?'

Silence greeted the question – a stab in the dark,
but Luc sensed he'd struck true. Devil's gaze didn't
waver from his, yet he couldn't tell what was going
on in the mind behind the eyes.

Sensing the clash between her father and him,
Louisa squirmed around to stare up at Devil's face,
then she looked across at him, her block firm between
her pudgy hands, lips parted as those huge eyes
searched his face. Then she flopped back, with force,
and pointed her block at him.

'Dgoo!'

It sounded very like 'Do!' – a dictate handed down
by some imperious empress. Startled, Devil glanced
down, a grin dawning.

She turned her head, pointed the block at him,
frowned direfully and repeated her stern order.
'*Dgoo*!'

It came out with even greater force – as if to underscore
that, Louisa repeated it, then grabbed her block with both
hands, wedged a corner into her mouth, and, with every
sign of dismissing them – mere ignorant males – from her
mind, settled her cheek against Devil's waistcoat and
chewed, and pondered other things.

At less than one year old, there was absolutely no
possibility she could have understood any of what
they'd said. Yet when Devil raised his head and met
his gaze, Luc widened his eyes in instinctive fellow
feeling.

The tension, the battle of wills, that had raged,
restrained but nonetheless real, between them
moments before, had evaporated, replaced by a wary
sense of unease.

219

Luc broke the ensuing silence. 'I'll try to do as you ask . . .' —he drew breath— 'but I won't promise, at least not as to when.'

They were talking about a declaration, not of financial status, but of emotional reality – a reality neither of them, it seemed, had yet put into words. Almost certainly for the same reason. Neither of them wished openly to acknowledge the vulnerability they both knew to be fact – and in both their cases, there was no one, in truth, who could force them to it.

Except that Devil had used the misunderstanding over his wealth to pressure him, and he – with Devil's daughter's help – had now turned that pressure back on Devil.

Acknowledging that, Devil grimaced, then inclined his head. 'Very well – I'll accept that much reassurance. However' —his green gaze steadied— 'you asked for advice, and on this subject I can claim to be an expert. The longer you leave it, the harder it gets.'

Luc held that compelling gaze for some moments, then nodded. 'I'll bear that in mind.'

Louisa turned her head and stared soulfully at him – as if practicing snaring men's hearts.

On leaving St. Ives House, Luc took himself off to his club for sustenance in the form of a neat lunch and the company of various friends. Suitably refreshed, he returned to Upper Brook Street.

Amelia was out with Louise, parading in the park. Luc considered, then returned to Mount Street and sent his grooms scurrying; five minutes later, he set out in his curricle to extract his bride-to-be from the center of the by now sure to be avidly interested *ton*.

He spotted her strolling the lawns on Reggie's arm, bringing up the rear of a group that included, among others, his sisters, Fiona, and Lord Kirkpatrick. Two younger sprigs he couldn't place were hovering earnestly at Anne's and Fiona's elbows.

Drawing his greys to a stamping halt by the verge, Luc grasped the moment to study the group. Emily and Mark, Lord Kirkpatrick, had grown progressively close, more discernibly easy in each other's company – definitely more oblivious to those around them. That was shaping up nicely. As for Anne, as he had hoped, in Fiona's brightly chattering presence, she was less reserved, although, from the look of concentration on the face of the young man at her side, she was still distinctly quiet. The others of the group were of similar age, similar station; there was no threat there – no wolves in sheep's clothing or otherwise.

He shifted his gaze to Amelia. In a white muslin gown sprigged with bright blue, she was a sight for sore eyes – and more. He felt a tug at his heart, in his gut; his gaze roamed her figure, sleek yet distinctly more mature than those of the younger girls around her. She must have felt his gaze, for, quelling her flighty ribbons, blowing in the breeze, she looked around – straight at him.

Her smile – spontaneous and unreserved in the instant before consciousness of where she was intruded – warmed him. She turned to Reggie, pointed to the carriageway; with a word to the others, they left the group and strode, swift and eager, toward him.

His impulse was to descend and meet her, however, a single glance around confirmed that, as he'd feared, they were the unrivaled center of attention. Every eye that could reasonably roll their way was fixed on them.

He nodded to Reggie. Reaching down, he grasped the hand Amelia held out to him. 'Step up. Quickly.'

She did, without question; he drew her up to the seat beside him. As she sat, he looked at Reggie. 'Can you manage with that lot – and tell Louise I'll return Amelia to Brook Street within the hour?'

Reggie, struggling to hide a grin, opened his eyes wide. 'Within the hour?'

Luc narrowed his eyes at him. 'Indeed.' He glanced at Amelia; she met his gaze. 'Hang on.'

She did; he backed the curricle, then flicked the reins and set the greys pacing. Without a single glance right or left – refusing to allow anyone to catch his eye, wave, and detain them – he guided the greys, not down the Avenue but straight out of the park.

Amelia turned his way as they passed through the gates, a smile on her lips, an intrigued light in her eyes. 'Where are we going?'

He took her home – to his home, Calverton House – to his study, the one place he could think of where no one would interrupt, where they could discuss the necessary arrangements, and he could distract her if need be.

Cottsloe opened the door to them; stepping back, he beamed. 'My lord. Miss Amelia.'

Speculation flared in Cottsloe's eyes, stoked by the fact that he, Luc, had Amelia's hand firmly in his. He led her into the front hall. 'You deserve to be among the first to know, Cottsloe – Miss Amelia has done me the honor of consenting to be my wife. She will shortly be Lady Calverton.'

Cottsloe's beaming smile threatened to split his round face. 'My lord – Miss Amelia – pray accept my heartfelt congratulations.'

Luc grinned. Amelia smiled. 'Thank you, Cottsloe.'

'If you don't mind me asking, my lord ...?'

Luc caught Amelia's eye, saw the same unvoiced question there. 'Next Wednesday. A bit rushed, but summer's nearly here.' His gaze locked with Amelia's, he raised her hand to his lips. 'And there seems no reason to dally.'

Her eyes widened; he could sense the questions rising in her mind. He glanced at Cottsloe. 'We'll be in the study. I don't wish to be disturbed.'

'Indeed, my lord.'

He turned and, Amelia's hand still locked in his, strode down the hall. Flinging open the study door, he went in, towing Amelia behind him – then he turned, pushed the door shut, twirled her about and backed her against the panels. Sank one hand into her golden curls and kissed her.

Ravenously.

Surprise froze her for an instant, then she kissed him back – wound her arms about his neck and invited him to devour.

And he did. The taste of her, the softness of her mouth, willingly yielded, was nectar to his soul; just over a day had passed since he'd last had her in his arms, yet he was already starving.

Hungry, and greedy, too.

She was very ready to appease his appetite – and hers. He felt her hands slide down his chest, then lower; he grasped her waist, lifted her, then used his weight to hold her trapped against the door, her head

223

just lower than his, her hands no longer able to reach his hips.

Draping her arms over his shoulders, holding him to her, she gave her full attention to the kiss – as did he.

They were both gasping, his chest heaving, her breasts rising dramatically, when they finally broke the kiss. They didn't move apart – didn't move at all – but remained, foreheads touching, gazes meeting fleetingly from under heavy lids. Lips separated by a breath.

While they waited for the thunder in their ears to subside.

Eventually, he murmured, 'I've seen your father, and Devil, too.'

Her eyes opened wide. 'Both?'

He nodded. 'We discussed things . . .' He touched his lips to hers, savored their warmth, their clinging softness. 'We went over all the points that needed to be addressed.' Angling his head, he nudged her chin up, and set his lips cruising the sensitive skin beneath her jaw.

'And?'

'And there's nothing – no one – standing in the way of our wedding.'

He felt the tension – pure anticipation – tighten her spine.

'They agreed to Wednesday?'

He nodded. 'Wednesday.' Raising his head, he looked into her bright eyes, then bent his head again. 'On Wednesday next, you'll be mine.'

Chapter Eleven

That evening, Amelia and her mother attended Lady Hogarth's musicale. On the list of social events Luc most hated, musicales ranked at the top. Consequently, he went to dinner with friends, then ambled around to Watier's.

An hour later, inwardly disgusted, he handed his cane to Lady Hogarth's butler. The man bowed, silently indicating the long corridor that led to the music room. Hardly necessary; a pained cauterwauling emanated from that direction. Suppressing a wince, Luc strolled toward the screeching.

Reaching the arched doorway, he paused and reconnoitered; the room was packed with ladies, mostly matrons, some of Amelia's age but few of the younger set. There were other balls on tonight; his mother and sisters had planned to attend two. Lady Hogarth's event had attracted those who considered themselves musical aficionados or who were, like Amelia and Louise, in some way connected.

There were few gentlemen present. Grimly accepting he'd stand out like a crow among seagulls, Luc waited until the soprano was well launched, then strolled nonchalantly to where Amelia was seated along one wall.

She saw him, blinked, but managed not to gawp. Louise, beside her, glanced around to see what had distracted Amelia; her gaze fell on him – her eyes narrowed.

He'd been a tad late – an hour late to be precise – in returning her daughter that afternoon. Amelia had slipped straight upstairs; he hadn't waited to exchange words with Louise. Her expression stated she had no difficulty guessing precisely what to make of that.

Bowing, first to Louise, then Amelia, he stepped into the space beside Amelia's chair, resting his hand on its back.

And pretended to listen to the music.

He hated sopranos.

Luckily, the recital lasted only another ten minutes. Just long enough for him to fabricate an answer to the fraught question of what had possessed him to appear.

As the applause died, Amelia twisted in her chair and looked up at him. 'What ...?' Her hand rose to grip his on the chair back.

He'd met her gaze, but her touch distracted him. He looked at their hands, after a frozen instant managed to catch his breath, then smoothly turned his hand, closing his fingers around hers. Beneath his fingertips, the feel of the ring he'd placed on her finger that afternoon elicited a primitive jolt of satisfaction.

'There's no difficulty – no problem.' He answered the question he'd seen flaring in her eyes. Meeting them again, he bent closer. 'I wanted to warn you I've placed a notice in the *Gazette* – it'll appear tomorrow morning.'

226

Glancing at the female crowd about them, most only just noticing his presence, knowing the hiatus that had permitted him even this much private speech would continue for mere seconds, he added, 'I didn't want you to be taken by surprise when half the *ton* descends on Brook Street in the morning.'

She studied his eyes, then smiled – a natural, artless smile, yet behind it he sensed a lingering trace of that other smile that never failed to tease him.

'I'd assumed you'd do something of the sort, but thank you for the confirmation.' She rose, shaking out her turquoise silk gown.

He caught her slipping shawl, draped it over her shoulders. She looked back at him, smiled again – this time, in commiseration. 'I'm afraid we're for it.'

They were; those who'd attended the Hightham Hall house party had had a whole day to spread their news. Expectations were running high; his appearance tonight had only fanned the flames.

Besieged, he had no option than to stand by Amelia's side and deflect the arch queries as best he could. His temper growled, but he reined it in, aware its irritation was entirely his own fault. The temptation to see her, to confirm that she was there, happy and content – that she'd recovered from being introduced to the concept that a desk could be used for activities other than writing – had crept up on him, niggling until it had seemed the easier of all evils simply to give in. Having surrendered to such weakness, this – coping with the avid interest of the matrons – was the price he had to pay.

Having appeared at all, he felt compelled to remain and escort Amelia and Louise home; his social mask anchored in place, he stoically remained by Amelia's side and refused to be drawn, refused to be tempted into any confirmation of what the *Gazette* would reveal tomorrow.

Tomorrow was soon enough for these harpies to learn of his fate. They could gloat then, out of his sight.

Amelia held to the same line, neither confirming nor denying what everyone suspected was the truth. Tomorrow they'd all know, and she'd have to share; tonight was her moment to hug the knowledge to herself, to savor her victory.

Incomplete though it was. Yet she'd never imagined that he'd fall in love with her just like that, purely because she suggested they marry. But they'd soon be wed, and she'd have time and opportunity aplenty to open his eyes, to lead him to see her as something more than just his bride.

She was used to social discourse, accustomed to the frequent need to slide around or ignore impertinent questions. Dealing with the inquiries of the many who flocked about them, those who'd spoken stepping back to let others take their place, was as easy as breathing. Under cover of the incessant conversation, she slanted a glance at her husband-to-be.

As usual, she could divine little, not now, not in public. Yet in those private moments they shared ... she was becoming more adept at reading him then. The hour and more they'd spent that afternoon in his study had been one such moment. One thing she was now quite confident of: he had never given his heart to any other woman.

It was there, hers to claim if she was willing to brave the fates and seize it. She knew him well; at some instinctive level she sensed his mind, was already close enough to him to, sometimes, know what he felt. That afternoon, when he'd had her laid across his desk, his to savor and take as he wished, there'd been something in his eyes, some recognition that with her, between him and her, there was something more than the merely physical.

The suspicion that he might already have recognized some deeper link between them had intensified later, when, with her slumped, deliciously exhausted, on his lap, he'd slipped the pearl-and-diamond ring – the betrothal ring that had been in his family for generations – on her finger. The moment had, at least for her, shimmered with emotion; she was willing to wager he hadn't been immune.

A first glimmer of the ultimate victory she sought, or so she hoped.

Her gaze had remained on his face too long; he turned, met it, raised a brow. She only smiled and turned back to the matrons eager to extract her news. And let her mind dwell on that ultimate victory.

The evening was drawing to a close when Miss Quigley approached. Although as curious as the others, Amelia and Luc's putative relationship was not uppermost in her mind. 'I wondered, Miss Cynster' —Miss Quigley lowered her voice, turning a little aside from the rest— 'did you by any chance see Aunt Hilborough's lorgnettes lying about anywhere at Hightham Hall?'

'Her lorgnettes?' Amelia remembered them – anyone who'd met Lady Hilborough would; she wielded the item more to point than to look. 'No.' She thought back, then shook her head decisively. 'I'm sorry. I didn't.'

Miss Quigley sighed. 'Ah, well – it was worth

inquiring.' She glanced around, then lowered her voice further. 'Mind you, now I've learned Mr. Mountford is missing his snuffbox, and Lady Orcott her perfume flask, I have to say I'm beginning to wonder.'

'Good heavens.' Amelia stared. 'But perhaps the items were misplaced ...?'

Miss Quigley shook her head. 'We sent back to Hightham Hall the instant we reached London. Lady Orcott and Mr. Mountford did the same. You can imagine – Lady Hightham must have been quite beside herself. Hightham Hall has been searched, but none of the missing items were found.'

Amelia met Miss Quigley's serious gaze. 'Oh dear.' She looked to where Louise stood not far away, chatting to some others. 'I must tell Mama – I doubt she's checked her jewelry case, let alone all those other little things one takes. And Lady Calverton, too.' She looked back at Miss Quigley. 'Neither she nor her girls are here tonight.'

Miss Quigley nodded. 'It appears we all need to be on our guard.'

Their gazes met – neither needed to specify just what they needed to guard against. There was, it seemed, a thief among the *ton*.

At eight the next morning, Luc sat alone at his breakfast table and studied his copy of that morning's *Gazette*.

He'd deliberately risen early – long before his sisters would be up and about. He'd come down to see – to stare at, to ponder – his fate, his destiny, printed in black-and-white.

There it was – a short, sensible notice informing

230

the world that Lucien Michael Ashford, sixth Viscount Calverton, of Calverton Chase in Rutlandshire, was to marry Amelia Eleanor Cynster, daughter of Lord Arthur and Lady Louise Cynster of Upper Brook Street, at Somersham Place on Wednesday, June 16.

Laying the paper down, he sipped his coffee, and tried to define what he felt. The primary emotion he could identify was a simple one: impatience. As for the rest . . .

There was a great deal more swirling inside him – triumph, irritation, anticipation, deprecation – even a faint lick of desperation, if he was truthful. And underneath them all ranged that unnameable force, grown stronger, more powerful – more compelling, more demanding.

Just where it would lead him – how far it would drive him – he didn't know.

His gaze fell to the paper, to the notice therein.

A moment later, he drained his mug, rose and strolled from the breakfast parlor. He paused in the front hall to collect his riding gloves.

It no longer mattered where the path led – he was committed, publicly and privately, and despite all uncertainties, he did not, not for a minute, question the rightness of his direction.

The future was his, to make of it what he pleased.

Drawing his gloves through his hands, he grimaced. Unfortunately, his future now contained her, and she wasn't a force he could completely control.

The clop of hooves on the cobbles reached him; with a nod to the footman who hurried to open the door, he strode out of his house.

Pausing on the porch, he lifted his face to the morning sunshine and mentally looked ahead, weighed up the immediate future. When all was considered, he still felt the same.

Impatient.

While Luc rode in Hyde Park, not far away, a young lady entered the garden at the center of Connaught Square, and approached a gentleman garbed in a long, drab driving coat standing beneath the branches of an ancient oak.

As she neared, the lady inclined her head stiffly. 'Good morning, Mr. Kirby.'

Her voice squeaked.

Kirby stirred and nodded brusquely. 'What did you get this time?'

The young lady glanced around, nervousness escalating in the face of Kirby's dismissive contempt. He watched, unmoved, as she lifted a bag – a cloth sack of the type maids used when shopping; fumbling within, she drew forth a snuffbox.

Kirby took it; he glanced around, confirming they were unobserved, then raised the box so the light struck the miniature painting on the lid.

'Is it . . .' The young lady swallowed, then whispered, 'Do you think it will be worth something?'

Kirby lowered his arm; the box disappeared into one of the capacious pockets of his coat. 'You have a good eye. It'll fetch a few guineas. What else?'

The lady handed over a perfume flask, crystal with a gold lid, a pair of lorgnettes, old but riddled with small diamonds, and a pair of small candlesticks, silver and finely wrought.

Kirby briefly assessed each item; one by one, they

disappeared into his pockets. 'Quite a nice little haul.'
He saw the young lady flinch, observed her dispas-
sionately. 'Your excursion to Hightham Hall was well
worthwhile.' Voice lowering, he added, 'I'm sure
Edward will be grateful.'

The young lady looked up. 'Have you heard from
him?'

Kirby studied her face, then calmly replied, 'His
latest communication painted a grim picture. When
such as Edward are cast off' —he shrugged— 'it's not
easy for them to find their feet in the gutter.'

The lady sighed despondently and looked away.

Kirby was silent for a moment, then smoothly said,
'I've heard rumors of a wedding.' He pretended not
to notice the stricken look in the lady's eyes as she
swung to face him; instead, drawing that morning's
Gazette from another pocket, he gave his attention to
the item he'd circled. 'It appears it'll be held at
Somersham Place next Wednesday.'

Lifting his gaze, he fixed it on her face. 'You'll be
attending, I'm sure, and that's an opportunity too
good to miss.'

One hand rising to the lace at her throat, the lady
shook her head. 'No – I *can't!*'

Kirby studied her for a moment, then said, 'Before
you make that decision, hear me out. The Cynsters
are as rich as bedamned – wealthy beyond belief.
Word has it Somersham Place is crammed full of
objects and ornaments collected over the centuries by
members of a family who've always had the means to
indulge their expensive tastes. Anything you pick up
there will be worth a small fortune, yet it'll be one
small item from a sprawling mansion filled to bursting with similar things. The chances are one or two

things will never be missed.

'And we shouldn't forget that Somersham Place is only one of several ducal residences. On top of that, there are the residences of other family members – not all, perhaps, will be as richly endowed, but all will contain artwork and ornaments of the highest standard – of that you may be sure.

'Now, let's contrast this with Edward's dire situation.' Kirby paused, as if selecting his words, censoring his knowledge; when he continued, his tone was somber, subdued. 'It would not be untrue to say Edward's case is desperate.'

Fixing the young lady with a hard and steady gaze, he went on, 'Edward has nothing – as he wrote in his letter to you, his brother has refused to support him, so he's reduced to eking out a living in any way he can. A rat-infested garrett, stale bread and water his only food, he's at the limit of his resources and in a very bad way.' Kirby heaved a tight sigh and looked across the square at the houses fronting it. 'I seek only to help him, but I've already given all I can – and I don't have access to the places, to the homes, to the people who own things it won't hurt them to lose.'

The young lady had paled; she swung away – Kirby reached out to haul her back, but she turned back of her own accord, wringing her hands. He lowered his arm unobtrusively.

'In his letter, he only asked me to get those two things – the inkstand and the perfume flask. He said they belonged to his grandparents and had been promised to him – they were his, all I did was to bring them to you so he could have them.' The lady lifted her eyes, beseechingly, to Kirby's face. 'Surely, if he believed those two things would see him through, then together with the other items' —she nodded at Kirby's pockets— 'the ones I've just given you, and the others, too, then Edward should have enough to survive for a few months?'

Kirby's smile was rueful, patronizing, but understanding. 'I'm afraid, my dear, that Edward is, in his present arena, no more up to snuff than you. Because he so desperately needs the money these items will bring, he cannot get much for them. That's the way such things work.' He paused, then added, 'As I said, he's in a very bad way. Indeed . . .' He seemed to recollect himself and stopped, then, after transparently wrestling with his conscience while the young lady watched, he sighed and met her gaze. 'I should not say such a thing, yet I greatly fear I cannot answer for what he will do if we cannot get him decent funds soon.'

The young lady's eyes grew round. 'You mean . . . ?'

Kirby grimaced. 'He won't be the first sprig of an aristocratic house who couldn't face life in a foreign gutter.'

One hand rising to her lips, the young lady turned away. Kirby watched from under hooded lids, and waited.

After some moments, she drew in a shaky breath, and turned back to him. 'You said anything, any little item from Somersham Place, will be worth a small fortune?'

Kirby nodded.

'So if I take something from there, and give it to you, then Edward will have enough to live on.'

Kirby's nod was immediate. 'It'll keep him from starving.'

'Or doing anything else?'

'That's in the lap of the gods, but at least it'll give him a chance.'

The young lady stared across the square, then she drew in a breath, and nodded. 'Very well.' Lifting her chin, she met Kirby's gaze. 'I'll find something – something good.'

Kirby studied her for a moment, then inclined his head. 'Your devotion is to be applauded.'

Briefly, he told her where to meet him, where and when she should bring her next contribution to Edward's well-being. She agreed and they parted. Kirby watched her cross the square, then turned and strode in the opposite direction.

Why the devil had he decided on Wednesday?

Returning to Calverton House on Monday afternoon, Luc stalked into his study, shut the door, then flung himself into an armchair and stared at the empty hearth.

If he'd said Monday instead ...

He'd avoided Upper Brook Street on the day the notice announcing their nuptials had appeared in the *Gazette*. Predictably, all fashionable London, or so it had seemed, had descended on the Cynsters to congratulate Amelia and gossip about the wedding. Even here, at Calverton House, his mother had been besieged by callers throughout the morning; after luncheon, she'd shrewdly decided to join Amelia and Louise in Brook Street, so the wishful could have at them all at once.

Saturday evening they'd spent under the full glare of avid – not to say rabid – scrutiny at Lady Harris's soirée, one of the last major engagements before the *ton* retired to their estates for summer. The weather had already turned warm, the ladies' gowns commensurately revealing. To his relief, Amelia had restrained herself; she'd appeared in a demure sheath of gold silk to parade on his arm, ineffably calm and courteous to all those who paused to wish them well.

He hadn't had a chance for so much as a moment in private with her. Lecturing himself that the evening was, after all, a once-in-a-lifetime occasion, he'd accepted the fact with what he'd thought at the time to be reasonable grace. The intent look Amelia had bent on him when they'd ended the evening and parted, under her mother's watchful eye, had suggested that she, at least, had seen past his mask – sensed the restless dissatisfaction he'd concealed.

Deciding he wasn't averse to her sensing his impatience, he'd called the next afternoon – Sunday – expecting to whisk her away, to spend at least some moments alone with her, moments with her attention all his, only to discover the females of her family had congregated to confer and plan the wedding.

Vane, having escorted his wife, Patience, to the gathering, was leaving as he arrived. 'Take my advice – White's would be much more to your taste.'

It had taken less than a second for him to consider, and disgustedly agree. White's at that hour was thoroughly unexciting; it was, however, safe.

On Sunday evening, he and his mother had hosted the more or less traditional formal dinner for the families of bride and groom. He'd never seen his staff so excited; Cottsloe spent the entire evening beaming fit to burst. Mrs. Higgs exceeded her own high standards; despite once again being denied any chance of

237

a private word with Amelia, he had to admit the evening had gone well.

Devil, of course, had been present. They'd come upon each other in the drawing room later in the evening. Devil's eyes had searched his, then he'd grinned. 'Still not broached the painful subject?'

He'd calmly turned to survey the company. 'You can talk.' He'd waited only a heartbeat before adding, 'However, I can assure you no mention of that particular topic will occur before the wedding.'

'Still determined?'

'Absolutely.'

Devil had sighed exaggeratedly. 'Don't say I didn't warn you.'

'I won't.' Turning, he'd met Devil's eyes. 'You could, of course, send me pointers . . .'

Devil had humphed and slapped his shoulder. 'Don't press your luck.'

They'd parted amicably, their common difficulty a bond. The fact had only served to raise the issue more definitely, embed it more firmly in his mind.

He would have to tell her sometime.

The knowledge only fueled his impatience.

He'd called in Upper Brook Street that morning, early enough, so he'd thought, only to have the butler, old Colthorpe, gravely inform him that Amelia and Louise were already in the drawing room with four other ladies.

Swallowing his curses, he'd considered sending in a note, asking her to slip away. Then the front door bell pealed. Colthorpe had caught his eye. 'Perhaps, my lord, you might prefer to wait in the parlor?'

He had, listening as the bevy of elegant matrons who'd come to call were shown into the drawing room. In to see Amelia.

With a growing sense of disappointment, and a hollow, indefinable unease, he'd accepted the inevitable and departed the house. He hadn't left a note.

He'd gone to his club; various friends had taken him to lunch. Some would travel down to Cambridgeshire tomorrow, as would he; that afternoon had been the last time they and he could celebrate as all bachelors. And celebrate they had, yet although he'd laughed and outwardly enjoyed their company, his mind had already moved on – his thoughts had been fixed not on old friends, but on the woman who would be his wife.

Eyes trained unseeing on the cold hearth, he tried to decide what he felt – how he felt. Why he felt as he did. When the clock struck six, no further forward, he rose and went up to change.

Lady Cardigan's grand ball had one thing in its favor – it was a ball, it therefore featured dances. Times during which he would have Amelia in his arms, albeit in the middle of a dance floor. In his present state, he was thankful for even that.

'Are you all right?' she asked, the instant they stepped out in the first waltz. 'What's the matter?'

He stared – very nearly glared – at her. 'Nothing.'

Amelia let her joyful mask slip long enough to flash him a disbelieving look. 'Don't.' She deliberately used his earlier injunction. 'I can see it in your eyes.'

They were not just dark but turbulent; the sight left her certain something was wrong. In her opinion, they were too close to the vital moment – exchanging their vows – to let anything stand in their way.

'Stop being difficult.' She felt her own chin setting

239

and had to force her features to ease.

When he simply hid behind his impassive mask, she drew a deep breath, and broached what she'd decided had to be the problem. 'Is it money?'

'What?' He looked thunderstruck, but that might simply be his reaction to any lady discussing such a subject with him.

'Do you need funds for something – now, before the wedding?'

His features were no longer impassive. He looked as horrified as she'd ever seen him. 'For God's sake! *No*. I don't need—'

His eyes flashed. She'd obviously hit a nerve, but remained unrepentant. 'That just goes to show that you ought simply to tell me, rather than leave me to guess.' She waited while they went through the turns at the end of the room, conscious of his arms tightening, drawing her close – and then of him forcing them to ease so they wouldn't cause a sensation.

'So what is the matter then?' she demanded as, in acceptable order, they swung back up the room.

He looked down, trapped her eyes. 'It's not money I need.'

She searched his eyes, somewhat relieved. 'Very well – what then?'

Exasperation and frustration reached her clearly, yet he didn't rush to answer her. They were halfway back up the room before he replied, 'I just wish it was Wednesday already.'

Her brows rose; she smiled spontaneously. 'I thought it was brides who were eager for their wedding.'

His midnight blue eyes locked with hers. 'It's not the wedding I'm eager for.'

240

If she'd had any doubt of his meaning, the expression in his eyes – not just heated, but knowing, awakening – quite deliberately stirring – memories of their previous intimacies – dispelled it. Warmth, definite but not too intense, rose in her cheeks, but she refused to lower her eyes, refused to play the innocent when, thanks to him, she was no longer that. 'Are you sure you want to travel on that afternoon?' Brows lightly rising, she held his gaze. 'We could always remain at Somersham for the night.'

The line of his lips eased; the intensity in his eyes did not. 'No. With the Chase only a few hours away ...'

The waltz ended and the music died; he whirled her to a halt, caught her hand. Trapped her gaze as he brushed a kiss on her fingers. 'It'll be infinitely more appropriate for us to retire there.'

She had to quell a shiver – an instinctive reaction to the subtle suggestion in his voice, to a situation that was looming as an unknown. While he'd let her organize the wedding entirely as she pleased, he'd insisted that after the wedding breakfast they would leave for Calverton Chase. Her first night as his wife, therefore, would be passed in his ancestral home.

A sense of, a commitment to, starting out as they meant to go on seemed to hover between them, as if they both knew it in themselves, and now recognized it in the other.

Somewhat cautiously, she acknowledged the fact with an inclination of her head, a smile, not light but intent, curving her lips. He saw – distracted, he glanced up as others bustled toward them – quickly looked back and nodded, his eyes serious as they touched hers.

With that mutual, unvoiced agreement, they turned to smile and chat with those who gathered about them.

The evening progressed as such evenings had before, but this time it was only during the two waltzes they shared that they were private enough to talk – and during their second waltz, neither bothered with words.

She was breathless when that waltz ended, prefectly ready to stand beside the dance floor and chat to acquaintances while the tension that had seized her nerves, that had sent tingling anticipation spreading over her skin, slowly faded.

Toward the end of the evening, Minerva approached; leaving Luc to deal with Lady Melrose and Mrs. Highbury, Amelia gave his mother her attention. They quickly confirmed the members of his family who would be attending the wedding; Minerva was about to move on when Amelia saw her gaze lock on the pearl-and-diamond ring Luc had given her.

Smiling, she extended her hand, displaying the ring. 'It's lovely, isn't it? Luc told me how the betrothal ring was passed down through the family.'

Minerva studied the ring, then smiled warmly. 'It suits you perfectly, dear.' Her gaze moved on to her son; her smile faded. 'If you don't mind, Amelia, I'd like a quick word with Luc.'

'Of course.' Turning back to the wider conversation, Amelia drew the two ladies' attention, releasing Luc to his mother.

Luc turned to Minerva; she put her hand on his arm and urged him a few steps away. He leaned closer when she spoke, her voice low.

'Amelia just showed me her ring.'

Before he could stop himself, he'd stiffened. His

mother fixed him with a sharp glance.

'It seems,' she continued, 'that Amelia believes it to be the betrothal ring passed down over generations of Ashfords.'

He held her gaze; after a long moment, he grudgingly admitted, 'I mentioned the betrothal ring when I gave her that one.'

'And doubtless left her to make the connection herself?' When he said nothing, she shook her head. 'Oh, Luc.'

It wasn't quite condemnation he saw in her eyes, but whatever it was, it made him feel twelve years old. 'I didn't want her to worry about where the ring came from.'

Minerva's brows rose. 'Or to think too far along those lines?'

She waited, but he refused to say more, to justify his stance or his behavior.

After a moment of reading his eyes – she was one of the few who could regularly manage it – she sighed. 'I promised not to meddle, and I won't. But beware – the longer you delay making your revelation, the more difficult it will be.'

'So I've been told.' They were talking of two different revelations, but one led inexorably to the other. He looked at Amelia. 'I promise on my honor I will tell her. Just not yet.'

He glanced at Minerva; again she shook her head, this time with a latent smile. Pressing his arm, she stepped away.

'You'll go to the devil in your own way. You always have.'

He watched her walk away, then rejoined Amelia.

*

243

Early the next morning, Amelia left for Somersham Place in company with her father and mother, her brother Simon and her younger sisters Henrietta and Mary, their butler Colthorpe and various family servants. The latter were to lend their support to the staff at the Place, Devil's principal residence, a huge sprawling mansion that in many ways represented the heart of the ducal dynasty.

They arrived late in the morning to find other family members already in residence, among them Helena, the Dowager, Devil's mother, and old Great-aunt Clara, summoned from her home in Somerset. Lady Osbaldestone, a distant connection, rattled up in her coach on their heels; Simon dutifully went to help her into the house.

Honoria and Devil had come down the day before with their young family. Amelia's twin, Amanda, and her new husband, Martin, Earl of Dexter, Luc's cousin, were rushing down from their home in the north; they were expected later that day. Catriona and Richard had sent their regrets – coming down from Scotland at such short notice, with a new baby to boot, had simply been impossible.

Luc, his mother, Emily, and Anne were expected later in the afternoon. By dint of careful questioning, Amelia discovered that Luc had been given a room in the opposite wing to hers, as distant as possible. Which in a house the size of the Place, was distant indeed; any notion she might have entertained of visiting him that night was effectively quashed.

The company were just sitting down to luncheon when the rattle of wheels on gravel heralded another arrival. A few minutes later, two light voices were heard, earnestly, just a little nervously, greeting Webster.

Amelia set down her napkin and exchanged a smile with Louise. They both rose and went out to the hall; guessing the identity of the latest arrivals, Honoria also rose and followed more slowly in their wake.

'I do hope we were expected,' a girl in a faded carriage dress, thick spectacles perched on her nose, told Webster.

Before Webster could reply, her companion, in a similarly faded dress, piped up, 'Actually, you might not remember who we are – we have grown somewhat since we last visited.'

Louise laughed and swept forward, saving Webster from potentially embarrassing assurances. 'Of course you're expected, Penelope.' She enveloped Luc's youngest sister in a fond embrace, then, passing Penelope to Amelia, turned to the other. 'And as for you, miss, no one who lays eyes on you ever forgets who you are.'

Portia, the third of Luc's sisters, wrinkled her nose as she returned Louise's embrace. 'As I recall I was a grubby little squirt last time I was here, so I was hoping he might.'

'Oh, no, Miss Portia,' Webster assured her, his customary magisterial calm in place but with a twinkle in his eye. 'I remember you quite well.'

Emerging from a wild hug with Amelia, Portia pulled a face at him, then turned to greet Honoria.

'Indeed, my dear.' Honoria's eyes danced over Portia's jet-black hair, not curly but falling naturally in deep waves, 'I really don't think you can hope to be forgotten. Any crimes you commit will haunt you forever.'

Portia sighed. 'With these eyes as well as the hair, I suppose it's inevitable.' The black hair and dark blue eyes that in Luc were so dramatically masculine, in Portia were startlingly feminine. A born tomboy, however, she'd never appreciated the fact.

'Never mind.' With a smile, Amelia linked one arm in Portia's and slipped her other arm around Penelope's waist. 'We're just sitting down to lunch, and I'm sure you must be starving.'

Penelope pushed her spectacles up on her nose. 'Oh, we're always interested in food.'

Amelia spent the rest of the afternoon greeting arrivals and helping relatives to their rooms. She had little time to think of the wedding other than as a list of things to be done; even when, later in the afternoon, she tried on her wedding gown for a final fitting, with Amanda, Louise, and the rest of her aunts looking on, not the slightest hint of nervousness assailed her.

Later, she and Amanda retired to her room, to lie on the bed and talk – as they always had, as they always would, married or not. When, weary from traveling, Amanda dozed off, Amelia silently rose and crept from the room.

She'd wandered this house from her earliest years; slipping out through a secondary door into the grounds without being seen was easy. Under the welcoming cover of the thickly leaved oaks, she crossed the lawns to the one place she was sure of being alone, of finding a moment of blessed peace.

The sun was sinking, but still shone strongly between the trees as she crossed the clearing before the small church. Built of stone, it had stood for centuries, and seen scores of Cynster marriages, all of which, so the story went, had lasted through time.

That wasn't why she'd chosen to marry beneath its ancient beams. Her parents had been married here; she'd been christened here. It had simply seemed right, the right place to end one phase of her life and embark simultaneously on the next.

She paused in the tiny porch and felt the peace reach for her, the heavy sense of timelessness, of grace and deep joy, that permeated the very stones. Reaching out, she pushed the door; it swung soundlessly open and she stepped in. And realized she wasn't the only one who had come seeking peace.

Luc stood facing the altar; hands in his breeches pockets, he looked up at the oriel window high above. The jeweled colors were magnificent, but it wasn't them that filled his mind.

He couldn't put his finger on what did, couldn't sort one feeling from another, pull one strand free of the turbulent whole – they'd all merged, all subsumed beneath, feeding into, one overriding compulsion.

To have Amelia as his wife.

It would happen here, tomorrow morning. All he had to do was wait, and she would be his.

The violence of his need rocked him, even more so when examined in a place such as this, where there was nothing and no one to distract him from seeing the whole, from acknowledging the frightening truth.

Even more, this place, silent witness to the unions of centuries, steeped in their aura, at some level resonant with the power that flowed through those unions, connecting the past with the present, flowing on to touch the future – facing the fundamental reality of life seemed natural, even necessary, here.

He'd always felt there was something about Somersham Place; he'd visited intermittently over the years, always dimly aware of that special something, but only now did he see it clearly. Only now, with his mind – and if he was honest, his heart and his soul – attuned to the same drumbeat, the same driving need, the same warrior's desire.

Quite when it had grown so important to him, he didn't know. Perhaps the potential had always been there, just waiting for the right circumstance, the right woman, to give it life, to set it free.

To rule him.

He drew breath, refocused on the altar. That was what, when he married her tomorrow, he would be accepting. When he made his vows, they would not be just to her, not just to himself, but to something beyond them both.

Air stirred behind him; he looked around, and saw Amelia closing the door. Smiling gently, calmly, she came toward him; he turned and faced her.

She halted before him, close, but with space yet between them. She studied his eyes, her composure unruffled. Curious, but not demanding.

'Thinking?'

He'd been drinking in the sight of her face; he brought his gaze to her eyes, then nodded. Forced himself to raise his head and look around. 'It's a wonderful old place.' He looked back at her. 'You were right to choose it.'

Her smile deepened; she, too, looked around. 'I'm glad you think so.'

He didn't want to touch her – didn't want to risk it; he could feel desire humming through his veins, feel need prickling his skin. 'I'd assumed we wouldn't meet, at least not alone.'

'I don't think anyone imagined we would.'

He met her gaze, knew what she was thinking. For one instant, he considered telling her the truth, all of it. Getting it off his chest before tomorrow ...

But she still had to say 'I do.' Tomorrow.

He grimaced, gestured to the door, 'We'd better get back to the house, or some bright soul is going to realize we're both missing, and imaginations will run riot.'

She grinned, but turned and preceded him up the aisle. He reached past her to open the door – she stayed him, one hand on his arm.

Their eyes met, held – then she smiled, stretched up, and touched her lips to his. Kissed him gently, lightly; the battle to suppress his reaction left him reeling.

Before he lost the fight, she drew back, met his eyes again.

'Thank you for agreeing to my proposal, and for changing your mind.'

Amelia held his gaze – black as night – then smiled and turned to the door. After an instant's hiatus, he opened it. She went out, waited for him to follow and close the door, then, very correctly, side by side, they walked back to the house.

Chapter Twelve

The next morning dawned fine; a playful breeze wafted about the lawns and set the tone for the day. It flirted with curls and ribbons, ruffled ladies' gowns, teased flounces and frills. People laughed; the breeze caught their mirth and dispersed it impartially over the richly dressed throng – the relatives and close connections invited to witness the ceremony.

It went forward without a hitch, without a single moment of awkwardness or panic. Once the gay crowd had assembled in the small church, gentlemen filling the aisles while their ladies took the pews, Luc stepped forward to face the altar, Martin, his cousin, Amelia's brother-in-law, by his side. Martin was in turn flanked by Simon, Amelia's brother, a nineteen-year-old stripling Luc had, courtesy of their families' closeness, even before the last few months considered in the light of a brother.

Martin, glancing first to his right, then his left, was moved to comment. 'This is becoming incestuous – you do realize after today we'll not only be cousins, but brothers-in-law, too?'

Luc shrugged. 'We always shared excellent taste.'

Simon snorted. 'More like you've both inherited a familial tendency to succumb to the charms of women with whom no sane man would dally.'

Thus spake a Cynster; the obvious riposte rose to Luc's lips, but as he glanced across to deliver it he caught Martin's eye – saw the same thought mirrored in his cousin's face. They both knew the truth; they exchanged knowing smiles, then faced the altar again, by mutual agreement leaving Simon to learn of his fate by himself.

At that moment, from the mansion's front porch, Amelia, on Arthur's arm, stepped out on her journey into marriage. Attended by Amanda and Emily, she glowed with confidence, with the certainty of having finally achieved that of which she'd so long dreamed, with the satisfaction of having brought her dearest dream one step closer to full reality; indeed, she felt sure she was more than halfway there.

As they crossed the lawns and passed under the ancient trees, she leaned close to Arthur. 'Thank you.'

Returning her smile, he raised his brows. 'For what?'

'Why for having me, of course, and taking care of me for all these years. In a little while, I'll no longer be yours, but Luc's ... responsibility.'

She looked ahead, briefly sobering. She'd added the last word to soften the truth, but she knew what that truth was, and Arthur, a Cynster to his bones, knew, too. She glanced again at him, but his smile hadn't faltered.

'I'm glad you chose Luc – there may be ups and downs, but at base he's the kind who will never turn his back on his duties. His responsibilities.' Arthur patted her hand. 'And that augurs well.'

The church lay before them; Amelia grasped the moment to draw in a deep breath, to draw to herself the blessings of the years, then they entered, paused for only a moment, then, with a serene smile, radiant once more, she walked up the aisle to Luc's side.

He was waiting. Their eyes met, held, then he took her hand and she stepped up beside him; together they faced the altar.

Mr. Merryweather led them through the ceremony, delighted to be marrying another of the generation he'd baptized. They made their vows in strong, clear voices, then it was over, and they were man and wife.

She put back her veil, and Luc drew her to him, bent his head and set his lips to hers. A gentle kiss but a lengthy one; only she could feel the reined strength in the fingers curled about hers, sense the power of all he suppressed.

When he lifted his head, their eyes met, searched – briefly noted the underlying emotions that, despite their outward calmness, seethed behind their experienced facades – then, those facades firmly in place, they turned as one to receive the congratulations of their families and friends.

Luc hadn't believed impatience could ever escalate to this extent, to the point where it was a physical thing – a ravening beast inside him, clawing and howling for succor, for satisfaction. He hoped – prayed – that the promise of the fact she was now his, legally before God and all men, would be enough to see him through the day. As they stood side by side, accepting the wishes of those who crowded around to kiss Amelia and pump his hand, clap his shoulder, he was acutely aware of his inner tension, of how his nerves leapt, flexed – how they remained poised for action.

He wanted nothing more than to seize her, to lock her to his side, clear a path to the door, find a horse, and be far away from here – to whisk her away from this place that was hers, to a place that was his.

The sheer primitiveness of the feeling left him breathless, stunned – for the past decade, he'd thought himself an elegant sophisticate; what presently raged inside him was not sophisticated at all.

But he had a whole day to survive, and survive it he would. He had absolutely no intention of allowing anyone to know just how affected he was. Anyone other than Amelia, whose wide, cornflower blue eyes said she knew – and wasn't quite sure what she felt about it, how to interpret it – just as well. Other than Martin, who met his gaze, and smiled a too-knowing, too-understanding smile.

He'd briefly narrowed his eyes, but Martin guessing he could live with; the fact only confirmed that Martin knew what he was going through, which he only would had he gone through it himself.

The thought, if not precisely encouraging, at least made for resignation. If Martin had survived, he could, too.

A June wedding possessed numerous advantages, one of which was the chance of staging the wedding breakfast outside. The wide lawns of the Place provided a perfect setting; during the ceremony the staff had assembled long tables lined with chairs under the spreading branches bordering the main lawn.

The breakfast with its inevitable toasts turned into a riotous event. Because their families had always been close, their members so well acquainted, an informality prevailed that couldn't otherwise have been.

Amelia was thankful for the relaxed atmosphere, grateful when the breakfast slid into the easy, familiar comfort of a large family gathering. She was conscious of Luc's tension – conscious of the fact he was suppressing something – and she didn't know, couldn't think, what it was. She worried that it derived from their agreement – that now he'd actually done it and married her for her dowry, he wanted to depart, get away, leave behind the public charade they were enacting.

Everyone, of course, imagined they were in love, that being the norm for marriages celebrated here. In one respect, that was true – she was quite sure she was in love with him. She was equally sure the other half of the equation was possible, and that, given time and her devotion, it would come to be. But it wasn't there, in existence, yet; she could imagine the fact grated on Luc's pride, grated on his conscience ... that was what she sensed from him – a wish to leave, to put this day behind them.

As it was, they both knew their duties; the informality of the day made them easier to bear.

Once the meal was at an end, she and Luc parted, going in opposite directions around the long table, greeting, talking with and thanking their guests. Others rose, too; most of the gentlemen stood to stretch their legs, then gathered in small groups, discussing this and that, passing the time – getting out of the ladies' way.

One gentleman left a group and came to meet Amelia. She smiled and held out her hand. 'Michael!

I'm so glad you could come. Honoria tells me you've been very busy these last months.'

Michael Anstruther-Wetherby, Honoria's brother, grimaced as he pressed her hand. 'The way she puts it, I feel like an old man, buried among files and papers in the depths of Whitehall.'

She laughed. 'Isn't that true?' Michael was a Member of Parliament, one expected to go far; involved in numerous committees, he was widely tipped to step up to the ministry sooner rather than later.

'The papers and files unfortunately are. As for the age, I'll thank you not to be a minx.'

She laughed; he smiled and glanced about, giving her a glimpse of the silver at his temples, glinting through his otherwise thick brown hair. Michael was handsome in a quiet, inherently strong way. A quick calculation told her he must now be thirty-three. And still unmarried, yet to advance in his career as everyone fully expected – and as he was backed by both the Cynsters and his grandfather, the redoubtable Magnus Anstruther-Wetherby, that seemed a foregone conclusion – then he would have to bestir himself on the matrimonial front. Cabinet ministers were expected to be married.

'Magnus is over there.' Michael directed her gaze to the old man grumpily still at the table – Magnus was a martyr to gout and could not stand for long; he had Lady Osbaldestone beside him, to keep him in line. Amelia waved; lifting his huge head, Magnus nodded, bushy brows drawn down as they almost always were. Amelia grinned and turned back to Michael.

He was studying her. 'You know, I can remember

both you and Amanda when you first put up your hair
– at your first *informal* ball.'

She thought back; the memories made her smile.
'Honoria's first informal family gathering in the
music room at St. Ives House. How long ago that
seems.'

'Six years.'

'A bit more.' Her gaze went to her twin, leaning,
laughing, on her husband's arm. 'How young
Amanda and I were then.'

Michael grinned. 'Six years is a long time at this
stage in your lives. You've both blossomed, and now
you're moving on. Amanda to the Peak District, and
I hear you'll be in Rutlandshire?'

'Yes – Calverton Chase isn't far from here.'

'So you'll have your own establishment to run – I
know Minerva's more than ready to hand over the
reins.'

Amelia acknowledged that with a smile, her
thoughts shifting to the future, to what now lay before
her. To the next stage. 'I expect there will be quite a
lot to do.'

'Indubitably – I'm sure you'll handle it wonderfully. But now I fear I must leave you. There's a
matter I must deal with in Hampshire, one I must
attend to in person.'

'A constituency matter?'

His brows quirked. 'Indeed – you might well call it
that.'

He bowed, then, with his practiced, easy smile,
stepped back, saluted her, and strolled away across
the lawn. Amelia saw Devil cross to have a last word;
from the way Magnus followed his grandson's depar-
ture, Michael had already taken his leave there.

Scanning the crowd surrounding the tables, filling the shade with color and laughter, Amelia located Luc. He'd been checking on his sisters. Anne, Portia, and Penelope, together with Fiona, invited and allowed to attend as a special treat, were sitting about one end of the long table with others of similar age, including Amelia's younger cousins, Heather, Eliza, and Angelica. Simon was presiding at the very end; he exchanged some negligent remark with Luc, who laughed, clapped him on the shoulder, and left him.

Moving along the table, Luc heard his name called, in an imperious accent he knew better than to ignore. Looking over the heads, he saw the Dowager watching; he made his way to her.

'Come.' She waved. 'Give your arm. We will stroll and you can tell me how lucky you are to have married my niece, and how you will extend yourself to the utmost to keep her happy.'

Outwardly smiling, inwardly alert, Luc helped Helena from her chair, then dutifully gave her his arm; by mutual accord, they strolled away from the gathering into the relative privacy deeper under the trees.

'You will be happy, you know.'

The comment caught him unprepared; he glanced at Helena, and found himself trapped in her pale green eyes, eyes that he knew from experience always saw too much. She was worse than his mother; very little escaped the Dowager Duchess of St. Ives.

She smiled, patted his hand, then looked ahead. 'When you have witnessed as many weddings as I, you simply know.'

'How ... comforting.' He wondered why she was telling him – wondered what she knew.

257

'Just like this place.' Helena gestured to the church, standing quiet and peaceful, basking in the sunshine, its moment past, its job done. 'It is as if the very stones possess some magic.'

He was struck by how close to his thoughts of yesterday her observation came. 'Have there never been any less-than-successful Cynster marriages?' He knew of at least one.

'Not that were celebrated here. And none in my time.'

That last was said with decision, as if warning that if his and Amelia's union did not live up to expectations, they would have to answer to her.

'That other you are thinking of – Arthur's first marriage – was not celebrated here. I was told that Sebastian forbade it, and in truth, Arthur refused to request the boon.'

And if Helena had been old Sebastian's duchess at the time, rather than a young girl in France, Luc felt sure that ill-fated union would never have been permitted at all.

'You are ...' —he struggled to find words, settled for— 'a believer, are you not?'

'*Mais oui*! I have lived too much, seen too much, ever to doubt that the power exists.'

He felt her green gaze, sensed her gentle amusement, but refused to let her catch his eye.

'Ah,' she said, facing forward again. 'You are resisting – is that it?'

As usual in conversations with Helena, one came to the point of wondering how one had come to this. Luc said nothing, reacted not at all.

She smiled again, patted his hand. 'Never mind. Just remember – whatever is not yet resolved between you, the power is there – you can accept it and wield it anytime you choose. No matter the difficulty, all you need do is ask, and the power will deliver it up to you – right the wrong, ease the way, whatever is necessary.'

She paused, then, amusement again in her tone, she continued, 'Of course, to call on that power you first need to acknowledge it exists.'

'I knew there was a catch.'

She laughed, and turned them back toward the tables. '*Eh, bien* – you will manage. Trust me – I know.'

Luc raised his brows fleetingly; he wasn't going to argue.

He did, however, wonder if she was right.

It was finally – at last! – time to leave. The afternoon was waning; Amelia disappeared indoors and changed into a new carriage dress of cerulean blue, then returned to the lawns. To Luc's side.

There was a moment of crazed jostling over her bouquet – her throw went wild, it landed in a branch, then fell onto Magnus's head, eliciting much laughter and a host of ribald suggestions. Then the younger crew, after hugging them and bidding them farewell, went down to the lake. Their elders remained in their chairs under the trees; the others – the Bar Cynster and their wives, Amanda and Martin, all crowded around, kissing Amelia, shaking Luc's hand – and offering more suggestions, to Amelia as well as to Luc. At last, they let them go, standing in a group to watch as Luc and Amelia, accompanied by Devil and Honoria, strolled to where the Calverton traveling coach stood before the porch, horses prancing.

259

The distance was sufficient to render the moment private.

They reached the carriage; Honoria, suspiciously misty-eyed, drew Amelia into her embrace. 'It's almost seven years since I first met you, here, on the gravel beside a carriage.'

Their gazes met; both remembered – then they smiled, touched cheeks.

Honoria whispered, 'Remember – whatever you do, enjoy it.'

Smothering a laugh, Amelia nodded; she was about to climb into the carriage when Devil caught her, hugged her, kissed her cheek, then tossed her up.

He turned to Luc. 'From now on, you get to catch her when she tumbles out.'

Luc glanced at Amelia – she grinned and settled back on the seat. Making a mental note to ask for an explanation later, he kissed Honoria's cheek, then held out his hand.

Devil gripped it; their gazes met, locked. 'I'll see you in town in September.'

Luc inclined his head. 'Indeed – we can catch up, and no doubt Gabriel will want to make a start on his new idea.'

'Presuming the preconditions have been met.'

One boot on the step, Luc raised a brow. 'Of course. And I daresay we'll be able to compare notes, you and I.'

They were much of a height. Devil held Luc's midnight blue gaze, his own pale gaze steady, then inclined his head, accepting the challenge. 'As you say.'

With a nod, Luc climbed up; Devil shut the door.

'Good-bye!' Honoria waved.

'Good luck!' Devil added.

The driver cracked his whip – the coach lurched, and rolled forward; slowly gathering speed, it rolled down the gently curving drive. Honoria and Devil stood side by side and watched until the avenue of oaks intervened, blocking the coach from sight.

Honoria heaved a sigh. 'Well, that's it for a while.' She turned to her spouse. 'And what was that all about? On what subject do you and Luc expect to compare notes?'

His gaze on the distant avenue, Devil paused, then looked down at his duchess. His wife. Looked into her misty grey eyes, the clear steady eyes that had first trapped his hardened heart.

'Have I ever told you that I love you?'

Honoria blinked, then opened her eyes wide. 'No. As you very well know.'

He could feel his face hardening. 'Well, I do.'

She – the mother of his three children, who now knew him better than anyone else in the world, even better than his mother – studied his eyes, then smiled. 'I know. I always have.' Linking her arm in his, she turned, not back to their guests but toward the rose garden around the side of the house. 'Did you think I didn't?'

He considered, allowing her to steer their steps. 'I suppose I always assumed you'd guessed.'

'So why the sudden confession?'

That was much harder to explain. They stepped down to the sunken garden, strolled past the rioting roses to the seat at its end. Honoria neither spoke nor prompted. They sat; together they looked back at the house – their home – steeped in the glories of the past, full of the laughter and cries of their children, the future incarnate.

'It's like a rite of passage,' Devil finally said. 'But not one that's connected with any other. At least, that's how it is for me – and some others.'

'Like Luc?'

Devil nodded. 'It's easier, for us, to live the reality rather than declare it, to acknowledge it in our hearts but not put it into words. Basically, to act the part without owning to the label.'

Her eyes on the house, Honoria followed his thoughts, tried to understand. 'But ... why? Oh, I can understand at first, but surely, over time, as you admit, actions speak the truth and the words become redundant—'

'No.' Devil shook his head. 'Those particular words never become worthless. Or easy.' He glanced at Honoria. 'They never lose their power.'

She could feel it now as she met his gaze. Understanding dawned; misty-eyed again, she smiled. 'Ah – I see. Power. So, to you, putting the fact into words—'

'Saying them out aloud.'

'Uttering them, declaring the truth, is like ...' She gestured, knowing what she meant yet not able to describe it.

Devil could, did. 'It's like giving an oath of fealty – not just by one's actions acknowledging your sovereign, but offering your sword and accepting and acknowledging another's power to rule you.' He met Honoria's gaze. 'Men like me – like Luc – we're conditioned never to give that final, binding oath, not until we're forced to it. To do so willingly goes against every precept, every ingrained rule.'

'You mean you – and Luc – are rather more ... primitive than most?'

Devil narrowed his eyes. 'It's possibly more accurate to say our instincts are less flexible. We're both heads of our houses, both raised to protect all that's ours – and we've both been raised knowing others are depending on us to do just that.'

She thought, then inclined her head. Then she smiled, turned into his arms, unsurprised when they immediately slid around her. Drawing his head to hers, she murmured, 'So ... does that mean I rule you?'

His lips, an inch from hers, curved wickedly. 'That's the only mitigating factor. Love may rule me, but only because it also rules you.'

Honoria closed the distance, set her lips to his, then let him take as he wished – she didn't care as long as that power still ruled, as long as love was there between them.

The essence of the present, an echo from the past, and a never-ending promise for forever.

The Calverton coach paused at the main gates of the Place, then rolled through, turning left onto the road that would eventually lead to Huntingdon. From there, they would head northwest through Thrapston and Corby, along decent roads. Lyddington lay north of Corby; Calverton Chase lay to the west of the small village.

Amelia had traveled the same road many times on visits to Calverton Chase. She assumed some of the anticipation gripping her was because the well-known destination had, mere hours ago, become her home.

The rest – the bulk – of that anticipation could be attributed to the Chase's owner. Luc sat beside her; anyone viewing him would think him relaxed. She knew better. She could feel the tension holding him, locked tight, a brittle net striving to contain some unseeable power.

She hadn't heard all of Devil's words, hadn't understood what she'd caught. The exchange had distracted Luc, left him thinking, far away ...

Grasping his sleeve, she shook. 'Did Devil guess?'

Luc turned his head and looked at her; his expression remained blank. 'Guess?'

'That we arranged our marriage – that money was at the heart of it.'

He stared at her for a long moment, then shook his head. 'No.' Resting his head against the squabs, he studied her; the light in the carriage wasn't strong enough for her to read his eyes. 'He didn't guess that.'

'What was he talking about, then?'

Luc hesitated, then answered, 'Just the usual saber rattling your cousins enjoy. Nothing of any concern.'

He paused, wondering if, given his state, given the brutal desire riding him, he dared touch her, then he reached out with one hand and cradled her jaw, savoring the delicate curve. Battling the impulse to seize – reminding himself she was already his.

Sliding his fingers farther, he curved them about her nape and drew her to him. Bent his head and brought her lips to his.

And kissed her.

Fought to hide the shudder of awareness that racked him when she offered her mouth, when she sank against him.

Succeeded well enough – grappled and clawed and hung on to enough control to keep the kiss light. To draw back, lift his head, touch his lips to her forehead. 'If you're not tired – worn down with smiling, laughing, and playing the delighted bride – you ought to be.'

She looked up, met his eyes, smiled.

Before he could think – reconsider – before she could speak, he murmured, 'Thank you.'

Her smile filled her eyes with a light – a simple joy and delight – he longed to drown in. 'It went very well, I think.' She spread one small hand on his chest. 'It was just as I wanted it – not fussy or elaborate, but simple.'

To him, there'd been nothing simple about it. He made himself return her smile. 'I'm happy if you are.'

She stretched up to touch her lips to his. 'I am.'

The feel of her in his arms, the look in her eyes . . . he glanced across at the green fields rolling past. Drew in a breath. 'We've close to another four hours of this. We should be there by seven.'

Looking down, he met her eyes, then bent his head and kissed them closed. 'Rest.' Lowering his voice, he murmured, 'The entire staff will be waiting to greet us when we arrive, and they'll have dinner waiting.'

He was reminding himself more than her, but she nodded, and, eyes obediently closed, settled her head on his chest, in the curve of his shoulder. The simple acceptance of his edict went some way to appeasing his more primitive self – that self he was becoming increasingly familiar with the more time he spent around her.

Leaning back, settling her in his arms, feeling her body ease against his, he ruthlessly focused on the argument that having her well rested on their wedding

265

night was preferable to the alternative. Preferable to having her now.

She must truly have been as worn-out as he'd suggested; she fell into a dozing slumber within a mile.

Leaving him to stare, unseeing, out of the window, a prey to thoughts he'd never imagined he'd have, to longings he didn't fully understand – to emotions stronger and wilder than any he'd felt before.

Emotions strong enough to rule him.

The touch of Luc's lips on hers woke Amelia; she clung to the kiss until he lifted his head, then glanced around.

'We just cleared the gates,' he informed her.

Which meant she had ten minutes in which to make herself presentable. Reluctantly leaving the warmth of his arms, she sat up, stretched, then straightened her bodice and shook out her skirt.

Noted that her bodice was still neatly done up; Luc had made not a single rakish move toward her since they'd been wed.

'We're nearly at the curve.'

His voice gave no indication of what he was thinking or feeling, indeed, if he was thinking or feeling anything at all. But his warning had her shuffling along to peer out at a sight she'd particularly wanted to see.

To savor – the first glimpse of her new home, spread out, pale stone faintly golden in the westering sun, sheltering in a dip below a rise some way ahead. For a time, the house would remain visible from the carriage as the road ran parallel to the rise on the opposite side of a shallow valley, a vista engineered to give visitors an appreciation of the quiet beauty of the Chase – an established, elegant mansion set in a rich and luxurious landscape.

The fields around the house were a verdant green, the vibrant color slowly fading to darkness as the sun set and the light waned. The house glowed through the dusk, as if the stone was lit from within, promising warmth to the traveler, and even more to those returning to its fold.

Long and large, the mansion comprised two stories with dormers atop; the facade was classical in design with twin columns supporting a central portico. However, the facade was not straight, but a shallow inverted V, the central block containing the portico at the apex, the ends of the long east and west wings angled forward toward the valley.

There'd been a house on the site for centuries; the central block had been built and rebuilt many times before the newer wings were added.

Beyond the end of the east wing stretched the darker green of trees – the old demesne, now woodland. To the west of the house lay the fields of the home farm, the roofs of stables and barns standing out amidst the green. Presently invisible behind the house were the formal lawns and gardens. Gazing out of the carriage, Amelia thought of them – thought of all the hours she'd spent there in the past, then let the memories fade.

Turned her mind to the future, thought of her dreams, embodied in the house before her; this was where she would make those dreams come true.

Watching the same scene from behind her, Luc let his gaze dwell on the house – his home. Eyes narrowed, he confirmed the slates on the west wing

267

had been repaired and the wall damaged by a fallen tree nearly a decade ago rebuilt. The sight unexpectedly touched him; it now looked as it had when he could first remember seeing it, in his grandfather's time.

The decay of his father's term had already been partly erased; those had been some of the urgent orders he'd dispatched the day after he'd learned of his new wealth. The day following the dawn on which he'd agreed to marry Amelia, to take her hand and see what they could make of the future.

Together. Here.

His gaze shifted to her; the possessiveness that seized him was disorienting, disconcerting. He leaned back, shifting his gaze ahead as the carriage swept on. Trees intervened as the road curved again and dipped into the valley; Amelia sighed and sat back, her gaze still on the window, her expression soft and eager.

The coach rattled over the stone bridge, then traversed the shoulder of the rise, the horses leaning into the traces for the long, sweeping approach to the house.

Five minutes later, the coach rocked to a halt before the portico of the Chase.

He'd been correct in his prediction; not just the indoor staff, but those who worked in the gardens, stables, and kennels as well, were lined up to greet them. The groom opened the door and let down the steps; Luc stepped down – a spontaneous cheer rose from the assembled throng.

He couldn't help but grin. Turning, he handed Amelia from the coach; as she stepped down and stood beside him, her hand in his, the cheers rose to new heights. Caps were tossed high – everyone was beaming. Conscious of the clouds blowing up from the west, encroaching on the summer twilight, Luc led Amelia forward. Cottsloe and Mrs. Higgs had left the Place immediately the ceremony had ended to ensure all was as it should be here, and to be ready to welcome them both to their new life.

Luc smiled as Mrs. Higgs rose somewhat shakily from her deep curtsy; with a gesture, he handed Amelia over to her. He and Cottsloe followed as Mrs. Higgs introduced all the indoor staff, then Cottsloe took the lead and did the same for those who worked outdoors.

The long line ended at the top of the portico steps where a youth struggled to hold a pair of enthusiastically eager Belvoir hounds. The animals wriggled and whined pitifully as Luc approached.

Amelia laughed and halted, watching as Luc patted them, and they slavishly adored him. Once they'd quieted, she offered her hands for them to sniff. She remembered them both. Patsy, Patricia of Oakham, was the matron of the pack and utterly devoted to Luc; Morry, Morris of Lyddington, was her oldest son and a reigning champion of the breed.

Patsy wuffed welcomingly and rubbed her head into Amelia's hand; not to be outdone, Morry wuffed louder and went to jump up – Luc spoke and Morry subsided, instead wagging his tail and rump so vigorously their poor handler was nearly brushed off his feet.

'Kennels,' Luc declared in a tone that brooked no argument, canine or otherwise. Both dogs seemed to sigh and desist; with a grateful look, the boy turned them away.

Luc held out his hand.

269

Amelia looked up, met his gaze – then smiled, and slid her fingers into his. They closed firmly; with a flourish, he turned her to their assembled staff.

'I give you your new mistress – Amelia Ashford, Viscountess Calverton!'

The roar that answered was deafening; Amelia blushed, smiled, waved, then turned and let Luc lead her on, over the threshold into their home.

The staff followed quickly, streaming past as they stood in the wide front hall listening to Mrs. Higgs's arrangements.

'I've held dinner back to eight-thirty, my lord, my lady, not being sure of when you would arrive. If that's all right?'

Luc nodded. He glanced at Amelia, then raised the hand he still held to his lips. 'I'll let Higgs show you up.' He hesitated, then added, 'I'll be in the library – join me when you're ready.'

She smiled, inclined her head; he released her.

He stood in his hall and watched her climb the stairs, already deep in discussion with Higgs; when she finally disappeared from his sight, he turned and strode for the library.

He would have preferred to show her up to their suite himself, but then Higgs's dinner would have gone to waste, and his servants would have had a field day with their nods, winks, and knowing chuckles.

Not that any of that had deterred him.

A glass of brandy in his hand, Luc stood before the long windows of the library and watched the western sky turn black. A summer storm was rolling in; his tenant farmers would be rejoicing. A flash of lightning, still distant, caught his eye.

He raised his glass and sipped, his gaze on the turbulent mass of thunderheads, evidence of a tempestuous force that mirrored the one roiling within him. The force of emotions, passions, and unslaked desire that, suppressed, had steadily escalated throughout the day until every muscle he possessed was rigid, locked in the fight to contain, to restrain, to keep the violence trapped, inside him. For now.

Turning from the window, he crossed to the hearth and dropped into an armchair before it. He didn't want to think of later. The sense, not of being out of control, but of not being fully *in* control haunted him. As if some part of him he'd never met before, some part he didn't recognize, was driving him. And he was helpless to resist.

He could control his actions, but not change the result; he could dictate the path, but not the ultimate goal.

While his intellect resisted, some deeply buried part of his mind rejoiced, metaphorically threw back his head and laughed at the danger, eager to taste the unexplored, the implicit, untameable wildness, to pit his wits and strength against it, to experience the promised thrill.

He took a long sip, then lowered his glass. 'Thank God she's no longer a virgin.'

He was still sitting, sprawled in the chair, when the door opened and she entered. He turned his head, forced himself to remain still as he watched her cross the long room.

She'd changed into a gown of pale green silk, as delicate as a budding leaf seen through spring dew. The silk clung to her curves lovingly, the low, scooped neckline showcasing her breasts, the fine skin

271

over her collarbones, the delicate arch of her throat. Her golden curls were piled high; wisps bounced by her ears. She wore no jewelry bar the wedding band he'd placed on her finger earlier that day. She didn't need more. As she halted before the other armchair, facing him across the hearth, the light from the candelabra on the mantelpiece fell across her; her skin glowed like pearl.

She was his wife – his. He could barely believe it, even now. He had known her for so long, had considered her untouchable for years, yet now she was his to do with as he pleased – the primitive possessiveness the thought evoked was startling. Not that he would hurt her, physically, emotionally, or in any other way. Pleasure was his currency, and had been for a long time – long enough to know how broad a field physical pleasure truly was.

The thought of exploring that field with her ... he stopped trying to block the thought. His gaze on her, on her face, then slowly traveling down her body, he let his mind imagine ... and plan.

She remained standing before him, her gaze steady, her color even, no hint of any panic showing. Yet he was aware of her accelerating heartbeat as if it were his own, could sense her skin heating, saw her lips part fractionally.

Returning his gaze to her eyes, he tried to read them, but the distance defeated him. He'd kept his expression impassive, his eyes hooded. After an instant, she tilted her head, faintly raised one brow.

There was nothing he could tell her – wished to tell her – no words, no warning. He raised his glass to her, and sipped.

The door opened; they both looked.

Cottsloe stood in the doorway. 'Dinner is served, my lord. My lady.'

Impatience sank its claws deep; ignoring it, Luc smoothly rose, set his glass down, and offered Amelia his arm. 'Shall we?'

The glance she threw him was curious, as if she wasn't entirely sure what he was truly asking. But there was a smile on her lips as she set her fingers on his sleeve and let him lead her to the door.

Chapter Thirteen

He had absolutely no idea what Mrs. Higgs and Cook had prepared; he paid no attention to the food Cottsloe laid on his plate. He must have eaten, but as the storm gathered and built beyond the windows, he felt increasingly distanced, the violence outside calling to all he'd suppressed throughout the day until it – sating it – dominated his thoughts and his mind.

From the end of the table, shortened as much as possible but still able to seat ten, Amelia watched, and wondered. Over the years, she'd seen Luc in all his many moods – this one was new. Different.

Charged.

She could feel his intensity, crackling between them, feeding her own welling anticipation. An anticipation further buoyed by relief. His unexpected reserve, his eschewing of all loverlike gestures, had left her uncertain. Wondering if, now she was his wife, he was no longer as physically interested in her as he once had seemed. Wondering if that earlier interest had in truth been as potent as she remembered it. Wondering if it hadn't in some measure been feigned.

Glancing up the table, she watched him sip from a

crystal goblet, his gaze fixed on the windows, on the storm brewing outside. He'd always been enigmatic, cool, reserved; she'd assumed as they drew closer, his barriers would fall. Instead, the closer they grew, the more impenetrable his shields, the more of an enigma he became.

She wouldn't put it past him to pretend to a pretty passion as the easiest way to deal with her, to satisfy her within their marriage. She was not such an innocent as to think he couldn't, or wouldn't, do so if it suited him.

Cottsloe approached with the wine bottle; Luc glanced at her plate of poached figs, then shook his head. He went back to staring at the storm.

While the intensity between them, stoked by that brief, dark *impatient* glance, surged even higher.

Suppressing a smile, she set herself dutifully to dispense with the figs. She couldn't leave them untouched – Mrs. Higgs said Cook had slaved over every dish, and indeed, the quality had been excellent. Given that the cook's master had paid not the slightest heed, it behooved her to make the effort.

She'd probably need the strength.

The wayward thought popped into her mind, and nearly made her choke. But it was an indication of her underlying thoughts, and her expectations.

Ever since joining Luc in the library, she'd realized that, whatever else he might fabricate, this intensity – the attraction flaring between them – was not feigned. Not a construct created by a master seducer to dazzle her; the truth was, the master seducer wasn't thrilled.

That realization had sent her heart – and her hopes —soaring. He was giving an excellent imitation of a man driven, compelled, not by lust, but by something

275

more powerful. Neither the direction nor his goal discomposed him, but rather the degree of his compulsion; he was a man who controlled all things in his life – being driven . . .

That was why, at least in part, he'd been so keen to leave the Place, why he was now so impatient to have her to himself. To . . .

She stopped her mind at that point, refused to think further. Refused to dwell on the heady mix of curiosity and excitement rising within her.

The clang of her cutlery as she laid it on the plate had Luc glancing around.

Cottsloe immediately whipped away the plate; two footmen whisked away the covers. Cottsloe returned to offer Luc an array of decanters; he dismissed them with a brusque shake of his head. His gaze on her, he drained his goblet, set it down with a soft *clack*. Then he rose, walked down the table, took her hand, and drew her to her feet.

Met her gaze fleetingly.

'Come.'

Her hand locked in his, he led her from the room. She followed, quickly so he didn't tow her along. She would have grinned, but she was too keyed up, too much in the grip of that flaring excitement. The expression on his face had done that. That, and the fathomless darkness of his eyes.

He went up the wide stairs, keeping her beside him. If she was foolish enough to try to pull away . . . glancing briefly at his face, she felt he might even snarl. An animalistic energy poured from him; this close, she couldn't miss it, couldn't stop it from tightening her own nerves, from squeezing her lungs.

They reached the first floor. The main suite filled

276

the rear of the central block, in pride of place, jutting into the gardens behind the house. A short corridor ended in a circular foyer giving access to three rooms via carved oak doors. To the left lay the viscountess's apartments – a light, airy sitting room flanking a large dressing room and bathing chamber. To the right lay similar rooms – Luc's private domain. Between, directly ahead behind a pair of oak doors, lay the master bedchamber.

She'd seen the room – large, uncluttered, with an immense four-poster bed – earlier; she'd explored, enchanted by the position, surrounded by gardens with views on three sides.

Luc gave her no time to admire anything now – he flung open one door, towed her through, paused only to glance around to ensure no maid still lingered, then he heeled the door shut and she was in his arms.

Being kissed – no, *ravished*.

Every link with reality was swept away in that first hot rush. He'd swept her literally off her toes; she was locked so hard against his steely frame, his arms banding her, she couldn't breathe – had to take her breath from him. Had to appease the greedy, hungry kisses, the starving urgency with which he kissed her; she offered her mouth, surrendered, tried to catch up – tried to orient.

He gave her no chance. He turned with her in his arms, took two steps, and set her back against the door – trapped her there. He ravaged her mouth; grabbing hold, her fingers sinking into the rigid muscles of his upper arms, she met him in a clash of tongues, in a hot world of whirling desire. She flagrantly incited, urged him further – wanted more.

Angling his hips, he pressed her to the door,

anchoring her as he drew back just enough to strip off his coat and fling it away. She fell on his shirt, popping buttons in her haste, in her need to have her hands on his bare chest. His erection rode hard against her mons; his fingers were busy with her laces.

Then his shirt was open; she wrenched the halves wide and spread her hands over him, over the acres of burning skin, sliding her fingers through the raspy curls. She devoured him with her hands while he devoured her mouth, while he conjured the hot, driving need between them, while he drew it up, and set it free.

Let it rage.

She was suddenly beyond hot; he was suddenly beyond urgent. He lifted his head. Her gown and chemise ripped as he yanked them down to expose her breasts; she didn't care – cared for nothing beyond her wanting, and its satisfaction. He dipped his head, set his mouth to her breast, suckled – and she screamed.

Felt her body arch as he suckled fiercely again, felt his hands on her, hard and demanding. No gentle lover, no soothing caresses, nothing but heat, possessive passion and a driving, urgent need.

A need that drove her, too, that had her gasping, fingers sunk in his hair, blindly holding him to her as he feasted.

Ravenously.

Cool air caressing her legs, then her thighs, told her he'd rucked up her skirts. For one instant, she wondered if he would take her there, against the door – then he cupped her and she stopped thinking.

His touch was knowing, blatantly possessive. He

opened her, thrust one, then two fingers into her, worked them deep. Then his thumb found that most sensitive part of her, and circled it, tormenting, while he worked his fingers within her sheath, matching his rhythm to that of his suckling—

She shattered, fractured – so fast, so intensely, she saw rapture like a starburst on the insides of her lids.

His hands and lips left her – too soon, too quickly. She was empty, aching – boneless, vanquished ...

Then she was gasping, falling; he swept her up in his arms and carried her to the bed. Laid her upon it and ruthlessly stripped her gown away. Stripped her naked. When she wore not a stitch to hide her from his gaze, black as night, burning with desire, he tumbled the heaped pillows, rearranged them, then lifted her and laid her among them. A sacrifice waiting, displayed.

She had no will to move, no strength even to lift a hand. He stalked back to the end of the bed, stood facing it, his gaze locked on her, traveling her body as if cataloging every last inch, every soft curl as he stripped off his shirt, flung it aside, then set his fingers to his waistband.

His face was graven, the features and planes so familiar, yet not. They'd been lovers before, yet it had never been like this – she'd never been able to taste desire, never been able to sense it like a shimmering aura around him, around her. Something heightened, something more – some meshing of physical and ephemeral needs that was both frightening and compelling had happened between them.

He kicked off his shoes; in a single smooth move-ment he removed his trousers, dropping them as he straightened. As he stood there, naked, rampantly aroused and intent, before her.

He knelt on the bed, his knee between her feet. The muscles in his arms and shoulders shifted, bunching like rock, flexing like steel. His gaze, locked on the curls at the junction of her thighs, lifted to her eyes.

'Open your legs.'

A deep, gravelly, command. An outright order.

She complied, not quickly but without hesitation; he'd clenched his fists – hard – to stop himself from reaching for her. She remembered the feel of his hands on her breasts, their driving urgency, the sheer strength in his fingers. She knew, as her gaze fell into the black of his and she shifted her thighs apart, that he didn't want to lay hands on her – not yet.

Not while this sheer, ungovernable force rode him.

The force that, as soon as her thighs were wide enough apart, had him on the bed, poised over her, arms braced, hands sunk in the pillows on either side of her shoulders. He settled his hips between her thighs, ruthlessly forcing them farther apart, wedging them wide.

His eyes locked on hers as the blunt head of his erection probed her slick flesh. Then he found her entrance; she caught her breath, trapped deep in the black fires of his eyes as he entered her – with one powerful, savagely complete thrust – one that stretched her and filled her, that had her arching, wildly gasping, hands gripping his forearms, nails sinking deep, her head pressing back into the soft pillows as he relentlessly pressed in.

Until he'd possessed her. Until he'd filled her so completely her every sense was filled with him.

Then he rode her.

She gasped, writhed beneath him, driven ruthlessly, relentlessly on. Hands spread on his back, feeling the unforgiving flexing of the powerful muscles bracketing his spine, she clung blindly and surrendered. His arranging of the pillows had had a purpose; they cushioned her, cradled her, tilted her hips and supported her so he could drive into her body harder, faster – deeper.

So her body could withstand his possession, could ride the force and the fury as he took her.

As he loved her.

It came to her in a blinding flash as she watched his face, passion blank, eyes closed, his every sense focused on their joining. The sheer force of his thrusts took him deeper yet; her body gave and she gasped, arched beneath him. He gasped, too, took every inch she offered, hung his head. Bent enough to take the tight peak of her breast, flagrantly offered as her spine bowed, her body supported by the pillows, into his mouth. Blindly, he feasted while his body plundered hers.

Fiery energy spread insidiously through her, down every vein, into her core. She felt it coalesce. Felt it build and swell with every deep rocking thrust, with every lightninglike flash of sensation he sent spearing through her.

Until she ignited, burned. Exploded. Until she lost every sense in the mindlessness of heat and wonder.

This time, he didn't leave her, but with guttural commands urged her on. Forced her on, begged her to stay with him.

And she did. Held to him, clung, senses wide-open, her body all his. Caressed him, eased him, offered herself to him. And he took, again, and again, and again—

A crash from outside echoed their gasps.

Outside the storm broke; inside, the wild energy swirled.

Beyond the windows, the wind lashed the trees and lightning cleaved the sky.

Inside, the rhythm of their loving escalated, step by relentless step.

Energy sparked through them, alive in shards of sensation, shimmering emotion, the brilliant colors of passion and desire. It grew until it was almost real – an incandescent glory. Intensifying, drawing in, it tightened about them – tightened their nerves, locked every muscle.

Then imploded.

And they flew. High on a crest of sensation that shattered every perception. High to a plane where emotions formed the sea and sensation the land. Where feelings were the winds and peaks grew from delight. And the sun was pure glory, exquisite and unshielded, an orb of power so intense it fused their hearts.

And left them beating as one.

When had it ever been like that?

Never.

Why had it come now? Why with her?

Imponderable questions.

Luc lay on his back amid the pillows, Amelia curled by his side, her head pillowed on his arm, one small hand spread over his chest. Over his heart.

The night was mild in the aftermath of the storm; he hadn't bothered to cover their cooling bodies. To hide their nakedness.

Fingers toying with her hair, he looked down – at

282

her, at her naked limbs twined with his, at the smooth, alabaster curve of her hip over which his other hand lay possessively draped. Felt something within him clench, then, very slowly, release.

It seemed so strange – that it was she, a female he'd known as baby, child, and girl. A woman he'd thought he'd known so well – yet the woman who'd climaxed beneath him last night, who'd taken his every thrust, who'd closed about him and taken him in, who'd accepted him no matter the raging power, who'd stayed with him throughout their wild ride on that tumultuous tide of desire . . . he didn't know her.

She was different – an elemental mystery, shrouded and veiled, familiar yet unknown.

Tonight, there'd been no gentle kisses, no gentling caresses, only that wild power that had driven him – and her. That she would like it – nay, covet it – that she would welcome it and so gladly let it swirl through her as it had through him, so it could sweep them both away . . . that had been a surprise.

From beyond the window came the light patter of rain; the storm had moved on.

Yet the power that had flowed between them and brought them together with such cataclysmic force was still there, but dormant. Quiet, yet still alive. It breathed as he did, flowed in his veins, possessed him.

It would until he died.

Did she know? Did she understand?

More imponderables.

Doubtless if she did, he'd know tomorrow morning, when she woke and started trying to manage him. Trying to wield the power that was, indeed, hers to command.

283

Letting his head fall back against the pillows, he listened to the rain.

Surrender.

Men were always so sure that women surrendered to them.

Yet men surrendered, too.

To that unnameable power.

Miles to the south, the winds of the storm bent the tops of the ancient trees surrounding the Place. Those stalwarts were too old, too established, to be made to bow in anything but a token way; the winds instead piled clouds before the moon and set the topmost branches lashing, creating a bleak landscape of violently shifting shadows.

The mansion lay in darkness. It was after midnight and all those residing under its wide roof had retired to their beds.

Except for the slight figure who emerged from the side door, struggling to close it against the wind, then fighting to pull the heavy cloak she wore tightly about her. The hood refused to stay up. Leaving it back, she set off across the narrow side lawn, quickly ducking under the trees; her reticule swung and bumped against her legs, but she ignored it.

Skirting the lawns, she headed for the front of the house – to the summerhouse at the edge of the trees facing the front facade, from the shadows of which Jonathon Kirby stepped.

She was breathless when she reached him. Without a word, she halted, caught her reticule, opened it, and drew out a slender cylinder. She handed it to Kirby, then glanced back, fearfully, at the house.

Kirby held the cylinder up to the fitful light,

examined the intricate chasing, hefted its weight.

The young lady turned back to him. Drew breath. 'Well? Will it do?'

Kirby nodded. 'It'll do very well.'

He slid the heavy cylinder, an antique saltcellar, into the pocket of his greatcoat. His gaze rested on the young lady. 'For now.'

Her head came up; she stared at him. Even in the poor light, it was obvious she'd paled. 'What ... what do you mean – *for now*? You said a single item from here would be enough to see Edward safe for some time.'

Kirby nodded. 'Edward, yes.' He smiled, for the first time letting the foolish chit see his true nature. 'Now, however, it's time for me to take my cut.'

'*Your cut*? But ... you're Edward's friend.'

'Edward is no longer here. *I* am.' When her expression remained stunned, Kirby raised his brows. 'You don't seriously think I'm helping a whipstraw like Edward purely out of the goodness of my heart?'

His tone made the truth painfully clear.

The lady stepped back, her eyes wide, fixed on Kirby. He smiled, even more intently. 'No – you needn't fear I've designs on your person.' He ran his gaze over her, dismissively contemptuous. 'But I do have designs on your ... shall we say, light-fingered talents?'

Her hand had risen to her throat; she had difficulty finding breath enough to ask, 'What do you mean?' She swallowed. 'What are you *saying*?'

'I'm saying I require you to continue to supply me with little items, just as you have for the last several weeks.'

Aghast, she managed a shaky laugh. 'You're crazed. I won't. Why would I? I only stole for

Edward to help him – you don't need any help.'

Kirby inclined his head; the twist of his lips suggested he enjoyed her distress – enjoyed putting her right. 'But the fact is, my dear, you stole. And as to why you'll continue to steal for me, that's very simple.'

His voice hardened. 'You'll do as I say, supplying me with select items from the wealthy homes you enter, because, if you don't keep me satisfied, I'll arrange for the truth to out – oh, not my part in it, but yours most assuredly – and that will cause a scandal of quite remarkable degree. You'll be banished from polite society for life, but even more, the entire Ashford family will be looked upon askance.'

He waited for full understanding to dawn, before smiling. 'Indeed, the *ton* has never shown sympathy for those who, however innocent themselves, sponsor thieves into its midst.'

The girl stood, so pale, so still, it seemed as if the rising wind might blow her over. It had already tugged her brown hair loose, left it lying in tumbled curls on her shoulders.

'I can't—' She choked, backed away.

Unmoving and unmoved, Kirby watched her, his gaze, his expression, granite-hard. 'You will.' He spoke with a finality that brooked no argument. 'Meet me in Connaught Square, same time as before, the morning after you return to town. And' —he smiled, all teeth— 'bring at least two worthwhile items with you.'

Eyes like saucers, the girl moved her head from side to side, wanting to deny him yet knowing she was caught. Then she gulped, whirled.

Kirby stood in the shadows and watched her flee, cloak billowing wildly. His lips curved in genuine amusement; when she disappeared around the corner of the house, he turned and headed off through the trees.

The girl pelted around the house, sobs coming hard and fast, tears streaking her cheeks. *Fool, fool, fool!* The litany sang in her head. She stopped, quivering, hauled her cloak around her and hugged it about her, head bowed, trying to calm herself. Trying to tell herself it couldn't be, that her good intentions – born of the *purest* motives – couldn't have gone so wrong. Couldn't have turned out like this. But the words in her head didn't stop; on a choked sob, she raised her head. She couldn't stay out – someone might see her. With dragging steps, she forced herself on, toward the side door and the safety of the house.

High above, an old nurse stood at a dormer window, frowning down at the empty lawn where the girl had been. The nurse had been up for hours; her employer had had one of her bad nights and had only just fallen asleep. The nurse had just reached her room; with no need of light, she'd started to undress, then a movement outside – too quick to be the play of shadows – had caught her eye and drawn her to the window.

Now she stood, thinking of what she'd seen. The girl fleeing, clearly distressed. That moment of stillness, then the effort to move on.

The girl was in trouble.

Brown hair, quite thick, long enough to cover her shoulders. Slight build, of average height. Young – definitely young.

And so vulnerable.

The nurse had lived too long not to know the odds; there would be a man in the story somewhere. Lips thinning, she made a mental note to mention – at the right moment – what she'd seen. Her noble employer knew the girl, she was sure. Something would have to be done.

Mind made up, the nurse finished undressing, lay down upon her bed, and fell sound asleep.

Luc woke to the sensation of a woman's hands on him. On his chest, sweeping across the wide muscles as if in gloating possession, then sweeping lower, over his ribs, then lower still, fanning over his hips. The wandering hands paused, then swooped inward, closing, warm and alive, blissfully firm about his morning erection.

'Hmm.' He shifted under her hands, and registered the warm weight of her across his thighs. She was straddling him, examining him – that last was enough to mentally jolt him to full awareness, to remind him who 'she' was.

He just managed to quash the impulse to open his eyes; his mouth was already dry – he wasn't sure he could handle what he might see. He fought to keep his expression slack, even though he doubted she was looking at his face. Keeping his breathing even was harder, especially when she started to caress, to fondle, to explore.

Abruptly, her hands left him. A bereft heartbeat later, they returned, palms flat to his skin, sliding slowly upward from his waist, up over his chest to curl over his shoulders. Even better, her body followed, and she lay atop him.

He had to look then. Cracking his lids open the

288

veriest fraction, he looked out from beneath his lashes. She was watching, waiting – blue eyes the color of summer skies, wide, warm, locked on his. And she smiled.

The quality of that smile very nearly did for him; he could feel his body hardening with self-imposed restraint. After the wildness, the unrestrained ardor of last night, a little gentleness might be wise. Flipping her over and sheathing himself inside her without further ado would be unlikely to gain him any points.

And would, if she'd already guessed the truth, be ridiculously revealing. He was supposed to be calmly in control.

There was an awareness in her eyes – one he was sure hadn't been there before. When her lids lowered, and her gaze fell to his lips, he had to wonder if she was about to tell him she'd seen through him completely and demand he now dance to her tune.

He braced himself, rapidly assembling arguments to back his denial – she made a soft purr in her throat and stretched up, set her lips to his.

In a soft, clinging, persuasive kiss – a subtle, gentle plea.

'More.' She whispered the word against his lips, then took them again, brushed her tongue over them, gently entered when he parted them to tangle with his tongue – then gave her mouth readily when he returned the pleasure.

'There's more, much more – and you know it all.' She angled her head and kissed him again. Her breasts, warm, firm feminine mounds, pressed to his upper chest; he felt her nipples hardening. His hands had risen instinctively to trace the long line of her spine, to curve about her bottom.

'I want you to teach me.' She drew back with a last, loving kiss, giving a gentle tug to his lower lip.

His head was reeling; that other part of him she'd already tempted, now cradled between her thighs, was throbbing unmercifully.

He blinked, dazedly, into wide sultry siren's eyes. 'You want me to teach you more?'

His voice was not his, slightly hoarse, raspy with the passion she'd already, very effectively, stirred to life.

'I want you to teach me' —she met his gaze boldly— 'all you know.'

The next fifty years might just be long enough, given he discovered things he hadn't known every time he was with her. Her – a woman who kept proving to be so much more than he'd ever guessed.

She seemed to take his stunned silence as assent; her lashes lowered, veiling her eyes. A very feminine smile curved her lips. 'You could teach me more now.'

The invitation was so shockingly blatant it took his breath away. Locked his lungs, his whole body, with the urge to react.

She lifted her lids, met his gaze. Raised her brows. 'If you feel up to it.'

He couldn't help it – he laughed, relaxing on the pillows. She grinned, and went to slide off him.

His arms didn't move; he held her where she was. He caught the flash of awareness that showed briefly in her eyes. Realized why she'd made him laugh – to ease the tension that had hardened his body, and made his strength – the promise of it, the threat of it – so much more overt. He was a great deal stronger than she was.

He noted her reaction for future reference; noted the need to go carefully until he knew which side of the coin she preferred. He didn't, yet, know her well enough to guess, but after last night ...

Her tongue passed over her lower lip; her eyes, bright, eager yet unsure, returned to his. 'Can we do it like this?'

He smiled, slowly. 'Oh, yes.'

She raised her brows, her own lips curving. 'How, then? Show me.'

Locking his eyes on hers, he ran his hands down from her waist, over her hips, then down to close over the backs of her thighs. He tugged them up, drew her knees to his sides. Leaving them there, he clamped his hands on her hips, and eased her down his torso, fraction by fraction, until he – and she – felt the marrying touch of their bodies.

He'd assumed she'd already be aroused; she didn't disappoint him. The entrance to her body was already slick, swollen soft; he guided her a fraction lower, until he could nudge into the wet heat, then he stopped.

'Put your hands on my chest and gradually sit up.'

She obeyed. The look on her face as she realized what would happen – what naturally did happen – was priceless. Halfway up, astride, half-impaled, she looked down at him, eyes widening as she realized she could control the speed at which she took him in. That she would be in control.

Then her lids fell, her arms locked, her knees clasped his sides. She slowly eased down, taking him in, more, and yet more, experimenting at the last, shifting on him until she'd taken him all.

He could barely breathe, but he met her gaze when,

muscles clamped about him, perched upon him, she opened her eyes and looked at him.

'What now?'

A laugh, even a pained chuckle, was out of the question. He was hanging on to his demons, and their need to ravish her, by a thread. 'Now you ride.'

She blinked, then her gaze cleared and she tried it.

And found it very much to her liking.

That was obvious from the soft sounds that poured from her throat as she let herself slide down upon him, from the delight in her face when she rose, only to sink down and take him again.

Amelia decided this was bliss. Sheer, unadulterated bliss. No morning in her life had ever been like this one, filled with discovery, filled with promise. She gave herself up to both, to learning all she could, experiencing all she could, to pleasuring herself, and him.

She enjoyed it. As much as she'd exulted last night, this, watching his face from beneath her lashes as she rode him, used her body to caress him, feeling him rampant inside her, filling her, stroking smoothly and deep, all at her command, was heaven indeed.

The morning sun rose, shining down on a rain-washed world. It shone in through the windows, across the bed. Fell across her and him, its gentle warmth a subtle benediction.

He'd raised his hands to her breasts, caressing, fondling; now they trailed away, down, tracing the curves and lines of her body, his eyes following, his attention that of a connoisseur assessing a new acquisition. An acquisition that gave him real pleasure; she didn't doubt that as the fever rose and spread beneath her skin and his face hardened with desire. His hands returned to her breasts, their touch harder, more demanding, then he shifted beneath her, half-rising, one hand at her back urging her forward so he could close his mouth over one tight nipple.

His suction there connected in some fashion she didn't understand with the slide of his body into hers. Heat built steadily until her fingers curled, trapping hairs on his chest. The hand at her back stroked down, over her fevered flesh to close about her hip.

And guide her. He limited her movement and instead moved with her, under her, thrusting into her willing body in a powerful, rolling rhythm that, this time, she was a party to. She adjusted to his beat; he continued feasting as she moved at his behest upon him.

The tempo built, and built, until she thought her heart would burst. That the tension coiling inside her would explode.

Then it did, shattering into shards of sensation and wonder, purest heat flowing away, under her skin, behind her lids. Pooling deep within.

He fell back, both hands closing about her hips as he ruthlessly held her down, held her so he penetrated her most deeply.

Luc lay on the pillows, chest heaving, and waited, teeth gritted, holding tight to every impulse he possessed, and watched her, watched her climax flow through her, savored her body's clasp as she closed tight about him, waited on the edge of oblivion until every last contraction faded.

The remnants of tension drained from her, and she slumped onto his chest. He held her to him and rolled, pressing her deep into the pillows.

Pressing deep into her.

Despite her satiation, she opened her eyes, blinked. He moved within her and she roused within seconds, matching him with a simple eagerness, an open giving, that made him shudder. He found her lips. They parted under his and she welcomed him in. They moved together, the pillows cocooning them in a world of their own.

A world of sensation untrammeled, a green field where the power flowed freely. The power that drove their mating, that, as before, tempted and promised an unstinting reward.

They took it, grasped it, let it possess them – let it fill them.

To bursting point. He drew away from the kiss long enough to gasp, 'Your legs – wrap them about my waist.'

She obeyed immediately. He groaned as he drove into her, deep toward her heart.

The power fused them. Rushed over them in a wave and took them both. Completely. Absolutely.

He yielded without question, knew she did the same. Heard her sweet cry as she tumbled into the void. He followed swiftly, holding her tight.

And knew in that instant of startling clarity that she, and that power, had become the linchpin of his life.

Chapter Fourteen

That revelation did not buoy his confidence. Some hours later, sitting in the breakfast parlor staring unseeing at the latest news sheet from London propped against the coffeepot before him, Luc had to wonder what madness had brought him to this. Not just married, but married to a Cynster.

It wasn't as if he could claim ignorance; he'd only known her all her life.

Yet here he was, on the morning after his wedding night, feeling as if *he* was the one in need of gentle reassurance. He stifled a snort, forced his eyes to focus on the print. His mind refused to make sense of the words.

It wasn't his sexual prowess that was in question. Or, indeed, hers. He didn't, in fact, know what his problem was – why he felt the need to tread warily, even gingerly, in this landscape that, despite being so familiar, had, since their wedding, subtly altered.

At least his mother had taken his sisters – all four of them – to London for the week, leaving him and Amelia blessedly alone to settle into married life. The thought of facing Portia and Penelope over the breakfast cups while he was in this less-than-certain state made him shudder.

He raised his cup, took a long sip, and tossed aside the news sheet.

Just as Amelia walked in.

He hadn't expected her to join him; he'd left her – he'd thought exhausted – a warm bundle in their bed.

She breezed in, wearing a delicate lavender sprigged gown; she smiled cheerily. 'Good morning.'

He nodded, hiding his surprise behind his cup. She turned to the sideboard; Cottsloe bustled up to hold her plate while she made her selections. Leaving the butler to pour and follow with her tea, she swept to the table.

To the chair on his right.

A footman hurried to hold it for her. She smiled and sat, thanking the footman, then Cottsloe sunnily.

At a look from Luc, Cottsloe and the footman effaced themselves. Luc returned his gaze to his wife. And her piled plate. The wifely duties she'd most recently been discharging had clearly given her an appetite.

'I expect you'll be busy this morning, catching up with business?' She glanced at him as she picked up her fork.

He nodded. 'There are always urgent matters to catch up with immediately I return here.'

'You spend most of the year here, don't you? Other than the Season, and later in the year?'

'Yes. I don't usually go up until the end of September, at the earliest, and try to get back by late November.'

'For the shooting?'

'More so I can oversee the preparations for winter and the hunting.'

Amelia nodded. Rutlandshire and neighboring Leicestershire were prime hunting country. 'I suspect we'll have any number of visitors in February.'

'Indeed.' Luc shifted. 'Speaking of riding, I must get off soon, but if you want me—'

'No, no – all's well. Your mother spoke with both me and Higgs before we left London, so we know where we are.' She smiled. 'It was sweet of her to hand over the reins so cleanly.'

Luc humphed. 'She's been waiting to hand them to someone she trusts for years.'

He hesitated, then reached out and caught Amelia's hand. She laid down her fork; he raised her fingers to his lips. His gaze on her eyes, he kissed her fingertips, then, curling his fingers around them, rose, pushing back his chair and stepping around the table, returning her hand to her with the words, 'I'm sure my household will be in good hands.' He paused, then added, 'I'll be back for luncheon.'

Whether her hands would prove to be 'good' or not, she didn't know, but they were well trained and eager. This was what she'd been born, raised, and trained for, to manage a gentleman's home.

Higgs appeared as she was finishing her tea. She returned the housekeeper's beaming smile. 'Perfect timing. Shall we start with the menus?'

'Indeed, ma'am, if you will.'

From previous visits, she knew the house reasonably well. 'We'll use the parlor off the music room.' She rose.

Higgs followed her into the hall. 'You wouldn't rather use your own sitting room, ma'am?'

'No. I intend keeping that private.' Completely private.

The parlor off the music room was a small chamber filled with morning light. It contained a comfortable chaise and two armchairs covered in chintz, and an escritoire against the wall, just as Amelia had recalled. She crossed to the escritoire and the spindle-legged chair before it; as she'd suspected, the escritoire held some paper and a few pencils, but clearly hadn't been used in years. Even better, it had a lock with a key.

'This will do nicely for my desk.' Sitting, she searched the papers for a clean sheet, then examined the pencils. 'I'll get some better things shortly, but this will do for today.' She smiled at Higgs and nodded toward the nearest armchair. 'Pull that closer and sit, and let's get started.'

Despite knowing the theory, despite having sat with her mother through innumerable household meetings, she was nevertheless grateful for Higgs's experienced common sense, and the woman's blatant support.

'Duck with cherries would be a wise choice to go with the rest. Now we have the werewithal to be a touch more extravagant, it only seems fair to give the master his due. Duck with cherries is one of his favorites.'

Amelia added the dish to her dinner menu. Higgs's mention of the family's improved circumstances hadn't escaped her. Higgs had to have been practicing the most severe economies for years; Luc had been right to inform her there was no longer any need. 'Can we add *crème brulée*, do you think? It should round things off nicely.'

Higgs nodded. 'A good choice, ma'am.'

'Excellent – so that's done.' Amelia set down her pencil and handed the sheet to Higgs. The housekeeper scanned it, then placed it in her apron pocket.

'Now, is there anything else I should know?' Amelia caught Higgs's eye. 'Anything less than satisfactory about the house or the staff? Any difficulty that needs dealing with?'

Higgs's beaming smile returned. 'No, ma'am – nothing at present. 'Deed, we were remarking in the hall only last night that now with the master married, and to you, miss – ma'am, I should say – who we all know and have seen grow from a wee girl, well!' Higgs paused to draw breath. 'There's not much more any of us could think of to wish for, and that's a fact.'

Amelia returned her smile. 'I know things must have been difficult in recent years.'

'Aye, they were that, and sometimes even worse what with Master Edward and all. But!' Higgs's bosom swelled; her face, which had clouded at thoughts of the past, cleared. 'That's all behind us now.' She nodded at the window and the glorious summer's day. 'Just like the weather, the family's come around, and we've got nothing but good times and pleasant surprises to look forward to.'

Amelia pretended not to notice the 'pleasant surprises,' doubtless an allusion to children – babies – hers and Luc's. She nodded graciously. 'I hope my tenure here as mistress will be a happy one.'

'Aye, well.' Higgs hauled herself up from the armchair. 'You've started out on the right foot – now it's simply a matter of keeping on.' She patted her pocket. 'I'd best get this to Cook, then I'll be at your disposal, ma'am.'

'I've a better idea.' Amelia rose, too. 'I'll come

with you, and you can show me around the kitchens. After that, you can take me around the house – I know the general layout, but there's many places I've never been.'

Places a guest wouldn't venture, but a mistress needed to know.

Like the attics.

Those of the west wing and half of the east were given over to servants' quarters – small cubicles, few larger than a cell, but Amelia was pleased to note as she walked down the narrow central corridor that each room had a dormer window, and every one she peeked into was not only neat and clean, but showed little signs of comfort – a looking glass, a framed picture on the wall, a jar acting as a vase.

The second half of the east wing's attics were given over to storage. After looking in, she agreed she didn't need a more detailed inspection. Luc had said he'd return for luncheon; she didn't want to appear trailing cobwebs on their first day as man and wife.

Returning to the central block, Higgs stood at the top of the main stairs and pointed out the rooms filling the top floor. 'Nursery's here at the front, and the schoolroom's right to the back. We've rooms here for nurse and governess – that's Miss Pink.'

Amelia recalled the shy, diminuitive woman. 'How does she manage with Portia and Penelope?' A wonder, for Luc's younger sisters were nothing if not handfuls.

'Truth to tell, I think it's more that they manage her – those two young madams are sharp as you please, but for all their willful ways, they've good hearts. I think they took pity on Pink the instant they set eyes on her, and there's no doubt she's as much of a blue-stocking as they'd wish for.'

300

'They like their lessons?'

'Devour them. And between you and me, Pink teaches them far more than young ladies need to know. Howsoever, as they've brains enough to cope without ending in a fever, Pink has served well. Because they like her, Miss Portia and Miss Penelope try to behave.'

Descending from the top floor, they commenced an inventory of the rooms on the first floor. Most of the reception rooms were on the ground floor, but the occasional sitting room was interspersed between the bedchambers along both wings.

'So we actually have a number of suites. Helpful, especially when we have older guests.' Amelia made a note on the tablet she carried.

A deep *bong* resonated through the house. Higgs lifted her head. 'That's the luncheon gong, ma'am.'

Amelia turned for the stairs. 'We'll continue this afternoon.'

She stepped into the front hall as Luc entered from the long corridor of the west wing. In breeches and hacking jacket, he appeared the epitome of an English country gentleman; the planes of his face, the long lines of his body more definitively declared his status.

Higgs bobbed, then bustled past him, heading for the servants' hall. Luc raised a brow at Amelia as he joined her. 'Have you seen all?'

'Barely half.' She led the way into the family dining parlor. 'Higgs and I will continue after lunch.'

She took her seat, once more on his right; she refused to sit at the end of the table when they were alone. Cottsloe appeared to agree with her; he'd set her place as she'd wished, even though she'd made no request. Shaking out her napkin, she glanced at

301

Luc. 'Is there any particular' —she gestured— 'element of household management you'd like to see changed?'

He sat, clearly gave the matter thought while Cottsloe served. When the butler stood back, Luc shook his head. 'No. Over the past years, we've reorganized virtually everything.' He met her gaze. 'Now Mama has handed over the reins, control of household matters is entirely in your hands.'

She nodded. Once they'd both started to eat, she asked, 'Is there any aspect of the estate presently on your plate you'd like me to take over?'

A delicate question, but Minerva wasn't young, and Luc was Luc. While his mother had undoubtedly fulfilled her duties unstintingly, she knew he would have transferred as many responsibilities as possible from Minerva's shoulders to his.

Again, he considered, then went to shake his head – as she'd fully expected – but stopped. 'Actually' — he glanced at her— 'there are a few things you could take over.'

She nearly dropped her fork. 'What?' She hoped her eagerness wasn't too transparent. It was essential to her long-term strategy that she establish herself as his wife, not only in the eyes of the staff and estate workers, and all others, but in Luc's eyes, too.

'The Autumn Gathering – it's an ... estate party for want of a better name, held in late September.'

'I remember,' she replied. 'I've been here for one, years ago.'

'Ah, but you wouldn't have been here for one in my grandparents' time. Now *those* were parties.'

She met his eye, grinned. 'I'm sure we could match them if we try.'

302

'Cottsloe was a footman, and Higgs was a parlor maid – they'd remember enough to resurrect some of the more unusual events.'

His eyes remained on hers; she inclined her head. 'I'll ask and see what we can organize.' She laid down her fork, reached for her glass. 'Was there anything else?'

Luc hesitated. 'This is more prospective. Mama visited the tenants, and I'm sure you'll do the same, but we're taking on more workers, not just on the home farm but on the tenant farms, too. There's a lot of children about. Too many to eventually work the farms in their fathers' stead.'

He picked up his glass, sipped, leaned back. 'I've heard good reports from various estates where schools have been set up for the workers' children. I'd like to institute something along those lines here, but I simply don't have time to look into it properly, let alone do the necessary planning.'

And if Devil and Gabriel had their way and co-opted him into the Cynster investment cartel, he'd have even less time for such activities.

He was watching Amelia carefully; he saw the spark of eagerness in her eyes.

'How many estates do you have?'

'Five.' He named them. 'Each is productive, and the returns are sufficient to justify the time and effort to keep them running smoothly.'

'That won't leave you much time for anything else.'

He inclined his head. 'I travel to each estate at least twice a year.'

She looked at him. 'I'll be coming, too.'

No question. Pleased, he inclined his head again.

303

'Your other estates – are any big enough to justify a school?'

'In the next few years, it's likely all will have sufficient numbers.'

'So if we trial the concept here, and work through all the problems, then we can later expand to your other estates.'

He met her now overtly eager gaze. 'It'll take time and considerable effort in each case. There are always prejudices to overcome.'

She smiled. 'I'll have more than enough time – you may leave the matter with me.'

He acquiesced with a nod, masking his satisfaction. The more she became enmeshed in his life, in the running of his estates and his household, the better.

His ride about the estate had brought home how many repairs and improvements were under way – works she'd undoubtedly think were being paid for by her dowry.

Convention stated that no woman had any right to know her husband's business.

Regardless, he couldn't imagine not telling her the truth.

That her dowry was a drop in the ocean compared to his wealth, that he'd known it from the dawn she'd offered herself – and her dowry – to him, that he'd been careful to allow no hint of the truth to reach her, even to the point of corrupting her father and making a pact with Devil ...

Could he rely on her temper to blind her to the real revelation therein?

He inwardly grimaced; she was a Cynster female – he had too much respect for her perspicacity on such subjects to risk it.

He had until September to make his confession.

Sufficient unto the day the evil thereof.

'My lord?'

He looked up to see Cottsloe standing by the door. 'McTavish has just come in. He's waiting in the Office.'

Luc laid down his napkin. 'Thank you.' He glanced at Amelia. 'McTavish is my steward. Have you met him?'

'Yes. It was years ago, however.' She pushed back her chair; a footman started forward – rising, Luc waved him back, drew out the chair.

Amelia stood and faced him, smiled into his eyes. 'Why don't I come with you and you can reintroduce us, then I'll leave you to your business while I continue with mine?'

He took her hand, set it on his sleeve. 'The Office is in the west wing.'

After meeting McTavish and casting a curious glance over the Office, Amelia rejoined Mrs. Higgs, and they continued their inspection. While the house was in excellent condition, and all the woodwork – floors and furniture both – gleamed with beeswax and care, virtually every piece of fabric was in need of replacement. Not urgently, but within the next year.

'We won't be able to do it all at once.' They'd completed their circuit of the reception rooms; in the main drawing room, Amelia scribbled a note putting the curtains in that room at the top of her list. Followed by the curtains in the dining room. And the chairs in both rooms needed to be reupholstered.

'Will that be all, ma'am?' Higgs asked. 'If so, would you like me to get your tea?'

She raised her head, considered; unlikely that Luc would wish for tea. 'Yes, please – send the tray to the small parlor.'

Higgs nodded and withdrew. Amelia returned to the parlor off the music room.

Leaving her notes – a considerable pile – in the desk, she retreated to relax on the chaise. A footman appeared with her tea tray; she thanked and dismissed him, then poured a cup and slowly sipped – in silence, in isolation, both very strange to her.

It wouldn't last – this had always been a house full of people, mostly females. Once Minerva and Luc's sisters returned from London, the house would revert to its usual state.

No – not so. Not quite.

That was, indeed, what this strange interlude signified – the birth of a new era. As Higgs had said, the weather had changed, the season swung around, and they were moving into a new and different time.

Into the period when this huge house would be hers to run, to manage, to care for. Hers and Luc's the responsibility to steer it, and the family it sheltered through whatever the future might bring.

She sipped her tea and felt that reality – the fabric of their future life – hovering, as yet amorphous, unformed, all about her. What she made of it, how she sculpted the possibilities ... it was a challenge she was eager to meet.

Her tea finished, the sunshine tempted her to try the French doors. They opened; she strolled out into the gardens.

As she walked the clipped lawns, then strolled along a wisteria-covered walk bathed in sunshine, she turned her mind to her master plan, to charting the immediate future.

Their physical relationship appeared to be taking care of itself, developing of its own accord – all she needed to do was devote herself as required, something she was perfectly willing to do, especially after last night. And this morning.

She grinned. Reaching the end of the walk, she turned into the crosswalk and continued on. She hadn't expected to feel so confident, to gain such a fillip from knowing she pleased him in their bed, from knowing that his desire for her was real – entirely unfeigned; if anything, it had grown rather than diminished since first they'd slaked it.

Another unlooked-for success had been his readiness to accept her assistance with the Autumn Gathering and his new idea about schools. It might simply be that he saw her as competent, and he was willing, given the burdens he already shouldered, to let her help; nevertheless, it was a start. A step toward true sharing, which was, after all, what a real marriage was about.

A real marriage – that was her goal, the absolute achievement she'd promised herself. The marriage she intended to have.

At the end of the crosswalk, she looked up and ahead – to the stables, and the long building that extended beyond. From there came the unmistakable yipping of hounds.

Luc's treasures. Lips curving, she set out to view them for herself. She was quite partial to dogs – just as well, for Luc's pack of prize Belvoir hounds had been his hobby since boyhood. A lucrative one – the pack would be a source of income now, both through being leased to the local hunt and through breeding fees and sales of the offspring of champions like Morry and Patsy.

The kennels, clean, well run, spic-and-span, were reached via the courtyard around which the stable was built. A narrow aisle ran down the center of the long building with pens giving off on either side; there she found Luc talking to Sugden, the kennel master.

Luc's back was to her; he and Sugden were discussing buying another breeding bitch. Sugden saw Amelia first, colored, closed his lips and nodded, tugging at his cap. Luc turned, hesitated, then raised a brow. 'Come to see my beauties?'

She smiled. 'Indeed.' That momentary hesitation hadn't escaped her – he was wondering if she was going to be upset at learning he was using her dowry to buy a breeding bitch. Letting real appreciation light her eyes – the entire pack were magnificent specimens – she nodded to Sugden and tucked her hand in Luc's arm. 'They seemed to be calling me. How many do you have?'

He moved down the aisle with her. 'They're just hoping you've brought dinner.'

'Are they hungry? When do they get fed?'

'Always, and soon. There are nearly sixty all told, but only forty-three actually run. The others are mostly too young. A few are too old.'

One of the 'too old' was lying curled on a blanket in the last pen, the one closest to the potbellied stove that in winter would heat the area. The pen door was wedged open; the dog lifted its head as Luc neared, and thumped its tail.

Luc crouched, patting the greying head. 'This is Regina. She was the matriarch before Patsy.'

Amelia crouched beside him, let Regina sniff her hand, then scratched behind the dog's ears. Regina tilted her head, lids heavy.

Luc sat back on his heels. 'I'd forgotten you like dogs.'

Just as well, for in winter they were forever around. He even brought some – the very young and very old, like Regina – into the house when it was freezing out.

'Amanda does, too – we always wanted a puppy, but it was never fair, not living in London all the time.'

He'd never considered – never thought that, although they shared such similar backgrounds in some ways, in others ... he couldn't imagine not having a sprawling country house like the Chase, or the Place, to call home. Yet she hadn't; while he'd spent his summers riding the wolds, she'd been visiting here, visiting there – no single place her own.

The tenor of the hounds' call changed. Luc glanced back down the aisle, then rose, and reached down to take Amelia's arm. 'Come on – you can help feed them.'

She stood eagerly; he steered her back up the aisle, took over from the lads whose chore it was to feed the dogs, then showed her how much to place in each bowl. She took to it with alacrity, quickly learning to gently tap the hounds' noses out of the way long enough to reach the bowls.

At the end of the aisle, opposite Regina, Sugden was checking the latest litter. The pups were six weeks old, not yet weaned. Sugden nodded at Luc as they approached.

'This lot's doing well – might even have another

309

champion here.' He pointed to one puppy who was nosing along the edge of the pen, wuffling and snuffling. Luc grinned; leaning over the low barrier erected to keep the puppies in, he scooped the questing pup up and showed him to Amelia.

'Oh! He's so soft.' She reached for the pup, took him in her arms; delight lit her face. When she cradled him like a baby and tickled his tummy, the pup closed his eyes and sighed.

Luc watched, struck – then he glanced around. When he looked back, Amelia glanced at him. 'Later, when they're grown, can we send one to Amanda?'

She looked down at the pup, continuing to ruffle the downy fur on its belly. Crooning softly. Luc looked down at her head, at the golden curls. 'Of course. But first, you'll need to pick out one for yourself.' He took the now-dozy puppy from her, held him up again, checked the splay of his legs, the size and formation of his feet. 'This one would be a good choice.'

'Oh, but—' Amelia glanced at Sugden. 'If he's a champion—'

'He'll be the very best dog to own.' Luc bent and returned the puppy to its mother. 'Belle will be honored.' He stroked the bitch's head. She closed her eyes, then turned her head and licked his hand.

Luc stood. He nodded to Sugden. 'I'll check with you tomorrow.'

Taking Amelia's arm, drawing her away from the apparently fascinating sight of her little champion suckling, he guided her up the aisle and out of the kennels. 'You'll have to think of a name for him. He'll be weaned in a few weeks.'

She was still glancing back down the aisle. 'Will I

310

be able to take him for walks then?'

'Little walks, more like gambols. Puppies love to play.'

Amelia sighed and faced forward, looping her arm through Luc's. 'Thank you.' She smiled when he glanced at her, stretched up and kissed him lightly. 'He's the most precious wedding gift you could have given me.'

Luc's expression clouded; she immediately frowned. 'I'm afraid I haven't got anything to give you in return.'

Wide-eyed, she met his gaze – but couldn't read it.

A moment passed, then he lifted her hand from his sleeve, raised it to his lips. 'You,' he stated, 'are more than enough.'

She assumed he meant her dowry, but as she searched his face, his eyes, she wasn't sure ... a wave of fine tension swept up her spine.

They strolled on and she faced forward, conscious of the tightness about her lungs. Wondered if she should tell him she didn't mind if he spent money on his dogs – wondered fleetingly if that was why he'd given her one, his latest champion. Dismissed the thought as soon as it occurred. She'd never known Luc to be devious – he was too damned arrogant to bother.

Should she speak? They hadn't mentioned her dowry since those early days, yet in truth, there was nothing to say. When it came to money, to how he managed their now-combined fortunes, she trusted him implicitly. Luc was definitely not his father; his devotion to the Chase, to his family, was beyond question.

Indeed, it was that devotion that had allowed her to

311

get this far – to be here, walking the grounds of the Chase, now her home, with him, now her husband.

She could feel his gaze on her face, could feel the heat of him, the sleekly muscled length of him, all down her side. Not a touch but the promise of a touch, and more.

Glancing up, she smiled, and tightened her hold on his arm. 'It's too early to go inside. Come and show me around the gardens. Is the folly on the rise still there?'

'Of course – it's one of the stated attractions. We couldn't let it fall into disrepair.' Luc turned toward the path leading up the rise. 'It's one of the best spots in the district from which to view the sunset.' He glanced at Amelia. 'If you want to indulge, we could go up there.'

Her smile deepened; she met his gaze. 'What an excellent idea.'

Chapter Fifteen

The idea inhabiting her mind had not been the same as the one inhabiting his; he'd actually imagined they'd watch the sun set.

The next morning, while he paced in the hall waiting for her to join him to ride about the estate – infinitely safer than walking the gardens or anywhere else with her – Luc was still mentally shaking his head, trying, largely unsuccessfully, to rattle his disordered wits back into place.

What with their visit to the folly – folly indeed! – it hadn't been his idea to risk being caught *in flagrante delicto* by one of his undergardeners – it was midsummer; they were out in force – or worse, by one of his neighbors, many of whom, with his permission, used the folly for the purposes of bucolic introspection. What they would have found would have opened their eyes – in some it would have caused heart failure.

What with that, and their subsequent late return, then the unexpected challenge of dinner and the fight to resist behaving as he had the night before and dragging her straight off to their room – only to succumb before they'd been in the drawing room for more than ten minutes – let alone the consequent events of the night, and the dawn, he felt thoroughly disoriented.

He was – had been – the gazetted rake, yet it seemed it was she who was set on corrupting him.

Not that he was complaining, at least not about the outcome, not even at the folly – he felt desire lance through him simply at the memory – yet it was all . . . so different from what he'd expected.

He'd assumed – been sure – he was marrying a stubborn but delicate flower, yet she was turning out to be a tigress. She certainly had claws – he had good cause to know.

The clack of her heels on the stairs had him turning. Looking up, he watched as she came gliding down. She wore an apple green riding habit; the color turned her curls a deeper gold. She looked up and saw him; her face lit with eagerness, and – or so he told himself – something else. An expectation that had nothing to do with their projected ride.

She stepped down from the stairs and came toward him; she halted, looking down, fiddling with the buttons on her glove. The morning sun shone through the fanlight behind him and poured over her.

For one instant, he couldn't breathe, couldn't think. The same feeling that had flooded him yesterday when he'd seen her cradling the puppy rushed over him again. A longing, deep-seated and absolute, a need to give her something even more precious of his to hold and croon over.

She grumbled about the buttons. The feeling ebbed, but didn't completely leave him. He hauled in a deep breath, glad she was distracted, then reached for her wrist. As he had before, he deftly slid the tiny buttons home. His eyes met hers; briefly, he raised her wrist to his lips, then closed his hand about hers. 'Come – the horses are waiting.'

In the forecourt, he lifted her to her saddle, watched critically as she settled her feet and gathered the reins. He'd ridden with her years ago. Her seat had improved since that time; she grasped the reins more confidently. Satisfied, he strode to his hunter and mounted, then with a nod, directed her down the drive.

Side by side, they cantered through the morning, through the landscape of wide green fields liberally splotched with the darker greens of copses and coverts. They headed south, occasionally jumping drystone walls; he knew every field, every dip, every wall for miles – he avoided any route he deemed too challenging.

If Amelia guessed, she gave no sign, but took each jump easily, with a confidence he found both reassuring and yet distracting. Another sign of difference, of the maturity the years had wrought in her – and changed her to woman, no longer girl.

The summer sky wheeled above them, a wide and perfect blue, with only a hazy wisp of cloud to veil the beaming sun. The chirp of insects, the flight of startled game as they passed a covert, were the only sounds they heard above the steady drum of their horses' hooves.

They went as far as the lip of the Welland Valley, drawing rein on the ridge to look down on the rich green land threaded by the river, a silver ribbon winking here and there.

'Where do your lands end?'

'At the river. The house lies in the northern part of the estate.'

'So those' —Amelia pointed to a cluster of slate roofs visible through trees— 'are yours?'

Luc nodded; he wheeled his dappled hunter in that direction. 'We're doing repairs to one of the cottages. I should look in on the work.'

Amelia set her bay mare to follow him along the ridge, then down the gentle slope to the cottages.

They were sturdy dwellings built of the local pink-brown stone. The central cottage of the three was being reroofed – it was presently roofless. Men were perched on the wooden skeleton, adding new struts; the sound of hammering filled the air.

The foreman saw them, waved, and started to climb down. Luc dismounted, tied his reins to a branch, then lifted Amelia to the ground.

'A huge branch went through the roof during the gales last winter. The house has been uninhabitable since.' With a nod, he directed her attention to one of the other cottages from which a tribe of small children spilled to stand gawking at them. 'The three families have lived squeezed into the two cottages for nearly six months.'

Luc turned as the foreman came up; he introduced Amelia. The foreman nodded, tugging his cap, then gave his attention to Luc.

Who'd been scanning the work through narrowed eyes. 'You're further on than I expected.'

'Aye.' The foreman joined him in surveying the work.

Amelia decided to leave them to it. She started toward the children; no sense wasting an opportunity to get to know the estate families.

'Mind you, if we hadn't been able to get that order in afore June, we'd have been nobbled. The timber merchant had just enough to see us through, but with all the repairs 'round about starting as soon as the weather turned, he was cleaned out in a week.'

'But you've made good progress nonetheless. How long before the slates go back on?'

Amelia let the voices fade behind her; reaching the nearest of the children, she smiled and bent down. 'Hello. I live up at the big house – the Chase. Is your mother in?'

The younger children stared, curious, bright-eyed. One of their elders, hanging back by the door, turned, and shouted, 'Ma! Her new ladyship's here!'

The information caused a minor panic. By the time Amelia had reassured the three young mothers that she wasn't expecting to be specially entertained, and had accepted a glass of lemonade and spoken to two old crones huddled by the hearth, a half hour had passed. Surprised Luc hadn't summoned her, she went back out to the stoop and looked around. The horses were under the tree, placidly grazing, but there was no sign of Luc. Then she heard his voice and looked up.

Her lord and master had dispensed with his hacking jacket; with his shirtsleeves rolled up, his kerchief loose about his neck, he was balancing on a cross-beam of the new roof. Hands on hips, he bounced, checking the beam, clearly caught in some discussion about the structure. Outlined against the blue sky, his black hair ruffling in the breeze, he looked sinfully beautiful.

Someone tugged timidly at her sleeve. Amelia looked down and discovered a moppet with curly brown hair and big brown eyes gazing up at her. The girl must have been about six, maybe seven.

The girl cleared her throat, cast a glance at her fellows; she appeared to be the ringleader. Drawing a deep breath, she looked up at Amelia. 'We wondered . . . are all your dresses as pretty as this one?'

Amelia glanced down at her summer riding habit; it was, she supposed, pretty enough but hardly in the league of her ball gowns. She debated her answer, remembered how precious dreams were. 'Oh, I have prettier dresses than this.'

'You do?'

'Yes. And you'll be able to see some when you come to the big house for the party later in the year.'

'Party?' One of the boys edged closer. 'The Autumn Gathering?'

Amelia nodded. 'I'll be running it this year.' She glanced down at the moppet. 'And we'll be having lots more games than before.'

'You will?'

The other children crowded around.

'Will there be bobbing?'

'And archery?'

'Horseshoes? What else?'

Amelia laughed. 'I don't know yet, but there'll be lots of prizes.'

'Do you have dogs for pets like he does?' The moppet slipped a hand into Amelia's. Her nod indicated Luc, still climbing about the roof. 'They sometimes come with him, but not today. They're big but they're friendly.'

'I do have a dog, but he's just a baby – a puppy. When he grows, I'll bring him to visit. You'll be able to see him at the party.'

The girl looked trustingly up at her. 'We have pets, too – they're 'round the back. Would you like to see?'

'Of course.' Amelia glanced at the small crowd about her. 'Let's go around and you can show me.'

Surrounded by the children, all now eagerly asking questions, she was led around the house to the small clearing at the back.

Luc found her there fifteen minutes later, peering into a chicken coop.

'We save the feathers for pillows,' her newfound best friend informed her. 'That's important.'

Amelia knew Luc was waiting – she'd known the instant he'd walked around the house – but she couldn't simply desert the children. So she nodded solemnly at little Sarah, then glanced at Luc. 'Do we have any contests for best – most handsome – chicken on the estate?'

Luc strolled forward, nodding to the children. He'd known them all from the cradle, had watched them grow; they were unafraid of him. 'Not that I know of, but I see no reason why we can't begin one.'

'At the Autumn Gathering?' Sarah asked.

'Well if I'm in charge,' Amelia said straightening, 'then things have to be as I say. So if I say there'll be a most handsome chicken contest, then you'd best start grooming Eleanor and Iris, don't you think?'

The suggestion gave rise to considerable discussion; glancing around, Luc noted the bright eyes, the gazes fixed on Amelia – the way the children listened and watched. She was completely at ease with them, and they with her.

It took him another five minutes to extricate her, then they were on their way. As they rode back to the Chase, he pointed out the other tenant farms they passed, but they didn't stop. The image of Amelia, not just with the children but also their mothers when they'd taken their leave, stayed in his mind.

An ability to communicate with servants was one thing, the ability to interact with farmers and their families, especially the children, on such an easy level was quite another. It wasn't one he'd thought of in respect of his wife, yet it was indeed essential. While Amelia might not have had a permanent home in the country, she did come from a large family, as did he. From birth, they'd always been with other children, older, younger – there'd always been someone's babies about.

Dealing with people of all ages was a knack he took for granted in himself; he couldn't imagine not having that sort of confidence. Assisting a wife who wasn't similarly endowed would have been difficult; as they trotted back into the Chase's stables with the lunch gong clanging in the distance, he was thanking his stars that he had, by sheer luck, chosen Amelia.

Only as he followed her into the cool of the house did he remember that she had chosen him.

And why.

The foreman's opening words replayed in his head; he hoped she hadn't heard. As they went upstairs to change, she chatted in her customary cheerful way. He concluded that she hadn't, and let the matter – and the niggle of guilt – slide from his mind.

Amelia recalled the foreman's words while she was stripping off her riding habit. There was something in what he'd said that had caught her attention, but she couldn't remember quite what . . .

Afore – before – June. That was it. Luc had authorized the critical order for timber at the end of May. From what she'd understood of his circumstances ... it had to be her dowry, or the promise of her dowry, that had enabled him to do so.

For some moments, she simply stood, half in and half out of her jacket, staring unseeing at the window, then Dillys came fussing, and she shook aside her thoughts.

There was no reason Luc shouldn't have taken her dowry for granted, not after she'd offered to marry him and he'd accepted. In their circles, that was all it took; from that moment on, short of her changing her mind and him agreeing to release her, her dowry had in effect been his.

And it had obviously been needed. Urgently. The foreman's words and the cramped cottages had confirmed that. The timber had been not only a sensible expenditure, but a responsible one.

As she stepped into a day gown and waited for Dillys to lace it up, she rapidly reviewed all she knew of Luc, and all she'd seen over the past few days – and concluded that he was as she'd always imagined him to be, a gentleman landowner who in no way shied from his responsibilities, not just to his family, but to all those he employed.

And of that, she thoroughly approved; there was nothing to upset her in that.

Nothing to account for the nebulous concern that something, somewhere, was not quite right.

The next morning they rode into Lyddington. The houses of the village lined the main street, with the inn, the bakery, and the church clustering around a neat green. An air of pleasant but sleepy prosperity hung about the place; although quiet, it was by no means deserted.

Leaving their horses at the inn, Luc took her arm and steered her toward the bakery, from which heavenly aromas wafted on the mild breeze. Amelia looked around, noting numerous little changes that had occurred since she'd last visited the village five years before.

Now, as then, the bakery made the most delicious, mouth-watering cinnamon buns; Luc bought two while she chatted to Mrs. Trickett, who owned the shop and manned the counter. Mrs. Trickett had been quick with her congratulations, leaving little doubt that the fact of their marriage was widely known locally.

'Lovely to discover it was you, my lady, coming to be the new mistress of the Chase – well, it's almost like you were one of us already.'

Returning Mrs. Trickett's beaming smile, Amelia made her farewells and let Luc lead her outside. Their eyes met as they went out of the door, but they only smiled and said nothing. If either of them had thought of it, they would have expected that reaction; she might not have lived hereabouts, but conversely she was no stranger.

They sat on a bench overlooking the green and gave their attention to the cinnamon buns.

'Hmm,' Amelia eventually said, licking cinnamon sugar from her fingers. 'Delicious. Every bit as good as they ever were.'

'Not much changes around here.' Luc had wolfed down his bun, then stretched out his long legs and leaned back.

She glanced at him and found his gaze on her fingertips, on her lips. Her smile deepening, she gave one finger a last, long lick. After a second, he blinked, then lifted his gaze to her eyes; she met it innocently. 'Should we wander and meet more people?'

They'd already met the innkeeper and his wife, but there were others in the village it would be polite to acknowledge.

Luc's gaze shifted past her. 'No need.' Gracefully, he drew in his legs and sat up. 'They're coming to meet us.'

She turned and saw the vicar's wife bustling up. Rising, she and Luc exchanged pleasantries with Mrs. Tilby, then that good lady begged Amelia's support for the local almshouse.

'Lady Calverton – I mean the *Dowager* Lady Calverton – is our patroness, of course, and we hope she'll continue in that role for many years, but we would be honored if you would join us, too, your ladyship.'

Amelia smiled. 'Of course. Lady Calverton will be returning from London shortly. I'll accompany her to your next meeting.'

The promise quite made Mrs. Tilby's day; she parted from them with flurries of farewells and an assurance she would pass their greetings on to her spouse. Finally leaving them, she paused to exchange nods with Squire Gingold, a large, bluff gentleman, before hurrying on her way.

Squire Gingold approached, eyes bright, a good-natured smile on his ruddy face. 'Felicitations, m'dear.' He bowed gallantly before Amelia; she smiled and bobbed a curtsy.

Turning to Luc, the Squire shook hands. 'Always knew you weren't blind, m'boy.'

Luc raised his brows. 'After all these years of

323

following my leads, so I would suppose.'

The Squire laughed and asked after Luc's hounds. He and Luc shared numerous interests and responsibilities relating to the local hunt; Amelia wasn't surprised when their conversation veered in that direction.

She didn't have time to get bored. A carriage drew up outside the inn; its door opened and three young ladies tumbled out, shaking their skirts, unfurling their parasols. Their mother, descending more leisurely, gathered them up, then the flock descended.

That was only the beginning. In the next hour, simply by dint of standing on the green, Amelia found herself introduced to the majority of their neighbors. Or, more accurately, reintroduced, for she'd met all of them previously; indeed, thanks to the numerous house parties she'd attended over the years at the Chase, she was even more familiar with the local gentry than she was with the villagers.

They all welcomed her warmly, familiarity lending an ease to the situation, making the wives even more eager to invite her to tea. She was a known quantity, one they found unthreatening.

When the impromptu gathering eventually dispersed, and she and Luc reclaimed their horses and mounted to ride home to the Chase for luncheon, Amelia noted his gaze resting on her. She caught his eye, smiled. 'That went even more easily than I'd expected.'

He hesitated, some thought, some consideration lurking in his dark eyes, then he wheeled his hunter. 'Indeed. But now we'd better hurry.'

She laughed. 'Why? Are you hungry?'

Luc watched as she brought her mare alongside.

324

'Ravenous,' he ground out, then tapped his heels to his hunter's sides.

She fitted so well it was frightening. Fitted his household, fitted his life – fitted him. She was like a natural complement, a lock to his key.

He hadn't foreseen it – how could he have? It had never occurred to him that married life – their married life – would be like this.

A ridiculously easy slide into relaxed contentment. They lunched; they had already fallen into an easy camaraderie. They already knew each other's likes and dislikes, were accustomed to each other's everyday habits. Although they didn't know each other completely – and that unknowing lent an edge, an uncertainty to an old family friendship converted into marriage – yet the familiarity, the ease ... the simple comfort of being able, already, to expect and receive routine understanding ...

He felt like he was being pulled into a whirlpool that was simply too good to be true.

He pushed back from the luncheon table. 'I need to check on the dogs.'

She smiled, and wriggled back her chair. 'I'll come, too – I want to see my puppy.' She paused, her eyes on his. 'Were you truly serious about that?'

Rising, he rounded the table to draw out her chair. 'Of course.' The champion puppy would serve as a substitute wedding gift until he could give her his real one – the necklace and earrings he'd had designed to match the pearl-and-diamond betrothal ring. But he couldn't give her the set until he confessed, or she'd think he was simply giving her part of her dowry back, a scenario he wasn't capable of stomaching.

325

She rose; he offered her his arm. 'I'm sure you won't begrudge him to the pack when he's needed.'

'You mean when they run? But they love to run, don't they?'

'It would kill a champion not to run when the scent's high.'

She continued asking questions about the care of hounds; when they reached the kennels, she made her way immediately to the litter pen. Her pup was at the front again; from where he'd stopped in the aisle to talk to Sugden, Luc watched her lift the pup out, crooning.

Amelia held the puppy, who seemed quite content in her arms, and talked to him. When Luc eventually came up, she turned. 'You said I could name him.'

Luc scratched the pup's head. 'You can, but he has to have a proper name for registering, one we haven't used before.' He nodded to the office at the end of the kennels. 'Sugden has the registration book – ask him to show it to you. You'll need to check the name hasn't already been used.'

She nodded.

Luc crouched and patted Belle, then checked over the other puppies. Then he stood. 'There are business matters I need to deal with – I'll be in my study. Check with Sugden, but your pup and the others can probably do with a little time outside.'

She glanced at him. 'Playing?'

He grinned, a little evilly. 'What else do pups do?' With a salute, he swung away.

Amelia turned back to her pup. Once Luc was out of earshot, she whispered, 'Galahad. He never was all that impressed with King Arthur, so he won't have used that name before.'

*

He'd been in his study for twenty minutes, poring over investment reports, when he rose to retrieve a ledger from the other side of the room – and saw her, on the lawn, puppies gamboling at her feet. Sugden and Belle watched from a distance; Amelia, golden ringlets dancing, the blue of her gown mirroring the blue of the sky, held center stage as, laughing, she mock-fought with the puppies over a length of knotted rope.

The pups fell over her feet as well as their own; they jumped up, pawed her gown, dug at her hem … she didn't seem to mind.

After a moment, Sugden called; Amelia looked up, then waved, and Sugden left. Belle put her nose on her paws and closed her eyes, like Sugden, convinced her puppies were safe.

Ledger in hand, Luc hesitated. Perhaps he should—

A knock on the door had him turning. 'Come.'

McTavish entered. 'Those estimates we were waiting on have arrived, my lord. Do you want to go over them now?'

He wanted to say no – wanted to put aside all work and join his new wife on the lawn and play with the puppies. He'd already spent all morning in her company; the revelation that he'd happily spend all afternoon with her, too, was damning.

'By all means.' He waved McTavish to the chair before his desk; carrying the ledger, he returned to his seat behind it. 'How much are they asking?'

It had all been so easy. So surprisingly straightforward.

Two mornings later, Amelia lolled in bed, smiling inanely at the ripples of sunlight dancing across the ceiling. There was a small pool at the end of the terrace outside the window; every morning, indeed, throughout most of every day, the sun reflected off the water, filling the main bedroom with shimmering light.

The main bedroom – hers and Luc's. The bed in which she lay was the one they shared, every night, and every morning.

Her smile deepened at the memories – of the nights, of the mornings. Only five had passed since they'd wed, yet in that respect she felt confident and assured. Just as in the wider sphere of his household, of the estate and their neighbors, she felt secure in her position as the new Lady Calverton; in all those arenas, their interaction, their relationship, was precisely as she'd wanted it, exactly what she'd wished to achieve.

As a first step.

She'd achieved that first step much sooner than she'd expected. Which left her facing the question of what next far earlier than she'd imagined. She could lie back and simply wallow, enjoy her achievement before girding her loins and broaching the next, far more difficult stage. However, she was twenty-three, and her impatience to have the marriage she wanted hadn't abated. She knew what she wanted – that and nothing less. Just the thought of it was enough to make her restless.

There was an underlying sense, not of dissatisfaction, but of something still missing from the equation of their marriage. Yet it wasn't simply a case of introducing the missing element.

It was there, already in existence; she was sure of that, at least with respect to her. She loved Luc, even though she hadn't yet made that plain. It was as yet too risky to make such a declaration; if he didn't love her in return – or wasn't yet willing to admit he did – a declaration from her would only create awkwardness. Worse, being him, he might dig in his heels and doggedly resist the notion completely.

Yet that had to be her next step – she needed to bring love – hers initially, his in response – into the open, lower her veil, persuade him to lower his shield. She needed to draw love up from where it lurked, unacknowledged, beneath the fabric of their interactions, and weave it into their lives, into their relationship so it became a vibrant part of the whole.

So it could contribute its strength and support.

She needed to coax, to convince, to cajole, to make him recognize it, and want it, too.

The question was: how? How did one encourage a man like him to deal with an emotion like love? An emotion he almost certainly would prefer to avoid.

She knew all about the way gentlemen like Luc, like her cousins, tried to slide around love. And Luc was unmanipulable; she'd always known the battle she now faced would be the most difficult.

So what was her best strategy?

Lying amid the rumpled sheets, the scattered pillows, she applied her mind to the question. Sifted through her memories, through all she'd learned of him in the past weeks ...

A plan took shape – a plan to educate Luc as to the full potential of their union using the only form of argument to which, on such a subject, he would listen. The only language guaranteed to capture his attention.

A wicked plan. Even a trifle underhanded – she was sure he would think so. Yet when a lady had to deal with a gentleman like him ... it was said all was fair in love as well as war.

And the perfect opportunity had just presented itself. To pursue such a plan, they had to be alone, without family or friends in the house. Once Minerva returned with Luc's sisters, the visits from their wider families would start, but she had four days before the others arrived.

Four days in which, already confident in her new role, she could turn her sights on something else.

On her husband.

Luc walked into the dining room and found it empty. The sound of the lunch gong had faded minutes ago; he wondered where Amelia was. Brows quirking, he walked to his chair and sat. Cottsloe had just poured him a glass of wine when footsteps sounded in the corridor.

Amelia's footsteps.

Sitting back, Luc lifted his glass and fixed his gaze on the doorway. Ever since he'd realized he had to draw a line, had to check his desire for her company, and her, and keep both within excusable limits, all had gone well. During the days, she flitted about his house and grounds, rode with him about the estate and played with his pups; each day saw her more and more occupied with the day-to-day business of being his wife.

As for the nights ... she welcomed him into her arms with open passion, with a desire so blatantly honest it seared his soul.

Her footsteps had halted, now they came on, and

she appeared in the doorway. She paused, looked straight at him, and smiled.

Luc blinked; before he could prevent it, his gaze raced over her – hungrily devouring. The gown she wore was of muslin so fine it would be translucent but for the fact the gown was overhung by a half gown of the same material. Two flirty layers – that was all that concealed a luscious form he now knew very well. A form his imagination could supply without conscious effort.

The peach-colored gown drew attention to her skin, so white, so perfect. She approached, and the upper swells of her breasts, revealed by the scooped neckline, made his fingers tingle, his palms itch.

Shifting his gaze, he forced himself to take a nonchalant sip of his wine as Cottsloe held her chair and she sat.

She smiled at him. 'Did Colonel Masterton find you?'

Luc nodded. The Colonel, one of their neighbors, had come looking for him that morning; Amelia had charmed the Colonel, then pointed him in the direction he himself had gone. 'He wanted to discuss the covert on the north boundary. We'll need to thin it this year.'

They discussed this and that; with an estate of this size, there was always something needing attention, and after the years of enforced parsimony, there was much to be done. While Amelia waxed lyrical about the new furnishings – he'd given her *carte blanche*, assuring her there were more than sufficient funds to do whatever she wished – Luc watched her face, drank in her animation.

Tried not to let his mind drift whither it wanted to go.

331

To her animation in another sphere, in other circumstances. To seeing it again, soon.

Her eyes were bright, her lips full and rosy. Being outside had lent a faint golden tone to the fine skin of her arms.

One errant curl, luscious golden silk, bobbed by her ear, again and again drawing his gaze. She always wore her hair up; the strand must have slipped loose. He glanced at the knot on the top of her head; it appeared well anchored, yet that teasing tendril ... he almost reached out and touched it, caressed it. Only just managed to stop himself.

Forced his gaze away – to her lips, then her eyes. Shifting, he leaned back, sipped his wine, and tried to keep the sight of her from sinking into his mind.

By the time the meal was over, he was decidedly warm, definitely uncomfortable, very ready to rise and depart.

He drew out her chair. She stood and smiled her thanks. 'I'm going to play with the puppies – are you heading for the kennels?'

He had been. He met her gaze. Their bodies were mere inches apart; he'd never been so conscious of a woman in his life. 'No.' He looked ahead, gestured for her to precede him. 'I've work to do in my study.'

She led the way from the room, paused in the corridor to throw him a smile. 'I'll leave you to it, then.'

With that, she walked away, her gown floating about her hips, her legs ...

Luc blinked, mentally shook his head, then swung on his heel and strode to his study.

Two hours later, he sat behind his desk – cleared,

tidy, all business disposed of. The first thing he'd done on entering the room had been to close the curtains across the window overlooking the lawn; ever since, he'd been fighting the urge to open them again. Who knew what he might see? For the past ten minutes, he'd been examining the embossed scroll-work around the edge of the leather inset on the desk top, his mind determinedly blank.

A tap came at the door – not Cottsloe's usual rap. He glanced up – as Amelia walked in.

She was frowning at the large ledger she held open in her hands. She'd been in the sun again; her pale skin was literally sun-kissed, a delicate peach.

Another curl had slithered loose and now bounced alluringly alongside the first, down one side of her face, swishing beneath the curve of her jaw to caress her throat.

She looked up, glanced around, confirming he was alone, then smiled, and shut the door. 'Good – I hoped you'd be finished.'

He managed not to glance at his pristine desk – no help there.

She raised the ledger. 'I've been checking the dogs' names.'

He waited where he was, waited for her to take the chair opposite. Instead, still studying the ledger, she walked around the desk and placed the book across the blotter, and leaned over it.

Close enough for him to sense the warmth of her skin, for the light scent she wore – some combination of orange blossom and jasmine – to wreath through his brain. He took a deep breath, fleetingly closed his eyes; gripping the arms of his chair, he surreptitiously edged it back.

'I've been looking through the names – is there any reason they're all "of Lyddington" or some such?'

She glanced at him; he met her gaze – which meant looking up. Standing as she was, leaning on the desk, her breasts, mounding tantalizingly above her low neckline, were at eye level. 'It's customary to give them such a tag to denote where they were whelped, usually the nearest town.'

His tone was even, commendably cool yet the temperature was steadily rising.

'Is it necessary?' She faced him, propped her hip against the desk's edge. 'I mean that the second half has to be the nearest town. Can't it be ... well, "Calverton Chase"?'

He blinked; it took a moment to get his brain to work – to follow her argument. 'The naming rules don't specify, not to that level. I can't see why, if you wished . . .' He focused on her. 'What name have you chosen?'

She smiled. 'Galahad of Calverton Chase.'

He half smothered a groan. 'Portia and Penelope will be your willing slaves – they've been at me for years to use that.' He frowned at her. 'What is it with females and King Arthur's court?'

Her eyes met his; her smile deepened. Before he knew what she intended, she slid onto his lap. His body reacted instantly; his hands closed about her hips.

Her smile only grew as she leaned into him. 'You'll have to ask Lancelot.'

She kissed him, but lightly, her lips toying with his. Then she drew back; the fingers of one hand slid into his hair as she twisted and leaned closer still, her breasts to his chest. 'It occurred to me that I haven't

334

thanked you properly for Galahad.'

He had to moisten his lips before he could say, 'If
you want to name him Galahad, you'd better add a
bribe.'

Her smile, her low chuckle, nearly brought him
undone. Lips parted, she leaned in. 'Let's see if I can
convince you.'

She put her heart and soul into it; his head literally
spun. Her lips tempted, teased, incited – and he
couldn't help but take, partake of what she offered,
slide deep into the warm cavern of her mouth and
savor all she was, all she would give him. He closed
his arms about her, then tipped her back so he could
plunder more deeply, more evocatively. She
welcomed him in, urged him on, fingers tangling in
his hair as her tongue dueled with his.

Outside, the warm, dozy afternoon took hold;
activities slackened; people rested. In the small room
with the curtains drawn, hands grasped, silk shushed,
and the temperature rose.

He'd taught her well enough not to rush; kissing
her, feeling the promise of her supple body, her
generous curves filling his arms, caressing his thighs,
was like drowning in a sea of sensual delight. She was
fluid, malleable – a mermaid tempting him to sink
with her deeper under the waves.

Into the oblivion of ecstasy.

The temptation whispered through his mind, pulsed
through his veins, throbbed beneath his skin. He was
on the brink of yielding when some remnant of self-
preservation reared its head.

Was she – could she possibly be – seducing him?

His instinctive reaction was to mentally smile and
push such a ridiculous thought aside. She was his

wife, here to thank him for an act of generosity; she was warm summer in his arms, full of the promise of life. The need to take, her and all she offered, was strong – and she'd made no demand. She'd simply offered . . .

Because she knew him too well – knew he would take if she offered, and resist if she demanded.

He kissed her more forcefully, deliberately setting her wits spinning while he tried to assemble his. Tried to decide if she was intent, following some plan of her own . . . even if she was, did he care?

Uncertainty reigned, then she kissed him back, and the feeling faded, along with his resistance. They both knew what lay between them, knew the power and the force, knew how it would consume them.

Wanted it – with one mind, one purpose.

He closed his hand about her breast and she arched in his arms; he ravaged her mouth as he filled his hand with her flesh. He drew her closer, tighter, deeper into his embrace—

They both heard the steps in the corridor – both stilled, then broke apart, eyes wide, widening . . .

A brisk tap fell on the door. A second later, the knob turned; the door opened and McTavish looked in.

He blinked, taking in the scene as Luc looked up and raised a brow.

'Oh, sorry, my lord.' McTavish blushed. 'I didn't think.' He nodded respectfully to Amelia, perched on the desk, watching as Luc pored over the ledger.

'Never mind.' Shutting the ledger, Luc waved McTavish to the seat before the desk. He turned to Amelia. 'That name seems in order.' He handed her the ledger. 'We can discuss the necessary payment later.'

Amelia saw the smoldering passion in his dark eyes – she saw the suspicion, too. Accepting the ledger, she smiled, and slipped from the table. 'Excellent.' She let just a touch of the purr she knew he would hear slide into her voice. 'I'll leave you to your business.'

With a smile for McTavish, she headed for the door, perfectly serene.

She might not have got all she'd wanted, but she'd gained enough to go on with. And who knew? McTavish might, indeed, have been sent by the gods.

Chapter Sixteen

'I'm going riding – I thought I'd go to that place on the river we used to go to years ago.'

Looking up from a financial report, Luc stared at the vision filling his study doorway. Clad in her pale green riding habit, Amelia smiled, then glanced down as she fiddled, as usual, with her gloves. Beneath her tight-fitting jacket, a froth of gauzy blouse showed, tantalizing in its transparency. Late-afternoon sun washed through the windows, bathing her in golden light, emphasizing the temptress role he was almost certain she was playing.

Gloves secured, she looked up, smiled again. 'I'll be back in time for dinner.' She started to turn away.

'Wait.' He was rising before he'd truly considered, but didn't stop. 'I'll come with you.'

She'd turned back; now she raised her brows. 'Are you sure ...?' She glanced at the papers he'd dropped on the desk, then met his gaze as he joined her. 'I didn't intend to disturb you.'

Looking into her eyes, he couldn't tell whether she was lying. Biting back the words: then you shouldn't have come within my sight, he gestured impassively on. 'I could do with a ride.'

Her eyes widened; her lips curved deliciously. 'I see.' Serenely, she turned and started down the corridor. 'Being out in the fresh air will be pleasant.'

He had no idea which way she intended that; gritting his teeth, he strode after her.

She'd already called for her mount; his hunter was quickly bridled and saddled, then they were away, galloping over his fields, heading south to the river. He knew the spot she was looking for; he led her straight there, to where a loop in the river left a finger of his land surrounded on three sides by water. Trees screened the base of the promontory; they left the horses there. Beyond the trees, the tip of the promontory was a secluded place, cushioned in lush grass, partially shaded by the reaching branches of the trees.

As children, this had been their spot for lazing, for paddling, for passing the days in idle talk, or in dreaming. They had occasionally been here in a large group, or had visited alone or with others, but they'd never come together, just the two of them, to this realm of childhood peace.

Ducking under a branch, he led the way, Amelia's hand in his; as they walked out into the thick grass, he could almost hear the high-pitched voices, the laughter, the whispers, the soft murmur of the water a constant counterpoint. He stopped in the center of the grassy area, and drew in a deep breath. It brought with it the scents of summer, of sun on leaves, of grass crushed beneath their feet.

'It's just like it always was.' Amelia slipped her hand from his and sank down on the grass, lush, green, and, courtesy of the warm day, dry. She looked up, met Luc's eyes, smiled. 'It was always so peaceful here.'

Arranging her skirts, she looked around, then hugged her knees, set her chin upon them, and fixed her gaze on the gently swirling water.

After a moment, Luc sat beside her. He stretched out, long legs toward the water, booted ankles crossed. Leaning back on one elbow, he, too, considered the river.

It was a constant, something that had been here over the generations, over the centuries – something that tied them to this land, to its past, yet whispered of its future.

She let the feeling sink to her bones, let the warmth in the air, the music of the river and the shifting leaves soothe and reassure. Confirm.

Eventually, she looked at Luc, waited until he met her gaze, then, smiling lightly, raised a brow. 'Well – can I call the pup Galahad?'

His midnight blue eyes darkened; she knew why, knew what he was recalling. The events of the past night when she'd paid the price he'd asked – and his bribe, too. This close, she could feel the sensual power that was his to wield, could sense, too, the rise of that other emotion, the one she sought to evoke, to provoke, to draw again and again into their encounters, until he recognized it and acknowledged it, too.

The former was the tension infusing his long limbs, hardening his muscles, sharpening the angles of his face. The other was more ephemeral, a distilled force, the very essence of power and compulsion.

She could see both in his eyes as they held hers.

'It's warm,' he said. 'Open your jacket.'

Such simple words; they sent desire flooding

through her. His gaze held hers; his tone – deep, quiet, controlled – was one she recognized. She now knew to obey him to the letter, that that was how the game was played. Assuming she wished to play ...

Her eyes locked with his, she uncurled her arms, sat up, and unhurriedly undid the buttons closing her light jacket. He hadn't said to take it off, so she didn't, perfectly willing to follow his experienced lead.

As her hands lowered, so did his gaze.

'Face me and tuck the halves back.'

She swung to him and did as he asked, so he had an uninterrupted view of what she wore beneath the jacket. Her blouse was of fine gauze, essentially transparent. She'd omitted to wear a chemise.

Luc's mouth went dry as he noted that last. His hand was reaching for her before he'd even thought. Gaze fixed, with his fingertips, he traced, then caressed, then closed his fingers about one pert peak. He took his time examining her, a sultan assessing a slave. Knowing she was naked under her skirts, knowing she'd be heating, softening, her body preparing to receive his.

When his hand was shaking with the effort of holding to his heavily restrained script, he let his gaze rise, to her throat, to where her skin glowed, lightly flushed. Lifting his gaze to her jaw, he saw the two ringlets she'd taken to letting loose bobbing by her ear.

He reached for them, wound them about one finger, then drew her evenly, steadily, toward him. Splaying one hand on his chest, the other curving about his shoulder, she met his gaze briefly, her eyes wide, pupils enlarged, circled by sapphire blue, then her lids fell and she let him pull her close, let him take her mouth.

Ravage it – he made not the slightest effort to hide the hunger eating him from inside out.

The hunger she'd teased and fed and incited. The hunger he was perfectly certain she'd seen in his eyes.

He kissed her as if she was indeed his slave; she met him, drew him in, urged him on. Hand curved about her jaw, he held her steady as he plundered, commanded, demanded the surrender she was so very ready to give.

His hand returned to her breast, his touch hard, driven. He kneaded, and she moaned. He found her nipple and tugged, tweaked, until her spine arched, her breath strangled, caught.

He lay back, grasped her hips and lifted her astride his thighs. Her hands started to slide down his chest.

'No. Sit still.' If she touched him ... he seriously doubted he'd remain in control, and he wasn't sure either of them could yet deal with that.

She obeyed, albeit reluctantly. The irony that this was one of the few areas in which he could count on her obedience hadn't escaped him; how long that would last he didn't like to think.

Pushing back the folds of her voluminous skirt, he quickly undid the buttons at his waistband, laid open the flap of his breeches, released his throbbing erection. On his chest, her fingers curled, but she didn't move.

'Gather the front of your skirt.'

She blinked, glanced at his face, then quickly complied, shifting on her knees to free the folds, lifting them.

As soon as there was no longer any fabric between

them, he slipped his hands beneath her skirts, gripped her naked hips, lifted her, then drew her ruthlessly down.

Impaled her upon him, sheathed his length in her very willing body.

She gasped, eyes wide; she'd expected him to touch her, not to simply take her. Fill her.

Luc felt the now-familiar bliss roll through him as she closed, hotter than summer heat, about him. Something in him eased, even while desire's tension increased.

He'd had her like this, above him, last night, while she'd paid the price for her teasing. The memory flared in her eyes as they met his; the vivid sensual recollection of how he'd had her ride him to oblivion – of how long he'd kept her there, trapped on the cusp of ecstasy while he'd sated his senses, his desires, with her, in her, drawing out the moment to a cataclysmic climax that had left them both shattered.

But that had been last night. He gripped her hips and held her down, allowing her no leeway to move. Then he undulated beneath her, holding her, guiding her, as he took his pleasure in her body – and gave her a new pleasure in return.

Amelia closed her eyes; she'd been shocked by the ease, by the rapidity and completeness of his penetration, unprepared for the crashing wave of sensation that had rolled through her and swept her wits away. Her breasts were full and aching; between her spread thighs, he moved rhythmically, buried within her, stroking deep. Not the usual thrust and retreat, but a subtler, deeper, more intimate movement.

Vulnerability and an aching, familiar need rushed up and over her, filled her, overflowed her heart. She

343

bit her lip against a whimper, a primitive sound of wanting; her fingers curled on Luc's chest. She started to lean forward, to press her hands flat.

'No. Stay as you are. Sitting up.'

His tone was definite, authoritative. She complied, straightening her spine, feeling him press deep inside her. Her fingers barely touched his shirt – she didn't know what to do with her hands ...

'Put your hands on your breasts.'

Startled, she lifted her heavy lids enough to look down at him, only then realized how rushed her breathing was. His eyes were dark, black as they captured hers; his chest rose and fell rapidly. 'Do it. Now.'

She did, not quite understanding; she cupped her breasts, uncertainly at first, then more firmly as her own touch added to the building pleasure.

'Knead. Gently.'

She obeyed, eyes closing, leaving him to move her upon him as he wished. When he told her to take her nipples between her fingers, she did, mimicking what he had so often done, squeezing, circling, squeezing again, knowing he was watching.

Then the glory descended; she felt her body tighten, coiling about him. Heard him gasp; he gripped her hips, fingers sinking, holding her down as he thrust deeper still.

And it took them, shattered them, fused them. Who went first, who followed, she couldn't tell.

She cried out, heard his answering groan. Felt the warmth within as he emptied himself into her womb, as her body rejoiced, rippling about him.

The tension faded, not so much draining away, as easing into the background, letting them, temporarily, free.

Luc slid his hands from beneath her skirts, followed her silken thighs to nudge her knees back, then he lifted his arms, drew her down, wrapped her close against his heart.

Listened to that organ pound in time with the beat he could sense where they joined. Waited as both slowed, his lips on her hair.

He had no idea what game she was playing, only that she was intent on gaining something through an escalation of their sexual play. He seriously doubted he'd approve of her goal, however, after what had passed between them last night, he'd realized that attempting to deny her – deny the passion she evoked – was a sure road to madness.

He wasn't capable of refusing what she offered.

That in itself was enough to shake him, to illustrate just how dangerous she and her latest direction was, how right he was to be wary. Unfortunately, his only option was to play her game. He glanced down at her golden curls, at the sliver of her face he could see. Her breasts were warm mounds pressed to his chest, her body a soft weight on his.

The passion she evoked, that she was so deliberately and repeatedly inciting, held a powerful compulsion. There was no name he could put to what it made him feel; it was brutal, violent in intensity, but not intent. It wasn't a power that demanded hurt to appease it, but something quite different. And when in the grip of that compulsion, he wanted only one thing.

To surrender to it. To ride its wild tide regardless of all else.

Condemned to madness if he resisted; insane if he gave in.

345

With her locked in his arms, he lay flat on his back, stared at the sky, and wondered how he'd come to this.

Midnight came and went, and if he hadn't definitively identified the answer, he was starting to suspect what it was. Amelia lay slumped beside him, sound asleep; knowing that – where she was, exactly what she was doing – freed his mind from its obsession with her, left him free to think.

That evening he'd let her retire without him, feigning a properly cool husbandly discretion. Her eyes had touched his, her lips had quirked as she'd turned and left him. At least she hadn't laughed.

He'd forced himself to wait for half an hour, then climbed the stairs to their bedroom.

She'd been waiting in the darkened room, clothed in moonlight and nothing else.

He'd taken her then and there, had her kneeling naked on the bed before him, gasping as he filled her and drove them both to ecstasy. Then he'd stripped and joined her on the bed, and made love to her thoroughly, to the depths of his soul, to the very limits of his expertise.

And there it was, the little word he was avoiding. Shying away from. Even thinking that much had him shifting restlessly. Made him aware of her hand on his chest, of how she habitually slept with it there, spread over his heart. He lifted her hand, placed a kiss in her palm, then replaced it and covered it with his.

Love. That was the simple truth. He could hardly go on denying it, unexpected though it was. For himself, he couldn't see that it would alter very much. It wouldn't alter his behavior, wouldn't change how he dealt with her. It might alter his perceptions, and his motivations, but that wouldn't show in the consequent actions. He'd always been able to conceal what he thought, and he'd been born with arrogance enough to do whatever he wished, whenever he wished, without any need for explanations.

Being under the sway of that dangerous emotion wasn't the end of the world. He could cope, and easily conceal the truth.

At least until he was sure enough of her to let her guess it, as she assuredly would when he confessed about her dowry.

Meanwhile ... there was her game to be endured. It had taken him some time to discern her direction. She didn't know he loved her, but she knew he desired her. Lusted after her to a highly uncomfortable degree. Given she was a Cynster female and as managing as they came, given she believed she'd arranged their marriage, given he was certain he'd hidden his secret well, she wouldn't be expecting to tie him to her with love.

She did, it seemed, expect to tie him to her with lust. With desire.

He had to admit her line of attack was sound.

Provoking him in venues more associated with forbidden lust than marital connubiality was a sure way to heighten the desire that flared between them. The surest way to stoke the fire. And no matter the actual outcome of her daytime plans, when they repaired to this room, she would reap her reward.

Every day, every night, saw the sexual stakes raised higher.

Today, he'd accepted that he was, regardless of his wariness, along for the ride. In whatever interpretation.

347

Aside from his damningly weak resistance, ultimately her game might work to his advantage. He wanted – needed – her to love him; he was too experienced to imagine lust or desire would do. It had to be love, openly acknowledged, freely given. Only that would be strong enough to allay his fears, soothe his vulnerability, allow him to confess his deception, to feel safe in doing so. To feel safe in acknowledging the reality of what he felt for her.

He didn't think she loved him yet, had seen no sign that she did. However much he lusted for her, she returned the passion, but that wasn't love – none knew that better than he. Once, he might have been gullible enough to imagine that for a woman, a lady like her, giving herself, her body, as she now did to him, unreservedly, was an indication of love. The experience of the last ten years had burned such innocence out of him.

Women, especially ladies, could be as lustful as any man. Even him. All it needed was a certain sense of trust, and unreserved surrender could come into play.

That wasn't, however, a bad place to start. The more frequently she gave herself to him like that, the more trusting she became, the closer they drew, the more emotionally attached; even he could sense that, and he was hardly an emotional being.

Her game could further his cause, too.

Her goal might be to bind him to her with lust, hers to command forevermore – his goal was to evoke love to keep her his, now and always.

Amelia had no real proof her plan was working, but there was a look in Luc's eyes when they rested on her when he didn't realize she knew he was watching that set her heart soaring.

Like now. From his chair at the end of the dining table, he watched as she snipped off a bunch of grapes and laid it on her plate. Luncheon today had been a light meal in deference to the heat outside. It looked set to be a long hot summer.

She popped a grape between her lips and glanced at Luc.

He shifted, looked away, reached for his wineglass.

Hiding a smile, she looked down at her plate. Selected another grape. 'How do the hounds fare in such weather?'

'They just lie around, tongues lolling. No runs or training in such heat.' After a moment, he added, 'Sugden and the lads will probably take the pack down to the stream later, once the worst of the heat's passed.'

She nodded, but declined to help him out with another question. Decided that her plan would be better served by silence, and by eating her grapes delicately, one by one.

Her plan was simplicity itself. Love existed between them – she recognized it in her, had always believed she could find it in him. But to evoke it, call it forth, not once but again and again until, stubborn male that he was, he acknowledged and accepted it, too – to do that, she needed his emotional shields down.

But they never were down, not ordinarily.

Only when they were physically entwined – only then could she sense the emotions that drove him, the power behind his desire, behind the tumultuous passion. By whipping passion to new heights, she'd hoped to weaken his shields so she could connect with those emotions he otherwise kept so hidden.

And she'd been right. It wasn't only that look in his eyes that had grown stronger by the day. Interlude by interlude, the emotional surge when they came together grew stronger, clearer, more powerful. It hadn't yet broken free, hadn't yet flattened his defensive walls and forced itself on his consciousness, but victory seemed only a matter of time.

It still amazed her that a man could be so hard, so ruthless, so passion-driven, so dominant and dictatorially inclined, yet when he touched her, there was care, protection, and a devotion in him not even the most ruthless passion could disguise.

That last made her shiver; she didn't try to suppress it. She glanced at him, saw he'd noticed; she smiled. 'Higgs told me the grapes are grown here, in succession houses. I never knew you had any.'

He met her gaze, watched her take another grape between her lips, then replied, 'They're to the west, between the house and the home farm.'

Her eyes steady on his, she asked, 'Perhaps you could show me?'

One black brow rose. 'When?'

She raised her brows back. 'Why not now?'

He looked at the windows, out at the lawns drowsing under the sun. He sipped his wine, then looked back at her. 'Very well.' He gestured to her plate. 'When you've finished.'

His eyes held hers – challenge accepted, another issued in return.

She smiled, and applied herself to her grapes.

They left the dining room; she linked her arm with his, and they headed down the corridor and through

350

the west wing. He opened the door at the end and she stepped outside; a warm breeze stirred her curls. She glanced at him as he joined her. He met her gaze; rather than offer his arm, he took her hand, and they set out, strolling across the lawn.

'The most direct route is through the shrubbery.'

He led her through the archway cut in the first hedge. Beyond lay a series of green courtyards opening one to the next. The first held a fountain in a central garden, the second a sunken pool in which silver fish flashed. The last played host to a large magnolia, its trunk thick, its branches twisted with age. A few late blooms remained, pale pink against the green foliage.

She eyed the tree; it was an ancient monster. 'I've never been this deep into the shrubbery before.'

'There's little reason to come this way unless you're heading to the succession houses.'

Luc drew her to an archway in the last hedge; she stepped through. Ahead stretched three long, low, elongated sheds with many glass panes in their roofs and walls. Paved paths led to doors set in the nearer ends of each; Luc steered her to the leftmost shed.

He opened the door; a gust of warm air, rich with the scent of soil, leaf mold, and rampantly growing greenery washed over them. A veritable jungle lay before them. Amelia entered; as Luc followed and closed the door, a faint ruffling of leaves high above drew her gaze. Slats in the roof were open, letting the breeze waft through.

She looked around, eyes widening at the sheer magnitude of the greenery. Then she realized. 'It's summer.' She glanced at Luc. 'Everything's growing.'

He nodded. A hand at her back, he steered her on. 'There's little to do at present but harvest the fruits. Later, it'll be cut back, but right now, everything's left to run riot.'

Riot indeed; they had to duck and weave to follow the paved path down the center of the shed. The jungle denseness extended to the door at the other end. Jettisoning any thought of an interlude in the succession house – there was barely room to stand – Amelia led the way out.

They emerged into a small paved area partially surrounded by low stone walls; shaded by large trees, the spot was distinctly cooler than the shed. Unexpectedly, it afforded a view over the shallow valley before the Chase. She glanced around, orienting herself. The home farm lay beyond the shade trees, with the kennels and then the stables farther back to the right. To the left lay the valley, slumbering in the summer heat.

She walked to the low stone wall beyond which the ground dipped toward the front lawn. Close by the shed, steps descended to a path leading to the front drive. 'I thought I knew most of the grounds, but I've never been here, either.'

Securing the shed's door, Luc glanced at her, then crossed the flags, halting directly behind her. Over her head, he surveyed the valley, the sight as familiar as his mother's face. 'You'll have plenty of time to become acquainted with every facet of the estate.'

A quiver of awareness shot through her; she hadn't realized he was so close. She went to turn; he stepped closer, trapping her between him and the thigh-high wall.

She caught her breath, went very still.

Raising his hands, he curved them about her shoulders, bent his head. He might have to dance to her tune; that didn't mean he couldn't lead.

He touched his lips to the point where her shoulder met her throat, and she shivered. Head lifting, tilting, allowing him access, she let herself lean against him, but she was far from relaxed.

Releasing her shoulders, he slid his hands down her arms, then slipped beneath to push his palms across her waist and lock her lightly against him. Paused for a moment to savor her body, supple and curvaceous, pressed to his, then, his jaw to her temple, he murmured, 'Why?'

After an instant, she murmured back, 'Why what?'

'Why are you, for want of a better word, seducing me?'

She seemed to consider. 'Don't you like it?' Her hands came to rest over his at her waist.

'I'm not complaining, but you could do with a few lessons from an expert.'

She laughed, interdigitating her fingers with his. 'What, then?'

'When you trap your quarry in a room with seduction in mind, it's a good idea to lock the door.'

'I'll bear that in mind.' There was laughter and something else in her voice. 'Anything else?'

'If intending to use any exotic location, it's wise to reconnoiter first.'

She sighed. 'I'd no idea a succession house could be so crowded.' After a moment, she added, 'Anyway, it's too hot.'

'You still haven't told me why.'

Amelia recognized the undertone in his voice, knew she would have to answer. 'Because I thought you'd like it.' That was at least partly true. 'Don't you?'

'Yes. Do you?'

She blinked. 'Well of course.'

'What do you like best?'

When she didn't immediately reply, he elaborated, 'When I touch your breasts, when I suckle them, when I touch you between your thighs—'

'When you come inside me.' She'd already been warm; she was getting hotter by the minute. 'When you're deep inside me and I can hold you there.'

A long pause greeted that. 'Interesting.'

She wasn't going to let the chance slide. 'What do you like best?'

After the most fleeting pause, he answered, 'Having you.'

'But how? Do you prefer me clothed, or naked?'

His laugh was short, gravelly. 'Naked.'

'And you? Clothed or naked?'

He appeared to have to think. Eventually, he said, 'Either. It depends. But if you want to know what I prefer above all else?'

'Yes.' She made the word quite definite.

'I prefer both of us naked, in our bed.'

Before she could ask her next question, he bent his head; his lips caressed her ear, then skated lower.

'Anytime, night ... or day.'

The words hovered in the air about them; the afternoon was peaceful, silent, still. The atmosphere was heavy with the sun's warmth, weighted with unvoiced suggestion.

It was difficult to breathe, not just because his hands lay heavy at her waist, not only because she could sense his strength, and that overwhelming sexual power he commanded, already surrounding her. She was already his captive in that regard; the challenge had been issued, but there was no decision to be made – she had to answer, had to accede.

'Yes.' She breathed the word, felt his hands, his fingers, briefly tighten.

Then he raised his head; hands sliding from her, he stepped back. Took her hand as she turned to him. His gaze, dark as night, touched her eyes, lowered to her lips, then he glanced at the house.

'Come.'

He led her down the steps, along the path to the drive and around to the front door. Unhurriedly. Far from easing her unaccountably tight nerves, his apparent lack of urgency only wound her tighter. His attitude was one of having the right, and the whole afternoon, to do with her whatever he wished.

As, indeed, he did.

They entered the front hall and heard distant voices – servants working in the cool of the house, busy and cheerful – but as they ascended the stairs, all sounds fell away.

Silence engulfed them; they neared their room and the world retreated.

This house was his, she its mistress. It was indeed their bastion, its walls designed to protect and nuture them. He opened the door, drew her into their room, shut the door behind them. The snib of the lock was a soft echo, a note signaling intent.

The curtains were drawn against the heat and the sun. Golden light filtered through, illuminating a haven of stillness, not hot, not cool. Theirs.

Amelia walked to the bed, stopped, and glanced back.

Luc followed, but halted a yard away. He shrugged

out of his coat, dropped it, then started on the buttons of his shirt.

His eyes held hers. With a faint arching of one brow, she followed his lead.

By the time her chemise hit the floor, he was already naked, lying stretched on the bed, leaning on one elbow watching her. He'd pulled the covers to the bed's foot, dispensing with most of the pillows, leaving a wide expanse of silk sheet.

Stepping around the bed, she ran her gaze from his bare calves to his shoulders. Her lips curved; she suspected he knew how magnificent he looked, fully aroused, shamelessly masculine. She felt his gaze on her body, on her breasts, her thighs, as she knelt, then climbed onto the bed.

He reached for her hip, drew her down to lie beside him.

Met her gaze, seemed to weigh the moment, then he raised his hand, and set his fingertips to her breast. His eyes locked on hers; he touched, traced ...

The afternoon dissolved into golden hours of delight, of profound sensual bliss. He led, she followed, yet who sat in the driving seat changed several times, turn and turnabout.

It was too hot to lie body to body, in full contact, for long. In the drawn-out, extended exchanges when she had him under her hands, when she took him in her mouth and pleasured him, for the first time in their lives she knew she had the whip hand. Because he allowed her to have it, to take it – to take him as she wished.

And she returned the favor, without reservation. Without intent beyond the giving.

It was too hot for either to think, to watch for hints

of the other's thoughts, the other's motives. By unspoken agreement, one she was as conscious of as he, they set aside all outward desires, disregarding their day-to-day hopes and fears, the needs and wants that drove them outside the doors to this room. By a deliberate joint act of will, they devoted themselves unreservedly to the moment, to the sensual, the physical, and what lay beyond.

The hours stretched, and they came together in simple, achingly sweet pleasure, again and again. They gave no thought to anything but that, the delight their bodies could give and receive. The only sounds to disturb the heavy stillness were their pants, their moans, groans, the faint, rhythmic slap of skin against skin, the soft shushing as they moved upon the silk sheet.

Outside, all lay still, slumbering under the relentless sun. In their room, heat swirled, and danced across their skins. Tongues lapped, languid and slow, bodies arched, bowed, limbs slid and shifted, fingers traced, drifted, hands cupped, caressed, touched, possessed.

And as the hours slid past, something else went with them – the barriers behind which they both, until then, had sought to hide. She felt him tremble, caught in the throes, felt him surrender, felt the last shield fall away.

Felt her own heart constrict so hard she thought it would shatter. Then the glory rushed in and swept her away.

In the end, between them nothing remained but simple honesty. Neither had gone searching for it – it was simply there, theirs. Golden and bright. Their gazes met – each recognized the uncertainty in the other, felt the same. They both drew breath, short, shallow, tight.

By mutual accord, gazes locked, together, they reached for it, claimed it, accepted it.

Accepted the fact that in doing so, they could never be the same, never retreat and return to how they had been before they'd closed the door.

They came together in a kiss, each needing the contact, wanting more. Her fingers sank into his hair, holding him to her; his speared through her long locks, tangled and tumbled.

He rolled and came over her, nudged her thighs wide. She parted them, cradled him. Arched when he entered her, sheathed him lovingly again. Lifted her knees and gripped his flanks as he moved within her, danced with him as the sheets heated and the musky scent of their desire swirled through the room.

Their tongues tangled, dueled; their bodies rode an uninhibited ride, slick and hot, and suddenly urgent. The abrasion of his chest against her breasts made her cry out, made her gasp.

He drank the sound, held tight to the kiss, slid his hands down, curved them about her bottom and held tight to her. The way she matched him, the way she held him within her, caressing him, wanting him, drove him wild.

The power flared between them, rushed through them, and they followed – higher, further, faster, deeper. No barriers, no restrictions, no thoughts, no regrets. Just a driving, untameable, irresistible need to give themselves up to the flames.

To dive into, to wallow, to glory, to burn in the pure heart of what they knew lay between them.

Chapter Seventeen

Men!

Thank heavens she was stubborn. Stubborner than he.

Toiling up the stairs to the top floor of the Chase, Amelia silently berated her lord and master. He of the masculine persuasion who, in this one matter, was proving to be unbelievably dense.

She couldn't believe he could be so stupid as not to comprehend what was in front of his nose!

After what had occurred on that overhot afternoon, anyone would think the true state of affairs between them ought to be obvious. They *loved* – were in love. She was in love with him; he *had* to be in love with her. She couldn't see any alternative – any other way it might be. Any other possibility to explain all that had occurred, and all that had flowed from it.

However, it was now two days – *forty-eight hours* – later and Luc had said not a word, given not a single sign.

What he was doing was watching her, carefully, which had ensured *she'd* said not a word.

She didn't dare.

What if the damned man really was so stupid that he didn't see the truth? Or refused to see it – that was much more likely. But if either was the case and she mentioned the word 'love', she'd lose every last inch she'd fought so hard to gain. His shields would go up, and she'd be shut outside.

She wasn't silly enough to take the risk. The truth was, she had time; only days ago she'd been congratulating herself on having got so far so fast with him. She – they'd – now gone even further, deeper into the mysterious realm that was love. The mysterious realm love was proving to be. Yet they'd only been married nine days.

It wasn't even the end of June.

So there was no justification for taking any risks by trying to force his hand.

Reaching the top of the stairs, she didn't bother to mute her, 'Huh!' As if she could force him to anything.

She'd just have to be patient and stick to her sworn path, cling doggedly to her goal.

'*I'm twenty-three!*' wailed in her mind.

Resolutely shutting the words out, she headed determinedly down the corridor that ran above the master suite.

'Higgs, have you seen her ladyship?'

The housekeeper was bustling down the corridor, her arms full of fresh linens, two parlor maids in tow.

'Not since just after luncheon, my lord. She was in her parlor, then.'

Amelia wasn't in her parlor now; Luc had just been there. Frowning, he turned toward the front hall.

The second parlor maid skidded to a halt and

360

bobbed. 'I saw her ladyship going up the main stairs, m'lord. When we was on our way to get these.' She lifted the folded linens in her arms.

'That would be about fifteen minutes ago, my lord,' Higgs called back.

'Thank you, Molly.' Luc strode for the stairs.

As he climbed, he slowed. Wondered why Amelia had gone to their apartments, wondered what she'd be doing when he found her.

Wondered what he would say – what excuse he would give for his appearance.

Reaching the first floor, he paused, then shook aside his reservation. He was married to the damn woman – he had a right to join her whenever he wished.

He strode straight to the bedroom, opened the door – one quick glance told him the room was empty. Disappointment tugged; he looked at the connecting door to her private rooms, then stepped into the bedroom and shut the door. She might have heard his footsteps in the corridor; if he came from this direction, it would appear he was just looking in on her.

But when he sauntered into her sitting room, that, too, was empty. Frowning, he returned to the bedroom, then checked his private room, a place he rarely used, but she wasn't there, either.

Returning to the bedroom, his gaze fell on the bed. Their bed. The bed in which, ever since that afternoon they'd spent in it, they came together without so much as a veil between them emotionally or physically. What reigned in that bed was the truth – what he didn't know, couldn't tell, was whether on her part it meant love.

For himself, he no longer doubted it, but that only

361

made his uncertainty greater, made his question more crucially important.

If what she felt for him was love, then he and their future stood on rock-solid ground.

If it wasn't love . . . he was in a hideously vulnerable position.

There was no way he could tell. No matter that he'd watched her like a hawk, he'd yet to see any outward sign that she loved him, any evidence that what she felt for him when she took him into her body was more than purely physical.

He stared at the bed, then turned away. For other men, perhaps that – her physical giving – would be assurance enough. Not for him. That belief was one he'd lost long ago.

From the door, he glanced back at the bed. What it now embodied both frightened and buoyed him. At least he had time – a few months. Until the end of September. No need to panic.

Marriage lasted for a lifetime – nothing in his life was currently more important than convincing Amelia to love him, and show it, at least enough so he would know. So he could feel confident, and emotionally safe, again.

Quitting their room, he headed back to the stairs, then paused, nonplussed. Where was she? Intending to descend, he reached for the balustrade – and heard a sound. Faint, distant; he couldn't place it. Then he heard it more definitely, looked up.

A second later, he left the downward flight and took the stairs up to the top floor.

The door off the gallery stood open. Beyond it, looking out over the valley, lay the nursery. He approached the door; courtesy of the runner, Amelia

362

didn't hear him. Leaning a shoulder against the door-jamb, he watched her.

She was half turned away, facing a large cot standing between the windows. Taking notes.

The sight made his heart catch, had him quickly calculating ... but no, not yet. The emotion that had surged was familiar; in the face of her occupation, it had scaled new heights. He wanted to see her with his babe in her arms – that want was absolute, intense, now an integral part of him. And, thankfully, one facet of his love for her he didn't need to hide.

She lifted her head; he considered the note tablet in her hand. As yet unaware of him, she read what she'd written, then slipped tablet and pencil into her pocket.

Leaving the cot, she moved to a low dresser under one window. She pulled out two drawers, peered in, then slid them shut. Then she looked at the window, studied it, reached out and tugged at the bars set into the frame.

His lips curved. 'They're solid. I can vouch for it.'

Releasing the bars, she glanced at him. 'Did you try to break out?'

'On more than one occasion.' Straightening, he strolled to join her. 'Me and Edward both. Together.'

She looked at the bars with new respect. 'If they withstood the pair of you, they must be safe.'

He halted beside her; she didn't turn and meet his eye. 'What are you doing?'

She gestured, went to step away, but he caught the hand that waved, slid his fingers around her wrist. She frowned, vaguely, at those fingers, then briefly at him. 'I've been making a list of all that needs doing. Higgs and I missed these rooms when we went around earlier.' She glanced about, waved with her other hand. 'This needs refurbishing, as even you must see. It's been what – twelve years? – since there were babies here.'

He caught her gaze, trapped it, without looking away, raised her wrist to his lips. 'You would tell me, wouldn't you?'

She blinked. 'Of course.' Then she looked at the window. 'But there's nothing to tell.'

'Yet.' He kept hold of her hand, wrapping his fingers around hers.

After a moment, she inclined her head. 'Yet.'

His gaze remained on her face, on her profile. Her jaw was set. 'When there's anything to tell, you will remember to mention it, won't you?'

She glanced at him. 'When there's anything you need know—'

'That's not what I said.'

Chin rising, she looked back at the window; he stifled a sigh. 'Why weren't you planning on telling me?'

It didn't really matter; if he was capable of keeping track of complicated investments, he was capable of working it out on his own, especially now she'd reminded him. But the fact she hadn't intended to tell him immediately ... what did that say of how she viewed him?

'As I said, there's nothing to tell yet, and when you *need* to know—'

'Amelia.'

She stopped, lips compressing. After a moment, she went on, 'I know what you'll be like – I've seen all the others, even Gabriel, and he's the most sensible of the lot. And as for you – I know you – you'll be worse than any of them. I've seen you for years with your sisters. You'll hem me in, confine me – you'll stop me from riding, even from playing with my puppy!' She tugged, but he didn't let her go; eyes flashing, she glared at him. 'Can you deny it?'

He met her gaze squarely. 'I won't stop you playing with the puppies.'

She narrowed her eyes but he didn't flinch, didn't shift his gaze. After a moment, he said, 'You do realize that if you were carrying my child, I would want to know, that I would care – not only because of the child, but because of you as well? I can't help you carry it, but I can – and will – keep you safe.'

Amelia felt something inside her still. There was a sincerity in his tone, in his eyes, that reached her, touched her.

Under her scrutiny, he grimaced, but his eyes remained on hers. 'I know I'll be obsessive, or at least that what I'll decree will seem so to you, but you have to remember that when it comes to pregnant wives, men such as I feel ... helpless. We can order our world much as we wish, but in that one arena ... everything we want, everything we desire, so much of what's at the core of our lives, seems to be placed in the hands of fickle fate, not only beyond our control, but even beyond our influence.'

He'd spoken from the heart. Such a simple admission, one she knew was true, but one men like he so rarely made. Her heart leapt. She turned fully to him—

A commotion outside had them both glancing at the window; they stepped closer and looked down. A large traveling coach rocked to a halt before the front portico; a procession of smaller coaches rolled up in its wake.

Figures streamed from the house; others jumped

365

down from the coaches. The Dowager Lady Calverton, her four daughters, and their entourage had returned from London.

Luc sighed. 'Our privacy is at an end.'

He looked at her. Amelia met his gaze, sensed his desire to kiss her, a desire that quivered in the air. Then his long lashes swept down; he released her and stepped back, waved to the door. 'We'd better go down.'

She turned, but instead of heading for the door she stepped closer, stretched up, and set her lips to his. Felt his immediate response, treasured the sweet moment, then she drew back.

Reluctantly, he let her.

She smiled and linked her arm in his. 'Yes, I will tell you, and yes, we'd better go down.'

'We went to Astley's Amphitheatre and Gunter's, too. And the museum.' Portia twirled before the windows of the drawing room; her hours in the coach had in no way dimmed her boundless enthusiasm for life.

'We went to the museum twice,' Penelope informed them. The light glanced off her spectacles as she looked up from her seat on the chaise.

Luc glanced at the slight, frail-looking figure sitting beside Penelope. Miss Pink appeared exhausted, as well she might – it sounded as if she'd been dragged all over London several times in the few days his younger sisters had spent in the capital.

'We could hardly waste the opportunity to see all we could.'

Luc looked at Penelope; she gazed back at him, brown eyes steady – as usual, she'd read his mind. It was, in his opinion, one of her least attractive habits.

'We all thoroughly enjoyed our time at Somersham,' his mother put in, 'and although the last days in town were busy with shutting up the house, it was a pleasant and eventful interlude.' Minerva sat in her customary armchair, sipping a cup of tea. Her gaze rested briefly on Emily, seated alongside Miss Pink, then she raised her eyes to meet Luc's.

He surmised he'd be hearing more about Lord Kirkpatrick shortly.

'I'm so glad you could all come to Somersham for the wedding.' Amelia sat in another armchair, likewise sipping tea.

'It was perfect – just *perfect*.' Portia continued to twirl. 'And seeing everyone again – well, we've known them all for years, but it was lovely to catch up and learn how people have got on.'

Luc leaned his shoulders against the mantelpiece – surrounded, as he'd been for the past eight years, by a sea of females. He was fond of them all, even Miss Pink, although they often laid seige to his sanity. And now he'd added another. One who threatened to be the most unnerving of the lot.

Portia was the most predictable. Ceasing her twirling, she swung to him. With her dark hair and deep blue eyes, she was the most physically like him; she'd also inherited the longer bones of his mother's family – she was taller than Emily, Anne, and Penelope. 'I'm going to visit the puppies. They must have grown enormously in the past two weeks.'

She bobbed a curtsy, then headed for the French doors giving onto the terrace and lawns.

Luc inwardly grimaced, but felt compelled to say, 'The largest male is already adopted – don't set your heart on him.'

Portia halted and looked back at him, brows high. 'I thought he looked a potential champion – have you claimed him, then?'

'No.' Luc nodded at Amelia. 'I gave him to Amelia.'

'Oh!' Portia's smile was genuinely delighted – in more ways than one. She beamed at Amelia. 'What have you called him?'

Luc shut his eyes fleetingly, inwardly groaned.

'He seemed very set on questing.' Amelia returned Portia's smile. 'He's Galahad of Calverton Chase.'

'*Galahad*!' Portia gripped the back of the chaise, her face alight. 'And Luc agreed?'

Amelia shrugged. 'The name hadn't been used before.'

Portia looked at Luc; from her expression she was busily making connections he'd much rather she didn't. Her eyes narrowed, sparkling with intelligent conjecture, but all she said was, 'Capital! I'm off to see this phenomenon.'

She strode for the French doors.

Penelope set down her cup, swiped up two biscuits. 'About time, brother dear. Wait for me, Portia – I have to see this, too.'

With a nod to their mother and Amelia, Penelope hurried out after Portia.

The energy level in the room subsided to more comfortable levels. Everyone smiled, relaxing a trifle more. Luc hoped Amelia, at least, imagined Penelope's comment referred to the puppy's name; he was fairly certain his irritating littlest sister had meant something more pointedly personal.

Minerva set down her cup. 'Of course, there were a few other events of interest during the past week beyond Astley's and the museum.' Together with Emily and Anne, she filled Luc and Amelia in, passing on the good wishes of various hostesses. 'When you return to London later in the year, you both, along with Dexter and Amanda, can expect to be besieged.'

'With any luck, some scandal will by then have reared its head, deflecting the interest of the fickle.' Luc straightened, adjusting one cuff.

Minerva shot him a cynical look. 'Don't wager on it. Given Martin and Amanda took refuge in the north, and you married at Somersham and headed immediately up here, the hostesses will be waiting for their moment.'

Luc grimaced; Amelia smiled.

Miss Pink, sufficiently restored from the rigors of the journey, rose and quietly excused herself; Emily and Anne, having finished their tea, decided to retire to their rooms.

'I've set dinner for six,' Amelia said, as they bobbed to her.

'Oh, good!' Emily said. 'We'll be famished by then.'

Anne smiled softly. 'It's so good to be home.'

The instant they'd quit the room, Minerva glanced at Luc. 'You may expect a letter from Kirkpatrick – by my guess, within the week.'

Luc raised a brow. 'He's that serious?'

Minerva's lips twitched. 'Impatient, my dear, as I would have thought you'd appreciate.'

He let that comment lie.

Minerva added, more seriously, 'An invitation to visit here would be appropriate, but I didn't want to say anything until I'd consulted with you.'

Her gaze had shifted to Amelia – who suddenly realized the implication; she waved. 'Of course.' She glanced at Luc. 'Late July or early August, perhaps?'

He met her gaze. 'Whatever you decide. We'll be here until late September.'

Amelia looked back at Minerva.

Who relaxed in her chair. 'We can decide once he writes – he definitely will.' Her lips curved. 'So that's Emily all but settled.' Minerva glanced at Luc, then back at Amelia, her smile deepening. 'I won't ask how you two are getting on – I'm sure you've been settling in and finding your feet without any great difficulty. Has it been very warm up here?'

Cursing her memory, which immediately focused on that long afternoon she and Luc had spent rolling on their bed, Amelia prayed she wouldn't blush. 'We did have a day or two when it was quite hot.' She fought not to glance at Luc.

Minerva rose. 'The chaos must have subsided by now. Time for me to go up and rest for an hour or so. Six, you said?'

Amelia nodded.

Minerva inclined her head to them both. 'I'll see you in the drawing room.'

She glided toward the door, then halted. Turned back, frowning. 'Actually, while we're alone . . .' She glanced briefly at the door, then continued, her tone serious, 'While I was packing, I found I was missing two items. A *grisaille* snuffbox – you know it, Luc – and a perfume flagon with a gold collar. They're both small things, but old and quite valuable.' She looked at Luc. 'Both were in my sitting room, and yes, they're definitely gone, not misplaced. Do you have any ideas?'

370

Luc frowned. 'We haven't taken on any new staff.'

'No. That was my first thought, too, but what with running shorthanded for years, everyone still with us has been with us all those years. It seems inconceivable it could be anyone within the house.'

Luc nodded. 'I'll check with Cottsloe and Higgs – it's possible we had someone through for the chimneys, or something similar.'

Minerva's face cleared. 'Of course – you're quite right. That's sure to be it. Still, it's a sad day when one has to guard such items every time someone unknown steps over the threshold.'

'I'll look into it,' Luc said.

Minerva nodded and left.

Amelia set aside her empty cup and rose. Both she and Luc remained standing, watching until his mother had passed out of sight beyond the open drawing room door.

Then they glanced at each other; their gazes met, held. They stood a foot apart. Luc reached out, sliding his fingers down over her wrist to twine with hers.

This close, in this light, and because he let her see, the desire that prowled behind his dark eyes was impossible to mistake.

Again she sensed his welling need to kiss her, to touch her – to take her in his arms; like a wash of heat against her skin, it awakened her, drew her to him. A shimmering aura, desire hung between them until, once again, she sensed him rein it in, suppress it.

His gaze still locked with hers, he lifted her hand, pressed a kiss to her knuckles. 'I'd better go and check what's going on in the kennels. Portia and Penelope have their own ideas about everything, and they're both termagants at heart. And then I really have to do some work in the Office.'

She accepted what he was telling her with an easy smile, but when he released her hand, she linked her arm with his and turned toward the French doors. 'I'll come to the kennels with you – I want to make sure your sisters don't spoil Galahad.'

When they stepped onto the terrace, she murmured, 'Let's go via the shrubbery.'

It was the longer way to the kennels; Luc hesitated, but acquiesced.

She let him lead her into the courtyards surounded by the high hedges. Let him lead her past the fountain, to the courtyard where the pool lay limpid under the last of the day's sunshine, where fish flickered and swished, silver flashes in the water.

Convinced him that taking her in his arms and kissing her – just for a little while – was something that despite the advent of his sisters could, with a little determination, still be squeezed into his schedule.

That evening, the magnitude of what Luc faced within his family became clear.

Sitting at the end of the long table, now comfortably filled, Amelia watched, and learned, and, despite having to struggle to keep her lips straight, felt for him.

He was out of his depth.

She'd never imagined seeing him like that – that such a situation could ever be – yet here he was, manfully trying to cope with four very different females, all of whom were under his protection. He was their guardian.

And his evening had got off to an unsettling start.

Handing a platter of beans to Emily, seated on her right, Amelia noted again the abstracted quality of Luc's eldest sister's gaze. Emily's thoughts were very definitely elsewhere, dwelling on exceedingly pleasant memories.

She'd had her suspicions of just what such memories might be; a nonchalant question when they'd gathered in the drawing room earlier and she'd drawn Emily a little apart, concerning Lord Kirkpatrick and Emily's feelings for him, had elicited such a glow in Emily's eyes, and her words, as to confirm just how definite matters had become between Emily and his lordship. Hardly a problem given Minerva was expecting an offer any day.

Squeezing Emily's hand, she'd smiled with feminine comprehension, then turned – to find Luc's dark blue gaze fixed on them. He'd excused himself to his mother and Miss Pink, and come prowling over; she'd been ready to step in should he attempt to interrogate Emily, but that damsel, a light blush to her cheeks, simply put her nose in the air and refused to be meek.

Instead, greatly daring, Emily had confessed that she found his lordship quite manly, indeed, all she could wish for in a husband.

Amelia saw Luc clench his jaw, probably wisely biting back a demand to be told all. She doubted he'd enjoy hearing it.

Emily's comment, and the fact she'd looked at Luc in its wake, evoked the inevitable comparison. Kirkpatrick was well enough, well set up and decently handsome, but to rhapsodize him when one had grown up with Luc – that was a clear demonstration of Emily's state.

It was Luc who was masculine beauty personified – grace, elegance and aristocratic polish doing nothing to hide the hard, sharp, darkly menacing qualities of steely strength and inflexible, arrogant will. It was Luc who had always sent a shiver down her spine.

And still did.

He'd noticed – his gaze had swung to her, sharpened.

'Dinner is served, my lord, my ladies.'

Cottsloe had bowed in the doorway, struggling not to beam. The whole family bar Edward was here, at home once more, and all was perfect in Cottsloe's world.

She'd been grateful for the interruption. Placing her hand on Luc's sleeve, she'd let him lead her in. Let him seat her at the end of the table, at the place she hadn't occupied since their wedding night.

The touch of his fingers trailing over her bare arm evoked a memory of past thrills; she'd considered sending him a frowning glance – instead, she got distracted, wondering . . .

Luckily, the meal provided a diversion, especially with Portia and Penelope present. Portia, fourteen, was a hedonist, bright, cheery, and sharply intelligent. With her looks and her tongue, and her quick wits, she was so much like Luc that of the four, he found her most difficult to deal with.

Portia tied him in knots. At every opportunity.

Despite that, the affection that flowed between them was apparent. It took Amelia most of the meal to realize that Portia had set herself to play the role of Luc's nemesis, at least within the family, making sure her eldest brother never got too arrogant, too above himself with masculine condescension.

No one else would dare, at least not to the extent

Portia did. She herself would never have opposed Luc so definitely as did Portia – not in public. In private ... in reality, she had more power than Portia over Luc, more chance of altering his entrenched behaviors where they needed adjustment. She wondered how, given that Portia was only fourteen, she might explain, might suggest that Portia could now leave her brother's arrogance in the delicate hands of his wife.

For unknowingly – Amelia was quite sure unintentionally – Portia was also grating on something else in Luc – the very thing that made him what he was, but which also gave rise to the worst instances of what appeared to be his masculine high-handedness.

She could see it, and was mature enough to value it where Portia did not.

Luc cared deeply for his sisters – not just in the general way of duty, because they were in his care, and had been for the past eight years – but in a manner that went to the heart of family, and what family meant to him.

As she watched him frown and snipe intellectually with Portia, Amelia was reminded of his earlier words about their potential offspring.

He would have to know – she would have to tell him as soon as she herself was sure. It was simply that important to him. So important it was the first thing he'd deliberately revealed now the barriers between them had come down. He'd asked, admitted more than he'd needed to – a confidence she knew how to value and knew she needed to return.

That unwavering, unreasoning, unconditional devotion was there in his expression, in the effort he made to cope, to remain as far as he could in control of his sisters' lives. With or without their consent.

Emily was almost at the point of stepping out of Luc's care, but he'd deal with that by passing her hand to Kirkpatrick. Until he did, however ... Amelia made a mental note to suggest to Emily she avoid giving her brother any potentially inflammatory information he didn't need to know.

Then there was Anne, who remained so quiet that everyone was forever in danger of forgetting she was there.

Anne was seated on Amelia's left. She smiled at her, then set herself to learn how Anne had found her first Season. Anne knew her, trusted her, confided in her easily; while she absorbed Anne's reactions, Amelia felt Luc's dark gaze resting on them and duti- fully made mental notes.

She was more than socially adept enough to, while listening to Anne, also glance at Penelope, the youngest, seated in the next chair. In terms of the number of words she uttered, Penelope could well have been judged 'quieter' than Anne. No one, however, was at all likely ever to forget that Penelope was present. She viewed the world through the thick lenses of her spectacles – and the world knew it was being weighed, measured, and judged by a shrewd and highly intelligent mind.

Penelope had decided at an early age to become a bluestocking, a woman for whom learning and knowl- edge were more important than marriage and men. Amelia had known her all her life, and could honestly not remember her ever being otherwise. Presently thirteen, brown-eyed and brown-haired like Emily and Anne, but possessed of a decisiveness and confidence her older sisters lacked, Penelope was already a force to be reckoned with, but just what she planned to do with her life, no one had as yet been informed.

Portia and Penelope got on well, as did Emily and Anne, but the older sisters were forever at a loss when it came to dealing with their juniors. Which threw an added burden on Luc's shoulders, for he couldn't, as a male in his position normally would, rely on Emily and Anne, or indeed on his mother, to keep the younger two within bounds – bounds neither Portia nor Penelope truly recognized.

And they encouraged each other. Where the elder girls shared aspirations, so, too, did Portia and Penelope. Unfortunately, their aspirations did not lie within the areas generally prescribed for gently bred young ladies.

As things presently were, the pair of them looked set to turn Luc's black hair grey. Amelia glanced at Luc's dark locks, inwardly frowned.

A moment later, she caught Luc's eye. She smiled, and reminded herself she was, after all, his wife.

Which meant she had a right and a duty to ensure his black hair remained just the shade it was for the next several years.

She'd come to that conclusion, made the resolution, by the time she climbed into their bed that night. Snuffing out the candle, she lay back, and considered the hurdles she'd decided to face with a welling sense of rightness.

One of those hurdles was gaining his agreement, his understanding, his acceptance of her help, but she was too wise, when he joined her half an hour later, to mention the matter.

He himself brought it up; halting in the dimness by the side of the bed, he reached for the tie of his robe. 'Did Anne give you any indication of how she felt about the Season – the *ton*?'

Eyes and the better part of her mind fully absorbed as he loosened the robe, then shrugged out of it, she murmured, 'If you mean how she feels about the subject of a husband, I don't think she does.'

He frowned, knelt on the bed, then slumped down beside her, propped on one shoulder on top of the silk sheet that covered her to her shoulders. 'Does what?'

'Have any real thoughts of a husband.' She twisted to face him. 'She's only what? Just seventeen?'

He raised his brows at her. 'You think she's too young?'

She met his gaze. 'Strange though the thought may be to you, not every girl dreams of being wed as soon as she's out.'

A moment passed, then, his gaze steady on her face, one dark brow arched higher. 'Didn't you have girlish dreams of being wed?'

She wondered if she dared tell him that the only dreams of marriage she'd ever entertained had transformed into reality. He was the only gentleman she'd ever dreamed of marrying. Nevertheless, as she felt between them the inexorable rise of the compulsion that now ruled them here, in their bed, where neither any more pretended otherwise, she was very glad – gave thanks to the gods – that she'd waited until she was twenty-three to tackle him.

'I'd be surprised if Anne doesn't have dreams of marriage, of what she wants her marriage to be. But I sincerely doubt – no, I know – that she's not yet thinking specifically about stepping into that sphere.

She will when she's ready, but it won't be yet.'

He studied her face, then lightly shrugged. 'There's no need for her to do anything in that arena until she wishes to.'

She smiled. 'Precisely.'

She lay still, watching, waiting, letting her gaze roam his face while heat and desire welled and swelled and grew between them. Waited for him to make the first move, confident that whatever route he chose to take, the outcome would be novel, and as exciting, fascinating, and enthralling as she wished. In this sphere, his imagination had, she suspected, no bounds. His understanding of what she would find thrilling and pleasurable had proved, thus far, to be one hundred percent reliable.

After a long moment, his lips curved; his teeth flashed as he smiled. Then he leaned closer, bent his head, and set his lips to hers.

He didn't touch her in any other way, simply kissed her – while they both lay naked with only the flimsiest barrier of silk between their heating bodies.

And the temperature steadily escalated. Rose as he demanded her mouth, then took rapaciously when she offered. Yet with not so much as a finger did he touch her.

His body was like a flame, a source of pure heat beside her; she could feel that heat, warm, alive and so well remembered, all down the length of her. Her skin itself seemed to yearn – to burn with the need to touch, and be touched.

A yearning that only grew.

Then he drew back, looked down. Hooked one long finger into the sheet, now tight about her swollen breasts; crooking his finger between her breasts, he

379

didn't so much as graze her skin as he drew the sheet down, easing it down to her waist.

His gaze touched her face, then he bent his head. And set his lips to her nipple. He didn't touch the soft skin of her aching breasts, but only the aureole – tortured the tightly budded peak until she arched and gasped.

The instant he released her, she slumped onto her back, giving him access to her other breast. He bent his head and repeated the exquisite torture until she cried out and reached for him.

He caught her hands before she touched him, locked them both in one of his. Anchored them above her head as he reached again for the sheet, and tugged it still lower.

To her hips.

This time, when he bent his head, his tongue touched her navel. Probed, circled, probed again.

She'd never truly considered that one of those spots that could make her weep with need; with her skin on fire, with her body burning with the need to feel him against her, with that confined, restricted caress, he proved her wrong.

When he next raised his head, he drew the sheet all the way down and away. Releasing her hands, he grabbed two pillows, simultaneously moving down the bed.

'Lift your hips.'

She did, knowing full well what was coming when he stuffed both pillows beneath her. She expected him to run his hands up her legs, to caress them. Instead, he grasped her knees – lifted them up and wide as he settled between, and bent his head to her.

Covered her with his mouth, caressed her with his tongue.

She smothered her cry, suddenly unsure.

He lifted his head to murmur, 'No one can hear.'

She hauled in enough breath to ask, 'Even if I scream?'

Dark satisfaction rumbled in his voice. 'Even then.'

He bent to his task; she lay back, and let the fire wash over her. Her skin was aflame, her nerves leaping, even though he was only caressing her there, at her core. He held her knees so wide her thighs didn't touch him; she could have reached the top of his head, but it seemed more important to close her fists tight in the sheet beneath her, as if she could thus cling to her wits, to the world as he wound her tighter and tighter.

Notch by steady, knowing notch ... until she fractured.

She saw stars, felt the heat and the force swirl through her body. Felt his satisfaction in the way his mouth worked on her, the way his tongue filled her.

Then the pillows were gone and he surged over her.

And he was inside her, all around her, surrounding her with heat, fire and flaming passion. He drove into her and she ignited; her skin, so long denied, like white-hot lava merging with his, her entire body hungry and greedy to touch, to take, to consume and be consumed.

She grabbed him, held him tightly.

Luc felt her nails bite as she writhed beneath him, riding the wave of ecstasy he'd conjured, as she strove as passionately, as desperately as he to reach the next pinnacle of promised delight.

Their bodies knew each other deeply, completely; they merged and fused, unrelenting in their need.

Consumed, consummating in that moment of

absolute trust, of abject surrender.

And then they were there, at the highest peak of earthly delight, and the inferno took them. They gave themselves up to it, bathed in the flames, and let the glory fill them.

The moment stretched, held, then slowly faded as, locked together, they tumbled back to reality. The fire waned, until it was nothing more than glowing embers, buried inside them.

It would never be anything less – their shared hearth would never be cold, never lonely; the fire that now smoldered within would always keep them warm.

Chapter Eighteen

The next morning saw the first of the visitations customary in county circles when welcoming a new bride into their midst. Squire Gingold and his wife led the charge, somewhat surprisingly accompanied by their two sons, both gangly youths, painfully shy.

Luc took one look at them, then sent a message summoning Portia and Penelope. Amelia, chatting with Mrs. Gingold, wondered ... yet although the Gingolds were pleasant, both bluffly good-natured, she couldn't believe Luc would encourage his sisters in that direction. The Ashfords were, regardless of any difficulties, of the *haut ton*.

Mrs. Gingold put her right. When Portia and Penelope appeared and curtsied to the company, the looks on her sons' faces made her sigh. She exchanged a meaningful glance with Minerva, then, lowering her voice, confided, 'Besotted, the pair of them. No more *nous* than helpless puppies, but it'll pass soon enough, no doubt.'

Not soon enough for Portia and Penelope – Amelia read their thoughts with ease. While she, Mrs. Gingold, Minerva, Emily, and Anne comfortably conversed, exchanging the London news as well as local tales, and Luc and the Squire, sitting apart, were deep in plans for new plantings and repairs to fences, she kept a watchful eye on Portia and Penelope, holding exceedingly reluctant court by the terrace doors.

They appeared every bit as arrogantly superior as their eldest brother, and had tongues to match.

She couldn't hear what was said, but when Portia, brows high, spoke haughtily to one of the young men, cuttingly enough to make his face fall, Amelia inwardly winced.

Luckily, before she felt compelled to rescue the poor youths from the torture they'd brought upon themselves, the Squire concluded his business with Luc and rose. Mrs. Gingold exchanged a resigned smile with Minerva, extended it to Amelia, and heaved herself up from the chaise. 'Come, boys. It's time we left.'

Despite all they'd suffered, the boys were reluctant to leave. Fortunately for them, their parents paid them no heed. The entire company swept out to the portico. Portia and Penelope peppered the Squire with questions, showering on him the eager interest they'd denied his sons. Mrs. Gingold climbed into her gig; one son took the reins while the other joined his father on horseback.

The Ashfords waved their guests away, then turned back inside. Minerva went off with Emily and Anne in tow; Luc disappeared into the shadows of the front hall. As Portia and Penelope were about to follow, Amelia looked toward the kennels. 'I'm going to walk around and check on Galahad. He and his brothers and sisters could probably do with a gambol.' She glanced at the girls. 'Why don't you come with me? I'm sure Miss Pink will excuse you for another half hour.'

'She will if we tell her we were with you.' Penelope changed directions. 'Anyway, you shouldn't take all the puppies out by yourself. There are too many to watch over all at once.'

'Indeed.' Portia swung away from the door. 'And they're still so helpless.'

Amelia grabbed the opening. 'Speaking of helpless puppies ...' She waited until both girls glanced at her. Held their gazes until comprehension dawned and they shifted and looked away.

'Well, they're just so *irritating*. And soppy about it, too.' Penelope scowled in the direction the Gingolds had gone.

'Perhaps, but they don't mean to be. And there's a difference between being civilly discouraging and actively taking slices out of their hides.' Amelia glanced at Portia; she was looking down the valley, her lips compressed. 'You could try being a little more understanding.'

'They're both older than us – you'd think they'd have more sense than to moon about us the way they do.' Portia's chin firmed; she glanced at Amelia. 'They can't seriously imagine we're flattered by such fawning.'

Neither had had a younger brother; both Edward and Luc were much older. When it came to youthful males, Amelia had considerably more experience than they. She sighed, linked arms with Penelope, then with Portia, and drew them toward the gravel walk leading around the house. 'They may be older in years, but in the arena of male-female relationships, boys, indeed, even men, are always backward. It's something you need to remember.

'In the Gingold boys' case, a little understanding now – and no, I don't mean being encouraging or even acquiescing but just dealing with them gently – may work to your later advantage. They'll likely always live in this area and may later be perfectly reasonable acquaintances; there's no need to give them poor memories of you. Furthermore, a little practice in dealing with male devotion, however misplaced, won't come amiss. When it comes your turn to make your bows to society, knowing how to deal with besotted young men . . .'

Amelia's voice faded as the trio walked along the path; from where he'd been waiting inside the front door, Luc risked looking out. The three were walking slowly, heads bent close – black, blond, and brown – Amelia lecturing, his sisters listening – perhaps reluctantly, but listening.

He'd been waiting to try to make precisely the same points, but he would not have been been anywhere near as successful.

Aside from anything else, he would never have admitted to being backward in the arena of male-female relationships.

Even if it were true.

He stood in the hall, the tension that had gripped him over the prospect of verbally wrestling with Portia and Penelope over their unacceptable behavior dissipating. With that fading, his mind returned to its usual obsession – that other female he'd yet to adequately deal with.

Suppressing a resigned grimace, he headed for the Office.

*

386

A week of long sunny days rolled by, punctuated by more visits as the families around about called to offer their felicitations and welcome Amelia. As she was already known to all, such visits passed in comfortable style, with easy familiarity. Outside such social interludes, a steady murmur of life filled the Chase – something Luc also found comfortable and familiar.

It was the way his home had always been, as long as he could remember it – the long corridors filled with the steady thrum of a large household, the laughter and whispers of his sisters, his mother's more measured tones, giggling from the maids, Higgs's brusque edicts, Cottsloe's deeper voice. To him, that murmurous sound – a sound containing so many other sounds – represented much of what he'd struggled for the past eight years to preserve.

The sounds of the Chase in midsummer embodied the essence of family, the essence of home.

And now there was another thread in the symphony, another player. Time and again, he found himself listening for Amelia's voice, listening as she interacted with, interjected, corrected and encouraged his sisters.

In company with Minerva, Emily, and Anne, Amelia returned their neighbors' visits, satisfying the social expectations. Both Emily and Anne watched and learned, taking more notice of Amelia's behavior than they ever had of their mama's.

The expected letter from Kirkpatrick arrived. Minerva was simply pleased; with the confidence of one experienced in such things, she assumed everything would go smoothly. And there was no reason it wouldn't.

387

Emily, however, was understandably keyed up; she started worrying over things that didn't need worrying about. Luc steeled himself to speak with her, to somehow allay her feminine fears – Amelia got there first, relieving him of the problem of dealing with something he didn't truly understand.

Emily responded to Amelia's calming comments, smiling and returning to her usual self almost immediately. Luc felt cravenly grateful.

He was likewise happy when he discovered Amelia encouraging Anne, not pushing, but supporting, which was exactly what he himself wished to do but couldn't easily manage. He was a male, after all; his sisters all had him pegged, although the manner in which each regarded him differed.

Which was why, when one night over the dinner table, Amelia stepped directly between him and Portia, he found himself reacting, not gratefully, but with a quite different emotion.

A dark glance, a flash of tension that flowed through him – although she now sat at the other end of the table, Amelia noticed. One brown brow rose faintly, but she kept control of the conversational reins she'd filched from his grasp.

However, later that night, as soon as they were alone, even before he'd brought up the subject, she did, explaining her reasoning, asking – outright – for his approval. He'd given it, for she'd been, as usual when it came to his sisters, right. Her insight with respect to them was more acute than his, yet when she explained, he saw what she saw and agreed with her tack.

Reluctantly, he stepped back and let her handle them, reassured when she grasped private moments here and there to keep him informed.

Gradually, in such small increments that at first he didn't notice, the burden of dealing with his sisters lifted from his shoulders. He relaxed – and then he noticed. That he was less tense in their presence, that relaxed, he took greater joy in their company. He didn't love them any the less, but from one step back, his view of them was clearer, less clouded by his instincts, by the fraught knowledge they were solely his responsibility.

Legally, they still were; in reality, that responsibility was now shared.

The realization made him pause, again evoked a reaction, a concern he couldn't easily shrug aside.

When he walked into their bedroom later that night, Amelia was already abed, lying back on the pillows, her curls a gilded frame for her face. Calmly expectant, she watched him approach. He halted by the side of the bed, caught her gaze.

Reached for the tie of his robe. 'You've been very helpful with my sisters – all of them.' He shrugged out of the robe, let it fall. Watched her gaze drift down from his face. 'Why?'

'Why?' Her gaze didn't leave his body as he joined her on the bed, then she reached for him and lifted her eyes to his. 'Because I like them, of course. I've known them all their lives, and they need, perhaps not help, but guidance.'

She watched while he slid down beside her, and skin met skin, then she lifted a hand and brushed back the lock of hair that had fallen across his brow. 'Your mother ... it's been a long time since she had to deal with such things, and such things have changed with the years in many cases.'

'So you're doing it for them?'

She smiled, settled invitingly back, her fingers trailing down his cheek. 'For them, for you, for us.'

He hesitated; the 'for you' he'd hoped for, hoped he understood. Wasn't about to ask. 'Us?'

She laughed. 'They're your sisters, we're married – that makes them my sisters-in-law. They're family, and they need advice – advice I can give. So of course I'll do what I can to ease their way.'

Her hand slid into his hair, firmed as she drew his head to hers. 'You worry about them too much. They're clever and bright – they'll do perfectly well. Trust me.'

He did. His lips closed on hers, and he let the matter slide. Let another take its place. Let the power and the passion strip away their thoughts, let sensation and emotion rule, let their bodies fuse in concert with their souls.

Later, when moonlight painted a swath across their bed, he lay with Amelia asleep beside him and tentatively adjusted his thoughts.

He cared deeply for his sisters; Amelia knew that. He'd wondered what her motives in assisting with them were. A telling reaction; when it came to her and what was now between them, he could barely believe how far his uncertainty stretched. He'd imagined it possible that in seeking to control his sisters as well as his household, she was seeking, ultimately, to control him.

His position – his very self – was so deeply rooted in his home, in his family, that controlling both would effectively give her considerable influence over him. While he'd expected her to rule his household, he hadn't foreseen her helping with his sisters.

More fool him, but he was starting to suspect he'd been – was still being – foolish on a wider front.

He'd long recognized love for the power that it was, had always been wary that it would prove strong enough to rule him. As, indeed, he now knew it was.

She'd always been a terribly managing female, one as stubborn as he, yet she'd been the only woman he'd ever truly wanted, ever wanted as his wife. And now she was.

His wariness, his distrust – his continuing uncertainty – all stemmed from the fact that he didn't know *why* she'd chosen to marry him. He'd assumed, imagined, guessed – all wrongly, it now seemed.

He still didn't know.

But finally, belatedly, very likely foolishly so, he was starting to believe that it wasn't a wish to rule him that drove her.

The next afternoon, Amelia was sitting in her parlor toting up her household accounts when Higgs looked in.

'A curricle's coming up the drive, ma'am. Dark-haired gentleman, dark-haired lady – not anyone from 'round about but I do think I might have seen them at your wedding.'

Mystified, Amelia set down her pen. 'I'll come and see.'

She was expecting Amanda and Martin, together with her parents, Simon and her aunt Helena, all who'd been visiting at Hathersage, Amanda's new home which Amelia had yet to see, in a few days. Concern over what had brought anyone else earlier made her walk quickly to the front hall.

Cottsloe opened the front door and she stepped

out, raised a hand to shade her eyes against the slanting sun, and searched the long, curving drive. She spotted the curricle starting the long climb toward the house.

Stepping back, she glanced at Cottsloe. 'Please tell his lordship that Lucifer and Phyllida have arrived.'

Turning, she went out onto the portico to greet her cousin and his wife.

'What's wrong?' she asked the instant Lucifer stepped down from his curricle.

His gaze went past her to the groom hurrying up to take charge of his horses, then shifted to the portico where Cottsloe waited, a footman hovering, about to come for their luggage. Turning to her with his customary rakish smile, he enveloped her in a hug, planted a kiss on her cheek. 'I'll tell all later, when it's just you and Luc and me.'

'And me.' Phyllida prodded his back.

Lucifer turned and lifted her down. 'And you, of course. That goes without saying.'

Phyllida threw him a look, then embraced Amelia. 'Don't worry,' Phyllida whispered. 'No one's in any danger.'

Lucifer was scanning the surrounding fields. 'Superb country.'

Phyllida and Amelia exchanged glances, then linked arms and headed for the house. 'Now, quite aside from that,' Phyllida said, 'you must tell me everything. I'm here in lieu of everyone still in the south. How are you getting on?' Glancing ahead, Phyllida saw Luc step onto the portico. 'Ah, here's your handsome husband. He's almost as hideously handsome as mine.'

392

'Almost?' Amelia laughed. 'Each to our own taste, I suppose.'

'Indubitably,' Phyllida replied.

Luc lifted a brow as they neared, his gaze alert, serious; Amelia signaled with her eyes, murmured 'Later' as she slipped past to give her orders to Higgs.

There was plenty to talk about, laugh about; a late-afternoon tea and subsequently dinner sped by. Luc and Lucifer denied any interest in port, so the family settled comfortably in the drawing room.

Eventually, the girls and Miss Pink retired; after a few minutes, Minerva followed them upstairs. Luc rose as the door closed behind her. Crossing to the sideboard, he poured brandy into two glasses, handed one to Lucifer, then sank onto the arm of Amelia's armchair.

He sipped, then asked, 'What's the problem?'

Lucifer circled the room with his gaze, then looked at Luc.

'No one can hear us. All their rooms are sufficiently distant.'

Lucifer nodded. 'Right then. Our problem isn't clear. The facts, however, are these. After your wedding, Phyllida and I returned to London, intending to spend a week or so there, in my case, touching base with my various contacts.'

Luc nodded; he knew of Lucifer's interest in silver and jewelry.

'One afternoon, while looking over an old acquaintance's stock, I came upon an ancient silver saltcellar. When I asked where the dealer had got it, he admitted it had been brought to his back door by one of the "scavengers", his term for those who receive

393

goods with no declarable provenance.'

'Stolen goods?'

'Usually. Generally the better dealers avoid such goods, but in the case of the saltcellar, the dealer hadn't been able to resist.' Lucifer's brows rose. 'Luckily for us. The last time I saw that saltcellar it was at the Place. It was presented to one of my great-something-grandfathers for services to the Crown.'

Amelia sat forward. 'It'd been stolen from Somersham?'

Lucifer nodded. 'And that wasn't all that was taken. I retrieved the saltcellar, and we took it back to the Place. We arrived there to find Honoria seriously vexed. That morning she'd received three letters from various family members who'd stayed overnight. They were all missing small items – a Sèvres snuffbox, a gold bracelet, an amethyst brooch.'

'That sounds like the same thief who's been filching items from all over London.' Luc frowned. 'There's some reason you've come all this way to tell us.'

'Indeed, but let's not jump to any conclusions, because, frankly, we don't have sufficient facts. However, the reasons I've come to you are twofold. First, the losses at Somersham were already public knowledge before Devil and Honoria heard of them, so they haven't been able to keep things within the family, as they would have preferred.'

Lucifer held up his hand to stop Amelia when she would have asked why. 'The bald facts of the scattered thefts are that, if you chalk the losses at the Place up to the same account, then there appears to be only one common factor, only one group who attended all the affected events.'

Silence gripped the room. For long moments, no one broke it. Lucifer looked steadily at Luc, who returned his regard.

'The Ashfords,' Luc finally said, his voice even, uninflected.

Lucifer grimaced. 'On the face of it, yes. Devil and Honoria have returned to London – they'll do what they can to dampen speculation there. Luckily, with the Season virtually at an end, if we can deal with it – whatever it is – swiftly, there won't be much damage.'

To Amelia, Luc seemed preternaturally still.

'We can't afford another scandal – not after Edward.'

Lucifer inclined his head. 'We knew you'd feel that way, which is why I drove up here and Devil headed back to town. We need to identify the culprit, so we can deal with the situation as we'd prefer. And, if necessary, minimize any damage.'

His gaze distant, Luc nodded; he raised his glass and sipped.

Phyllida, until then silent, stirred. 'You haven't told them the rest.'

Lucifer glanced at her, then grimaced; he looked at Amelia and Luc. 'When we were discussing all this – Devil, Honoria, Phyllida, and I – we'd forgotten there was someone else in the room. Great-aunt Clara. As usual, she confounded us all by telling us she rather thought her nurse-cum-companion might have seen something helpful. Luckily, Althorpe, the nurse, isn't anywhere near as vague as Clara – when we spoke to her, Althorpe remembered the incident clearly.

'It was the night of your wedding, and she'd been up late settling Clara. When she got back to her room, she saw a young lady rushing back to the house. It was after midnight. Althorpe is adamant the young lady was older than a schoolgirl, but not by much, and was distraught. Very much upset.'

'Could she describe this young lady?' Amelia asked.

'She was looking down on her – she didn't see her face. What she did see was thick brown hair, possibly shoulder-length – the lady was wearing a cloak, but the hood had fallen back.'

'Brown hair,' Luc murmured. He took another sip of brandy.

'Definitely. Althorpe was quite clear on that – not black, not blond. Brown.'

It could be one of my sisters.

Luc had made the comment, drawn the inevitable conclusion. Amelia knew how much it had cost him to do so.

Neither Lucifer nor Phyllida had said anything more; they'd all retired, sober and absorbed.

Now, lying in their bed, she watched Luc walk slowly toward her. His face was shuttered; he was further from her – and withdrawn to a greater distance – than at any time since they'd first spoken of marriage.

Her heart ached for him. After saving his family from the disaster of his father's depredations, steering them through the grim scandal of Edward's making, after working so hard and finally succeeding in getting all back on an even keel ... only to have all his efforts swamped by this.

The implicit threat was all too real. If it came to pass ... for him, it would be a serious blow.

She waited until he joined her beneath the covers, then took her courage in her hands, and baldly asked, 'Who do you think it is? Emily or Anne?'

That stillness that sometimes came over him swept him. He said nothing, just lay stiffly beside her. She bit her lip against the nearly overwhelming urge to speak, to reach for him. To dismiss and push her question away.

Then he exhaled. 'I think ... ' He paused, then his tone changed, 'I wondered if it could be Mama.'

It was he who reached for her, his hand finding hers, covering it, then gripping, holding tight. 'I wondered if ... well, you know how many families face a problem like that, one they hide and never speak of.'

That was a possibility she hadn't considered. 'You mean' —she turned to him, easing closer, seeking to comfort simply by touch— 'if she'd developed a habit of picking up things that caught her eye and not even really knowing?'

He nodded. 'The girl the nurse saw could have been something quite different – nothing to do with the thefts.'

Amelia thought of his mother, intelligent, calm, and wise. 'No. I can't see it.' She made her tone as definite as she felt. 'Those other older ladies who start taking things – from all I've heard, they're quite vague, not just about what they've taken but generally. Your mother's not like that, not at all.'

He hesitated, then said, softly, 'She's been through a lot over the years ... '

Amelia considered Minerva's quiet strength. She pressed closer; under the covers, she lifted a hand to his chest. 'Luc – it isn't your mother.'

Some of his tension left him, but not all. He released her fingers, lifted his arm over her, letting her snuggle against him, draping his arm so he could hold her there.

Accepting her comfort, her help, not shutting her out.

Amelia closed her eyes in mute thanks, then she felt his lips press the curls at her crown, felt the weight of his head as he rested it against hers.

After a long moment, he spoke. 'If not Mama, then it must be Anne.'

Chapter Nineteen

They didn't put it into words, but come the morning they had a tacit agreement that together they would face whatever developed in this latest threat to the Ashfords, and overcome it.

Both Emily and Anne had been at all the gatherings from which items had disappeared. Impossible to believe Emily, so caught up in her romance with Kirkpatrick, had spent any time filching small objects of value. Anne, on the other hand, so quiet and retiring . . .

In the depths of the night, Luc had asked, 'Do you have any idea why she might do such a thing?'

She'd shaken her head, then stopped. Eventually murmured, 'The only reason I can think of is that she believes she needs money for something, something she can't approach you, or me, or your mother about.'

Luc hadn't argued. But before they'd finally fallen asleep wrapped in each other's arms, he'd murmured, 'One thing – we can't broach the matter to her without real proof. You know what she's like.'

He hadn't elaborated, but she'd understood. Anne's

quietness wasn't like Penelope's. Penelope often remained silent simply because she saw no reason to waste her words. With Anne, being retiring was a form of self-effacement, a means of hiding in plain sight. Anne was inherently nervous; it had always been clear it would take time and steady encouragement to make her comfortable in society.

An unfounded accusation would destroy Anne's fragile confidence. If she learned that they – her family, her brother and guardian – suspected her of stealing ... regardless of the right or wrong of the matter, the outcome would be disastrous.

The morning's gathering about the breakfast table maintained its customary tone – bright, breezy, lots of feminine chatter. Today, there was a rumbling masculine counterpoint; Luc and Lucifer sat at one end, discussing something – Amelia couldn't hear what. Phyllida and Minerva were swapping household tales. Miss Pink was keeping an eagle eye on Portia and Penelope, biding her time before herding those two damsels upstairs for their lessons.

Amelia turned to Emily, on her right; Anne sat on her left. 'I was thinking it might be a good idea to check over your wardrobes.' With a glance, she extended the comment to Anne. 'You may well need more gowns to see you through the summer, and we should be looking ahead to when we return to town in autumn.'

It took Emily a moment to draw her mind from its now habitual preoccupation; Lord Kirkpatrick and his family had been invited to visit in a few weeks' time. She blinked, then nodded. 'I hadn't really thought, but you're right. I wouldn't want a panic over gowns while Mark's here.'

Amelia hid her smile. 'Indeed.' She looked at Anne. 'We should check your things, too.'

Anne smiled and nodded her agreement.

Perfectly readily, without the slightest hint of trepidation.

Amelia glanced down the table. At the other end, even though his conversation with Lucifer hadn't faltered, Luc had been watching, following her tack. She met his dark gaze; although he didn't precisely nod, she sensed his agreement to her plan.

If Anne had been stealing things, what was she doing with them? If her actions were purely an irrational compulsion, then the items would be hidden somewhere, most likely in her room. With Emily, Portia, and Penelope forever about, let alone the maids and Mrs. Higgs, anywhere else seemed unlikely. And even if Anne had somehow managed to sell some items, as the matter of the saltcellar seemed to suggest, she couldn't possibly have sold everything.

'Is there much to see in the village?' Phyllida asked.

Amelia looked up. 'Not really, but it's a pleasant place. We could go riding that way after lunch, if you'd like.' She nodded down the table at their spouses. 'They'll no doubt be occupied elsewhere.'

Phyllida grinned. 'Indeed. After lunch, then.' She pushed back her chair.

The table broke up. Phyllida and Minerva went out for a stroll in the gardens. Miss Pink ushered her charges up the stairs to the schoolroom. Leaving Luc and Lucifer still talking over their coffee cups, Amelia, Emily, and Anne headed off for the girls' rooms.

The necessity of examining their gowns wasn't a complete fabrication. It was Emily's and Anne's gowns that had first alerted Amelia to the family's straightened circumstances – she'd noticed fabrics being reused, gowns recut and refashioned; it had been cleverly done but having been in such frequent contact with the family, she'd seen and guessed the truth.

Now, there was no reason the girls couldn't have new gowns, that their wardrobes couldn't be improved to a level commensurate with their social standing. The girls themselves knew nothing of that, but Amelia did.

She directed them first to Emily's room. Emily opened her wardrobe doors wide, Amelia sank into an armchair by the window, Anne plopped down on the bed, and they all settled to enjoy themselves.

Forty minutes later, they'd exhaustively examined the contents of Emily's wardrobe and dresser. Amelia had extended their purview to include all garments, shoes, accessories of all kinds; every drawer and box in Emily's room had been looked into, the contents picked over.

Glancing down at the tablet on which she'd jotted various notes, Amelia nodded. 'Very well. We'll arrange to get all these things. Now ...' She waved to the corridor.

Without further direction, they decamped to Anne's room next door.

There they repeated the exercise, this time with Emily perched on the bed and Anne at the wardrobe doors. Amelia watched Anne closely as she pulled out gowns, shawls, and spencers. Not a glimmer of self-consciousness, not a trace of guilty fear, showed in

402

Anne's sweet face – just a shy delight at being included in such an undertaking.

Again, the contents of every drawer, every hatbox and bandbox were examined; all Amelia discovered was that Anne needed more silk stockings, a new pair of evening gloves, and a new cherry red shawl.

Holding the old one up, Anne studied it in dismay. 'I've no idea ... it was old, of course, but I can't think why the weave should have given way like that.'

Amelia shrugged. 'Silk sometimes does that – just gives way.' Although the fabric of the shawl looked like it had been worried and wrenched. 'Never mind. We'll get you a new one.'

Emily sat up. 'Until you get a new shawl, you won't be carrying your red reticule – the one that matched it. Can I borrow it? It's just the right shade to go with my carriage dress.'

'Of course.' Anne looked up at the shelf above the wardrobe's hanging space. 'It should be here some-where.'

Amelia glanced down at her notes. Emily and Anne shared clothes and accessories freely, a fact that had further disguised the lack in their wardrobes from the eagle eyes of the *ton*'s matrons. She scribbled a reminder to make sure Anne had all she needed to go on with, given all indications were that Emily would shortly be leaving home.

'I'm sure it was here.' Stretched on her toes, Anne pushed things this way, then that. 'Ah – here it is.'

She pulled the reticule free by its strings; with a grin, she swung and let it fly across the room to Emily on the bed.

Emily laughed and caught it, then her face

registered surprise. 'It's heavy. What on earth have you got in it?'

As she felt the contents of the reticule through the layers of red silk, Emily's expression grew more puzzled.

Amelia glanced at Anne, but the only expression on her face, in her brown eyes, was one of complete bemusement. 'A handkerchief, some pins. I don't know what could be heavy . . .' But they could all now see the shape under Emily's hands. 'Let me see.'

Anne crossed to the bed, to Emily's side; Amelia rose and joined them. By then, Emily had tugged the reticule's strings loose; she eased open the top and looked in. Then, frowning, she reached in and pulled out—

'A quizzing glass.' Emily held it up. They all stared at the ornately chased stem, at the tiny jewels winking along its length.

'Whose on earth is it?'

It was Anne who asked the question. Amelia looked at her – closely, sharply; no matter how hard she looked there was nothing but total befuddlement in the younger girl's face.

'And how did it get there?' Anne glanced back at her wardrobe, then swept around and returned to the shelf. Without Amelia suggesting it, Anne hauled all her reticules, all the hatboxes they'd already examined down. When the shelf was bare, she pushed aside the boxes and knelt beside the mound of reticules. She opened each one, and shook out the contents. Handkerchiefs, pins, a comb, two fans.

Nothing else.

Sitting back on her heels, Anne looked across the room. 'I don't understand.'

Neither did Amelia. 'It's not your mother's, is it?'

Emily shook her head, still studying the quizzing glass. 'I don't think I've seen anyone else with it either.'

Amelia took the quizzing glass. It truly was heavy; she couldn't imagine any lady carrying such a thing. Anne had drawn near, frowning at the glass – entirely at a loss.

'It must have been put into your reticule by mistake.' Amelia slid the glass into the pocket of her day gown. 'I'll ask around – the owner shouldn't be too hard to trace.' She looked around. 'Now, have we finished going through everything?'

Anne blinked, then looked about, somewhat dazedly. 'I think so.'

Emily gathered up the red reticule and jumped from the bed. 'I've just remembered – it's our day to do the vases.'

Amelia manufactured a smile. 'You'd better get going then – there's less than an hour to luncheon.'

They left the room; Anne closed the door. Emily popped into her room to leave the red reticule there, then rejoined them as they headed down the corridor. Amelia hung back as the two girls went ahead down the stairs; at the bottom, they turned and waved, then continued on to the garden hall.

On the last stair, Amelia paused. Emily had smiled, Anne had not. Doubtless, Emily had already dismissed the quizzing glass from her mind; she had too many far more pleasant matters to dwell on. Anne, however, was worried. Possibly a little fearful. But so she would be; despite being quiet, she was not unintelligent. None of Luc's sisters was.

Amelia stood in the empty front hall, hand on the

newel post, gazing unseeing at the front door, then she sighed, refocused, stepped down from the stairs, and headed for the study.

Luc looked up as Amelia entered the study. She saw him seated behind his large desk, but didn't smile. He watched impassively as she closed the door, then crossed the room.

As she neared, he realized her expression was unfamiliar – reserved, almost somber.

'What's the matter?' He couldn't hold back the question, started to rise.

She met his gaze, waved him back. He subsided into his chair; she passed the chair before the desk, continued around it. Reaching him, lips tight, she turned, sat on his lap, then leaned into him.

His mind streaked in a dozen different directions; an odd fear clutched his heart. Bad news – that was all he could think. He closed his arms about her, gently, then more firmly; she snuggled closer, deeper into his embrace, her cheek to his chest. He laid his jaw against her curls, feeling them slide like silk against his chin. 'What?'

'I went with Emily and Anne to check through their things – you heard me organizing.'

'You found something.' The vise about his heart slowly closed.

'Yes. This.' She lifted her hand and showed him an ornate quizzing glass. 'It was in one of Anne's reticules.'

His heart grew cold, then colder; he forced himself to take the quizzing glass. He held it up, squinted when he saw the stones flash. 'Diamonds?'

'I think so. And I don't think it's a lady's – it's too heavy.'

406

'I don't think I've ever seen it before.'

'I haven't either. Nor have Emily and Anne.'

Luc felt cold tension flow through him; it kept him so silent and still, Amelia eventually glanced up.

He met her gaze; her eyes were wide, as blue as the sky. A little shock, and a ton of worry, shadowed the blue. He clung to the contact and forced himself to say, 'So it's Anne, and we have another Ashford scandal.'

He saw the frown flow into Amelia's eyes before her brows drew down.

'No.' She shook her head brusquely. 'Stop leaping to conclusions.'

'Leaping . . . ?' He felt a flash of temper. Knew it was irrational. 'What the hell am I – is *anyone* to think—'

Amelia struggled to sit up, to draw out of his arms.

He immediately tightened his hold. 'No. Sit still.'

She complied – he suspected because she had to – but her accents were clipped when she tersely informed him, 'I'm sure it's not Anne. Or Emily, for that matter.'

He felt a little of the icy tension seep away, felt the vise ease a notch. 'Why? Tell me.'

She hesitated, then said, 'I'm not a mind reader, but I'm not hopeless at judging people and their reactions either. Anne was truly surprised, totally puzzled over the quizzing glass being in her reticule. She hadn't known it was there – I'm sure she didn't recognize it, meaning she literally had never seen it before. Anne's shy – she's not experienced enough to hide her feelings. And the most telling fact of all was that she didn't need to give Emily the reticule – she could easily have said it wasn't there, or she'd look it out later, or ... a host of things.'

Luc struggled through her words, then admitted, 'I'm lost – explain.'

She did, sitting in his lap within the circle of his arms. When she finished, she sat still, waited ...

After some moments, he forced himself to take a tight breath. 'Are you sure ...?'

'Yes.' She looked into his face, held his gaze. 'I'm quite certain that whoever took that quizzing glass, it wasn't Anne or Emily.'

He tried to find some wavering in the steady blue of her eyes. 'You're not just saying that ...?' He gestured with one hand; even though it was behind her back, she understood.

The stubborn set of her chin and lips softened. She laid a hand against his cheek. 'I might' —she paused, then continued— 'turn a blind eye to some things if I thought it was in your best interests, that it would help you or our family, but this ...' She shook her head; her eyes held his. 'Telling you it wasn't Anne when it was wouldn't help, and might instead lead to a great deal more harm.'

Her words sank into him, slowly eased the vise open, let his blood flow again and warm him, driving away the chill.

He drew a deep breath. 'You're sure.' No question; the answer was in her eyes.

She nodded. 'Not Anne. Not Emily.'

He let the knowledge buoy him for a heartbeat, then asked, 'If not them, then who? How did this' —he lifted the quizzing glass— 'get into Anne's reticule?'

Amelia looked at the glass. 'I don't know – and that's what truly worries me.'

*

The luncheon gong summoned them from the study fifteen minutes later. They left the room together, leaving the quizzing glass in a locked chest.

Amelia checked her reflection in the mirror in the front hall, cast a quick glance around, then tugged her bodice properly into place.

Luc fought to keep his lips straight; the look she shot him as she turned and caught him doing so suggested he hadn't succeeded.

The dining room quickly filled. After seeing Amelia to her chair, Luc strolled the length of the table to his place at its head. The meal passed swiftly; the usual chatter prevailed. He watched Anne; for the most part, she kept her eyes cast down, answering any questions but with a frankly distant air. Her expression was serious, she volunteered nothing, but Lucifer and Phyllida were present; Anne's behavior could simply be due to her shyness.

He wondered if he should speak with her ... unfortunately, both she and Emily regarded him with a certain awe, quite different to how Portia and Penelope reacted. Any questions from him might totally undermine Anne's confidence.

On his left, Lucifer sat back. 'If it's convenient, I wouldn't mind going over those investments with you this afternoon.'

Luc hesitated, then nodded. Amelia and Phyllida were making arrangements to visit the village; they'd doubtless take Emily and Anne with them. Portia, Penelope, and Miss Pink were heading off for a ramble to the folly; his mother would, as she usually did, rest through the afternoon.

Setting down his napkin, he pushed back his chair and looked at Lucifer. 'No time like the present.'

409

Lucifer grinned. Together they rose, strolled up the room, both, entirely independently, putting out a hand to their respective ladies' shoulders as they passed. Both Amelia and Phyllida looked up with identical, confident, wifely smiles, then went back to their arranging.

Luc and Lucifer quietly left the room.

'Where's Anne?' Amelia asked when she and Phyllida met Emily in the stables.

'She's gone to Lyddington Manor to visit Fiona – she'd forgotten she'd said she would.'

Amelia digested that while they mounted. The Manor wasn't far; Anne would be safe there. Remembering Fiona's bubbling presence in London, and how it had helped Anne cope with the *ton*, Amelia was happy to see the friendship remain strong.

She, Phyllida, and Emily indulged in a quick gallop to shake the fidgets from their mounts, then settled to a more comfortable amble along the lane to Lyddington. The day was fine, the sun warm on their faces. Birds trilled and swooped. All seemed right within their world.

In the village, they left their horses at the inn and wandered the green, then repaired to the bakery to purchase some pastries. They consumed the delicious morsels on the seat in the sun, then simply sat and mused about life. About children. At Amelia's behest, Phyllida brought her up to date on her sons' development; Aidan and Evan were growing apace.

'They're scamps. I know they're quite safe at the Manor, but . . .' Phyllida gazed down the green, into the distance. 'I do miss them.' Smiling, she glanced

410

at Amelia. 'Mind you, I'm quite sure Papa, Jonas, and Sweetie will have spoiled them dreadfully by the time we get back.'

Her gaze moving past Amelia, Phyllida murmured, 'We've company. Who's this?'

It was Mrs. Tilby; the vicar's wife joined them in a voluble froth of greetings and declarations. She seemed quite keyed up; the pleasantries aside, she told them why.

'Things are going missing. A host of small items – well, you know how it is when you're not quite sure when you last saw something. We only realized when we gathered for the Ladies' Guild meeting yesterday – it's not the sort of thing one worries about until one realizes it's an epidemic. Well, one hardly likes to think what might disappear next.'

Her heart sinking, Amelia asked, 'What things have gone missing?'

'Lady Merrington's small enamel box – it used to sit on the windowsill in her drawing room. An engraved crystal paperweight from the Gingolds', a gold letter opener from the Dallingers', a gold bowl from the Castle.'

Those were all houses she, together with Minerva, Emily, and Anne, had visited in the last week.

Phyllida's dark eyes touched her face, then Phyllida turned to Mrs. Tilby. 'And these things have only recently gone missing?'

'Well, dear, that's what no one can truthfully say. What we do know is that they've vanished now, and no one knows where they've gone.'

Amelia and Phyllida had to hold their tongues and disguise their impatience, until, late that evening, they

411

finally got their husbands to themselves. Then they poured out their story.

Lucifer frowned. 'It doesn't make sense. In order to sell such things, they'd have to go to London.' He glanced at Luc.

Who shook his head. 'I can't see rhyme or reason to it either.' He took a sip of brandy, his gaze going to Amelia, curled in one corner of the chaise. 'That is, of course, assuming they're stealing for the monetary value of the things.'

Lucifer inclined his head. 'Assuming that.'

Amelia felt the weight of Luc's gaze; she turned her head and met it. He was waiting for her to tell Lucifer about the quizzing glass. She returned his dark gaze steadily and kept her lips firmly shut.

'There's another, more pertinent point to consider,' Phyllida said from the other end of the chaise. 'The thefts are still going on.'

'Which means' —Amelia took up the thread of the argument she and Phyllida had already thrashed out— 'that the thief is still active. We therefore have a chance of catching them, unmasking them, and setting matters straight.'

Lucifer nodded. 'You're right.' After a moment, he mused, 'We need to think of a way of drawing whoever it is into the open.'

They tossed ideas about but could see no immediate way forward. Still turning the matter over in their minds, they retired to their beds.

'Why didn't you tell them?' Luc slumped on his back beside Amelia in their bed. She'd snuffed the candle; faint moonlight, silvery and insubstantial, filtered through the room.

412

'Why didn't you?'

He took a moment to consider her tone, but why she should be annoyed with him he couldn't imagine. 'I'm hardly likely to tell a tale that seems to definitively implicate one of my sisters. Especially when, according to you, she's not the thief.'

'Well! There you are.' After a moment, she continued, in a fractionally less belligerent tone, 'Why did you imagine I'd think differently?'

He suddenly wasn't sure whether there was any ice at all, thin or otherwise, under his feet. 'Lucifer's your cousin. A Cynster.'

She looked at him. 'You're my husband.'

He could feel her gaze but didn't turn to meet it. He stared instead at the canopy while he tried to understand. 'You're a Cynster born and bred.' He knew what he thought that meant, but was too wary to put it into words.

She turned fully, coming up on one elbow so she could – frowningly – study his face. 'I might have been born a Cynster, but I married you – I'm an Ashford now. Of course I'm going to do all I can to protect your sisters.'

He had to meet her gaze. 'Even to the extent of being not quite open with Lucifer?'

She returned his regard. 'If you want the truth, the question never even occurred to me. My loyalty now is to you, and beyond you, *our* family.'

A knot of tension buried so deep he hadn't until that moment been aware of its existence unraveled, flowed away. Left him. Her declaration rang in his mind; the set of her jaw and lips stated she was unwaveringly steadfast, her position solidly fixed.

He had to ask. 'Can you really do that – switch

413

allegiances? Just like that?'

Even in the dimness, he could interpret the look she bent on him; she thought he was being unforgivably dense.

'*Of course* women can do that – we're expected to do that. Just stop and think how complicated life would be if we couldn't – or didn't – do that!'

She was right; he was being – had been – unforgivably dense. 'I didn't think ... men aren't conditioned to change loyalties like that, especially not family ones.'

One sharp pointy elbow came to rest on his chest. She leaned over him. 'It always falls to the ladies to handle the more difficult tasks.'

Now she was closer he could see the exasperated affection in her eyes. She couldn't fathom why he hadn't understood; she thought he'd been obtuse, unthinking. Not true, but now he did comprehend, finally saw what the truth had to be ... raising his hands, he framed her face. 'Just as well.' He drew her closer. 'Thank you.'

Before she could ask what he was thanking her for, he kissed her, long, lingeringly – thoroughly. She murmured incoherently and pressed nearer. Releasing her face, he slid his hands down her body, gripped her waist and lifted her across, setting her down atop him.

Drawing back from the kiss, he murmured, 'If I could make a suggestion ... ?'

Given his erection was now cradled between her thighs, Amelia had little doubt of what direction his suggestion would take. 'By all means.' She set her lips to his. When she finally drew back, she invited, 'Suggest away.'

He did; she'd never doubted the quality of his expertise, nor the tenor of his imagination. The activities he scripted made her forget all else – the thief, protecting Anne, all else to do with his family – while she devoted every part of her mind, every part of her body, to just one thing.

The most important thing.

Loving him.

She loved him. She must.

A true heart and a backbone of steel; he'd always known she possessed both, but in recent times had focused more on the difficult latter rather than the highly desirable former.

Now both were his because she was. He finally understood all that that meant – all *she* meant by that.

The realization left him giddy.

Now he could confess, tell her all and everything he wished, all he felt she had a right to know. And all would be well. As Helena had told him, once he accepted the power, it was his to wield.

Wield it he would.

The only question was when.

Her parents, Amanda, Martin, Simon, and Helena herself were all due to arrive that afternoon.

The day was filled with preparations; Amelia rushed to and fro, giving orders here, checking details there. Lucifer and Phyllida smiled understandingly and took themselves off for a picnic. Reluctantly accepting that his time was not now, Luc retreated to his study, leaving Amelia in absolute control.

For which Amelia was grateful. As keyed up as she, the staff rallied around; when the youngest stablelad, whom she'd set on watch, came running with the news that the first coach had appeared across the valley, all was in readiness.

Exchanging a triumphant glance with Higgs and Cottsloe, she hurried upstairs to change her gown and tidy her hair. Descending ten minutes later, she just had time to winkle Luc from his study before a crunch of gravel and the clatter and stamp of hooves heralded the first of their expected guests.

Hand in hand, they strolled out to the portico to see Martin, Earl of Dexter, descend from the carriage, then extend his hand to his countess. The instant Amanda's feet touched the ground, she looked up, and beamed. 'Melly!'

The twins met at the bottom of the steps, flying into each other's arms. They hugged, kissed, laughed, waltzed, then held each other at arm's length – and started talking, simultaneously, in a welter of half sentences they never seemed to feel the need to finish.

'Did you hear about—?'

'Reggie wrote. But how was—?'

Amanda waved. 'The journey was easy.'

'Yes, but what about—?'

'Ah, that! Well—'

Shaking his head, Martin climbed the shallow steps to Luc's side. The cousins exchanged smiles, with a spontaneous return to the camaraderie of their youth clapped each other's shoulders, then turned to survey their still chattering wives.

After a moment, Martin lifted his gaze, surveying the rolling green of the valley. 'This place looks even more prosperous than I remember it.'

Luc inclined his head. 'We are doing quite well.'

Martin had never known of the Ashfords' travails. If his cousin, who would remember the Chase in its glory days, could detect no lingering sign of their past plight, Luc was content to let that past die. The Ashfords had survived, that was what was important; his gaze resting on Amelia's golden head, he inwardly acknowledged that his house was only growing stronger. Day by day, by every day that she was his.

Another carriage appeared on the long slope traversing the other side of the valley; Martin nodded at it. 'That'll be the Dowager. Simon's traveling with her. Arthur and Louise are bringing up the rear.'

The sun slowly sank, gilding the V-shaped facade of the Chase; the afternoon stretched and lengthened with the shadows, the hours filled with warmth, joy, and unalloyed happiness as Amelia's family arrived and settled in.

Everyone gathered for afternoon tea; it was then that Martin and Amanda made their announcement. Amanda was expecting their first child. The gathering erupted with a fresh outpouring of joy, of exclamations and congratulations. Luc watched Amelia hug her twin, watched the ladies crowding round to kiss and hug each other delightedly. Turning from the sight, he beckoned Cottsloe and sent him to fetch champagne.

Cottsloe rushed off to obey. Given he could count perfectly well, Luc returned his gaze to Amelia. She noticed; she cast him a quick glance, one he couldn't be sure he read correctly – imploring?

The champagne arrived; rising, he went to the sideboard and busied himself pouring the delicately fizzy liquid into the glasses Cottsloe hurriedly fetched. Simon came up to help distribute the glasses.

The instant Simon left him, Amelia appeared at Luc's shoulder. He paused in the act of pouring. Her

417

hand closed over his wrist as their eyes met.

'Please don't say anything. I'm not sure!'

He read her eyes, then, lips curving, bent his head and brushed a kiss to her temple. 'I won't – stop worrying. This is their moment – they married a month before we did. We'll make our own announcement, in our own time.'

She searched his eyes, his face, then her brittle tension left her. She released his wrist; he finished pouring, then handed the glass to her.

She took it. Her eyes held his. 'Thank you.'

His lips curved. 'No – thank you.'

For one moment, they were the only people in the room, then Simon returned and gathered the rest of the glasses bar one. 'That's it, I think.' He turned back to the gathering in the center of the room.

Luc lifted the last glass, caught Amelia's gaze, then clinked the edge of his glass to hers. 'Come.' His arm sliding around her waist, he turned to company. 'Let's drink to the future.'

She smiled, leaned close for a moment, then together they returned to their guests.

The next hour winged by; at the end of it, everyone started to consider retiring to dress for dinner. Miss Pink drew Portia and Penelope away; Simon stood and stretched. As he turned to the door, it opened; Cottsloe came in, located Luc, and approached.

'My lord, General Ffolliot has called. He's waiting in the hall.'

Luc glanced at the company. 'Our nearest neighbor.' He looked at Cottsloe. 'Show him in here – perhaps he'd like to join us?'

Cottsloe bowed and withdrew. Luc rose and

strolled up the long room.

The door opened again and the General came in. Of medium height and heavy build, the General's most notable features were his shaggy brows and his ruddy complexion. A genial but somewhat shy and retiring man, he readily took the hand Luc extended and shook it heartily.

'Afternoon, Calverton. Glad I caught you.'

'Welcome, General – can I invite you to join us?'

The General followed Luc's wave and saw the massed company, all smiling agreeably, further down the room. He visibly blanched. 'Oh – ah. Didn't realize you had company.'

'It's not a private gathering – can I offer you a drink?'

'Well . . .'

The General dithered; Luc had forgotten how awkward he sometimes was in the presence of strangers. He heard the swish of skirts as someone approached – he assumed it was Minerva, who always treated the General kindly. Instead, Amelia appeared by his side, smiling charmingly, slipping one hand into his arm, extending the other to the General.

'It's lovely to see you, sir – do let me convince you to join us.'

Hiding a smile, Luc stood back and left the field to her. Within minutes, the General was seated on the chaise, Minerva on one side, Louise on the other. Although initially nervous, the General was not immune to the combined wiles of the ladies present; he soon had a cup of tea in one hand, a cake in the other, and was listening with rapt attention to the Dowager Duchess of St. Ives's views on the pleasures of the surrounding countryside.

Arthur caught Luc's eye, a twinkle in his. Luc smiled, and sipped his tea. Eventually, when the Dowager had finished complimenting the General on his good sense in living in such a pleasant place, Luc asked, 'What was it you wished to see me about, General?'

The General blinked; his nervousness returned. He glanced around. 'Well ... not the sort of thing ... then again, well ...' After a moment, he hauled in a breath, and said in a rush, 'I just don't know what to think – or do.' His gaze appealed to Minerva beside him, then he glanced at Louise and Helena, all of whom looked encouraging. 'It's my wife's gold thimble – one of the few things I had left of hers.' He looked imploringly at Luc. 'It's gone missing, you see, and what with all this talk of a thief about – well, I didn't know who to see ...'

There was an instant of complete silence, then Amelia leaned forward and touched the General's arm. 'How dreadful for you. When did you miss it?'

'Such an unhappy occurrence,' Helena declared.

Emily and Anne, unbeknown to them both under heavy scrutiny, were unabashedly shocked. 'How terrible,' Anne murmured, her eyes wide, innocence writ in every line of her face.

The ladies rallied around the General; Luc noted the General's answers to the shrewd and necessary questions Amelia and Phyllida put to him.

It seemed the thimble, a simple unadorned gold one, had sat on the mantelpiece in the Manor's parlor ever since the General's wife had died. The last time he remembered seeing it was weeks ago.

'Not the sort of thing I look at every day. Just knowing it was there was enough.'

The only reason the General had come to them was for comfort; at no point did he cast any aspersions on anyone at the Chase. But once he'd left, not reassured but calmed and to some degree indeed comforted, the mood in the Chase's drawing room turned somber; Luc, Lucifer, Amelia, and Phyllida exchanged weighty glances.

Arthur, Minerva, Helena, and Louise all noted those glances, exchanged glances of their own, then Minerva rose and shook out her skirts. 'We'd best go up and change – Portia and Penelope will be down shortly, and they'll find us all still here, none of us dressed.'

The group broke up, everyone retiring to their rooms.

'We'll have to talk later,' Lucifer murmured as he went up the stairs beside Luc.

Luc nodded. 'And not just talk.' He met Lucifer's blue gaze, almost as dark as his own. 'We need to come up with a plan.'

Chapter Twenty

By general consensus, they waited until Emily, Anne, Portia, Penelope, and Miss Pink retired at the end of the evening before broaching the topic uppermost in all their minds.

Helena held up a hand the instant the door closed behind Miss Pink. 'You must start at the beginning, if you please. There is no point rambling about any bushes with such a matter, not when we are all family.'

Luc, Amelia, Lucifer, and Phyllida exchanged glances, then Luc complied. He sketched the known actions of the thief within the *ton*, then Lucifer and Amelia described the pieces of the puzzle they'd stumbled across.

Standing before the hearth, Luc concluded, 'We do not at present have any idea who the thief is. However, whether by design or sheer coincidence, his activities are making it appear that the culprit is ...' He paused, then, face hardening, went on, 'One of us. One of the Ashfords.'

Helena, more serious, more disapproving than Amelia had ever seen her, nodded decisively. 'Yes. It will be said it is one of your sisters. But as we have seen today, that is quite impossible.'

Luc studied her, then asked, 'Why do you say it's impossible?'

Helena stared at him, then blinked. 'Ah, I see – you wish me to state it. Very well. It is impossible that Emily or Anne could be the one who has taken the General's thimble because both are *jeunes filles ingénues* – they are not capable of dissembling to hide such a thing, not before me, and Louise and all here. This is not credible. Also, Amelia has said they did not know anything about the quizzing glass. It must be, I think, Lord Witherley's – I will look at it later. But again, neither their actions nor Amelia's reading of them supports the idea of either being involved. So they are not.'

Helena's expression grew somber. 'But that means we must find who is, and soon, for both Emily and Anne are ... susceptible. Their lives can be ruined by suspicion and rumor, if those are allowed to run amok.'

Luc inclined his head. 'Thank you. I agree. That is the situation in a nutshell.'

Martin, seated in an armchair, Amanda perched on its arm, looked at Luc. 'Do we know of anyone who would wish to harm the Ashfords?'

Luc met his gaze; Amelia watched the cousins' silent exchange, but it was Minerva who sighed, and said, 'There's Edward, of course.'

Everyone looked at her, but it was Luc whose gaze she met. 'Neither you nor I ever managed to understand him. Given what he's done in the past, how can we say he wouldn't do this – even this – too?'

Luc grimaced and looked at Martin. 'It won't, however, be Edward himself.'

Martin nodded. 'An agent, or agents. We all know it could be done.'

'Except,' Amelia put in, 'Edward doesn't have much money – not enough to pay agents.' She looked at Luc. 'Does he?'

'He has his allowance, but I doubt it'd stretch that far.'

'Actually, that would fit nicely.' Lucifer stretched out his long legs, crossing his ankles. 'Edward could simply suggest where these friends of his could pick up little items, and in doing so make him happy, too. Of course, that does presuppose Edward has those sorts of friends, and moreover, that they would be willing to consider his wishes.'

Luc shook his head. 'We were never close – indeed, we'd been deliberately distant for more than a decade. I've no idea of Edward's associates.'

Lucifer grimaced. 'If he is behind this, he'll be counting on that.'

Amelia didn't care who was behind the plot as long as it was ended. 'Regardless, we have to expose the thief who's here, on the ground, soon. We can't let things go until the rumors build and people start pointing fingers. The one most likely to be suspected is Anne, and' —her gaze sweeping the circle of faces, she saw comprehension and agreement— 'we can't let that happen.'

Arthur, sitting back, calmly watching, stated, 'We need a plan – one to flush the thief out.'

Martin leaned forward. 'We need to strike now, before he gets any inkling we might be after him.'

Luc met his gaze, nodded. 'So – how do we catch a thief?'

'That,' Helena declared, 'is simple.' When they all

turned her way, she raised her brows. 'We dangle before his covetous eyes something he will not be able to resist stealing.'

'A trap?' Luc considered, then asked, 'Baited with what?'

Helena calmly answered, 'With my pearls and emeralds, of course.'

The suggestion caused an uproar. Lucifer and Arthur forcefully declared using the Cynster necklace was out of the question.

Helena silenced them with a long, steady look from her pale green eyes. When all was again quiet, she evenly stated, 'The necklace is mine to do with as I please – Sebastian gave it to me all those years ago, and there never were any strings attached to it. There is nothing you can possibly suggest that would be more appealing to a thief. I agree that the necklace is now also a family piece, but as such, it is there, to my thinking, not just as a form of wealth, but to be used as need be for the family. This is one such occasion, when such a thing needs to be used.' Her gaze swept the company, then returned to rest on Lucifer and Arthur. 'It is my decision that it should be.'

Her tone reminded everyone that despite the fact Sebastian, her husband, Devil's father, was long gone, a great deal of power still remained at Helena's back. She was the Cynster matriarch; ultimately, none had the power to gainsay her.

Amelia noted that her mother, Phyllida – all the women – were, at least figuratively, squarely ranged behind Helena. She had taken a stand – declared what should be done; it was now up to the men to handle the rest.

Luc broke the ensuing silence. 'Assuming we

decide to bait a trap, how, exactly, are we to construct it?'

Lucifer reluctantly growled, 'We need some event – some occasion – that will appear to the thief to leave the door open.'

'If we're going to use that necklace, or something of the sort,' Martin smoothly said, 'we need to alert the thief to the possibilities, then lure him into a situation where we can catch him.'

'You need the bait and the trap,' Arthur said. 'You need to prime the trap, and then spring it.'

Luc looked at them all. 'So what's our trap?'

The discussions, suggestions, and arguments lasted for more than an hour. Amelia ordered the tea trolley replenished; Luc had the decanters brought in. They sat and argued, tossed ideas in, tossed them out. It was Minerva who finally suggested, 'We could have an open house of some sort.'

Amelia blinked. 'I've only recently joined the family – all the rest of you are here visiting . . .' She glanced at Luc. 'We could host a celebration of some sort, one for all the surrounding families.'

'And your tenants and the villagers,' Phyllida put in. 'That way, anyone could attend.'

'If you're determined to use the necklace,' Lucifer said, his tone underscoring his disapproval and his resignation, 'then it'll have to be an evening event – you couldn't wear that necklace during the day without being too obvious.'

Helena inclined her head. 'That is true.'

'A Summer Ball and Gala,' Amelia said. 'There's no reason we can't organize something like that quickly – an impulsive decision, an impromptu event. Nothing suspicious about that. The weather's been

426

glorious, you're all here visiting, so we decide to take advantage and host a ball for the neighborhood. To include everyone, we'll make it a whole evening, with the gardens open for dancing and fireworks, so there'll be plenty of opportunity for the thief to see the necklace.'

Everyone thought; everyone nodded.

'All right,' Luc said. 'Now for the details.' He fixed Helena with an even glance. 'How do you imagine it will be?'

She smiled, and told him. Despite Lucifer's growls, and Simon's, Luc's and Martin's frowns, everyone eventually agreed. Throughout the early evening, before the ball, Helena, flaunting the necklace, would move among the assembled tenants, villagers, and neighbors. At all times, she would be flanked by two of the other ladies, a normal enough situation; from a distance, at least two of the men would be watching her constantly.

Then, just before the ball was due to commence, Luc and Helena would meet on the terrace. Luc would comment on the necklace, suggesting the Dowager hand it to him after the ball for safekeeping – a suggestion Helena would openly dismiss, declaring it would be safe in her room.

'We can organize the fireworks to be lit then, so everyone will gather on the terrace and steps. That way, many people will be near enough to hear.' Amelia looked at Luc, who nodded.

'In the circumstances, I can appear to feel moved to speak, even surrounded by a crowd.' He glanced at Helena. 'If I understand this correctly, the necklace in question is of that ilk?'

Lucifer snorted. 'Believe it. Three long strands of

priceless matched pearls broken by three rectangular emeralds. Plus matching bracelets and earrings.' He glowered at Helena, then grimaced. 'Much as it pains me to admit, it's the perfect bait for this thief. Whoever they are, they've a nice eye for valuables, and that set can be broken up and restrung so easily, it would be child's play to do so and sell what would then be unidentifiable new necklaces. The emeralds, too, although distinctive, could easily be reset.'

Luc's expression turned grim. 'Definitely the sort of thing I would insist on having in safekeeping.'

Helena waved aside the caveat. 'Do not fear. By the time I am finished dismissing your so-kind insistence, everyone will know that the necklace will remain for that night in my room.'

'I still don't like that.' The objection came from Simon, standing, one broad shoulder propped against the end of the mantelpiece. He frowned at Helena. 'It's so risky. What if they harm you?'

Helena's smile turned gentle but did not disguise her steel. 'There will be no risk to me. The necklace will be strewn on the table in the middle of the room – just where a lady such as myself, careless with her wealth, might leave it. No thief is going to spare a moment to harm a small and frail old woman such as I. I will pose no threat to him.'

'Just to be clear on that issue' —Arthur had been following her dissertation closely— 'will you promise – in order to ease our no doubt irrational male fears – that you will not yourself in any way try to apprehend this thief?'

Helena met his gaze, then laughed. 'Very well, *mon ami* – I will promise you that. I will do nothing but watch – it will be up to you all' —she waved at the men— 'to catch this thief before he absconds with my treasure.'

'And if we don't,' Lucifer grumbled, 'we'll never hear the end of it.'

The clocks struck midnight. Helena rose; the other ladies followed, deeming their planning done. As she swept past Lucifer's chair, Helena patted his dark head. 'I have every confidence in you all, *mes enfants.*'

Lucifer, who when standing towered over Helena, as did every man in the room, looked thoroughly disgruntled.

By noon the next day, all the married men had accepted that shifting their ladies from Helena's plan was beyond their capabilities.

'We're going to have to cover every possible approach to the house.' Luc looked down at the plan of the house he'd unrolled on his desk. Lucifer and Martin flanked him, likewise poring over the diagram.

Simon stood opposite, his gaze flicking from the plan to their faces, then back again. 'There's really no other choice?'

'None.' Lucifer replied without even looking up. 'Take it from us – further argument is wasted effort.'

Arthur strolled up. He glanced at the plan, then sighed. 'I really hate to leave at such a moment, but those negotiations will not wait.'

Lucifer, Luc, and Martin all looked at him.

'Don't worry,' Luc said.

'We'll manage,' came from Lucifer.

'Especially given you got her promise not to tackle the thief herself.' Martin grinned. 'You've done your

429

bit – you can leave the rest to us.'

Arthur looked at them, then nodded. 'Very well – but send word to Devil if you do need help.'

They nodded.

Arthur pulled out his watch, checked the time. 'Well, I'd best go and see if Louise is ready to depart. We were supposed to leave fifteen minutes ago.'

He left them studying the house plan.

In the front hall, he came upon a scene of frenetic energy with maids and footmen dashing this way and that, streaming about the ladies gathered in the hall's center.

Louise saw him. 'There you are. We've been waiting for you.'

Arthur simply smiled.

Minerva, Emily, and Anne farewelled him with wishes for a speedy and safe journey.

A step beyond, the twins had their heads together. Arthur paused to take in the sight, one he'd seen so many times, then he slid one arm around Amanda's waist, the other around Amelia, hugged them both, and planted a kiss first on one forehead, then the other. 'Take care, both of you.'

They laughed, beamed, and kissed him back.

'Take care, Papa.'

'Come and visit again.'

Stifling a sigh, he released them, trying hard not to think that he had, indeed, truly let them go. He took Phyllida's hand and kissed it. 'You, too, my dear.'

Phyllida smiled serenely and kissed his cheek. 'Have a good trip.'

Arthur turned to Helena. 'As for you . . .'

Helena raised her brows haughtily, but her eyes danced. 'Me, I will do very well, I thank you. But you had best be away, or you will not reach London tonight.' Her smile softened; she gave him her hands and lifted her cheek for him to kiss. 'Take care.'

'That's my line,' Arthur growled, obliging with the kiss, then squeezing her hands before releasing them.

A renewed tide of 'good-byes' and waves carried them through the front door. Arthur led Louise down the steps to where their coach stood, heavily burdened.

He handed Louise in, then, with a last wave at the assembled ladies, who, he now noted, had been joined by their husbands and his only surviving son, he followed his wife into the carriage. The door was shut, the footman stood back. A whip cracked; the coach lurched, then rumbled forward.

They waved, then Louise sighed and sat back. Arthur did the same. Louise glanced at him. 'So, are you happy with your sons-in-law?'

Arthur raised his brows. 'They're both good men, and they're clearly ... devoted.'

'Devoted?' Louise's smile grew; she glanced away. 'Yes, I daresay you might call it that.'

Arthur shot her a glance. 'And you? Are you happy with them?'

'With Dexter, yes. With Luc ... I have absolutely no qualms – I never did. They seem to be settling together nicely, quite as well as I expected, but there's something not quite straight yet. However, I'm sure it, whatever it is, will sort itself out.' Louise faced forward. 'I asked Helena to keep an eye on them – I'm sure she will.'

Arthur studied her profile, then, as the coach turned up the long incline crossing the opposite face of the valley, he looked out at the Chase, basking in the sunshine. Wondered if he should write and warn Luc. Wondered where his own true loyalties now lay.

Louise glanced at him, then made a dismissive sound and patted his hand. 'Stop worrying – they'll do.'

Arthur humphed, settled back, closed his eyes. And decided they probably would – either fate or Helena would make sure of it.

They'd decided on the following Saturday evening for their Summer Ball. That gave them five days in which to prepare – possible, but only just. The first item that needed to be dealt with was the invitations; immediately after lunch, the ladies knuckled down and wrote them out, then co-opted every stableboy and groom to deliver them.

That done, they spent the next three hours disposed about the drawing room discussing and deciding and making lists. Portia and Penelope convinced Miss Pink that their education in ladylike endeavors could best be served by their attendance; their novel suggestions often induced much hilarity, but occasionally were incorporated into the various lists.

A list for entertainment, one for food, another for furniture, yet another for implements – crockery, cutlery, and glassware.

'We should have an Order of Ceremony,' Penelope stated.

When Minerva smiled, Portia weighed in, 'No – Pen's right. We need to make sure certain things get done by certain times, don't we?'

She looked about innocently. The assembled ladies exchanged glances. Neither Portia nor Penelope, Emily nor Anne was supposed to know . . .

Amelia asked, 'You mean for when the fireworks will be let off, and when the dancing will begin?'

'And when the food will be served and so on.' Portia frowned. 'I would think a list like that would be indispensable.'

Relief washed through the room; Portia and Penelope noticed, but when Phyllida and Amanda leapt in to agree with their suggestion, the moment slid away, along with their unvoiced questions.

When they were satisfied they'd identified all that needed to be done, and the four girls had gone out to stroll the lawns, Amelia relaxed in her chair, her gaze on Phyllida, on the chaise beside Amanda. 'I know you're eager to get back to Colyton. We can't ask you to delay—'

Phyllida cut her off with a wave. 'Alasdair and I discussed it last night. I do want to get back, but . . .' She smiled wryly. 'I'd never forgive myself – and he certainly wouldn't – if we left and things went wrong for want of a few extra hands.'

'Still, it's an imposition. You've already done so much—'

'Nonsense. You know we enjoy it. Besides, we've already sent messages. Alasdair sent his groom with dispatches to Devil in London, and Devil will send our news on to Papa and Jonas in Devon, so all's settled.' Phyllida leaned forward and squeezed Amelia's hand. 'Indeed, we feel so . . . *incensed* by this thief, so determined to have him caught, I doubt we'd leave even if you truly didn't need our aid.'

Helena nodded sagely. 'This thief, whoever he is, is beneath contempt. I do not believe he does not know that his actions will harm the innocent. I consider it an honor to have a part in arranging his downfall.'

Amanda murmured, 'Hear, hear.'

A moment later, they all smiled – at each other, at themselves – then they rose; skirts swishing, they headed upstairs to change.

Amelia took her lists to bed with her that night. Their bedroom was the only place she could be sure of meeting Luc alone, in absolute privacy.

The subject she had to broach demanded nothing less.

She waited until he stretched out beside her, large, lean and naked – she'd considered inquiring about nightshirts, but there was that old saying about one's nose and one's face, and the sight of Luc naked – lolling on the bed beside her naked – was not something she felt it incumbent on her to forgo – however, when he reached for the lists and filched them from her suddenly nerveless grasp, she discovered her mouth had dried, and her wits had wandered.

Clearing her throat, she focused on the lists – in his hands – and determinedly hauled her wits back to where they belonged. 'I tried to cut them down as much as I could, but that really is the least I think we need do.'

He glanced at her, then laid the lists on the covers over her stomach. 'Arrange for whatever you like. Whatever takes your fancy.'

He reached for her, drew her to him, found her lips with his. Kissed her longingly, lingeringly, until there was no doubt in her mind what his fancy was.

When he released her lips to tug the covers from between them, she clutched the lists, dragged in a breath. 'Yes, but—'

He kissed her again.

A minute later, she lifted the lists, reached back, blindly groping until she found the edge of the bed, then she opened her hand and let the precious lists fall to the floor. Safer there than on the bed. If they got tangled in the covers, who knew what state they'd be in come morning?

She reached for Luc's face, framed it as she kissed him back – let passion and desire flow through her to meet his.

His hands were everywhere, caressing, molding; his body flowed around and about hers. Then she was on her knees and he was behind her, his hands kneading her breasts as their loins came together and he slid deep within her.

She arched, heard her soft cry.

And they were caught in the heat, the power and the passion, their need, and the wonder that this, and the bliss it brought, was truly theirs.

Later, when they'd disengaged and were lying, slumped together beneath the covers once more, she moved her head and placed a kiss in the center of his chest. 'Thank you.' She smiled, realizing the ambuiguity but seeing no need to be more specific. Settling deeper into his arms, reveling in the way they instinctively tightened about her, she sighed contentedly. 'I will try to keep the expenses down.'

Stillness swept him, like a curtain sweeping down his body. A reaction to the mention of money, an awkwardness she could understand.

'Amelia, there's—'

'No reason to stint.' She touched her lips to his chest again. 'I know. But there's also no reason to run the estate too close to the edge. I'll manage.' Sleep was dragging at her; she patted his chest, then settled her hand where she liked to leave it, spread over his heart. 'Don't worry.'

Her murmur was almost inaudible; Luc inwardly cursed. He debated shaking her awake, forcing her to listen while he told her the truth ...

The soft huff of her breath stirred the hairs on his chest. Her hand grew heavier where it lay over his heart.

He drew a breath, let it out, and felt the stillness leave him. Felt her warmth wrap about him, sink through him.

Relaxing into the bed, he set himself to decide exactly where, when, and in what order he'd confess ... and fell asleep.

He *should* have told her. If not last night, then certainly this morning. If not all the truth, then at least the fact she didn't need to watch her pennies, and why.

Instead ...

Luc stood at the window of his study, staring out at the lawns while in his mind he relived that morning, when he'd woken and found Amelia gone.

Sheer panic had gripped him – she was never awake before him – then he'd heard her bustling in her dressing room. An instant later, she'd swept back into the bedroom, already dressed, ready to plunge into her day. Greeting him brightly, she'd rounded the bed and retrieved her lists.

She'd chatted happily about all she had to do; there'd been not the slightest trace of worry or reticence in her face, in her blue, blue eyes. She'd been genuinely on top of the world – *their* world – regardless of any monetary constraints. She'd barely

436

paused for any response from him; he simply hadn't had the heart – the intestinal fortitude, the necessary steel – to cut through her bubbling busyness and force on her a confession that, in that instant, had not seemed so terribly urgent.

'These figures.'

He turned. Seated behind his desk, Martin tapped the report he was wading through. 'Are they accurate?'

'As far as can be ascertained. I had them confirmed by three independent sources.' Luc hesitated, then added, 'I usually bank on 50 percent of what I'm told to expect.'

Martin raised his brows, calculating, then gave a low whistle and returned to the report. Opposite him, seated before the desk, Lucifer was similarly engaged in plowing through the details of a number of investment opportunities Luc had assessed; absorbed, one hand sunk in his black locks, Lucifer didn't look up.

Luc returned to the vista beyond the window. And saw Penelope emerge from the direction of the kennels, a wriggling puppy – Galahad, Luc felt certain – in her arms. Stepping onto the lawn, she set Galahad down; he lived up to his name, immediately dashing around, nose to the ground, tracking something.

Penelope sank to the grass and watched him with, as in most things she did, serious and unwavering concentration. Behind her, following her onto the wide lawn, came a bevy of the younger hounds – those yet too young to run with the pack – with Portia and Simon supervising.

Portia was supervising the hounds. Simon, his hands sunk in his pockets, appeared to be supervising Penelope and Portia.

That seemed a trifle odd. Simon was nineteen, nearly twenty, and had already acquired a degree of social polish. Emily and Anne were much closer to his age, yet these days he more often than not gravitated to the environs of Portia and Penelope whenever they were out of the schoolroom ... the explanation for that occurred to Luc even as the thought formed in his mind.

Given they suspected there was someone in the vicinity who was ill-disposed toward his family, his sisters in particular, and that Portia and Penelope were frequently out of doors, one step away from running wild, he could only be grateful for Simon's hovering presence.

As he watched the trio on the lawn, it became obvious Portia did not share his view; even from the study, he could see the haughtiness with which she stuck her nose in the air and said something – something cutting enough to make Simon scowl.

Penelope ignored the pair of them. They continued to snipe at each other over her head. Making a mental note to mention to Simon that arguing with either of his younger sisters was an activity best avoided, Luc turned and strolled to an armchair and the reports he'd yet to peruse.

As one, he, Martin, and Lucifer had taken refuge in his study; beyond the doors, pandemonium – and their wives – reigned. It was, they knew without stating it, best to keep their heads down.

At Devil's suggestion, Lucifer had asked to be given a general overview of Luc's investment strategy. Martin had pricked up his ears, and asked to be included in the fun. He presently had them both working through the reports he'd used to decide on

438

his last three investments – all speculative, all potentially high-yielding, all presently bidding fair to adding considerably to his wealth.

Glancing at Martin's and Lucifer's bowed heads, Luc smiled, settled into the armchair, and gave his attention to what might be his next venture.

Entirely unexpectedly – quite how it happened he wasn't sure – Luc found himself walking in the cool of that evening with Helena on his arm. When she directed him – imperiously as usual – to the shrubbery, his antenna rose, but he complied. With the westering sun gilding the tops of the high hedges, he escorted her into the first courtyard, then through to the next, to where the rectangular pool lay reflective and still.

Helena gestured to the wrought-iron seat set before the pool. He led her there, then waited while she sat. At her wave, he sat beside her, fixed his gaze on the pool, and waited, determinedly impassive, to hear whatever she wished to say.

To his surprise, she laughed, genuinely amused.

When he looked at her, she caught his eye. 'You may lower your shield – I am not about to attack.'

Her smile was infectious, yet ... he knew well enough not to relax.

She sighed and shook her head at him, then looked out over the pool. 'You are still in denial.'

He wondered if feigning ignorance would get him anywhere; he doubted it. Sitting back, stretching out his legs, crossing his ankles, he followed her lead in watching the fish streak like quicksilver through the dark water. 'I'm very happy – we both are.'

'That does not require saying. Yet ... you are not,

to my thinking, as happy as you might be, as you would be, if the truth was faced.'

He let silence stretch, acknowledging the reality in her words. 'In time, I daresay we'll come to it.'

Helena made a sound not generally associated with Dowager Duchesses. '"Come to it" – what does that mean? I will tell you this, time will not help you. Time will only deny you days of happiness you might otherwise have.'

He met her gaze, saw something in her pale eyes that was both humbling and compelling.

She smiled, shrugged, looked back at the pool. 'It happens to us all – we each have to face it. For some, it's easier than others, but each one must at some point understand and knowingly accept. At some point, we each have to make the decision.'

He hadn't thought . . . he started to frown.

Helena glanced at him; her smile deepened. 'Ah, no – one cannot escape. That is true. One can only accept and reap the benefits, or instead, spend one's life fighting the invincible.'

He laughed, albeit wryly. He understood all too well what she meant.

She said no more; neither did he. They sat as the shadows lengthened, both, he was sure, dwelling on only one thing. Eventually, she rose; he did, too. He gave her his arm, and they walked back to the house.

On Friday morning, from the window of his study, Luc watched Amelia and Amanda playing with Galahad, wondered, briefly, what confidences they were sharing. Briefly recalled his conversation with Helena, but a more immediate duty beckoned.

Carrying the paperweight he'd fetched from the

windowsill back to his desk, he anchored the last corner of the plan of the house and grounds.

'They're setting up the tables here.' Martin pointed with a pencil to the western edge of the lawns. 'And there'll apparently be a fiddler and drummer over here – far enough from the house so their noise won't interfere with the quartet in the ballroom.'

Lucifer glanced at Luc. 'Are any of the people they've hired – musicians, extra hands to help in the kitchen or anywhere else – unknown to you or your staff?'

Luc shook his head. 'I checked with Higgs and Cottsloe. Everyone they've brought in are locals – none has been out of the area this year.'

'Good.' Lucifer studied the layout of the house and the gardens surrounding the lawns. 'If you were going to break in at night, from which direction would you come?'

'If I knew about the hounds, from here.' Luc pointed to the area to the northeast beyond the rose garden. 'That's woodland, quite dense. It's a remnant of the original demesne and has never been cleared. It's readily passable, but the trees are old – even in full daylight, the paths are shadowy and dark.'

Martin nodded. 'True. But if you didn't know about the hounds, then this would be the better way in.' He traced a path from the west boundary of the gardens, across the lane to the home farm, then along the edge of the shrubbery. 'Or, alternatively, if one came down from the ridge, then late at night coming in beside the stables might seem wise.'

'Good cover all the way,' Luc agreed. 'However, I can assure you the hounds will send up an alarm if anyone approaches along that route.'

Lucifer grimaced. 'We'll have to hope he's smart enough to realize about the hounds.'

His hands in his pockets, Luc stared at the plan. Martin glanced at him. Luc met his gaze. 'I'd better warn Sugden. If anyone does come that way, and the hounds set up a cry, Sugden can release them. They'll run any intruder to earth, and hold him until we get there.'

Lucifer grinned. Evilly. 'Nice idea.'

'Another thought,' Martin offered. 'Let Patsy and Morry charm the children at the gala. They're well behaved enough. Sugden could keep them on their leashes and show them off. No one would think that odd, given they're champions. And it would serve to draw our thief's attention to the existence of the kennels.'

Martin straightened, meeting both Luc's, then Lucifer's dark eyes. 'While it might satisfy us to run the felon to earth, it would be better all around if we could catch him in the act first.'

Luc nodded. So did Lucifer.

They all turned back to the plan.

'All right.' Luc pointed to a bedchamber on the first floor. 'That's the room Helena's in. So how are we going to protect her?'

They spent most of the morning discussing the possibilities; they'd had to wait until then to learn all that their wives' had planned, and, most importantly, the when and where of each organized activity.

With all the details in place, they'd hatched their own plans. During the gala and ball, there'd be the three of them, plus Simon, Sugden, and Cottsloe, all keeping watch over Helena. Later, once the guests

442

were gone, Amelia, Amanda, and Phyllida would watch from various places inside the house, while Martin, Sudgen, and Lucifer patrolled the grounds, leaving Luc and Simon – presently the most familiar with the house and the rooms everyone was in – to guard the long corridors.

Once they'd finalized their arrangements, they'd dispersed. Luc had gone to the kennels to speak with Sugden and run a quick eye over the pack.

Returning to the house, he hesitated, then strolled to the music room. He paused in the corridor outside the door ... from the parlor beyond came Amelia's voice. And Phyllida's and Amanda's. Grimacing, he walked on.

Climbing the main stairs, he paused at the first floor, then, jaw firming, took the flight to the top floor.

Portia, Penelope, and Miss Pink were downstairs, eschewing lessons with books for more practical demonstrations; the upper central wing stood empty. Luc strolled to the nursery, opened the door, and went in.

Nothing had yet changed – he hadn't expected it would have; Amelia hadn't yet had time to put her plans into place. But she would. Soon.

Walking to the window, he looked down over the valley, and pondered that fact, what it would mean, how it made him feel.

A son – that was the least fate owed him after leaving him to manage alone with four sisters. His lips twisted; in truth, he didn't care. All he wanted was to see Amelia with his babe at her breast.

His conversation with Helena had cast a new slant – he hadn't considered that Amelia, too, would have her own decision to make.

She'd already made it – of that he felt certain. She was committed to him, had changed her allegiance and was carrying his child. She was his. At some primal level, he'd known that for some time – now he believed it.

His rational logical mind had at long last caught up with his primitive self.

Satisfaction and contentment welled, laced with escalating frustration. Now he was waiting to tell her all, fate was conspiring to delay his declaration.

She was rushed off her feet with preparations, dozy when he joined her in their bed at night, in the morning leaping out of it before he'd woken to plunge back into the whirl.

Given what she and all that lay between them now meant to him, given how important acknowledging that had become, grabbing a few rushed minutes with servants and family distractingly hovering to make such a vital declaration was, to him, unthinkable.

When he finally confessed to the ultimate surrender, he at least wanted to be sure she was paying attention – and would remember it later.

Impatience gnawed; frustration gnashed. He stared out at the valley. His jaw set.

Once the thief was caught, he would insist she refocus every last shred of her attention back on him.

And then he would tell her the simple truth.

Three little words.

I love you.

Chapter Twenty-One

'A word of advice, *ma petite.*'

Amelia glanced up from the lists scattered across her desk. Helena stood in the doorway, smiling fondly.

She quickly reorganized her lists. 'On what ...?'

'Ah, no. My advice does not concern any of our arrangements' —Helena dismissed the lists with a wave— 'but a subject much more dear to your heart.'

'Oh?' Amelia stared.

Helena nodded. 'Luc. I believe he wishes to tell you something, but ... there are times when even men such as he are uncertain. My advice is that a little encouragement would not be out of order, and may gain you more than you think.'

Amelia blinked. 'Encouragement?'

'*Oui.*' Helena gestured, supremely Gallic. 'The type of encouragement likely to weaken a husband's irrational resistance.' Her glorious smile dawned; her eyes twinkled as she turned away. 'I'm sure I can leave the details to you.'

Her lists forgotten, Amelia stared at the empty doorway. Now Helena mentioned it, Luc had been

... hovering for the past few days. They'd both been so busy with their visitors and their plans to catch the thief, their private lives, what lay between them, had necessarily been set to one side, in temporary abeyance while they tackled the threat to their family.

Yet ...

Sudden impatience seared her. Stacking her lists, she closed the desk, rose, and headed upstairs.

Luc entered their bedroom that night to discover Amelia not in bed as she usually was, but standing by the windows looking out over the moonlit lawns. She'd already snuffed the candles; in her peach silk robe with her hair tumbling over her shoulders, she stood silent and still, absorbed with her thoughts.

She hadn't heard him enter; he grasped the moment to study her, to wonder in which direction her thoughts lay. Throughout the evening, he'd caught her studying him, as if seeking to read his mind. He assumed she was keyed up, increasingly tense as they all were. By this time tomorrow, they'd be watching for the thief who, intentionally or otherwise, was threatening the Ashfords. Expectation, anticipation, had already started to course through their veins.

He watched; she remained quiet, statuelike, limned by the silvery light slanting through the window.

Temptation whispered ... but now, tonight, was not the time to speak. They had tomorrow, tomorrow night and whatever it revealed, to live through. After, later, once they had that business settled and could devote themselves once more to their own lives, to their future ...

Impatience welled; he subdued it, stirred and walked toward her.

She sensed him, turned – smiled and walked into his arms.

Slid her arms about his neck, stepped close, lifted her face, met his lips as he bent his head and set them to hers.

He closed his hands about her waist, anchoring her before him as he savored her mouth, took his time in the claiming, blatantly taking all she offered, all she freely yielded, her breasts warm mounds pressed to his chest, her slender limbs a silk-clad promise whispering against him.

Releasing her waist, he slid his hands down, around, tracing, then cradling the globes of her bottom, kneading, then lifting her to him so the ridge of his erection rode against her.

She murmured, drew back from the kiss, not away but so their lips were just touching, brushing, caressing – teasing their senses, breaths mingling as desire rose between them. Drawing one arm down, she slid her hand beneath the edge of his robe, splaying her palm on his chest, hungry, greedy, eager to touch. She lowered her other arm, braced that palm against him, easing back, not out of his embrace but to create a gap between them.

That she wanted to follow a different route to the one he'd intended he understood; it nevertheless took a few heated moments before he could force his hands to obey and ease their grip, let her stand again. He didn't let her move away but that wasn't what she wished – the instant she could, she slid her hands down, searching . . . for the tie of his robe.

He felt the tug, then release – felt, between them, her hand shift again, felt the shimmer of her robe under his hands, over her skin.

447

From beneath his lashes, he watched her smile – gloried in the open, uninhibited expectation in her face as she sent both hands sliding up to his shoulders, pushing the halves of his robe wide. She didn't immediately push the robe off but instead paused to admire, to look, to savor all she'd uncovered.

He knew better than to move – knew he was supposed to let her have her way. That had never been easy – he usually cut short her play – yet tonight, bathed in moonlight, he mentally – sensually – girded his loins, held back the urge to distract her, forced his hands not to tighten and haul her against him.

Let her touch, caress, then kiss as she would.

He had to close his eyes, felt tension coil about his spine as she licked, then grazed one tight nipple. Felt her hands, small, eager and wanton, slide greedily over his chest, over his abdomen, skating inexorably lower. Her lips, her hot, wet, open mouth, followed, trailing fire down his body.

His fingers had turned nerveless when she slid from his hold.

When her hands, then her avid mouth traced the line of his hips, then moved inward.

His mouth was bone dry, his eyes tight shut when she finally closed her hand about him. His fingers slid into her hair, tangling in her curls, as she lovingly traced, then closed her hand again, played and tantalized as he himself had taught her, until he thought he'd die.

When she went to her knees, bent her head, and took him into her mouth, he was sure he would.

The thunder of his heart filled his ears as she ministered to his wildest fancy. He'd never let her before, not as she was, not in this position – he'd thought he hadn't even given her the idea – dimly wondered how she'd guessed.

Instinct seemed a dangerous, possibly threatening, conclusion. Especially when she angled her head and took him deep, and his fingers spasmed on her skull in reaction. He felt, rather than heard, her soft, victorious exhalation when next she paused for breath.

Before he could react her hands and mouth recaptured him – his awareness, his senses. She held him captive, tortured him lovingly, pressed ever more flagrantly evocative caresses on him.

Chest laboring, he opened his lids enough to look down through the screen of his lashes, enough to watch her, bathed in moonlight, the skirts of her robe a shimmering pool in which she knelt, her golden curls softly lustrous, shifting against him as she loved him.

He'd taught her how; she'd learned well. Every too-knowing touch, every scrape of her nails, every long, liquid stroke of her tongue, wound him tighter, and tighter, until his spine quivered with tension, until his awareness was hard-edged, crystal sharp. Yet still she pushed him further.

Until his fingers gripped hard on her skull, until he closed his eyes, head lifting, chest seizing . . .

Until he had to wonder what had changed.

Something had.

She'd always been physically willing, even eager, yet tonight, she was assured.

Confident.

He could feel it in her touch.

Could see it when she finally – *finally* – released him and lifted her head. He hauled in a tight breath

449

and looked down as she sat back on her heels and, hands braced on his thighs, with calm deliberation considered the outcome of her efforts; her serene smile declared that outcome met with her satisfaction.

He groaned and reached for her – she put out her hands and caught his wrists, rocked to her feet and smoothly stood. Then she released his hands, grasped the sides of her loosened robe and spread them wide – and stepped into him.

Deliberately, with a calm intent that strangled his breath, set her body skin to skin with his. Sinuously shifted, her skin like burning silk as she used her whole body to caress his. Reached between them and adjusted his throbbing erection so she could better shift and slide against it. Draping one arm about his shoulders, she hooked one knee about his thigh, then evocatively – like some eastern houri pandering to her master – undulated against him.

Her hips, her breasts – her spread thighs, the curls between – all contributed. All added to the call, the primitive invocation that reached deep within him, harrying instincts buried under centuries of sophistication until they rose with a roar and poured through him.

Shattering every last vestige of control, drowning every glimmer of civilized man.

Left him revealed – him and his needs – laid bare, exposed. Before her, and him.

Left him reeling, but she was there – calming, urging, reassuring ...

He dragged in a huge breath, bent his head, and set his lips to hers as she offered them. It required no thought for him to push back the sides of her robe, reach under and slide his hands over her back, down,

450

over her bottom, possessively gripping, then releasing to lower and grip the backs of her thighs, and lift her.

She wrapped her arms about his neck, clung tight, wrapped her legs about him, knees bent, her heels in the small of his back – and he was inside her. She gasped, pulled back from the kiss, caught her breath, eyes closing as he pulled her hips into him, pressed deep inside her body, then anchored her, her body open and filled to the hilt with him. Let her feel the vulnerability she'd chosen, let the experience – of her giving, of the hot slickness of her sheath clamping tight all around him, of the shivery pleasure that always rushed through him when they joined – sink to his bones.

Only when he'd drunk his fill, let his senses wallow, only when he sensed she'd done the same and had caught her breath – only then did he move.

Or rather, move her. He stood rock-still and shifted her upon him. With her legs so high she had no leverage, had to accept what he did, all he did – all he pressed on her. He moved her only enough to wind her tight, until he felt desire sink its talons deep. Her arms tightened about his neck. She sank her teeth into his shoulder.

Inwardly smiling, he drew her down again, and stepped out. Walked, slowly, deliberately, working her up and down in his arms, matching that rhythm to his strides.

Until her breathing turned ragged, until she clung, fingers sinking into his shoulders, until she whimpered – not with pain but desperation.

Without allowing himself to think, he walked to the head of the bed, turned and sat, shuffling back, supported by the pillows piled high against the headboard.

She tried to wriggle, to unwind her legs – he tightened his hold on her.

'No. Stay as you are.'

She forced her heavy lids up just enough to blink at him.

'I want to watch you.'

His gravelly admission sent a quiver of anticipation through her; she licked her lips, her gaze dropped to his, but he made no move to oblige.

Instead, he lifted her again, brought her down again, and again, working her on him, working himself inside her, deeper, then deeper still. Her breasts, skin flushed, rode against his chest, nipples hard as pebbles, adding another layer of sensory delight.

Eyes locked on her face, he kept her moving, even when he felt her body coil and tighten, even when her spine arched and she cried out, and shattered, fractured, climaxing wildly on him, about him.

He paused, held her down, filling her while he savored the tight ripples of her release, savored the lush, rich softness that followed, that beckoned ...

But he wanted more tonight. She'd offered. He'd accepted. Tonight, whatever he wished, he could ask for and receive, for she would give.

And in return, she would know, see, all he'd held close, hidden behind his shield, for he no longer had any shield, any protection – she'd ripped it away, sent it spinning – left him no option but to show her all he truly was.

In this arena as well as that other.

He picked up her movements again, let her ride through her climax, didn't stop, gave her no surcease. When she was once again aware, when her senses again stirred and she opened her eyes, blinked, stared at him, he stopped, held her down. Let her feel his strength buried inside her.

Amelia licked her lips; her eyes, fixed on his, were wide.

'I want you.'

Her answer was breathy. 'I know.'

His lips twisted. 'Wrong answer.'

She felt her lips flicker in response. Her eyes only grew rounder. 'How?'

The midnight glitter of his eyes, the controlled hardness of his hands, of all his body, the reined passion, the potential, the promise of what would come, was nearly overwhelming. She searched the dark turmoil in his eyes, then managed to lick her lips. Deliberately leaned her forearms on his upper chest and leaned close, whispered against his mouth. 'Tell me.'

He kissed her, deeply, one hand rising to cradle her head, holding her still as he ravished her senses. He was hot and hard inside her, sunk to the hilt within her; his probing tongue, hot, insistent, demanding, underscored the fact. Underscored her position, the blatant, unforgiving vulnerability.

The kiss ended almost savagely.

From only inches apart, their gazes met, held – their already ragged breaths mingled.

'Curled over your knees in the middle of this bed.'

She struggled to breathe, couldn't think beyond the moment. His gaze dropped to her body; she'd never seen his eyes so dark, never known his body to be so hard, so tense, so coiled. So full of leashed passion. That body would shortly be wrapped about her, driving into her, the passion pouring through her.

When he joined with her as he wished. Uninhibitedly possessive.

One hand was in the small of her back, supporting her. The other slid down from her head; he delicately lifted one lapel of her robe.

'Leave this on.'

She couldn't manage a nod; barely able to breathe, she eased her legs from behind his back.

He lifted her from him. Set her on her knees. Wasting no time on trying to form a thought, she turned, moved to the middle of the wide bed, sat back on her ankles, freed her robe from under her. Seizing the moment to catch her breath, with unimpaired dignity she arranged the robe about her, fully open but draping from her shoulders to pool around her, concealing her back and feet. That done, she spared not a glance for him but bent from the waist, curled down, folding her arms in front of her knees, relaxing into that position.

She felt him shift as she did – when she peeked through the curtain of her hair he was no longer sitting against the pillows. His weight bowing the bed told her he was kneeling behind her; she felt his heat as he drew near, but he didn't, immediately, touch her.

Whether he intended to wind her nerves tight with expectation, or was simply clinging to his own tenuous control, it didn't matter. Her body started to pulse with that familiar emptiness; her skin flushed with the need to feel him wrapped about her.

She sensed, through the fine barrier of her silk robe, when he settled close behind her, knees widespread, when he reached out toward her head.

With one hand, he gathered the wild jumble of her

454

curls, the thick fall that lay covering her nape. He gathered, then, slowly, deliberately, wound his hand in the massed locks.

Gently drew her up, back, until she was kneeling almost but not quite upright. Releasing her hair, his palm slid beneath, cupping her nape, his long fingers cruising, caressing, up and down the slender column of her neck.

He reached around her, ran his other hand, possessively assessing, from the base of her throat to the damp curls between her thighs. Although the fall of her robe covered her back, in front, she was naked, exposed to the night, to his touch.

His hand rose, to explore, to possess. To trace, tweak, knead her breasts until they were swollen and aching anew, until her nipples were so tight any touch was close to painful. His hand drifted down to splay across her stomach, to knead evocatively until she moaned, then, his other hand lightly gripping her nape, he sent his questing fingers sliding down, spearing through her curls to find her, pressing between her thighs to expose and circle the throbbing flesh, to stroke and probe until she arched, gasped.

'*Please.*'

His hands left her.

The sudden loss of his touch left her reeling. Disoriented.

'Bend down.'

She did, eagerly, sinking down over her knees, heart thundering, pulse hammering. Wanting.

Simply wanting.

He lifted the back of her robe to her hips, exposing her bottom. Both hands spread, touched, reverently traced. Firmed, became more possessive as he stroked, fondled, caressed, lit fires beneath her already dewed skin. The contrast of heat against the cool air sent shivers up her spine while poised behind her he surveyed her as if she was his slave.

She wished she could see his face, wondered if he'd chosen this position so she wouldn't be able to. Wondered, fleetingly, why.

Then his fingers traced her cleft, slid down between her thighs.

Her thoughts fled; her lungs seized. She closed her eyes, nerves tightening with expectation.

He found her swollen softness and opened her. Probed, then he shifted, muscled thighs surrounding her, trapping her. His hands closed about her hips, holding her, anchoring her; the broad head of his erection nudged into her.

Then he sank home. Deep. Then deeper still. Filling her body, filling her senses.

Her sigh shivered through the night. Pure relief. She closed her eyes, laid her head on her forearms.

Prepared to be ravished.

And she was.

Fundamentally, elementally, profoundly. He demanded her body and she gave it, surrendered it without reserve. Without reserve he claimed her, every inch of her, his hands tracing, possessing even while he rode her.

Hard, fast, deep. Into an oblivion so all-consuming long before they reached the crest there was no sense of him and her, no separation of their souls as they traversed the sensual landscape, as, uninhibited, they flew higher and higher.

The end, when it came, was beyond even glory, steeped in much more than sensation. It was as if, together, they'd reached some place, some plane they hadn't before attained – that hadn't before been open to them.

When finally he withdrew from her, turned her into his arms and slumped back on the bed, they were still there, still floating in that blessed peace.

In that place where the world couldn't touch, and only fused souls could reach.

Gasping for breath, chests heaving, they both simply lay, touching, hands searching, fingers twining, struggling, both of them, to understand.

To comprehend.

A declaration without words, unspoken but absolute. When, at last, they turned to each other, when, at last, their gazes met, they didn't need words to assure themselves of that.

Just a look, a touch, a kiss.

A trust. Given, taken, reciprocated.

Amelia curled into Luc's arms; they closed about her. Closing their eyes, they slept.

The sleep of the exhausted. Luc might have suspected he was growing old – Amelia was once again awake and out of bed before he'd stirred – except he remembered, very clearly, all that had happened in the night.

Lying back on the pillows, arms crossed behind his head, he stared unseeing at the canopy. About him, the bed lay in utter disarray, vivid testament to the physicality of their union.

But it wasn't that – not only that – that colored his memories of the night.

She'd given herself to him, joyously surrendered, not just physically, not even just emotionally, but in some deeper, more profound way. And he'd taken,

457

accepted, claimed. Knowingly. With the same unswerving commitment.

Because she and all she offered was all and everything he would ever want.

That much was clear. What was less easy to assimilate was the conviction, based on no logical earthly fact, that the past night had been scripted, that it was part of some ceremony, part of their marriage, and would have needed to occur at some point.

As if their actions – her offering, his accepting – just as they had at the very start, in that moment in his front hall in London when those same actions had sealed their fates, were the true underlying reality of their relationship.

And she knew it. Even though he'd said not a word, she understood . . .

Had she taken the lead again?

Voices reached him – Amelia talking to her maid. Grimacing, he threw the sheets back, rose, found his robe, then stalked to his dressing room.

His impatience to tell her what he needed more than ever now to say had scaled new heights, but the day was going to be a long one – there was no way he could wring from it time to tell her, not properly, not until all the rest was settled.

She – and he – deserved better than a distracted, 'Incidentally, I love you,' while hurrying down the stairs.

Dressed, he returned to the bedroom just as she, ready for the day, came through from her rooms. She smiled, met his eyes. He waited by the door as she approached. Held her gaze when she halted before him. Saw blazoned in the blue of her eyes a serenity, a confidence.

Her decision, her commitment – her understanding of him.

The certainty rocked him; he drew a tight breath.

The chatter of maids in her rooms, clearly waiting to tidy the bedroom, reached him; he glanced toward the connecting door, then looked down, met her eyes. 'Once this is over, we need to talk.' He lifted a hand, briefly traced her cheek. 'There're things I need to tell you, things we need to discuss.'

Her smile held the essence of happiness. She caught his hand; her eyes on his, she touched her lips to his palm. 'Later, then.'

The brief contact sent heat racing through him. Her smile widened and she turned to the door. He opened it; she stepped out into the corridor.

He watched her hips sway beneath her blue day gown, then drew breath, took a firm grip on his impulses, and followed her.

Chapter Twenty-Two

The day flew. No one stopped for luncheon; Higgs set out a cold collation in the dining room and people helped themselves when they could. Restrained pandemonium reigned, yet when six o'clock struck and the first of the guests arrived in the forecourt, everything was in place. Higgs, beaming, hurried to the kitchens while Cottsloe strode proudly to the door.

Amelia rose from the chaise on which she'd only just sat. She'd been on her feet the entire day, yet the excitement in the air, which had laid hold of the whole household – the look in Luc's midnight blue eyes as she took up her stance by his side before the fireplace – were more than worth the effort, quite aside from trapping the thief.

The guests rolled in, guided through the front hall and into the drawing room to greet Luc and herself, and then be introduced to the rest of the family, both immediate and extended, standing and sitting about the huge room. Minerva, Emily, and Anne were primed to take over the introductions so Amelia and Luc could concentrate on welcoming the steady stream of their neighbors and tenants. Phyllida stood near Emily, ready to lend assistance should the younger girl encounter any difficulties, while Amanda did likewise with Anne, shy but determined to carry her role.

In the midst of them all, Helena sat beside Minerva on the chaise, her pearl-and-emerald necklace resplendent, displayed to advantage against a deep green silk gown. With her dark hair streaked with silver, her pale green eyes and her inherent presence, Helena drew everyone's gaze. No one was the least surprised to learn she was the Dowager Duchess of St. Ives.

Watching her aunt exchange nods with Lady Fenton, a haughty local matron, and then make some remark, very much in the *grande dame* style, instantly reducing Lady Fenton to dithering nervousness, Amelia had to look quickly away. Smiling widely, she turned to greet the next of their guests.

Portia, Penelope, and Simon patrolled before the long windows, open to the terrace, efficiently herding those with all introductions complete out into the gardens where the first act of the revelries would take place. Within an hour, a goodly crowd had gathered, eagerly sampling the delicious morsels provided by Higgs, washing them down with ale and wines.

When the incoming tide slowed, the front doors were shut; a stablelad sat on the portico steps to direct any latecomers around the house, and thus to the festivities. Together, Luc and Amelia led their assembled families out onto the lawns to mingle with their guests.

The sun was slanting through the trees, just gilding the tops of the shrubbery hedges as they went down the terrace steps. The air held the warmth of a summer's day; the breeze was a caress wafting the scents of grass and greenery, of stocks, jasmine, and the multitude of roses blooming throughout the gardens.

Luc caught Amelia's eye, lifted her hand to his lips briefly, then released her. They parted, each strolling into the crowd, exchanging greetings with their tenants and the villagers, the majority of whom had walked to the Chase, bringing their families as suggested to join in the fun.

While he chatted, Luc kept Helena in sight. She was easy to pick out in her gown, the solid hue distinctive. Amid the lighter, pastel colors, she was a dramatic highlight; as intended, she was the cynosure of all eyes.

She carried off her role with shameless abandon; no one watching her would suspect her primary aim was to display her necklace rather than boost her haughty self-importance. The fact there were always two of their ladies flanking her, like acolytes attending a master, only emphasized the image of commanding arrogance she projected.

As he tacked through the crowd, he saw the others – Martin, Lucifer, Simon – like him, scanning the throng. On the outskirts, Cottsloe kept watch from the terrace, while Sugden stood in the shadow of the shrubbery, keeping an eye on Patsy and Morry, and on everything else.

The dogs were greeting countless children. Luc headed that way, intent on asking Sugden if he could identify a number of men he himself could not. Nothing immediately worrying about that – all invited had been told to bring any houseguests. It was summer, and many country families had friends or family from London or elsewhere staying.

Moving through the crowd, Luc saw General Ffolliot standing to one side watching the fiddlers play. He changed course and joined him, nodding genially.

'Just watching our two.' The General indicated Fiona and Anne, arm in arm, watching the dancers.

Luc smiled. 'I'd meant to thank you for allowing Fiona to spend so much time with us in London. Her confidence is a boon to Anne.'

'Oh, aye – she's confident enough, is Fiona.' After a moment, the General cleared his throat, and somewhat diffidently asked, 'Actually, I'd meant to have a word myself, but that business of the thimble distracted me.' He shot Luc a glance from under his shaggy brows. 'You haven't heard anything about Fiona having dealings with any man, have you?'

Luc raised his brows, genuinely surprised. 'No. Nothing.' He hesitated, then asked, 'Have you reason to suspect she has?'

'No, no!' The General sighed. 'It's just that she's ... well, changed since she's returned home. I can't put my finger on it ...'

After a moment, Luc said, 'If you like, I could mention your concern to my wife. She's close to both Emily and Anne. If Fiona has mentioned anything ...'

The General studied his daughter, then gruffly said, 'If you would, that would be most kind.'

Luc inclined his head. A moment later, he parted from the General, and continued to where Sugden stood, Patsy's and Morry's leashes in one hand.

The hounds leapt and whined when they saw him, then sat, front feet dancing, ears back, tails wagging furiously. Smiling, he ran his hand over their heads, stroked Patsy's ears, sending her into a state bordering on ecstasy. 'These two have proved popular.'

'Aye – the kiddies love 'em, and the gents can't resist admiring them.'

Luc patted Morry. 'How could they not?' His tone altered. 'Have you seen anything amiss?'

'Not amiss, but there's a few here I can't place.'

Between them, they put names to all they could.

'That still leaves five men we don't know.' Impassive, Sugden had his eye on one.

Luc looked down at the dogs. 'We have four ladies we can't place, either, and there're still people arriving.'

'And from what you said, we've no idea when or from where this bounder will arrive anyway. He might not come via the front door.'

'True.' Luc focused on a small procession heading their way. Amelia and Portia were in the lead, holding hands with two children; a small tribe followed at their heels. 'What's this?'

It appeared Amelia had intended to head straight for the kennels; noticing them watching, she veered their way. With a wave, she indicated her entourage. 'We're taking the children to see Galahad.'

Luc recognized the children from the cottages by the river. 'I see.'

The older children stopped to pat Patsy and Morry; the younger ones followed, as did Portia and her charge. The girl with Amelia slipped away to join the group. Sugden talked about the pack; Luc drew Amelia aside.

She turned to him. 'I'll just take them in to see the puppies, Galahad in particular – I promised.'

He hadn't considered Amelia – or Portia – being anywhere but among the guests on the lawns – in full view. He couldn't, in all conscience, desert his watch on Helena to escort them to the kennels. Still, realistically, what harm could befall them in his kennels? He nodded, inwardly grim, but hiding it, or so he thought. 'Very well – but don't dally, and come straight back.'

She met his eyes, then smiled, stretched up, and kissed his cheek. 'Don't worry. We won't be long.'

The children were ready to move on; hands were retaken, the procession re-formed and headed on toward the kennels.

Luc watched them go, then turned to Sugden, who was also watching the group heading into his domain – unsupervised. 'Give me the leashes – I'll take Patsy and Morry. You go and watch that lot.' As a sop to his pride, he added, 'You may as well check around the kennels while you're there.'

Sugden nodded, unwrapped the leashes from his fist, then hurried off to catch up with the children.

Luc settled the leashes about one hand, then looked down at his favorite hounds. 'I'm the host – I can't stand here like a post. So we're going to wander through the crowd. Try and keep your noses to yourselves.'

With that probably useless admonition, he resumed his perambulation about the lawns.

Amelia wasn't surprised when Sugden caught up with them in time to swing the kennel doors open. She turned to the children. 'Now we need to be quiet and not excite the pack. We have to go right to the end to see the puppies. All right?'

They all nodded. 'It's the firs' time we seen the

465

whole lot, all together,' the little spokeswoman whispered. She clutched Amelia's hand tighter; Sugden waved them in and the procession stepped out, marching two by two down the central aisle.

Amelia heard soft 'Oohs' and 'Aahs'; she glanced back and saw many of the older children studying the hounds with rapt attention. The oldest boy, at the rear, turned and spoke to Sugden, following them. Sugden shook his head. 'Nay – best not to pat these. If you do, they'll expect to be taken out, and then they'll be right grumpy when we leave without 'em.'

The boy accepted the prohibition with a nod, yet his gaze went back to the older dogs, many coming to the front of the pens to watch them pass, ears lifting, heads cocking with curiosity. Facing forward, Amelia wondered how many lads Sugden used in the kennels. Perhaps he could use one more?

Then they reached Galahad; from that moment on, none of the children had eyes for much else. They were captivated; the pup took their attention and worship in his stride, wuffling about their feet, sniffing hands, licking this one, then that. Fifteen minutes passed in a blink; noticing Sugden shifting, Amelia reclaimed Galahad, tickled his tummy, then sent him back to his mama. Then she firmly reversed her entourage, and they filed, satisfied, whispering and exclaiming among themselves, out of the kennels, back into the deepening twilight.

The children streamed on, down the short path leading back to the lawns. With pretty thanks and bobbed curtsies, the two girls who had clung to Amelia's and Portia's hands made their adieus and scampered after their elders.

Sugden nodded to Amelia and Portia as he swung

the doors shut. 'I'll just be checking 'round about. Make sure all's tight.'

Amelia met his glance, nodded. 'We're going straight back.'

She turned, noting Portia's quick frown. Linking her arm in Portia's, she steered them both down the path in the children's wake. She was about to make some inconsequential remark to distract Portia from Sugden's sudden attention to security when Portia stiffened.

Looking up, Amelia saw a gentleman standing by the side of the path just ahead. They were nearly upon him yet until then, she hadn't noticed him, large though he was; he'd been standing so still in the shadows of a large bush, he'd been all but invisible.

Portia slowed, uncertain.

Amelia called up her hostessly armor, put on her lady-of-the-manor smile, and halted. 'Good evening. I'm Lady Calverton. Can I help you?'

A flash of teeth was followed by a neat bow. 'No, no – I merely thought I heard dogs and wondered ...'

A London accent, cultured enough, yet ... 'My husband's kennels are extensive.'

'So I see.' Another flash of teeth; the gentleman bowed. 'My compliments on the evening, Lady Calverton. If you'll excuse me?'

He barely waited for any nod before strolling off, back onto the lawns, into the crowd. Amelia watched him go. 'Who is he – do you know?'

She and Portia walked on more slowly in the same direction.

Portia shook her head. 'He's not from about here.'

Amelia couldn't recall being introduced to him. The man was as tall as Luc, but much more heavily built; not the sort of figure one forgot. From what she'd seen in the shadows and fading light, he'd been reasonably well dressed, but his coat hadn't come from a tailor patronized by the *ton*, nor had his boots – she was quite sure of that.

Portia shrugged. 'I daresay he's come with the Farrells, or the Tibertsons. They have relatives from all over staying every summer.'

'Doubtless that's it.'

She and Portia merged with the crowd, increasingly festive. Amelia glanced at the sky, but it was still too early for the fireworks; at this time of year, the twilights stretched for hours.

They drifted to the area where dancers twirled to the music of three fiddlers. Others ringed the dancers, clapping and smiling, laughing and joking. Despite being created to serve an entirely different purpose, the evening looked set to be a resounding success on the social front – everyone was having a thoroughly good time.

The dance ended; exhausted, dancers sagged. The fiddlers lowered their bows, but only to agree on their next piece. Then they set to again. Laughing, some dancers staggered off while others took their place, twirling and whirling through a sprightly gig.

Cool fingers slid around Amelia's hand.

She looked up to find Luc beside her.

He met her gaze. 'Come – let's join in.'

She hesitated; on her other side, Portia drew her hand from her arm and gave her a nudge. 'Yes. Do. You're supposed to lead the way.'

Glancing at her, Amelia caught the glare Portia directed at Luc. She swung to him, but he merely raised a brow, drew her to him, and swept her into the dance.

468

'What was that about?'

'That was Portia being her usual opinionated self.' He added, 'You'll get used to it.'

The resignation in his voice made her laugh. He raised his brows, whirled her through the steps; she'd danced such country measures often, but never before with him.

When the fiddlers finally consented to release them from their spell, she was breathless. And not all of her affliction was due to the dance. Luc steadied her, held her – far too close but then who was watching? – while she supposedly regained her breath and whirling wits. She read the truth of his motives in his eyes, pretended a haughty frown. 'It's not considered wise to render your hostess witless and incapable.'

His long lips quirked as he released her; his expression suggested he didn't agree. He glanced at the crowd, at the sky. 'Not long now.'

She drew in a breath, refocused her mind on their plan. They strolled the crowd; the instant the sky was a deep enough blue, they climbed to the terrace. Luc gave Cottsloe the order to proceed with the fireworks; Cottsloe signaled the gardeners, who hurried to set up the displays.

The crowd didn't need any orders; everyone recognized the preparations, glanced around, then moved toward the terrace and the steps. She and Luc shared a glance, then parted. Amelia went to find Helena. Five minutes later, when she guided her aunt to the balustrade to one side of the steps from where she would get the best view – and the crowd would have the best view of her – they were nearly ready to start.

She and Helena took up their position; an instant later, with a hum of anticipation rising from the crowd, Luc strolled nonchalantly out from the ball-room to join them. He nodded to Helena, his gaze coming to rest on her necklace.

He frowned, hesitated, then said, 'I'd be much obliged, ma'am, if you would give your necklace to me at the end of the night. I'll sleep better knowing it's under lock and key.'

Helena waved dismissively, haughtily patronizing. 'You need not concern yourself, Calverton. I have had this piece for an age – no harm has ever befallen it.'

Luc's lips thinned. 'Nevertheless—'

Helena spoke over his clipped protest, raising her voice to declare, 'Indeed, *I* will not sleep well if it is not with me, in my room.' With another dismissive wave, she turned to the gardens. 'Do not concern yourself.'

Luc had to accept her refusal; that he didn't do so happily was transparent. Amelia saw, from all around, glances thrown at Helena – at the necklace; countless heads came together in whispered confabulation. The rumors of the thief already circulating would ensure Luc's attempt to protect the fabulous necklace gained due notice.

A flash of fire at the bottom of the lawn drew all eyes, then the first rocket streaked upward. Amelia watched it, then glanced sideways at Helena's face, briefly lit. Nothing other than haughty disdain showed on her aunt's features, but then Amelia felt Helena's hand reach for hers, felt her squeeze briefly, triumphantly.

Smiling, Amelia returned her gaze to the fireworks, and, just for those moments, let herself relax.

*

470

None among the crowd on the terrace, all eyes trained on the fireworks, saw the gentleman Amelia and Portia had encountered close his fingers about a young lady's elbow. No one saw her turn, or the shock that filled her face. The man nodded silently at the other young lady who stood beside the first, oblivious, entranced by the spectacular display.

The man tugged; the young lady turned back to her companion, gently unwound their arms – caught by the beauty of a streaking rocket, the other barely noticed. The lady stood for a moment, then, with obvious reluctance, obeyed the man's unvoiced command and edged back. The crowd adjusted without truly looking; the man drew her to the rear, to where the wall of the house cast deep shadows.

The young lady glanced furtively left and right. 'We can't talk here!' Her voice was a breathy squeak, tight with panic.

Kirby glanced at her face, his own hard, devoid of feeling, then he bent so she could hear his reply. 'Perhaps not.' His eyes caught hers as they flicked to his face, trapped by the menace in his tone. He let her hang for a moment on the sharp hook of fear, then murmured, 'The instant the fireworks finish, we're going to walk, quickly and quietly, to the rose garden. To preserve your reputation, I'll let you lead; I'll be directly behind you. Don't think to attract any attention. Pray no one stops you.'

He paused, searching her face, her eyes; what he saw satisfied. 'No one will disturb us in the rose garden. There, we can talk.'

He straightened; the lady shivered convulsively, but she remained, still as the grave, beside him.

Until the last rocket burst and the crowd softly sighed.

She slipped away through the crowd, quickly but unobtrusively using the moment of milling, of everyone deciding what to do next, to slide from the terrace, through the crowds gathered below it, and into the shadows shrouding the walk leading along the east wing to the walled rose garden.

Her face was chalk white when she reached the archway in the stone wall. One brief glance confirmed her tormentor was a man of his word; he was all but at her shoulder. Gulping in a breath, she hurried under the arch, keen to get away from all eyes.

All who might see and guess her terrible secret.

She stopped as Kirby joined her, swung to face him. 'I told you – I can't steal anything more. I just *can't*!' Her voice rose hysterically.

'Quiet, you little fool!' Kirby took her elbow in a merciless grip and propelled her down the central path, away from the entrance.

He stopped at the end of the garden. The roses were in full spate; they were surrounded by huge bushes, arching canes supporting fist-sized blooms bobbing in the light breeze.

They were alone; no one would see or happen upon them.

The young lady swallowed; dizzy, she felt ill, faint, panic choking her breathing, fear chilling her.

Releasing her, Kirby stared down at her, eyes narrowed.

She wrung her hands. 'I told you.' Her voice broke on a sob. 'I can't take anything more. You said one more thing, and I gave you the thimble. There's nothing more—'

472

'Stop sniveling.' Kirby cut across her words, cut her like a whip. 'There's patently more, but if you want free of me, I'll offer you a deal.'

The young lady quivered, then drew in a small breath. Steeled herself. 'What deal?'

'That necklace – the one the old Dowager's wearing.' Kirby ignored the slumping of the lady's shoulders, the hopeless denial in her eyes. 'I need a lot more, but I'll settle for that.' He studied her, unmoved by the tears that welled in her eyes, ignored the shaking of her head. 'I could milk you for years, but I'm willing to cut our association short if you get me that bauble. You heard the old dear – it'll be lying in her room tonight just waiting for you to pick it up.'

'I won't.' The lady straightened, tried to raise her head. 'You lied before – you won't keep your word. You've kept drawing me along, first telling me it was all for Edward, later saying you'd go if I just got one thing more ... and here you are, still, asking for that necklace. I won't steal it – I don't believe you!'

That last was uttered on a spurt of defiance. Kirby smiled. 'The worm turns at last. I won't pretend you're wrong, given the situation, to distrust my assurances. However, you're overlooking one thing.'

The lady tried to keep her lips shut, tried to deny the need to know. 'What thing?'

'If you steal that necklace under my orders, because I've blackmailed you into it, and you give it to me, then I *have* to go away. Because if anything went wrong and you pointed the finger at me, then *I'd* be the one in trouble, not you. No one would worry about you in the least. *I* would be the obvious villain. You would be viewed as nothing more than the silly chit you are.' He let his words sink in, then added,

'Getting that necklace for me is the surest way to protect yourself from me for all time.'

He let silence stretch while she fought an inner battle against a conscience that had risen far too late to save her. The story he'd so glibly spun had holes he could drive a coach and four through, but he doubted she'd see them, or the danger one hole in particular posed to her.

She hadn't been the sharpest apple in the basket to begin with; with fear and panic clouding her mind, she wouldn't be able to see her way clear. See her way to safety.

Eventually, as he'd expected, she clasped her hands even tighter, and looked up at him. 'If I get you the necklace, you swear you'll go away? That once I hand it to you, I'll never see you again?'

He smiled, held up his right hand. 'As God is my witness, once you bring me that necklace, you'll never set eyes on me again.'

The fireworks were a wondrous success, a perfect moment bringing the first half of the entertainment to an end. When the last flare died into the now-midnight black sky, the entire gathering sighed. Then, slowly, collected itself.

As their neighbors filed back into the ballroom for the formal part of the evening, Luc and Amelia stood on the terrace steps and farewelled their happy and tired tenants, the villagers and other local attendees.

After expressing their delighted thanks for the evening, groups wended their way through the gardens, around the wings to the drive where some had left their gigs and farm carts; others headed on foot past the stables and the home farm, still others onto the path leading past the folly on the rise, carrying sleepy children home.

When the last had departed, with a contented sigh of her own, Amelia turned and let Luc lead her inside.

The rest of the evening went precisely as planned. The string quartet that earlier had entertained the older ladies not given to strolling the lawns now provided the company with waltzes and cotillions. Their neighbors laughed and danced, and the hours inexorably rolled by.

This, however, was the country. By eleven, all the guests had gathered their parties and departed; many had some way to drive to reach their beds. The family retired upstairs, as they normally would. Everyone smiled and wished all others a good night – everyone watched Luc's four sisters and Miss Pink disperse to their rooms before dropping their own masks.

But that was all they dropped. They couldn't be sure the villain wouldn't hide in the house; no matter that the ladies' skins crawled at the thought, they did not, by word or deed, allow any inkling of their plans to show.

Minerva and Amelia walked Helena to her room. With fond good nights, Minerva parted from the other two before Helena's door, and went on to her own room farther down the west wing. Amelia entered Helena's room with her; she sat and chatted idly about the events of the night while Helena's maid tended her mistress and prepared her for bed. The maid dismissed, Amelia came to the bed. She squeezed Helena's hand and leaned over to kiss her cheek. 'Take care!' she whispered.

'*Naturellement*.' Helena returned the kiss with her

usual unwavering confidence. 'But the necklace,' she whispered back. She gestured to the round table in the center of the room. 'Put it there so I can see it.'

Amelia hesitated, but the necklace did have to be left out somewhere – the maid had as usual locked it away in Helena's jewel casket – leaving the key in the lock – and if she didn't put it where Helena wanted it, her aunt would only wait until she left the room, get out of bed, and do it herself.

With a reluctant nod, she crossed to the casket, unlocked it, and retrieved the necklace. She left the matching bracelets and earrings where they were; if anything went wrong, something would remain of her grandfather Sebastian's gift. As she draped the fabulous strands of the necklace across the polished surface of the table, the value of the piece had never seemed so clear – so much more than material wealth; the magnitude of the risk Helena was so selflessly taking gripped her.

Fingers sliding from the necklace's iridescent strands, she looked across the room at Helena, propped high on the pillows in the shadow of the bed. She wanted to thank her, but this wasn't the time. With a last, shaky smile, she nodded. Helena imperiously waved her to the door.

She left, closing the door softly behind her.

Elsewhere in the huge house, the servants had cleared and cleaned, then, under Higgs's and Cottsloe's watchful eyes, they'd retired to their own quarters. Cottsloe did his rounds as usual; the house was locked, the lights doused in the usual pattern.

That done, Cottlsoe retired – to the kitchen, to keep watch. Higgs had already taken up her post at the top of the servants' stair, to guard against anyone hiding in the servants' quarters and sneaking into the house that way.

The family had retired to their rooms, but not to their beds. As the clocks around the house struck twelve, they all emerged, silently sliding through the shadows, nodding at each other as they passed on their way to their assigned positions.

Lurking in the shadows before the upstairs parlor door, Luc wondered as Portia's and Penelope's apparent lack of awareness. It appeared they hadn't realized anything was afoot. That seemed, to him, so utterly unlikely, yet they'd given not the slightest hint that either was even suspicious.

Easing his shoulders against the door, he mentally set his younger sisters to one side – they were in their rooms on the top floor – they couldn't easily get down without passing either him, Higgs, or Amelia; he had absolute faith that none of the three of them would let Portia and Penelope past them.

Perhaps his younger sisters truly were, even now, falling asleep?

Stifling a disbelieving snort, he listened ... but all he heard was the sounds of the house settling into its usual nighttime repose. He knew every creaking board, every squeaky tread on every stair; if any creaked in any unusual way, he would know. Helena's room lay to his left, midway down the west wing. Simon was concealed just before the stairs at the wing's far end; if the thief came that way, Simon would let him pass and follow.

Luc would do the same if the felon chose the main stairs as his route to Helena's room. Amelia was the only other watcher in the corridors on this floor – she was to Luc's right, in the east wing, hovering just past Emily's and Anne's rooms. Anne's was the farthest. Although none of them believed she was involved ... if by chance there was some connection, he and Amelia wanted to know of it first.

Not that they'd discussed it, or even said so much in words, however private – they'd simply exchanged a glance, then Amelia had claimed that position as hers.

His mind drifted to her – his wife and so much more – to all he wanted to say to her as soon as fate gave him a chance ...

With an effort, he yanked his wits back, focused them on the game at hand, one too fraught with danger to risk distraction. Lucifer was prowling downstairs; Martin was hovering in the shadows of the shrubbery. Sugden was out somewhere near the kennels. From a room at the end of the west wing, Amanda was watching the valley and all approaches from beyond the home farm. Phyllida was in hers and Lucifer's room, which happened to command an excellent view of the rose garden and the gardens farther along, beyond the east wing.

Night fell like a shroud over the house.

Through the depths of the night, they waited for the thief to show his face.

Two o'clock came and went. At a quarter to three, Luc left his position briefly; moving soundlessly through the corridors, he alerted Simon to cover the whole of the west wing, then checked with everyone else, eventually returning to his watch. They were all wilting. No one had voiced it, yet every one of them was wondering if they'd misjudged, and the thief would not, for whatever reason, appear.

Time drifted on; staying awake became increasingly difficult.

Propped up in her bed, Helena had much less difficulty than any of her guards in keeping alert. Old age left her less inclined to sleep, more inclined to lie in peace and sift through her memories.

Tonight, she lay on her pillows and kept watch over her necklace, and remembered. All the good times that had followed the moment when she'd received it – the moment when she'd most unwillingly accepted it, outwitted by Sebastian, and fate.

All the wonders of life, and love.

She was far away, reliving the past, when the door of her wardrobe, directly across the room, swung slowly open.

Chapter Twenty-Three

Helena watched as a cloaked figure stepped gingerly from the depths of the wardrobe. Glancing fearfully at the bed, the figure hesitated – too small and slight to be a man, but the cloak's hood was up, hiding all clues to identity.

Reassured by Helena's stillness, the figure drew itself up, then glanced around; its gaze fell on the table.

Lit by the faint moonlight slanting through the open window, the pearls glowed with an unearthly radiance.

The figure inched nearer, then nearer still. Then one small hand came out from beneath the cloak, fingers extending to touch the iridescent strands.

Helena saw the fingers shake, saw the last moment of hesitation. Realized in a flash who the figure must be. There was a wealth of kindliness in her voice when she asked, '*Ma petite*, what are you doing here?'

The figure's head jerked up. Helena pushed upright in the bed. The figure uttered a strangled squeak, halfway to a shriek; frozen, she stared at Helena.

'Come.' Helena beckoned. 'Do not scream. Come and tell me.'

Heavy footsteps shook the corridor. The figure's head jerked toward the door, then she rushed – first this way, then that – in total panic.

Helena muttered a French curse and struggled to rise from the bed.

The figure yelped, rushed to the open window. She leaned out – the room was on the first floor.

'No!' Helena ordered. 'Come back!' Centuries of command rang in her voice.

The figure turned uncertainly.

Simon burst through the door.

With a shriek of pure fear, the figure jumped out of the window.

Simon cursed and rushed to look.

'Good God!' He stared. 'She's landed on the loggia.' Leaning out, he waved. 'Come back here, you little fool!'

Helena rolled her eyes. Shrugging on her robe, she hurried to join him. The sight beyond the window made her lay a hand on his arm. 'Don't say anything more.'

But Simon had already fallen grimly silent.

Outside, the cloaked figure, weaving and staggering, was attempting to walk one of the beams of the loggia that extended away from the house over the flagstone terrace. If she overbalanced and fell, broken limbs would be the least of it.

The figure teetered precariously; time and again, she swayed, arms flailing – every time, she regained her balance. The heavy cloak swung about her legs, a dangerous encumbrance. Under her breath, Helena prayed.

'My stars,' Simon breathed. 'I think she's going to make it.'

'Don't speak too soon and tempt fate.'

In the gloom of the gardens, they could just make out Martin hovering by the shrubbery, and Sugden on the path to the kennels. Both remained frozen, silent witnesses to the girl's perilous flight. No one made the slightest sound, the slightest movement, did nothing to distract her.

After what seemed an eternity, the wildly lurching figure reached the end of the beam where it joined with an upright support. Simon tensed; Helena sank her fingers into his sleeve. 'You are *not* following her.'

Simon didn't even glance at her. 'Of course not. No need.'

They waited silently as the figure grappled and grasped, then partly swung, partly fell, partly scrambled to the ground, landing in an ungainly heap.

Simon immediately leaned out of the window. 'She's on the ground by the loggia outside the music room!'

His ringing call propelled everyone into action. The girl jumped to her feet and tore off toward the shrubbery.

Then she saw Martin closing from that direction.

With a shriek, she pivoted and fled in the opposite direction, toward the rose garden and the darkness of the wood beyond.

She was almost there, almost to the path that led into the shadows, when she ran directly into Lucifer, who'd left the house through the front door and circled around the east wing.

*

Luc heard Simon thunder to Helena's room, but no one had passed either him or Simon, so how ...? Via the window? But Martin, Sugden, or Phyllida would have seen ... how had anyone got past them all?

Striding into the west corridor, he saw Simon dash into Helena's room. He paused, poised to react, then he heard Simon speak. Confused, Luc waited – there was clearly no drama occurring in the room, no danger to Helena.

What the devil was going on? He was about to stride to Helena's room and find out when he heard Simon's call.

'She's on the ground by the loggia ...'

She.

The word stopped him in his tracks. The possibilities crashed down on him. *Could* they all have been wrong? Had Anne gone out of her window and around the outside of the house? Or had she not even been in her room but in Helena's?

Swinging around, he strode for the east wing.

Amelia was hovering outside Anne's door; she'd heard Simon's call but the house was too massive for her to make out his words. But she saw Luc coming, understood enough. She didn't hesitate.

She opened Anne's door. 'Anne?' No reply. The bed was draped in dense shadows. 'Anne!'

'Huh? What ...?' Pushing her thick brown hair from her face, Anne groggily sat up, peering at Amelia. 'What's the matter?'

Amelia beamed at her. Relief and newfound excitement rushed through her. 'Nothing, nothing – nothing to worry about.'

Sounds from outside reached them; Amelia rushed to the window, flung back the curtains, threw up the sash. Behind her, she heard Luc reach the room and step inside.

'What's going on?' Anne asked from the bed.

After the faintest pause, Luc replied, 'I'm not sure.'

Amelia heard the profound relief in his voice, could feel the irrational dread lift from his – *their* – shoulders. Holding back the curtains, she leaned out as Luc joined her. A second later, Anne, dragging a robe about her, pushed in alongside.

The sight that met their eyes was at first incomprehensible – a trio of figures wrestling on the lawn, detail obscured by the dense shadows cast by the huge trees of the wood. Then the trio resolved into two larger figures supporting the third toward the house; the smaller figure resisted, but weakly.

Beneath them, a door opened; Amanda stepped onto the terrace. She waved to the group. 'Bring her here.'

They changed direction; a moment later they passed out of the shadows and features became clear. Martin and Lucifer were gently but determinedly escorting a slight female, cloaked, shaking her head, sobbing hysterically. Her hood had fallen back revealing lustrous brown locks.

Luc frowned. 'Who is it?'

Amelia suddenly realized.

It was Anne who answered, staring at the figure round-eyed. 'My God – that's Fiona! What on earth is going on?'

It was the third time she'd asked, but the explanation wasn't going to be easy, and they didn't have all the answers.

'We'll explain tomorrow.' Luc swung around and

484

strode out of the room; they heard him running down the corridor toward the stairs.

Amelia started after him.

'Amelia!'

She turned back, met Anne's eyes. 'I truly can't stop now, but I promise we'll explain all tomorrow morning. Please – just go back to bed.'

Fervently hoping Anne would do so, Amelia hurried out, closing the bedroom door behind her. She started down the corridor, then remembered Emily. She paused by Emily's door, listening, then eased it open. She tiptoed in, just close enough to be sure Emily was still sound asleep – doubtless dreaming innocent – or possibly not so innocent – dreams.

Inwardly sighing with relief, she retreated, then hurried on toward the stairs. At their head, she came upon Helena and Minerva being escorted down by Simon.

Simon looked up. 'They've got her.'

'I know. I saw.'

Minerva sighed. 'The poor child. We'll have to get to the bottom of this, for I simply will not believe it was all her doing. She was *never* a bad girl.' She paused, one hand gripping the balustrade, a frown forming in her eyes. Then she glanced upward. 'Someone should check on Portia and Penelope.' Minerva glanced at Amelia.

She nodded. 'I will. Then I'll come down.'

Minerva resumed her descent. 'Tell them they must stay in their beds.'

Already headed up the stairs, Amelia doubted any such injunction was likely to stop those two; to her mind, their only hope was that they'd slept soundly and hadn't been disturbed.

That hope was dashed the instant she cracked open Portia's door – and discovered Luc's younger sisters fully dressed, leaning far out of the window, presumably watching Fiona being led into the house two floors below.

She stepped inside, shut the door with a click. 'What do the pair of you think you're doing?'

They glanced back at her; not a glimmer of guilt showed in either face.

'We're observing the culmination of your plan.' Penelope turned back to the window.

'They've got her inside.' Portia straightened, then walked to Amanda.

Penelope followed. 'I really didn't think the plan would work, but it has. I did think it might be Fiona – she was at all the places where things were taken, after all.' She fixed her spectacled gaze on Amelia's face. 'Do we have any idea why she did it?'

Amelia had no idea where to start in the task of putting these two in their place. She wasn't even sure it was possible. Nevertheless, she drew a deep breath. 'I bear a message from your mama – you're to stay in your beds.'

Both girls looked at her as if she'd run mad.

'What?' Portia said. 'While all this is going on—'

'You expect us meekly to close our eyes and fall asleep?'

One breath wasn't going to be enough. 'No, but—'

Amelia broke off, raised her head. Listened.

Portia and Penelope did, too. An instant later, they all heard it again – a muffled scream. They rushed to the window.

'Can you see . . . ?' Amelia asked.

They all scanned the gardens, even darker now; the moon was rapidly waning.

'There!' Penelope pointed across the lawn to where two struggling figures were just discernible on the path beside the rose garden.

'Who . . . ?' Amelia asked, but the clenching of her heart told her.

'Well, if Fiona's downstairs,' Portia said, 'then that must be Anne.'

'The fool!' Penelope said. 'How senseless.'

Amelia didn't stop to argue; she was already out of the door.

'No – just think,' Portia said. 'That man must be part of the syndicate—'

Amelia left them to their deductions – they were better at it than her – and with luck it would keep them where they were, arguing, well out of harm's way. She plunged down the main stairs, screaming for Luc, knowing she dared not stop to explain.

As far as she'd been able to see, the man – whoever he was – had his hands around Anne's throat.

'*Luc!*' She hit the front hall at a run, skidded on the tiles as she turned and flung herself down the east corridor. Via the garden hall was the fastest route to Anne – she took it without thinking.

She burst onto the lawn, much closer to the struggling pair – still struggling, thank God! As she pounded on, she realized, and called, 'Anne! *Anne!*'

The larger figure stilled, then the configuration rearranged itself – then with a curse she heard, the man flung Anne aside and raced for the wood.

She was gasping when she reached Anne; at least the blackguard had flung her onto the lawn, not into the stone wall. Anne was coughing, gasping, struggling to sit up. Amelia helped her to sit. 'Who was it? Do you know?'

Anne shook her head. 'But—' She wheezed, then tried gamely again, 'I think he was among the guests last night.' She hauled in another breath. 'He thought I was Fiona.' Her fingers clutched Amelia's. 'If you hadn't called ... he was trying to kill me – her. As soon as he looked and realized I wasn't her ...'

Amelia patted her shoulder. 'Stay here.' She looked at the darkness of the wood. She had to make an immediate decision. Had Fiona taken the necklace and passed it on before being caught? She didn't know. Nor did Anne. 'When Luc comes, tell him I've followed the man – I'm not going to tackle him, just keep him in sight until Luc and the others reach us.'

Freeing her fingers from Anne's, Amelia rose and ran on. The path led straight into the wood; the trees closed around her, enclosing her in gloom. She hurried on, no longer running but moving fast, her slipper-shod feet padding all but silently on the leaf-strewn paths. She knew these woods, not as well as Luc did, but better than anyone who'd only recently come to the area possibly could.

There were only so many ways the man could go; it was easy to guess he'd veer to the east, putting as much distance between himself and the Chase as he could. She doubted he'd keep running – crashing along the narrow tracks would invite pursuit – so with luck ...

Ten minutes into the wood, her decision bore fruit. She caught a glimpse of a large shadowy figure through the trees ahead. A minute later, she saw him clearly.

He was walking, striding along, quickly but without panic.

Silent and determined, she settled to track him.

*

Astonished, Anne watched Amelia disappear into the wood, her throat too raw to voice any protest. As soon as she'd caught her breath, she struggled to her feet and limped back to the house.

She didn't have to go far to find Luc. He was standing on the path outside the east wing, looking up at the window high above from which Portia and Penelope hung, yelling and gesticulating toward the rose garden and the wood.

They saw Anne, and shrieked, 'There she is!'

Luc swung around, then he was beside her, hugging her, holding her. 'Are you all right?'

Anne nodded. 'Amelia ...'

Luc felt his heart plummet. 'Where is she?'

He held Anne away from him and looked into her face.

She coughed, then hoarsely enunciated, 'In the woods – she said to tell you she wasn't going to try and catch him, just keep him in sight until you came ...'

He smothered a curse – an expression of sheer horror Anne didn't need to hear. Amelia might not intend to catch the man, but he might catch her. He pushed Anne toward the house. 'Go inside – tell the others.'

His mind was already with Amelia. Turning, he raced for the wood.

Amelia slipped along beneath the trees, increasingly cautious. While the wood at first had felt, if not comfortable, then at least familiar, the trees had grown progressively denser, older, the paths beneath their gnarled branches more dark, the air more weighted with age. Ahead, she could hear the regular

489

thud of the man's boots; he wasn't trying to skulk but was steadily tramping on. A quick mental survey had suggested he intended keeping to the wood to where it ended on the rise above Lyddington.

He was clever enough to recognize the unwisdom of rushing – one trip over a tree root could incapacitate him and leave him waiting for his pursuers to rescue him. Also clever enough to take the least exposed route to see him safe home, assuming he was staying somewhere about Lyddington.

The more she thought of how clever he was proving, the more uneasy, the more wary she became. But the thought of the Cynster necklace, the notion of following him to his lair, and then waiting to point the way to Luc and the others who she was sure must be close on her heels kept her putting one foot in front of the other.

Then the ground started to rise. She glimpsed the man ahead and above; she craned her head, trying to fix his direction – her foot hit an exposed root. She stumbled. Swallowing a curse, she fetched up against a nearby bole – and snapped off a dry twig.

The sound cut through the heavy air like a pistol shot.

She froze.

About her, the forest seemed to stir, menacingly breathe. She waited – only then remembered that her gown, the walking gown she'd changed into, was primrose yellow. If she was visible from where he was . . .

Then his footfalls started again. The same steady rhythm, in the same direction.

She drew breath, waited for her pulse to slow, then went on, even more cautiously than before.

He was following a rough track that led up a short rise, then dipped into a heavily wooded dell. She was deep in the trees before she realized she'd lost the repetitive tramp of his footsteps. She stopped. Strained her ears, but heard nothing beyond the usual woodland night sounds. A distant hoot here, a furtive rustling there, the creak of branches rubbing high above. Nothing that signified man.

Yet ... she couldn't see how she'd lost him.

Ahead, the track widened; stepping even more warily, she went on. The track opened into a small natural clearing closely ringed by trees.

Again she paused and listened; hearing nothing, she walked forward, her slippers whispering on the soft leaves.

She was almost across the clearing when sensation swept her spine.

She glanced back.

Gasped.

Whirled to face the man she'd been following.

His bulk blocked the path between her and the Chase. He was tall and wide, with close-cropped dark hair ... her mouth dropped open as she recognized the man she and Portia had met near the kennels.

He smiled – evilly. 'Well, well – how helpful.'

Her heart thumped, but she snapped her lips shut and lifted her chin. 'Don't be daft! I have no intention whatever of helping you in any way.'

Her only hope was to keep him talking – here and as loudly as possible – for as long as she could.

He took a swaggering step forward, eyes narrowing when she only tilted her chin higher; she'd had years of dealing with men who sought to intimidate with sheer size. Apparently accepting she was not about to make a bolt for it – into the dense woods – she knew how far she would get – he halted and looked down at her, lip curling with contempt.

'Ah, but you will help me, you see – to a nice slice of your husband's wealth. I don't know what happened back there' —with his head, he indicated the Chase— 'but I'm experienced enough to know when to cut my losses.' His chilling smile returned. 'And when to seize an opportunity fate throws my way.'

He tensed to step forward and grasp her arm; she stopped him with an utterly patronizing look. 'If you really are clever enough to know when to cut and run, then you'd better start running. There's absolutely no possibility my husband will pay very much for my safe return, if that's the direction your mind is taking.'

His smile didn't waver; he nodded. 'That's my tack, right enough, but you can save your breath – I've seen the way he looks at you.'

She blinked. 'You have? How?'

The look he gave her suggested he wasn't sure what her tack was. 'Like he'd cut off his right arm before he'd let you go.'

She fought not to grin delightedly. 'No.' Lips pinched, she stuck her nose in the air. 'You're quite wrong you know – he never did love me. Our marriage was arranged.'

He gave a disgusted snort. 'You can stow the guff. If it'd been Edward, I might have believed you, but that brother of his always was a painfully straight dealer. Arranged or not, he'll pay, and pay well, to have you back unharmed – without any public fuss.'

His eyes narrowed to mean and heartless shards as he emphasized the last words. He went to step

492

forward.

Again she stopped him, this time with an abject sigh. 'I can see I'm going to have to tell you the truth.'

She glanced up through her lashes, could see the urge to get on, get away, taking her with him, war with the need to know why she thought his plan doomed. He knew better than to argue, but ...

'What truth?'

It came out as a growl, a warning to be quick.

She hesitated, then asked, 'What's your name?'

His eyes glittered. 'Jonathon Kirby, although what that's got to do with—'

'I do like to know to whom I'm confessing.'

'So tell me – and make it quick. We don't have all night.'

She lifted her head. 'Very well, Mr. Kirby. The truth I apparently need to confess to you concerns the how and why of my marriage. Which is also the reason my husband won't pay any great sum for my return.'

She rushed on, speaking the words as fast as they came into her head, knowing she had to keep him there for just a little longer – Luc and the others couldn't be far away. 'I said our marriage was arranged, and it was – for money. He doesn't have much – well, that's an understatement – he doesn't really have any, not ... well, what one might call cash as such. Land he has, but you can't eat land, can you? – and you certainly can't gown girls for their come-outs in hay – so you see, it was imperative he marry for money, and so we did, so he got my dowry, but with all the urgent bills and the repairs and so on – well, if you've been about here for more than a day,

493

you must have seen the working gangs – so what I'm trying to say is that there's hardly any left, and he won't pay you much because he can't.'

She had to pause for breath.

Kirby stepped menacingly nearer. 'I've heard enough.' He leaned close, thrust his face close to hers. 'What sort of fool do you take me for? I checked – of course, I did!' His voice dripped scorn. 'As soon as I realized the possibility might arise to cozen one of his sweet little sisters. No joy there, but his wife's an even better mark. I don't even have to try to charm you, and you won't be on my hands for long. The man's as rich as bloody Croesus and he worships the ground you walk on – he'll pay a small fortune for you, and that's *precisely* what I'm going to demand.'

His features had contorted with some ugly emotion; Amelia set her jaw and stared him down, her belligerence fueled by desperate necessity, and the irrational irritation of knowing she was half-right and he was half-wrong. '*You're* the fool if you believe that!' Eyes narrowing, she planted her fists on her hips and glared. 'We didn't marry for love – he does not love me.' A complete and utter lie, but she could put her heart and soul into her next declaration: 'And he's next kin to a pauper – he hasn't a coin to bless himself with. I'm his *wife*, for heaven's sake! Don't you think I'd know?'

She flung her arms wide on the words – and glimpsed something from the corner of her eye. Until he'd stepped close, Kirby had blocked her view of the path into the clearing; looking past him, she saw Luc, standing motionless at the clearing's edge, his dark gaze locked, not on Kirby, but on her face. On her eyes.

494

For one instant, time stood still. Her heart contracted; she felt ...

Kirby read her face.

He turned with a roar.

Amelia jumped, gasped, skittered back as Kirby flung himself at Luc, one huge fist rising, swinging.

She screamed.

Luc ducked at the very last minute; she didn't see what happened, but Kirby's body jerked, then the big man bent foward, only to straighten abruptly as Luc's fist connected with his jaw.

She winced at the sound, quickly scuttled farther away as Kirby staggered back. The close-packed trees gave her little room to move, but although Kirby's gaze flicked to her, he kept his attention on Luc.

Who, after one glance at Amelia, stepped into the clearing. That one graceful step held immeasurably more menace than anything Kirby had done.

Kirby groaned, slumped, then straightened; a knife flashed in his fist.

Amelia gasped. Tensed.

Luc stilled, his gaze on the blade, then he resumed his slow, prowling approach.

Kirby crouched a little, spread his arms wide, started to circle.

Luc drifted aside.

Amelia pressed back among the trees ... a too-recent memory of Amanda with a knife at her throat flooded her ...

Kirby lunged with the knife. Luc weaved back, just out of reach.

Horrified, Amelia stared – Kirby was quite plainly aiming for Luc's face. Her husband's beautiful fallen-angel face. A face Luc himself barely noticed, and

495

certainly – contrary to what Kirby was imagining – felt no vanity over protecting.

She was very attached to that face – exactly as it was.

Jaw setting, she glanced around. Her gaze fell on a fallen branch – a nice, stout oak branch – large enough for a cosh, small enough for her to heft – best of all, close enough and free of debris so she could lift it undetected.

Kirby's back was to her. The branch was in her hands before she'd finished the thought.

She paused, gathered her strength, took one step as she lifted the branch high—

Kirby sensed her, started to turn—

She brought the branch down as hard as she could. It broke with a satisfying crack over Kirby's head.

He didn't go down. But he wobbled.

Very slowly shook his head.

Lips grimly set, Luc stepped forward, caught Kirby's wrist, holding the knife at bay. With his other fist, he delivered the *coup de grâce* – Kirby dropped like a stone to the leaf-strewn ground.

Clutching the remnants of her club, Amelia stared. 'Is he . . . ?'

Luc glanced at her, then bent and removed the knife. 'Unconscious. I don't think he'll wake for a while.'

In the distance, they heard voices, calling, coming nearer, yet here and now, there was just them.

And the silence.

Still ringing with all she'd said.

She frantically replayed all she'd gabbled to Kirby – how much had Luc heard? He could have been there for some time . . . but he couldn't possibly believe . . . think *she* believed . . . ?

496

She dropped her club, pressed her hands together, cleared her throat. 'I—'

'You—'

They both stopped, gazes locking – locked. She felt like she was drowning in the intensity of his eyes. Her lungs seized, as if she stood teetering on the brink of . . . happiness or despair, she wasn't sure which.

Stiffly, Luc stepped nearer, reached for her hands. Then he sighed and hauled her into his arms. Crushed her close. 'I want to *shake* you for running off alone into danger.' He growled the words into her curls, his arms an iron cage about her.

Then she felt his arms ease.

'But . . . first . . .' He drew back, looked into her face. 'I have to tell you something – something I should have told you long ago.' His lips twisted. 'Two somethings, if truth be told. And they are the truth – the real truth.' He drew in a breath; his eyes held hers. 'I—'

'Hroo-hroo! *Hroo*!'

Luc turned; they both stared. '*Damn*!' Releasing her, he faced the path; a steady crashing and rhythmic thudding were rolling toward them. 'They've let the dogs out.'

On the disbelieving words, hounds came bounding up, a veritable tide, joyous and excited, thoroughly delighted to have found their master. It wasn't just a few dogs, however, but the entire pack. Luc stood before Amelia; clutching the back of his coat, she pressed close, not frightened but in danger of being batted off her feet by so many whipping tails and bumptiously overjoyed canines.

'Down!' Luc thundered. '*Sit*!'

Eventually, they did, but clearly believed they were

497

due a great deal more thanks for having acquitted themselves so well.

Luc had just restored some semblance of order when the human tide descended. Portia and Penelope, more familiar with the woods, led the way, running and ducking branches ahead of Lucifer, Martin, Sugden, and a disgusted Simon.

They were all out of breath when they piled into the clearing.

'You got him!' wheezed Portia, one hand clutching her side.

Luc glanced briefly at Kirby, then Amelia, then he looked at his sister. 'We did.' He continued to look at Portia. 'Who let out the pack?'

'We did, of course.' Penelope's tone stated that the decision had been fully evaluated and only a fool would dare challenge it. 'They all reached the first fork, and didn't know which way you'd gone. The dogs were the only way to trace you.'

Luc looked at her, then sighed. Patsy pressed close, pushing her nose into his hand, whining with quiet joy.

'What's the story, then?' Arm braced against a tree while he struggled to catch his breath, Martin nodded at Kirby's slumped form.

Luc looked down, then shook his head. 'As to that, I'm not sure – but his name's Jonathon Kirby ... and I understand he's acquainted with Edward.'

Which, of course, told Amelia just how much of her tirade Luc had heard – all of it. She was still wincing at the thought when, hours later, she finally climbed the main stairs and headed down the short corridor to their rooms.

Dawn could not be far off.

Getting back to the house had proved an unexpected effort, not least because, with the villain caught and answers to all their questions doubtless to come, the determination that had fueled them all night abruptly waned. They slumped. Their feet dragged.

Luc dispatched Sugden, Portia, and Penelope to return the pack to the kennels. They went ahead, the hounds still alert, ready to dash off after anything at the slightest excuse.

Kirby, roused ungently, was too groggy to walk unsupported. Martin, Lucifer, and Simon took turns chivying him along in Luc and Amelia's wake; Luc was the only one who could lead them unerringly through the woods back to the Chase.

They'd arrived half an hour earlier to questions and exclamations. Portia and Penelope had said only that all was well before continuing to the kennels to help Sugden quarter the pack.

It was Helena who, in matriarchal fashion, eventually took charge. She pointed out that Luc himself was the local magistrate, that apparently there was a perfectly sound cellar below stairs in which Kirby – unanimously referred to as 'the felon' – could be incarcerated for the time being, until they wished to question him further, and that, meanwhile, they all needed their rest.

As usual, Helena was indubitably right, yet Amelia hoped that before she and Luc fell asleep ...

She didn't actually know what he wanted to tell her. Not absolutely. Yet entering her private sitting room, she was all but floating on her hopes and dreams. Two things, he'd said. In her heart, she knew what one of those things was.

The ultimate victory in her long and tireless campaign beckoned.

Triumph was a powerful drug. It seeped through her veins as she undressed and got ready for bed. She started brushing her hair, impatience escalating; to distract herself – she didn't know how long it would take Luc to organize the cellar and lock Kirby in – she tried to fathom what else – what other secret – Luc might wish to confess to her.

It couldn't be very serious, surely.

But why now? What had Kirby said to precipitate . . .

Her hand slowed, then lowered. She stared unseeing at her mirror. She and Kirby had discussed only two points. Whether or not Luc loved her enough to pay well for her return.

And whether Luc was, or was not, rich.

As rich as bloody Croesus.

Kirby had said he'd checked. He'd sounded very sure, and he was, after a fashion, clever. 'As rich as bloody Croesus' . . . it wasn't easy to imagine him making such a big mistake . . .

The months rolled back. In her mind, she revisited all the evidence she'd garnered, all she'd seen with her own eyes, everything that had led her to believe Luc and the Ashfords were very far from rich.

She couldn't have been wrong . . . could she?

Of course not! He'd all but admitted she was right . . .

No, he hadn't. Not as such.

Not ever.

The marriage settlements – by his insistence written in percentages so no real amount, no value of his estate had been there to read. She'd assumed the amount had been small.

What if it had been large?

All those repairs – the lumber ordered early, within days of that dawn she'd first spoken of marriage, of her dowry.

What if he hadn't married her for that?

She refocused on her reflection, then gave a shaky laugh. She was imagining things. The events of the night had left her overwrought, small wonder ...

What if he hadn't married her for her money?

A tap fell on her door.

Distracted, she called, 'Come in.'

She looked around as Higgs stuck her head past the door.

'I was just off to bed, my lady, if there's nothing else you need?'

'No, Higgs. And thank you for all your support this evening.'

Higgs flushed and bobbed. 'My pleasure, ma'am.' She started to back out of the room.

'Wait!' Amelia waved. 'One moment ...' Swiveling on her dressing stool, she faced Higgs. 'I have a question. When I first arrived, that first morning we discussed the menus, you mentioned we could now be more extravagant. What did you mean?'

Higgs came in, shut the door, clasped her hands. Frowned. 'I don't rightly know as it's my place to speak—'

'No, no.' Amelia smiled reassuringly. 'There's no difficulty – I just wondered why you'd thought that.'

'Well, you know about the master's father, about how he died, and ... all that?'

Amelia held her breath. 'About how Luc's father left the family in dun territory?' When Higgs nodded, she exhaled. 'Yes. I know about that.' She hadn't been wrong. It was all a silly misunderstanding of Kirby's—

'And then, at last, after all his hard work, the master's ship came in, and he said we didn't need to watch our pennies any longer. His investments had made him and the family rich. That was *such* good news! And then he was marrying you—'

'Wait.' Her mind literally reeled. Investments? Lucifer had asked Luc about investments . . . 'These investments . . . when did that happen? Can you remember when you heard?'

Higgs frowned, clearly counting through the days. Her eyes narrowed . . . 'Yes – that's it. The week after Miss Amanda's wedding, it was. I remember I had Miss Emily's and Miss Anne's gowns to see to when Cottsloe came and told me. He said the master'd just heard.'

She felt so dizzy it was a wonder she remained upright; her emotions swung crazily, from ecstatic happiness to fury. She plastered on a smile, brittle, but enough to reassure Higgs. 'Ah, yes. Of course. Thank you, Higgs. That will be all.'

Graciously, she nodded; Higgs bobbed and departed, closing the door.

Amelia set down her brush. One point she'd never understood swam into focus. Luc had been drunk that dawn she'd waylaid him; she'd realized at the time it had been a supremely un-Luc-like happening. He hadn't known she would materialize and offer to rescue him financially – he'd been drunk in celebration of the fact he'd *already* rescued himself from what, she now suspected, had been a much worse situation than even she had guessed.

For a full ten minutes, she stared, unseeing, across

502

the room, while all the pieces of the jigsaw settled into place, and she finally saw the full picture, the real truth of their marriage and what had brought it about, then, determined, she rose and went into their bedroom.

Five minutes later, Luc climbed the main stairs and headed down the corridor to their rooms. As he walked, he loosened his cravat, leaving it hanging about his throat. Outside, dawn was tinting the sky; he assumed Amelia would be asleep, exhausted ... he'd have to wait until tomorrow to talk to her. But he would; hopefully she'd be sufficiently curious over his 'somethings' to stay in bed long enough for him to confess.

Reaching for the doorknob, he made a silent vow that he wouldn't leave their apartments before he'd told her all.

He opened the door and entered, pushing it shut as he walked in, glancing down at a stubborn cuff button.

Belatedly registering that a candle was still burning ... and that Amelia wasn't in bed but standing by the window—

He looked up.

Ducked.

Something crashed on the floor far behind him, but he didn't look back. Amelia had a heavy paperweight clutched in her fist when he grabbed her, wrestled her back against the wall and pinned her there.

Her eyes, narrowed, blazed with blue fire. 'Why didn't you tell me?'

Furious, but far from cold, her tone gave him hope. 'Tell you what?'

The unwise words were out before he'd thought.

'That you're *filthy* rich!' Eyes spitting fury, she heaved against him. 'That you were even before we wed.' She struggled like a demon. 'That you weren't marrying me for my money! You let me believe you were, while all the while you – *oooof*!'

'Stand *still*!' Locking his hands about each of hers, he forced them back against the wall, one on either side of her head, leaned into her enough to subdue her – to keep her from damaging herself. Or him. He looked down into her furious eyes, her stubborn face. 'I've been *meaning* to tell you.' Not like this. 'I told you I had things to confess. That was one.'

Amelia narrowed her eyes to shards. Pinned him with her gaze. Refused to let her elation show – *refused* to let him off the hook – the hook he'd caught himself so wonderfully on. 'And the other?'

He narrowed his eyes back. 'You *know*.' After a moment, he added, 'Despite all you said to Kirby, you damn well know.'

She lifted her chin. 'I might guess, but with you that's plainly not the same as knowing. You'll have to tell me.' She held his gaze. 'Spell it out. In simple words. Crystal-clear phrases.'

His jaw set. Trapped between the wall and him, she'd never been more aware – of him, of herself – of the physical and ephemeral powers that flowed between them. The blatantly sexual and the flagrantly emotional – both had always been there, but only now were they fully revealed. Only now fully acknowledged.

So powerful now that anything else was unthinkable.

He'd come to the same conclusion. His eyes still

locked on hers, he drew breath. Spoke, his tone deep, low, intense.

'I let you believe I was marrying you for your dowry – that that was my reason. That was the first confession I wanted to make – that that wasn't true.'

He paused. She clung to his gaze, willed him to go on, curled her fingers and when he permitted it, twined them with his.

His gaze dropped to her lips, then returned to her eyes. 'My second confession was the real reason I agreed to marry you.'

When he said nothing more, his gaze lowering again, she prompted, 'What was it – your real reason?' The most important question in the world to her – the one she'd finally realized fifteen minutes ago actually existed to be asked.

He drew breath, lifted his gaze once more to her eyes. 'Because I love you – as you very well know.' The muscle along his jaw shifted, but he spoke the words clearly, his midnight blue eyes locked on hers. 'Because you are and always have been the only woman I ever wanted as my wife. The only woman I wanted to see here, ruling this house – the only woman I ever imagined finding in my nursery, holding my child.'

His lashes fell, hiding his eyes. He moved perceptibly – distractingly – closer. 'Incidentally, once we've dealt with Kirby, perhaps we should make some announcement—'

'*Don't* try to distract me.' She was well and truly wise to his ways. She tugged her hands and he freed them, simultaneously removing the paperweight. He reached to the side and set it on the dresser; she stretched up and wound her arms about his neck.

505

Touched her lips to his chin. 'You'd just got to the best part of your confession. Telling me how much you love me.'

Invitingly drawing him nearer, she kissed him, long, lingeringly, knowing, now, just how to incite but keep the flames at bay. He leaned into her, let her have her way, let their fires ignite ...

She drew back, but not far. 'Tell me again.' Her eyes locked on his as he straightened. His hands slid down, around.

His long lashes lifted; he met her gaze. Let her see what burned in his eyes. Then he looked at her lips; his quirked. 'I'd rather show you.'

She laughed. Let him bend his head and take her lips, take her mouth.

Let him lift her in his arms and carry her to their bed.

Let him love her. Loved him back.

With all her heart, as unreserved as he.

They needed no words – they spoke a language that required no words to communicate, to touch, to give, to open their hearts and share – yet at the last, as the silvery radiance of dawn poured through their windows and bathed their bed, as she lay beneath him, overburdened with sensual bliss, watched him above her, watched the sheer pleasure that washed through him as he savored her and all she gave him, and all he gave her, she reached up, drew his head down, lifted her own to whisper against his lips, 'I love you.'

His eyes flashed; he took her lips, her mouth hungrily, drank deep as he took her. Released her lips only when she arched, her body rising, clenching, senses flying high over the edge of the world as his words, deep, guttural, reached through the glory,

506

'And I'll always love you. Yesterday, tonight, tomorrow – *always*.'

'You'll never escape.'

As if to illustrate that point, Luc wrapped his long fingers in the strand of pearls interrupted by diamonds that he'd draped an hour before around Amelia's neck, and drew her to him for a long kiss.

She obliged most readily, sighed happily when he released her, sank deeper into the comfort of their bed.

It was midafternoon; outside their drawn curtains, the sleepy hum of a hot summer's day held sway. She'd retired after lunch to rest; he'd followed not long after, ostensibly to check on her. In reality to join her, but not to rest.

They were now completely naked, slumped on the rumpled bed, both at peace. One hand lazily ruffling Luc's hair, with the other, Amelia toyed with the fabulous necklace he'd had made for her before they'd wed – and then had to hide until he'd confessed and could give it to her. It matched her 'betrothal' ring, and the earrings he'd left on her dressing table yesterday, after Kirby had been taken away and Martin and Amanda, as well as Lucifer and Phyllida, had left.

She smiled. 'In case you haven't noticed, I'm not running.'

He glanced at her. 'I had noticed, but I'd thought I'd make the situation quite plain.'

His *situation* was as plain as she would ever need it to be. She couldn't stop her smile deepening, couldn't hold back the happiness that welled and overflowed her heart.

Before any family members had left, they'd announced their impending good fortune, adding their own hope for the future to Amanda and Martin's. Everyone was delighted; Helena had nodded wisely, her eyes filled with something more profound than mere joy.

As for Kirby and poor Fiona, all had been revealed, and all, as far as possible, put right.

Amelia sighed. 'Poor Fiona. I still can't believe Edward could be so unfeeling as to exploit her in such a way. He delivered her into Kirby's hands, and he must have known what Kirby was like.'

'We'll never understand Edward.' Luc stroked her cheek. 'He saw and encouraged Fiona's infatuation purely for his own selfish ends. When we banished him, she became a ready tool for revenge. That's all he would have cared about – not her.'

Amelia shivered. 'I can barely believe he's your brother.'

'Nor can I. But he is. Don't hold it against me.'

She grinned and hugged him – all of him she could reach. 'I don't.'

Given Kirby had stashed almost all Fiona had stolen in his lodgings in London, allowing the items to be retrieved and returned to their owners, and given that it was summer and the *ton* were not gathered in sufficient numbers to make sensationalizing worthwhile, the combined resources of the Ashfords, the Fulbridges, and the Cynsters had been sufficient to smooth the entire episode over. The tale had been cast as merely an endnote to Edward's earlier, already weathered disgrace; the story had quickly acquired the patina of 'old news'.

Kirby, however, hadn't been allowed to escape.

Any leniency they might have shown was slain when, the morning after his capture, they'd seen the bruising around Anne's throat. Anne had been right; Kirby had intended to kill, as he thought, Fiona.

It had taken careful management on the assembled ladies' parts to keep Kirby alive long enough to be carted away from the Chase, but he had been, and their evidence had been heard by one of the circuit judges; Kirby was now in London awaiting his trial.

Now the house had settled into peaceful harmony, driven by the subtle heartbeat of country house life. The best of the summer stretched before them, and after that, the rest of their lives.

'The Kirkpatricks will be here tomorrow.' Luc glanced at her. 'Does Emily want us to host a ball?'

'From what I gather, Emily will be quite content if we simply leave her and Kirkpatrick alone.' Amelia grinned. 'They'll be here for a week – we can talk to his parents when they arrive and see what they think.'

Luc accepted her wisdom and lay back, his long body alongside hers, one hand splayed across her stomach.

They both simply lay there, quiet but not sleepy, content, sated – at peace.

Outside, a door opened. A second later, they heard voices. One male, grumbling, the other female, sharp and decisive. Dismissive.

Luc frowned.

Seeing it, Amelia murmured, 'I gather Simon is of the firm opinion that it's not safe for Portia to take the dogs out rambling in the woods. Not alone.'

After a moment, Luc murmured, 'But she'll have the dogs with her.'

'I don't think Simon believes dogs are protection

509

enough.'

Luc choked on a laugh. 'If he thinks to persuade Portia to that end, I wish him luck.'

The altercation outside rose to a high enough pitch to confirm his reading of his sister – and Amelia's reading of her brother. The voices faded as Portia strode toward the kennels, no doubt with her nose in the air, and Simon stalked after her, equally without doubt, grimly determined.

They exchanged glances, then relaxed and let contentment lap about them. Savored it, gloried in it.

'There's one thing you never did reveal,' Luc murmured.

Amelia hesitated. 'What?'

'Why you chose me, out of all the others you might have had, to be the recipient of your outrageous proposal.'

She heaved a heavy sigh, and rolled onto her hip, sliding one leg across his thigh, sliding one hand, fingers splayed, across his chest. She located one nipple under the black thatch, started to play as she lifted her face and smiled.

'I chose you because I'd always wanted you – why else?'

He shifted; one hand slid down her back to curve about her bottom. 'Ah, I see. Because you lusted after me.'

'Precisely.' She wriggled higher, brushing her breasts across his chest.

He closed his hand, lifted her, framed her jaw and brought her lips, willing and eager and loving, to his.

A minute slid by, then he released her, met her gaze. 'You're a terrible liar.'

She looked into his dark eyes, then sighed and

snuggled down on him. Lifting the pearls, she let them slide through her fingers. 'The truth, then.' She felt him glance down, around at her face. 'I plotted and planned to marry you.'

Glancing up, she met his eyes. 'I was always sure that if I could just get you to marry me, we'd have – find—' She gestured.

'This?'

'Yes.' She resettled her head on his chest, spread her hand over his heart. '*This* is what I always wanted.'

After a moment, he murmured against her curls. 'You were more farsighted than I – I'd never imagined such a state could exist.'

She hesitated, then asked, 'You don't mind that I stalked you and trapped you?'

'Had I known it was a trap, I would have sprung it anyway. *You* were what I wanted, and I didn't truly care how I got you.'

She grinned, looked up. 'So we both succeeded in our plans.'

His hand shifted, stroking her bottom. 'I think we've both proved there's victory in surrender.'

She laughed, then stretched up and kissed him. 'Yours, mine – and ours?'

His lips curved; he kissed her back. 'The ultimate triumph.'

Also available from

Piatkus by

Stephanie Laurens . . .

ON A WILD NIGHT

'Where are all the exciting men in London?'

After spending years in the glittering ballrooms of the ton, Amanda Cynster is utterly bored by the current crop of bland suitors. Determined to take matters into her own hands, one night she shockingly goes where no respectable lady ever should, but where many an intriguing gentleman might be found.

But titillating excitement quickly turns to panic when Amanda discovers she's quite out of her depth. She looks around for help – and is unexpectedly rescued by the Earl of Dexter. Lean, sensuous and mysterious, he has delayed re-entering society, preferring instead a more interesting existence on its fringes.

He's the epitome of the boldly passionate gentleman Amanda has been searching for, but although his very touch makes it clear he's willing to educate her in the art of love, Amanda has to wonder if such a masterful rake can be sufficiently tamed into the ways of marriage.

978-0-7499-3723-2

THE TASTE OF INNOCENCE

Charles Morwellan has no intention of following in the footsteps of his family – marrying for love – and therefore wants to find a bride before fate finds him. He is convinced that it was total devotion to love that caused his father to shirk the responsibilities of the earldom and is determined not to make the same mistakes. What Charlie doesn't realise is the woman he chooses, Sarah Conningham, wants nothing less than a love match and she has no intention of letting Charlie get away with pushing her out of his life. Now, it's up to Sarah to convince Charlie that you really can have it all.

978-0-7499-3863-5

WHAT PRICE LOVE?

Despite his dangerous air, Dillon Caxton is now a man of sterling reputation, but it wasn't always so. Years ago, an illicit scheme turned into a nefarious swindle, and only the help of his cousin, Felicity, and her husband, Demon, saved Dillon from ruin. Now impeccably honest, his hard-won reputation zealously guarded, he's the Keeper of the Register of all racing horses in England, the very register Lady Priscilla Dalloway is desperate to see. She has come to Newmarket, determined to come to the rescue of her horse-mad brother who has fallen into bad company

Together, Dillon and Pris uncover a massive betting swindle. Assisted by Demon, Felicity, and Barnaby Adair, they embark on a journey riddled with danger and undeniable passion as they seek to expose the deadly perpetrators. And along the way they discover the answer to that age old question: what price love?

978-0-7499-3712-6

SCANDAL'S BRIDE

'He will father your children . . .'

When Catriona Hennessy, honourable Scottish Lady of
the Vale, receives this prediction, she is exceedingly
vexed. How can she unite with a rake like Richard
Cynster – a masterful man with a scandalous
reputation? More shocking still is her guardian's will
that decrees that she and Richard be wed within a week!
Though charmed by his commanding presence, and
wooed by his heated kisses, she will not – can not – give
up her independence.

So she forms a plan to get the heir she needs without
taking wedding vows. Richard is just as stunned by the
will's command. Marriage had not previously been on
his agenda, but lately he's been feeling rather . . .
restless. Perhaps taming the lady is just the challenge he
needs. But can he have the rights of the marriage bed
without making any revealing promises of love?

978-0-7499-3718-8

THE TRUTH ABOUT LOVE

Gerrard Debbington is one of the most eligible gentlemen in the ton, Gerrard is besieged by offers from London's most sought-after beauties, but as the ton's foremost artistic lion, there's only one offer he wants to accept – the chance to paint the fantastical but seldom-seen gardens of reclusive Lord Tregonning's Hellebore Hall.

That chance is dangled before Gerrard, but to grasp it he must fulfill Lord Tregonning's demand that he also create an open and honest portrait of the man's daughter. Gerrard loathes the idea of wasting his time and talents on some simpering miss, but with no alternative, he agrees . . .

Only Gerrard is stunned by the deep emotions Jacqueline Tregonning stirs in him. He is soon convinced that Jacqueline is the soulmate he needs as his wife.

978-0-7499-3727-0

THE PROMISE
IN A KISS

When a handsome man literally falls at her feet while
she's walking though a moonlit convent courtyard,
Helena knows he must be there for a scandalous liaison.
Yet she keeps his presence a secret from the questioning
nuns – and for her silence the stranger rewards her with
an enticing, unforgettable kiss. What Helena doesn't
know was that her wild Englishman is Sebastian
Cynster, Duke of St. Ives.

Seven years later, Sebastian spies Helena from across
a crowded ballroom. This heiress is dazzling London
society with her wit and beauty, tantalising all the
eligible men with the prospect of taking her hand in
marriage. But Helena is not looking for just any
husband. She wants an equal, a challenge – someone
who can live up to the promise of that delicious,
never-forgotten kiss.

978-0-7499-3724-9

WHERE THE HEART LEADS

Penelope Ashford may be rich, but she also has a social conscience. As Portia Cynster's younger sister, she is forceful, wilful and blunt to a fault – and she has for years devoted her considerable energy and intelligence to caring for the forgotten orphans in London's East End. But now her charges are mysteriously disappearing and, in desperation, Penelope turns to the one man she knows might be able to help her – Barnaby Adair.

Handsome scion of a noble house, Adair has made a name for himself in certain circles where his powers of observation and deduction have seen him solve several unsavoury crimes. Despite his skills – or perhaps because of them – he makes Penelope distinctly uncomfortable, but the stakes are too high. Throwing caution to the wind, defying every rule for unmarried ladies, she appears on his doorstep late one night determined to recruit his talents. However, soon the pair are in more danger than they could have ever imagined.

978-0-7499-0908-6

Praise for Stephanie Laurens